Books by Samantha Hickey

The Arbor Clan
Renewing the Arbors
Hunting the Arbors

The Moreau Lineage
The Forgotten Oath

Hunting the Arbors

Samantha Hickey

Text Copyright © 2026 by Samantha Hickey

Hunting the Arbors is a work of fiction. Names, characters, organizations, places, events, and incidents are either products of the author's imagination or used fictitiously. Any resemblance to actual persons, living or dead, is purely coincidental.

All rights reserved. No part of this publication may be reproduced, stored in a retrieval system or transmitted in any form or by any means, electronic, mechanical, photocopying, recording or otherwise without the prior intermission of the publisher.

Cover Design by: Phatpuppy Art Studios. Font by Catriona Crehan

ISBN-13: 979 8 9862744 4 7

To the wonderful friends I have found that have helped me grow as an author. Thank you for all the time and effort you have given me and my work.

Hunting the Arbors
SAMANTHA HICKEY

1

Declan crossed his arms, huffing as he watched the proceedings. Two hundred years ago, a hearing like this would have been held in an official yet informal location with no more than a handful of impartial seat holders on the World Council. It was only supposed to be a preliminary meeting to determine the facts and events of a potential case.

This, however, was a full-blown trial in an actual courtroom and it only added to Declan's ire at having to be here in the first place.

The room resembled a modern and democratic courtroom. Six Council members sat at a justice's bench toward the back of the room. At least more than one member was still required, but the whole point of having different points of view was lost since all of them were human magic users. Wizards. When had that started to be allowed? Five of the six were older men with long beards in various states of gray, only perpetuating the mortals' cartoonish ideas of their kind. The last, refreshingly, was a young woman. Still a wizard, but at least the panel wasn't completely one demographic. A clerk, transcribing the cases, sat to one side of the bench and two warlock bailiffs stood behind it, in addition to one posted at each exit.

But this was not the mortal justice system. There were no lawyers or plaintiffs in this room and no jury of peers either. The defendant, a young and nervous-looking vampire, walked through the gallery, past Declan, and up to the booth facing the bench of Council members.

The vampire was dressed nicely for the occasion, if not a bit outdated, even compared to Declan who hadn't needed to pull out his only suit and tie in over twenty years. He wore brown tweed slacks with a button-up shirt and tie. His face had that pale, deathly pallor vampires got after a while, but his eyes were still bright red so he couldn't have been more than a few hundred years old. Not even out of his fledgling stage. He politely removed his newsboy hat as he approached the accused's box, attempting to tame the dark mess of hair that had been hidden underneath.

The vampire's eyes darted to a row of seats encircling the room from above, the occupants peered down on the proceedings below. That part of the room was dimly lit, but Declan was sure he recognized a couple faces, including Icelyn's. If she was up there, then that could only mean those seats were for the World Council heads—in particular, by those present, the leaders who were neither human nor wizard.

Declan sat among the dwindling group of those awaiting their time in front of the judges. They were all on benches behind the current defendant, separated from the public crowd and caged in by a decorative railing. None of them were authorized to leave, for any reason, without express permission from the bailiffs.

The oldest and most grayed of the six judges, seated in the

center, addressed the vampire defendant without glancing up from the papers in front of him. "Please state your name to confirm." His tone was clinical, almost bored, like he had repeated this sentence at least a hundred times today. If the size of the crowd earlier was any indication, it was possible he had.

"Cyrus N-Nightshade," the vampire stammered.

The only woman on the panel sat next to the Merlin double, taking the place of the second-in-command. She never looked away from Cyrus, and her gaze had Declan squirming in his seat. She wore all white, which meant she should have been part of the most devout of the light magic factions. Her dark hair was done up in a crown of braids, and he couldn't deny she was appealing. Her face was calm and serene, and normally Declan might have argued that her presence was a comfort to those on the stand, but there was something about her eyes and her almost-smile as she stared at the accused that unsettled him—bright and sparkling, as if she enjoyed these hearings.

To Merlin's credit, Cyrus, the poor creature, actually seemed scared of him. "You are here today because you are accused of having sired another vampire without permission of the World Council. Do you have evidence to suggest this is false?"

Declan snorted. That couldn't be the reason he was here. Fledglings were supposed to be under the purview of the vampires, not the Council. Since when had it been illegal to create new members of any group anyway? Still, his stomach sank as his thoughts wandered home where his own two apprentices were waiting for his return.

The young vampire wrung his hands and licked his lips. Declan looked around the room but, to his astonishment, no one appeared to share his amusement. "Well, no. I did sire a vampire," Cyrus answered the bench, "but I brought her here to register her, like I'm supposed to. I don't understand what I did wrong."

The old wizard finally removed his attention from his paperwork. "Where is your fledgling now?"

A young lady, golden curls hanging over her shoulders in gentle waves, stood up a few benches over from Declan. She was clearly a freshly made vampire, her lips and complexion still rosy with life and her eyes the bright red of a fledgling. She wasn't very tall, and she raised her hand meekly to be seen across the room. "Here, sir."

The wizard snapped his fingers, and the two warlocks at the exits and two more entering the room, moved to obey. Two stalked over to the girl, pulled her hands behind her back, and handcuffed her before dragging her toward one of the side doors. She looked back to her sire, eyes wide as she called to him, but, to Declan's relief, she did not fight the warlocks as they hauled her away. He would have hated to see things escalate into violence.

The other two warlocks had also detained Cyrus, who could do nothing to help the poor girl. He had been cuffed with basic restraints since there was no need to use silver. Vampires couldn't cast spells, and any magic he had would be useless against the warlocks flanking him. The white wizard continued to stare, almost without blinking. Declan tried not to cringe.

"Cyrus Nightshade," Merlin said, addressing him once again without acknowledging his presence, "you are guilty of violating World Council laws"—Declan could have sworn he saw the white wizard's face twitch at the corners of her mouth and around her eyes as she barely held back a smile—"that state no mortals are to be turned to any group without express permission of the Council—"

"But our numbers are dwindling and her turning was consensual," Cyrus argued. "She was sick and would have died if I hadn't turned her!"

The young vampire's arguments were ignored. "As punishment," the wizard continued, "you and your fledgling, will be subject to servitude to the Council for the duration of her maturity, providing good behavior—"

"That's at least a hundred years if you won't let me teach her!"

"Your assignment will be provided to you within twenty-four hours."

With a wave of the wizard's hand, Cyrus was dragged off without ceremony or acknowledgment from anyone other than the white wizard sitting at Merlan's side. Declan hoped Cyrus and his fledgling would be reunited, but it didn't seem likely.

This was unfathomable. It was a blatant overstep into vampire affairs. The Council Declan had helped set up hundreds of years ago would not have interfered like this. The sole purpose of the Council was to help all the different magical creature factions navigate living together, hidden inside mortal societies. Each faction—druids, fae, werewolves, vampires, the Holy Order, and wizards—still governed their own people. Cyrus Nightshade's case should have been handed off to Ophelia for disciplinary action since his "infraction" wasn't a Council issue, but a vampire one.

Declan looked up to the shadowed seats above the room, expecting Ophelia, the head of the vampire faction of the Council, to intervene. Instead, she sat rigid, hands gripping the arms of her chair as she glared at the proceedings below her, but did nothing. How had these wizards gained so much power that even Ophelia didn't dare oppose them?

Her face dropped ever so slightly, electric blue eyes meeting Declan's. He had known Ophelia since she had been turned. She was petite, barely above five feet tall and, with the right clothes, could easily present as a man or a woman, though she preferred a highly feminine appearance. She was a force to be reckoned with: smart, resourceful, and possessing skills in diplomacy that could build or destroy kingdoms. Today, she attempted to appear unimposing, dressed in a sensible but likely very expensive dress. Her blonde hair was tied up into a neat and elegant bun. When she smiled sweetly, Declan had seen even the most distrusting of men bend to her will. Right now, she fixed Declan with a hard stare, her face a blank mask. He had seen that expression many times before. She was warning him.

"Declan Arbor," the old wizard called, shuffling his papers.

Declan turned his attention back to the courtroom.

"Take the stand, please." The older judge didn't look at him but the woman next to him perked up at the sound of his name and her dark eyes roved among those waiting their to be seen. It unsettled Declan to think she might be excited about his case specifically.

Uneasy, Declan rose to a cacophony of whispers. His return to the world of the living had doubtless stirred up a storm of gossip. He stepped up to the podium for the accused, hoping this would be easily cleared up with a simple explanation. "Your honors," he started, "I believe there has been some misunderstanding—"

The judges' heads snapped up, and the old wizard glared at him. "As an immortal, you went into hiding for two hundred years with no contact to this Council or any individuals on it. Protocol states you are to have two points of contact, and at least one of them is supposed to submit anonymous forms bi-yearly. Nothing has been turned in for you in all that time. Please educate this panel," he spat, "on which part of this we have been mistaken."

Declan gaped. "But that can't be right." His two trusted Council members had been Icelyn and Ophelia. He had been in regular communication with at least one of them and both had confirmed on multiple occasions they had submitted the correct forms. "I did follow the protocol. My two informed me they submitted those forms, each enchanted with their official codes to mark them as my designated contacts. They would both swear to it."

The old wizard glared at Declan but the woman next to him was smiling. Declan didn't like it. "Seeing as how there are no forms on file, that cannot be true. Due to the part of the law that keeps contacts anonymous, they won't be able to testify for you. Do you have any *other* proof of your observance of protocol?"

"No." He wanted to swear. As a fairy, Icelyn couldn't lie and he knew Ophelia had no reason to. He trusted them, but obtaining hard copies of the forms or any other kind of proof was out of the question. Regularly contacting them had been dangerous enough, but exchanging paper correspondences, which could be tracked, would have been reckless. And he couldn't call on his confidants to vouch for him without outing them to everyone. Icelyn and Ophelia had submitted the appropriate forms, Declan had no doubt, but they had been removed or, worse, destroyed for some reason.

"No." He scowled. "I have no other proof."

The old wizard nodded smugly. "Then let's move on to your other offenses."

Declan balked. Other offenses? What else could they accuse him of?

"You took on an apprentice without authorization sometime while in hiding and have failed to register her."

So they were going to try and get him on that too? Declan rolled his eyes, jamming his fists on his hips. "As that would have defeated the point of being in hiding—in fear for our lives, I might add—yes," he admitted with more than a little sass, "that is true."

His response was met with a sneer but was otherwise ignored. "You have also displaced the Winter Prince's mantle by taking him on as another apprentice, quite recently and also unregistered."

That was true, but the Council was splitting hairs. Declan was getting irritated at them sticking their noses into business that didn't pertain to them. Since Icelyn had agreed, however begrudgingly, to Galvin's apprenticeship, the Council had no authority to punish him for it.

Declan's struggle to stay silent about these absurd changes failed. "This Council not only dictates the laws of its affiliate factions but those of the fae as well?"

All six wizards on the judges' panel exchanged nervous glances. Merlin shifted in his seat, avoiding the gazes from the faction heads, where Declan had seen at least three fae rulers. Oberon was absent but, knowing him, that wasn't strange. Of all the fae monarchs, Oberon was the most likely not to do as he was told.

Declan had been right, though, and smirked at having caught the council red-handed: whatever power they had seized did not extend outside the mortal realm. That was good for the fae, but for all the magic users and creatures of the mortal realm, it was a problem.

"Of course not," the judge hissed, "but as an allied entity, their stability is of interest to us." Declan opened his mouth to argue more, but Merlin continued to speak over him. "Both apprentices will fall under review after submission of their registrations. As punishment, you will be officially stripped of all your World Council titles and offices. In addition, the Arbor Clan is being placed under probation until further notice."

Declan bit back his retort, mouth snapping shut. It was a much lighter punishment than the vampire before him received, and Declan had two illegal apprentices in addition to not following protocol. He would lose his authority on the Council and that could prove difficult if he wanted to contest his charges, though if he was being honest, the sentence wasn't unexpected. His power had mostly been honorary even before he went into hiding, but he had held enough clout to sway people to his side when necessary. *So they see me as a threat and need to take me down a few pegs before they can subjugate the druids.*

This farce made it clear the Council would have preferred if he, and his clan, had stayed dead. At some point during his absence, the Council had asserted themselves as the governing body of all the magic people who called the mortal realm home and saw Declan as a threat to their rule. Now that he had mysteriously returned, no longer preoccupied by imminent death, they had to minimize the damage by stripping him of influence and securing him and his apprentices under their thumb. On principle alone he wasn't okay with that.

"A probation officer will be assigned to you within the next twenty-four hours. You are to remain here until that has been finalized and you have discussed further instructions with them. They are to ensure the Arbor Clan is retrained to adhere to Council law. You are dismissed."

Declan glared at the panel of judges, his fists and jaw clenched to keep himself from making a scene. The whole performance had been ridiculous. He wanted to argue the legitimacy of the charges, the validity of the ruling, and the pompous reach the Council was displaying. As much as he would have loved to give them a real reason to fear his presence, this wasn't a fight he could win on his own. He and his apprentices had survived Mathias and Lucian by luck coupled with Alia and Galvin's grit, but now they were going to have to fight off the entire government. Plus, if the judges' command of the bailiffs were any indication, the Council now had control of the warlocks, who comprised the wizard military. Declan's actions here would directly affect Alia and Galvin, not just himself. He would need to bide his time for now, but the Council had not heard the last from him.

A warlock stepped up to Declan when he didn't move from the podium, still furious at the arrogant wizards on the panel. He looked up at the burly young man dressed all in black. His silver eyes and bangled wrist marked him as one of the special forces warlocks—Raptors, they were called. So he was still enough of a threat to make the judges pull out their big guns.

The Raptor, showing a surprising amount of respect, did not manhandle Declan like the other warlocks had with Cyrus and his fledgling. Instead, he gestured in the direction of the door, giving Declan the opportunity to obey willingly. There was no sense of a threat to comply either. He just stared down at Declan with a blank expression, waiting for him to acquiesce. Like a robot needing input before it responded accordingly.

Declan took a deep, calming breath before leaving the room with his Raptor escort. There wasn't anything more he could do here today. He had lost this battle, but he was not about to give up the war.

2

A bit more tweaking and Galvin was sure he could get the cellphones working in time for Declan's return. They would be impressive when he was done. He pulled one out of his tool bag and flipped it over in his hand. Mortals wouldn't even be able to tell the difference. He allowed himself a grin as he made his way down the hall toward Theo's lab. *These are going to be so cool!* He slid the phone back into the front pocket, thinking about how he could apply the same ideas to other electronics when he got the cellphones down. Alia's laptop had been on the fritz lately so she'd probably let him have it.

As he passed the open door to the Link Room, soft murmuring caught Galvin's attention. It sounded like Declan. Galvin was surprised he had made it back from the hearing so quickly. He stopped, grinning, and doubled back. "Things must have gone well if you're back already," he called, stepping inside. "That's a miracle. Things almost never go that smoothly with the Council. I figured you'd have to tell us you needed to stay longer."

But the room was empty. There wasn't much in it to begin with, just the portals linking all the major druid cities—the anchor groves—together. Three trees, carved to look identical to each grove's sacred tree, glowed quietly. The doorways in the trunks, which connected to the other anchor groves, were open and active. Everything looked as it should. Galvin frowned, sure he had heard Declan's voice.

More soft murmuring came from behind him, this time a woman. Galvin turned and nearly jumped out of his skin. Two hazy and translucent figures stood in the room with him. In front of him was a small but lovely woman in a dress with long flowing sleeves. The dress hugged her middle, displaying a petite frame. Her hair was dark and long, tied back from her face in a plait that cascaded down her back.

The second figure moved, making Galvin start. An undignified sound escaped him when he jumped again, dropping his tool bag at the sight of Tiberius.

Galvin stared open-mouthed at how different he looked. The face was the same—strong jaw, long nose—but with an easy smile Tiberius hadn't worn before. He was a lot more filled out than the sickly and thin man who had helped hunt Galvin and his friends down less than a month ago. His tunic stretched snug across his broad chest and around his thick arms. The heaviness sagging the shoulders of the man Galvin had met did not weigh upon this version. Instead, he had his fists propped on his hips and a laugh on his lips as he beamed at the lady in front of them.

Was this the Tiberius Declan had known? The person who had been Declan and Evelyn's best friend?

If this was the old Tiberius, then the lady had to be Declan's beloved Evelyn.

The lady stepped up to Galvin and Tiberius, and both turned to face her. Smiling up at them, deep blue eyes twinkling, she presented her closed hands to each of them. Her mouth moved as she spoke, but Galvin could only hear soft whispers that didn't quite form into coherent language.

Tiberius held out his hand to receive whatever the lady was about to give him, but she instead turned her gaze to Galvin. His heart skipped a beat as she watched him expectantly, though her gaze was a little off from meeting Galvin's eyes. He didn't know much about Evelyn, but he couldn't help but feel he didn't want to disappoint her. Without thinking, he offered his own open hand under her fist.

She opened her fingers and dropped a small round object into Galvin's palm. It was just as hazy and translucent as the figures and began dissolving into a cool, glittering mist as soon as it left her hand. Galvin squinted at the quickly disappearing image, trying to make it out, but it was gone soon after Evelyn had released it.

When Galvin looked back up, Tiberius was releasing the lady from a hug. She slipped out of his arms and stepped closer to Galvin. She leaned in, closing her eyes. Galvin felt the flush creeping across his face as her lips pressed against his skin. Her kiss was cool and light; more thought than a feeling.

The kiss was awkward for his height, her lips brushing his chin. *Of course, she's interacting with Declan.* His two-thousand-year-old mentor was slightly shorter than he was. For him, it would have been a true kiss.

Is this a memory? Ever since he and Alia had summoned that ghost in the old church, Galvin had been seeing an increasing amount of strange things.

Within moments of touching him, the images of Tiberius and

Evelyn dissolved, leaving as quickly as they had appeared. One last whisper called to him, the only word he had made any sense of so far. *Hurry,* Evelyn's gentle voice pleaded. As it faded, Galvin stood alone.

Galvin blinked, rubbing his fingers together over his palm where Evelyn had dropped her gift. He was disappointed he didn't know what it was supposed to be. The unfinished portal to Evelyn's temple, destroyed many centuries ago, sat dark and empty. Same as always.

It had to be a clue, right? He should probably tell Alia what he saw regardless.

He picked up his tool bag and left the Link Room. He hastened through the hallway and into the common room where Alia had said she was going to read.

She was on the couch with a book open in her lap. Her head had fallen back and her arms lay limp at her sides. Her auburn hair had been in the same braid for a couple days now, and her curls were starting to come free of it in little wild strands Galvin found adorable. Her breathing was soft and relaxed, but a small crease appeared between her eyebrows.

Galvin sighed and shook his head as he approached. This was the third time this week she had fallen asleep while studying. Her already fair complexion was losing what little color it had, making her freckles and the bags under her eyes stand out. She was working entirely too hard on training their new powers and researching Evelyn's disappearance. As much as she was pushing herself, Galvin worried about her health, but Alia was stubborn and argued she could handle it all.

He set his tool bag on the coffee table, then took the book from her lap and placed it next to his bag. Gently, he slid a hand under the back of her neck and the other behind her knees and guided her down across the cushions. She was light, despite her athletic build, and he moved her easily. Possibly, Galvin was getting stronger himself. Before releasing her head, he placed one of the sofa pillows under her for support.

Her hand slipped off the edge of the couch, dropping a gold coin to the floor. He tucked her arm back at her side and pulled one blanket draped over the back to lay over her. Then he knelt to find the coin.

Luckily, it hadn't rolled away and was right where she dropped it. It was the coin they had found while searching Lucian's rooms at the Ingadi Grove. Since then, Alia had carried it around with her, trying to puzzle out its significance.

It had landed with the Arbor Clan side facing up and, when Galvin picked it up, he flipped it to the Holy Order side. He ran his thumb over the symbol of the Healing Sects—a staff and two snakes—the group Evelyn had been a part of. The romantic inscription and the date of her wedding circled the symbols on each side.

Just in case anything happens, Evelyn's voice whispered to him. He looked up, glancing around for the source of the sound, but it was just Alia and himself. *Please, hurry...*

He rolled the coin again, but when it was clear he wasn't going to get any other messages, he put it down with Alia's book and notes on the table. Had the coin been what Evelyn had given Declan and Tiberius in the memory?

Alia would want to know what Galvin had experienced in the Link Room. She'd probably be able to make sense of it. He gazed at her, debating if he should wake her up and tell her.

She slept peacefully, her face relaxed and her chest rising and falling gently.

    Galvin stood up instead. He could tell her later. Right now, she needed rest. Quietly, he gathered his tool bag and left.

3

Alia breathed deeply, trying to release the tightness in her chest. She had no idea where she was or how she had gotten here. She wandered endless, winding hallways lined with empty rooms, looking for an exit door, a window, anything that would lead her out. There was no furniture, nothing on the walls, no way for her to tell if she was going in circles or not. The only light in the whole place was some sort of fait glow that seemed to follow her, leaving enough visibility to see where she was going. There was no other sound than her own breathing and muffled footsteps, both as quiet as she could make them but deafening in the overwhelming silence.

Where was Galvin? They hadn't been apart for weeks now, since they'd performed the upgrade spell on the Arbor Grove tree. The blending of their magic had been odd at first, but she was growing used to the connection developing between them. The constant presence of his emotions, and sometimes his thoughts, had become a comfort, but here she couldn't sense anything. "Galvin," she called softly, "where are you?"

A tingling started on the back of her neck, crawled across her shoulders, and prickled along her scalp. She halted and slowly turned in the direction her unease emanated from, straining her ears to find any sign of what might be here with her.

But there was nothing. She sensed something following her though. It felt predatory, hunting from the shadows. Waiting. The hair on her nape stood up and a chill ran over her body. It was right behind her. She whipped around, ready to fight whatever was coming after her.

She was alone.

Malicious laughter echoed through the hallways, making her heart race and sending more chills up her spine. She pressed her back against the nearest wall to prevent the menace from sneaking up on her. She scanned the hallways for any signs of her invisible stalker, too afraid to move. She saw nothing, but she could feel the other presence. Stalking her, hunting her down.

Pull yourself together. You're trained for this. She mentally shook herself, focusing on what Declan had taught her. *Breathe. Focus. Find something you overlooked. Any small detail.* But her inhale was shaky and she couldn't hold it for four counts. As she scanned again, she found nothing in the dim, nondescript hall. Nothing to help her break this loop she was stuck in. And she couldn't track what was stalking her.

This place was dangerous and the thing here with her meant her harm. She didn't know where to go, just that she had to get away. She pushed from the wall and hurried in a direction she thought she hadn't been down yet. It was difficult to be sure when every wall and room looked exactly the same. The laughter followed her as she searched. She was panting, hands trembling, more and more desperate to find anything to lead her out.

An icy breath dripped down the back of her neck, chilling her to the bone and making her body shake. "There's no way out," a voice whispered.

Alia froze, the blood draining from her face. She knew that voice.

"You won't escape me, not this time. Not from here."

Her gaze swung around, desperate to locate him. No matter which direction she turned, she couldn't find him. He remained out of sight, always behind her. Like a phantom, but much more dangerous. "No." Her voice unsteady as she tried to back away from her stalker. "You're dead."

He laughed again, this time right in her ear. She startled, screaming, and Lucian's hands grabbed her arms hard, his nails digging into her skin. He pulled her in close, pressing his face against her ear. She felt the wide grin across his face. "Am I?"

She squeezed her eyes shut, trying to block him out. *This can't be happening.* She pulled away, desperate to escape his grasp.

She sat straight up, gasping for air, her heart pounding. Her eyes darted over the room. She was on the couch in the Arbor estate's common room. The book she had been reading before falling asleep was now on the coffee table, the wedding coin resting on top, and someone had covered her in a blanket. The fire roared comfortably in the fireplace. Galvin was here, she could sense him nearby once more. Theo was always here because he wasn't allowed to leave. She was not alone. She was home, safe inside the protection of the Arbor Grove.

Declan still hadn't come home though.

Alia sank down on the couch, breathing deeply to calm herself. In through the nose slowly, hold, then out through the mouth slowly— her control restored. It had just been another nightmare. Lucian was dead. She had seen Declan kill him with her own eyes. He couldn't hurt her anymore.

She wasn't weak. She'd defeated demons. She was better trained than this. She needed to buck up.

Declan had told her to be kinder to herself. She had almost been Lucian's torture victim and a little residual fear and anxiety was a natural response to the magic he'd used. She knew her mentor was right, but she hated feeling like this: weak, terrified of nothing more than memories and shadows. It had been weeks since they had fought Lucian and Mathias in the Alaskan grove and she should be getting better, not worse. She needed to get over her fright. She wasn't weak.

She rubbed her face, trying to dispel the growing exhaustion. She had been losing more and more sleep as the nightmares worsened, which in turn only made the dreams more intense. She still felt the sting of his imaginary nails scratching her arms. She had to get some sleep so she could fully rest her mind and fight through any lingering trauma.

Declan would probably have a solution but did she really want to tell him she was struggling? He was so overprotective. She didn't want him surrounding her in Bubble Wrap because he was scared to lose her like he had lost her parents and every apprentice before them. She didn't want him to think that, no matter how strong she got or how much she learned, she wouldn't be able to cut it when the time came to face the world without a mentor. She would have to figure out how to tell him without triggering his concern.

She sighed, pushing herself up from the couch. Regardless of how tired she was right now, she did not want to go back to sleep. She shivered at the memory of those endless hallways and Lucian waiting for her. Declan was supposed to be home tomorrow; she just had to last until he got back.

In the meantime, she had better make some coffee. There was too much work to do in investigating Evelyn's disappearance to slack off. She scooped up the coin and slipped it into her pocket as she made her way to the kitchen.

A lot of coffee.

4

Since he was no longer spending his time trying to find a way to abdicate without the Queen's permission, Galvin had needed something else to occupy him when he wasn't training or looking into Evelyn's disappearance with Alia. Fascinated with mortal technology and wanting to figure out how the gadgets worked and why they were so sensitive to magic, he had started tinkering on anything the others would let him tear apart.

Declan had noticed his growing curiosity with mortal electronics so, wanting to encourage his interest and to save their current appliances, had taken him out to an old barn on the grounds. Inside was an amazing collection of stuff, thrown in and forgotten as the Arbor estate evolved through the ages. Declan gave him free reign to do whatever he wanted with whatever he found. It had all been stored away long enough no one would miss anything.

They searched the shelves of old machinery, relics from long gone eras, dirty and rusted from neglect, but Galvin was looking for something a little more modern. It seemed like everything now had some sort of electronic chip in it, and he wanted to learn how one worked; it was fundamental, if his idea had any hope of succeeding. Eventually he had found an old radio and an open workbench in the barn, and his hobby was born.

Learning to take things apart was easy. Putting them back together so they worked again? Not so much. Bits and pieces of junk scattered the surface of his workspace as he taught himself how the gadgets and devices functioned. Despite what he had heard from other fae growing up, mortals could be very smart. Slowly, he figured out how to put the machines back together and, most importantly, to operate again. Sometimes better than before he started.

It hadn't taken Galvin long to get the hang of reassembling things, and about a week ago, Theo had come out to visit him. Galvin stared at the unsocial half-dragon as he approached, his dark form emerging from the shadows appearing as unhappy to be there as Galvin was surprised to see him.

Theo was the definition of shadow. He controlled the darkness with an ease that still shocked Galvin, but Theo also *looked* like shadows. Black hair, dark clothes, and smokey swirls drifted up the left side of his neck and across his cheek to settle under one of his purple eyes. It was the only color on him: a purple staring out from the darkness, able to see you long before you ever saw him.

He leaned against a bench, crossing his arms, staring at the radio Galvin had just reassembled. "Not bad."

Galvin didn't know what to say. "Um, thanks."

Theo sighed and rolled his eyes. "Alia says you need magic tools. Until you get your own, I'll let you work in the lab—" Galvin's mouth fell open but Theo glared at him, pointing a clawed finger to cut him off before he could make an idiot of himself by squealing. "*If* you pick up after yourself. And keep the place clean. I don't want to see a bunch of bits and dirt everywhere. You break anything, you replace it," he growled.

Galvin snapped his mouth closed and nodded obediently, but he was practically bouncing in his seat with excitement. Theo's lab was a wizard's dream to work in. Altars for every occasion, his own library, an alchemical workbench. Theo had that place outfitted with anything and everything you could need for every type of magic known. He wouldn't willingly invite Galvin to invade his space; the half-dragon liked his solitude and rarely interacted with anyone other than Declan. His generosity had to be Alia's doing, but that didn't bother Galvin.

He'd ended up improving the radio. It sat now on the desk in his room, picking up stations operating on magic from the fae realm. All thanks to Theo's lab and tools.

Now, Galvin leaned in close, squinting as he brought his stylus down on the design. The tiny switchboard fizzled as he drew like he was welding. As he thought about it, that was what he was doing: welding magic into the electronics so the device would not only withstand the foreign energy but transmute it into something usable.

Galvin finished the delicate soldering and straightened up to examine his handiwork. The intricate symbols shone against the dark green of the plastic chip, already channeling magic from the fragile electronic components and changing it into what the hardware understood. Satisfied, he plugged the chip in with the rest of the components, secured the screen in place, and closed the outer shell. He held down the power button, a delighted grin spreading across his face when the smartphone's logo appeared as the device booted up. He was going to blow the others' minds with this one.

Galvin gasped and a cold sweat broke over him. His heart

started to race, jumping into his throat. The phone clattered on the table as he gripped the surface. He blinked, startled at the physical reaction that didn't match with his earlier enthusiasm. It was passing quickly, but the jolt of fear left him breathing hard and his hands shaking. It wasn't the first time this had happened. These feelings hadn't come from him, but the sensation was so intense he found himself frantically searching the room around him. These episodes were getting stronger; this was the most severe turn yet.

Theo entered the lab while Galvin was still trying to catch his breath, appearing without a sound and startling Galvin again. His black hair was brushed away from his face, but for function rather than aesthetic; Theo didn't do style, so any fashion choice he made had to be for a reason. He was wearing his usual pair of jeans but had added a dark hoodie sweater. Galvin had yet to see him change this look and figured he had an entire wardrobe of the same shirt and jeans. Only recently, as the weather cooled, had Galvin noticed the addition of warmer clothes. Apparently, dragons did not like the cold.

Theo slowed, his constant purple glare losing some of its usual harshness. "What's wrong with you?" Galvin had come to understand that, despite the coldness of the words and the glare—which was simply Theo's resting expression—this slight softening of his tone was Theo showing concern.

"I'm not sure anything is wrong," he answered.

Theo frowned, seemingly not convinced.

Galvin didn't blame him; he wasn't convinced himself. "Not with me, anyway." If his and Alia's connection was growing stronger, then something had scared her. He needed to check on her and make sure she was all right.

Galvin swiftly cleaned his area, storing his tools in his bag and placing it on the shelf Theo had hung just for him. He headed for the stairs, wondering where Alia was.

Theo cleared his throat. Galvin paused, one foot on the step, and turned back to the half-dragon. Lazily, he pointed to the table Galvin had just tidied and the phone forgotten on the surface.

Galvin laughed sheepishly, dashing back over to the table and snatching the phone up and stuffing it into his pocket. He smiled up at Theo, whose expression had returned to its typical resting glare. "Whoops, sorry about that."

Theo rolled his eyes, the only indication he wasn't nearly as angry as he always looked, and turned his focus to the research he had been studying for days.

Galvin tapped into the new yet somehow familiar connection to see if he could locate Alia. He took the stairs two at a time, closing the hidden door once he was in the hallway, as per his explicit instructions. Theo liked his privacy, and an open door invited interruptions.

Following the connection, Galvin rushed into the common room, but it was empty. The book and her notes were still open on the table. The blanket had been thrown over the back of the couch, but the sofa pillow remained on the cushions where he had slipped it under her head, though Alia wasn't anywhere in the room. He glanced around for any indication of where she had gone or what could have scared her so much.

The connection pulled on his senses again from farther through the house. He thought perhaps it was leading him to the stairs up to the first floor of rooms, but a gentle tug on the back of his neck directed his attention behind him. The only room in that direction was the kitchen, and he heard the small noises of someone moving about in it. He pushed through the swinging door and found Alia calmly pouring herself a cup of coffee.

In the evening? Alia never drank coffee in the evening.

"Hey," he greeted.

"Hey to you." She didn't look at him, continuing to stir the creamer in her cup before taking a big drink.

"Everything all right?"

She rose an eyebrow at his question. "Why wouldn't everything be all right?"

"But I thought..." he started, scratching his head. He got the distinct impression she was unhappy with him, but what had he done to irritate her? "But you were just..." He gestured to her before dropping his hands to his sides. What was happening here? He was sure the panic had come from their connection, but she seemed more ready to snap at him than scared. "There's nothing wrong? You're not upset about anything?"

Alia shrugged. "Nope." Her face relaxed as she pulled up a wall around her thoughts and emotions, blocking him out. She had gotten much better at that than he had in such a short amount of time. "Everything is fine."

So something *was* wrong and she was trying to hide it from him. She was paler than usual, dark bags under her eyes. It had to be connected to her retreating behind those mental barriers more often recently.

Plus, if everything were really fine, she would want to know what had happened to make him come check on her. The fact that she wasn't curious told him she knew exactly what had happened and didn't want to talk about it.

Alia didn't hide things often, especially not from him. She had no reason to. Whatever it was must be making her feel vulnerable, which was the one thing she didn't know how to cope with. He'd just have assure her she was always safe to confide in him.

But she wasn't ready, and he could be patient. "Hmm. Okay then. Have you heard anything from Declan?" Perhaps changing the subject would put her at ease.

"Not yet." She sighed, sinking into a chair at the island, rubbing her face. She looked exhausted and her defensive mental walls disappeared a little too quickly. Like it had been an effort to keep them up, one she couldn't maintain for long. "His hearing was last night; I would have expected him back today. You have more experience with the World Council. You don't think something happened?"

Galvin shook his head. "World Council trips always take a long time. Something is always getting delayed or ends up being more complicated than it needs to be. Nanny always planned for an extra couple of days when she had to attend Council stuff."

Alia gazed into a different dimension and worried at the handle of her mug. Her thoughts buzzed in her head so loudly Galvin could feel them. They were dark, but he didn't believe she was thinking about Declan. Her thoughts were like the inky black of fear. The same feeling he had gotten in Theo's lab.

He sat in the chair next to her, reaching a comforting hand out for her arm, his mind reaching out in a reflexive mirrored movement. "Please tell me what's wrong."

She shot him a glare, yanking away from his touch. "Nothing," she snapped. "I'm fine."

"C'mon. I can pick up your thoughts from across the room. Just tell me what's wrong."

The walls returned, blocking him out, and flames flickered

behind her hazel eyes. "You don't always have to know what I'm thinking!"

Galvin reeled back like she had slapped him, staring in shock at her outburst. She had never yelled at him before.

"I am allowed to have my own feelings without sharing everything with you!"

He pulled away, his stomach clenching. The connection wasn't always something either of them could control, but he had never pried into what he thought was personal. In the lab, he sensed genuine terror. They had promised to face things together, but she was breaking that promise, taking on whatever this burden was alone. Didn't she trust him to help her?

His eyes narrowed. She didn't have to say the words for the message to come through loud and clear. *Crowding.* "You're right," he admitted, his tone becoming polite but biting. He kept his voice hushed as he tried to project an outward calm. "You're allowed to have private thoughts. I apologize if you felt I was prying."

Galvin rose from his chair. If she didn't want his help, he couldn't force it on her. He had to wait for her to be ready to come to him. He started to walk out but paused at the swinging door. "If you need me, I'll be taking care of my chores before bed." He left without looking at her.

5

The World Council Offices were extensive, as was befitting the government entity it had become. Declan had witnessed last night at his hearing. Theo, who had managed to keep informed about world affairs better than Declan while in hiding, had tried to warn him the World Council was not the same as he had known it two hundred years ago, but he hadn't imagined it could've changed so much. Declan had thought it would still resemble that group of the world's magic leaders who had come together in a time of mutual need to offer support and order when the mortal world organized faster than all the groups of the magical world.

This was not that group. Not anymore. Now it was a large governing body that had swallowed up the separate factions under its rule. At least the ones in the mortal realm. Fae and dragons living in the fae realm remained autonomous, but all the supernaturals living in the mortal realm had either been wiped out or subjugated. Declan wondered what that meant for the fae and dragons living in the mortal realm. And where did angels and demons fall in this regime since they existed on their own planes separate from the mortal and the fae ones?

Still, the heads of the different factions had all had a place above the courtroom. Overlooking, but not part of, the decision-making. Symbolic then. A way to make it look like vampires, werewolves, and other non-human supernatural creatures had a say in their governing, when in fact all the authority had been seized by human wizards.

Whatever else, Declan needed to remember that governing bodies were only concerned with keeping power.

Declan approached the reception desk of the probation office where a mousy young lady frantically scribbled on the papers covering her desk. A hallway of doors lined the wall behind her, each with a name and title painted on the outside. She looked up as he approached, adjusting her big glasses, and stared at him expectantly. "Declan Arbor," he told her. "I'm supposed to report here this morning."

She blinked several times, her eyes darting back down to her work, but nodded in understanding. She thumbed through the files on her desk until she found what he guessed was his. Clutching it to her chest, she stood and backed away. "W-wait here please." Her voice squeaked, but she cleared her throat. "I-I'll inform her you are here."

Declan watched her scurry away, wondering what had just happened. He looked himself over but couldn't find anything wrong. He ran a hand through his brown hair, pushing the slightly shaggy mess away from his face. His shirt and jeans were clean and his sneakers were somewhat new. He had even checked himself in the mirror before he left his room to make sure his clothes weren't too old or too young for his mid-thirties appearance. He might have looked a little casual, but he didn't think he needed to dress up for a meeting with a parole officer.

He jumped as a dainty hand grabbed his arm, sharp nails digging into his skin. Ophelia stood next to him, one slender finger pressed to her mouth to signal him to keep quiet. She wore jeans, sneakers, and an oversized hoodie with the hood pulled over her head, but the tail of her blonde braid hung over her shoulder. Her face was clean of her usual makeup and paler than usual, illuminated by the indirect daylight filling the room from the large windows. Her eyes were rimmed deep red, and she blinked often. She was up way past a vampire's bedtime, and blood would begin to leak out of various orifices if she didn't sleep soon. Not only was it strange for her to risk being out at this time, but Declan had rarely seen her go out into public looking anything less than precisely put together.

She didn't give him the opportunity to speak before shoving a card into his hand and pulling him down closer to her. "We need to talk," she whispered. He could see blood inside her mouth as well. He was about to ask her when and where, but her eyes narrowed and she squeezed his arm tighter, shutting him up and leaving little half-moon shapes in the skin. "Not here," she snapped. "She has eyes and ears everywhere."

"Declan Arbor?"

Ophelia released his arm. He turned and straightened to see the young female wizard from the panel at his hearing. She was tall for a woman and would have towered over him had she not chosen flat shoes. She wore white again: a dress with a knit sweater to ward off the autumn chill. It was open at the top, hugging her rather busty curves. White was usually associated with the most peaceful, and usually modest, of magic sects, but from what he saw yesterday—and considering her outfit this morning—he had a hard time believing that of her.

Today, her smile was soft, the perfect image of gentleness. Was this the "she" who had eyes and ears everywhere?

Declan turned toward Ophelia, hoping to read in her face if he had guessed correctly, only to discover she had slipped away. Vampires were notoriously fast, but he was shocked at how she had managed to escape without being seen in the fraction of a second between the delivery of her warning and the appearance of this mysterious untrustworthy woman.

"Were you looking for someone?" the witch asked sweetly in his ear.

Declan jumped again, startled for the second time in nearly as many minutes, to find her standing right behind him, leaning in close. Any number of spells or abilities would allow her to move that quickly and silently, and he hoped it wasn't something she did often. Especially if he had to have prolonged interactions with her.

Her grin widened as she watched him under half-lidded eyes.

Declan recoiled and tried to put more distance between them. Chills ran down his spine but he forced himself not to visibly shudder. He needed to be polite, but something about her gave him the creeps.

"No," he said as casually as he could manage, tucking Ophelia's card into his pocket. "I thought I heard someone I recognized. Trick of the hallway." If Ophelia wanted to remain unseen, Declan wasn't going to be the one to give her away.

"Ah," she said, straightening and dismissing the incident. She held out her hand to shake Declan's. "My name is Camilla Edenbrach, but everyone calls me Grace. I am a white wizard, and I have been assigned to the Arbors as your probation officer as well as your World Council liaison while your clan is under strict supervision." Her grip was delicate, like her gentle façade, but firm. Her handshake told him she pretended to be weak to put people at ease but was not someone he wanted to trifle with.

"Nice to meet you, Grace," he said with a demure politeness. He had learned the best way to deal with people like her was to let them think they had control over you. "I'm rather new to this, so now that I've reported to you, what do I do?"

"Since you've fulfilled your obligations, that's it. You're free to go home."

Declan raised an eyebrow at her. There was no way that was all. "Really? That's it?" Why give him such a harsh sentence only to slap him on the wrist and send him back home?

"That's it," she repeated, beaming at him. "I'll meet you there in a few days and we'll get to work."

There it was. The catch. "Meet me where?"

"At the Arbor Grove, of course." Her smile dimmed when she saw the confusion on his face, but her eyes continued to glitter. "Oh dear, did no one explain it to you?" She sighed as if she were sad for him, but he got the impression she was enjoying this. He didn't have to ask what she meant because she continued eagerly. "I'm afraid your probation sentence is rather severe. The Arbors are required to have constant supervision until the Council deems you can manage your own affairs once more."

Declan's mouth fell open and he clenched his fists, trying to keep calm. Constant supervision? That was not going to work for him. If the World Council learned his clan's rules and ways, then nothing would stop them from subjugating the druids like he had witnessed with the vampires last night at the hearing. How was he supposed to keep the druid secrets secret with a World Council member living at the Arbor Grove? Not to mention Theo. If Grace discovered him, Declan would have a *real* reason to be in trouble.

This punishment had nothing to do with Declan or how he had handled being in hiding. Something much bigger was going on. No wonder Ophelia wanted to talk. This was bad.

Maybe he could just rely on the wards to keep Grace out; eventually she'd get so lost she'd be forced to give up and go home. But then the Council would just return with destructive magic to break through and he, Alia, and Galvin would all have to go back into hiding. If that happened, it would be worse than when Mathias was hunting them. The World Council no doubt had resources that would put Mathias and his demons to shame, forcing the druids to move much more often and live entirely off the grid. In the twenty-first century.

No, that wouldn't work. He was going to have to figure out another way to get rid of this lady. For now, he reached into his pocket and rolled a little charm reluctantly in his hand. It was one of several charms he had created to allow someone to come and go from the grove as they pleased. In his whole life, Declan had only ever given out four: to Ophelia, Icelyn, Theo, and Evelyn. The only non-druids he trusted with completely.

"There are wards around the grove," he explained, still fidgeting with the charm. "You will have to be led through them by a druid. There's a train station nearby, I'll pick you up there when you come in." He removed his hand, leaving the charm in his pocket. He wouldn't be giving out a fifth charm today. Not to Grace Edenbrach.

Her expression turned stiff, her eyes watching his fidgeting. Declan's stomach twisted, but he kept his face neutral.. He hoped she didn't demand more from him.

"How thoughtful. I will make note of your cooperation right from the beginning." Her voice took on a hard edge, and Declan doubted she would make any such notes. She spun on her heel and walked back in the direction of the offices. "I will send word when I'm scheduled to arrive. Don't be late." A dismissal if he ever heard one.

Declan clenched his jaw, his gaze going to the receptionist. She gave a little squeak when she saw his frown, hid her face, and buried herself in her work. He groaned. He wasn't half as bad as the actual criminals she'd probably seen, but she didn't seem to know that.

This trip just kept getting worse. At least he was free to go now. He hustled out of the probation office and back to his assigned room on the upper level of the building to collect his things. He needed to get home and warn the others they had dangerous company coming.

6

Alia leaned back in her chair and rubbed at her face, trying to clear the exhaustion. She had drifted off again while reading a book on Holy Order temple construction. Holy Gia, she was tired. All night she had dreamed about Lucian and gotten only a few hours' sleep. She was running on caffeine and stubbornness.

The nightmares were getting worse too. Each time she dreamed about the creepy house, Lucian gained a little more on her, finding her quicker. Before her dream yesterday evening she hadn't seen him but had felt him following her, reaching for her, a brush on her skin or her hair.

Now he was actually catching her.

She shivered, thinking about it. Between the nightmares and worrying about Declan, she had barely slept last night. She had thought research on Evelyn would keep her awake but, in hindsight, the library probably wasn't the most stimulating place. Her eyes kept drooping and her notes had descended into illegible scribbles. What could be read made little sense. She couldn't keep going like this forever. She needed a distraction. And she needed help.

Galvin had already offered help. Her stomach twisted with guilt as she remembered. She should've told him what was wrong when he asked. At the time, it had seemed so intrusive for him to use their connection to check on her wellbeing, but now she wished she had the comfort he had been trying to give. She didn't know why she'd gone off on him. Of all people, she knew he wouldn't judge her, but she didn't want anyone to see her in such a fragile state. Especially not him.

It was probably a good idea to apologize. Maybe if he forgave her, they could do some training. That would certainly keep her awake.

Or make the fatigue worse.

She scoffed. Nothing could possibly be worse than the way she felt right now. Declan would know how to help, and she just had to last until he returned.

He should have been home yesterday, but she still hadn't heard from him. Galvin had said she shouldn't worry yet. Delays were normal when dealing with World Council. But Declan should have checked in if he was going to stay longer.

Alia took a deep breath. It was too early to worry. She should focus on finding Galvin.

She tried tapping into their connection to track him, like he had to find her in the kitchen yesterday evening. She managed glancing touches on what felt like him but couldn't pinpoint a solid location. She only sensed his general presence on the grounds but nothing more specific.

Alia dropped her head back, rubbing her tired eyes, and groaned. Just another thing she couldn't do without proper sleep.

She'd have to think her way to him. That shouldn't be too difficult.

When he was angry or frustrated, Galvin tended to go to the training field, and he had been plenty upset after she snapped at him. The training field was a large, stadium-sized area down the path from the mansion. It was set up so druids could practice fighting and magic skills in a safe, designated place. There was even stadium seating so others could watch the spectacle. According to Declan, it had once been an enjoyable pastime for many of the active and civilian druids as well as the friendly mortals who lived in or near the Arbor Grove, not unlike the Roman gladiator games of old but without the slaves or death. Alia headed that way, figuring it was the best option to check first.

Her deduction proved correct. She found Galvin in the arena, great burning plumes covering his hands and practice swords as he went through one of the fighting katas Declan had taught them. She was happy she didn't have to search anymore, but the size of those flames proved how angry he was with her. Galvin's fire magic was directly connected to his emotions.

Declan had explained that all magic was, on one level or another, connected to emotions. While, with proper training emotions could lend an extra amount of strength and power to spells and abilities, unchecked they could easily overwhelm a caster and lead to disastrous results. Galvin had taken Declan's instruction seriously and worked to control his new powers while remaining calm and collected. He was making progress, but his flames when clear headed were much smaller than the ones currently engulfing him.

Galvin dropped his stance when he spotted her and the flames dwindled to a flicker in his hands. He stared at her, his face a hard mask.

She tried a small smile and a wave in the hopes of softening his mood. Like a peace offering.

He sighed, walking over to the bench to drop his practice swords and get a drink of water. Despite the cool air this morning, he had worked up a sweat. As he wiped the moisture from his face with a towel, it occurred to Alia he wasn't the skinny, clueless prince who had come to their door all those weeks ago. Now he had a full set of druid tattoos—white, almost sparkling with his exertion—down his left arm and circling his torso to disappear under the band of his shorts at his hip and reappear down his right leg. They were a mirror image of the black tattoos spiraling down Alia's right arm and left leg. Galvin still had all the glory of his fae heritage: high cheekbones, large eyes, towering height, and lean muscles. But lately his arms and chest had started to fill out with more brawn, softening the fae features with his human bulk. His hair had grown out too, just enough to cover his pointed ears.

His coloring had also changed. Ever since his grandmother had taken back the mantle of prince, most of the frost in his hair and eyes had melted, revealing jet black strands and deep blue irises. A few flakes lingered in both but now the snow was more of a dusting than the full, defining color it had been. The effect gave his hair a nineties boy band kind of look and the snowflakes deepened the blue of his eyes and made them sparkle. Frost sometimes gathered on his face too but Alia only noticed it when he was relaxed.

The best part was Galvin didn't even realize he was good-looking. He had spent his whole life thinking the only reason anyone liked him was because he was a prince. That might have been true to an extent, but it wasn't the whole truth. Alia remembered Bianca, who may have ultimately been after Galvin in order to become the crown princess, but she had also clearly wanted him for him. She'd made a special task force to chase them all the way across the world to get him.

Galvin was handsome. If he and Alia ever got the chance to interact with the rest of the world, girls would probably throw themselves at him. Much to his discomfort, most likely. When they had hidden from Bianca's soldiers at the train station and Alia had pulled him close, only *pretending* to kiss him, he had freaked out.

"Why are you staring?"

Alia shook her head, heat rising to her cheeks in the early autumn sunlight. "I was looking for you. You missed breakfast."

"I wanted to get out here before it got too hot. Besides, I didn't want to *crowd* you."

Alia winced. She deserved that. She hadn't said those words but it had been what she felt at the time. "I'm sorry. I shouldn't have snapped at you. It was mean and uncalled for. I was wrong."

He looked sideways at her. He was trying not to cave easily, making sure she knew her reaction hadn't been okay.

She clasped her hands together, pouting up at him with the biggest eyes she could make. She was selling it hard and had no regrets. Her goal now was to make him laugh. "Please, am I forgiven?"

He rolled his eyes, letting out a huff, but a smile spread across his face. "Is that the face you use on Theo to convince him to do your bidding?"

Alia waved the idea off—"Of course not. Humor doesn't work on Theo"—and resumed her puppy-dog stare. "Please?"

Galvin turned his face away, covering his mouth to hide that it was working. "Yeah, I suppose." He cleared his throat and faced her again, opened his arms, cocked his head to the side, and motioned her in. "Give us a hug then."

Alia wrapped her arms around his waist; she couldn't reach his neck without him bending down. He dropped his arms over her shoulders and hugged her tight. She closed her eyes, laying her face against his firm chest, enjoying the affectionate touch. He smelled cool, sharp, and earthy like the evergreens of his homeland. It was a nice hug and she let herself relax in his arms.

Then the moment was over. He squeezed her, smashing her head against him. She squirmed, playfully admonishing him. It felt good, like it had been weeks since she'd had a proper laugh, though it had probably only been a few days.

He released her with a gentle shove. "Does that mean you're ready to tell me what's wrong?"

Alia's gut clenched and started pushing the dirt around with the toe of her shoe. Reflexively, she erected her mental shields. Why was she so scared to tell him?

"I haven't been sleeping well." She skirted the whole of the truth with a small piece of it. "I keep waking up because of these awful nightmares. Declan said they could happen. That Lucian's magic tends to trigger something like a trauma response in his victims. It's not a big deal. It'll pass soon."

When she looked up, Galvin was frowning at her, his brows furrowed. Immediately she felt self-conscious. She stuffed one hand in her pocket and fidgeted with the coin, while the other rubbed the back of her neck. She avoided meeting his eye.

He touched her shoulder, stopping her from putting any more distance between them. She hadn't noticed she had been backing away. "You know you can tell me anything." His other hand tilted her chin up.

All Alia saw was concern in his eyes, and the fear began to

ease in her. A warmth grew in her stomach and burned on her cheeks. She could feel a little of her old self return along with something else. Something she didn't dare put a name to.

"Together, remember?" he asked.

She took a deep breath and sighed out the frustration and fear. She was being ridiculous. She had just told herself to confide in him. "I remember. It's just lingering magic from Lucian's attacks. It should pass." She mentally kicked herself. Why was she chickening out *again*?

"As long as you're sure."

The anxiety was returning, though perhaps not quite as strong as before. "So." Alia changed the subject before she could dwell too long on dark thoughts and to distract Galvin from asking more questions. "Would you like a sparring partner?"

His face split into a dark grin. "You're on."

Alia followed him into the ring, rolling her shoulders, and stretched out her hips and legs to warm up. She put away all other thoughts, emptying her mind and prepping for the quick thinking she would need for the fight. Even a practice fight. She fell into her stance, loose and ready.

Galvin took his own stance but did not rush in like he often did. He was learning to overcome his rashness, and she was proud of his progress. They each waited, watching for the slightest indication of an opening in the other's defenses.

Alia felt the familiar rush of adrenaline, her heart quickening to pump more blood through her system. She breathed through the change, even and controlled, and her senses heightened in response to the increased circulation. Time seemed to slow ever so slightly, enough to make this waiting game with Galvin feel like it was taking forever, but he kept his cool. Good.

A whisper in the back of her mind sent her heartbeat racing erratically. "You can't beat me," Lucian's voice echoed from their standoff at Ingadi. Alia gasped, blinking the memory out of her head.

Except, when she opened her eyes, it was Lucian who rushed in to meet her. His black hair was slicked back like a greaser from the fifties and his eyes were solid black, mouth open wide in a fanged smile as he ran toward her, laughing.

Alia shoved her shock away, glaring and ready to fight. He came in with a wide punch and the obvious goal of opening her defenses.

Alia wasn't falling for it. She dodged the hesitant punch easily and thrust her own counter into his ribs through the gap his attack made in his own defenses. She struck with her full strength, making him grunt and buckle to his knees. She didn't wait for him to recover, throwing a knee up to strike him in the face.

Lucian's eyes went wide and he barely managed to get his hands up in time to block, grimacing with shock and fear, and a grin pulled at the side of her face. *Good, you should be scared.*

"Whoa, Alia," Lucian said with Galvin's voice, grabbing her arm. "Hold on."

She growled, plunging her folded elbow down toward his head. If he thought he could fool her with Galvin's voice, he was seriously mistaken. Power surged inside her. A crackling snapped in the air around them, dancing over her skin as she struck him hard, splitting the skin and sending him tumbling and twitching to his side on the ground. Red blood dripped down his face from the open wound as he tried to regain his senses. She pinned him, pulling her fist back for a final blow.

Lucian's hands shot up, palms open in surrender. "Alia! Stop! What are you doing? Stop!"

She blinked again, and it was Galvin underneath her. His hair stood on end and blood seeped from a blackened split on his cheek. He panted, terrified, his hands still raised. Alia lowered her fist, uncurling her fingers, and slowly sank into the grass next to him.

What had she done? She had fully attacked Galvin. She had hurt him. She had gone ballistic on him because of a flashback. "Oh my God, I'm so sorry." Tears pricked at her eyes and she started to stand. She needed to be anywhere else right now.

Galvin sat up and took hold of her arm. "Don't do that," he pleaded. "Stop shutting me out, please."

She lowered herself back down and pulled her knees up to her chest.

"What is happening to you? I can't help if you don't let me in."

"I don't know," she said from under her knees.

"Can you explain what that was? It was like you couldn't even tell who I was."

She peeked at him from around her arm. Her gut clenched when she saw how badly she had hurt him. "We need to get that taken care of—"

"It's fine," he snapped, fixing her with a stern glare, "it's split skin. I'll probably have a black eye. It won't kill me in the next few minutes while you tell me what you saw to make you go mental."

"Lucian," she admitted. "I had a flashback of Lucian."

Galvin was silent for a moment, then he scooted next to her and wrapped his arm around her shoulders. "Alia. I'm sorry. That's..."

Her gut twisted but she didn't push him off, just folded farther into her herself, pulling her mental walls up around her for protection. She couldn't let him see her weak.

"Declan says what Lucian did to me was traumatic." She was reminding herself as much as telling Galvin. "And that it's common to have flashbacks and trouble sleeping for a while afterward. That this is normal, and I'll recover." She didn't dare tell him the nightmares were getting worse or she was afraid to sleep. She didn't want him to see how small and scared she really was. She was supposed to be tough, strong.

This is normal. I'll recover.

Galvin was silent again. He hadn't moved his arm from her shoulders but left it there like they were relaxing in the warm sunshine on any normal day. A crispness in the air brought the scents of old wood and stones across the training grounds from the village ruins surrounding the Arbor Grove. Alia took a deep breath, releasing some of the tension in her body.

"Are you sure that's all?"

"Yeah," she lied, "Declan says I'll be fine. It'll get easier."

"You know I'm here for you?"

"Yeah." She smiled at him. "Thanks. I'm okay."

7

Declan emerged from the grove tree and stomped across the magically glowing clearing, through the gardens, and toward the house. The whole situation was absurd and the more he thought about it, the angrier he got. Probation? He shook his head, huffing. Yeah right. This had nothing to do with rules or Declan coming out of hiding. Something was brewing on and he was going to get to the bottom of it.

In the meantime, if he had to suffer that woman at their home, then he would warn the others and they all needed to take care of some things before she arrived. They were going to have to hide everything. If the World Council thought he was going to roll over for them, they were sorely mistaken.

He crossed the terrace, shoved open the doors to the ballroom, and stormed inside, muttering under his breath about the audacity of power-hungry dictators. His thick hiking boots echoed as he stomped through the big open space. Didn't they know he was there when the

Council was formed? They couldn't use rules he had helped make against him.

Except the rules didn't apply anymore. The game had completely changed.

Theo was the first one he saw in the hallway. He approached as if he'd known Declan had returned. With Theo's sensitive dragon hearing and keen smell, it was likely true. He paused when he noticed Declan's stormy attitude. "What happened?"

"Go get the others for me," Declan told him, heading toward the stairs. "Bring them to my office and we'll all talk there."

Theo nodded obediently before heading out the way Declan had just come. Theo was the biggest secret they had to hide. Declan *had* broken the laws for him, which the Council did not need to know.

Declan's march up the stairs lost some bluster as he considered what to do. It was going to hurt Theo, but he couldn't imagine another solution. He went straight into his office, threw his overnight bag into the corner, and tossed his probation paperwork onto his desk. He sank into his chair, dropping his face in his hands. What a mess. How had things gotten so bad while he was in hiding? Two hundred years was evidently longer than he realized. Long enough for groups like the wizards to seize sizable amounts of power.

Alia soon led the pack into the office, and Declan was taken aback by her appearance. She and Galvin wore workout clothes dampened with sweat. A half-burned gash cut across Galvin's cheek. Alia's auburn hair was tied in her usual braid but several curls escaped. They must have been on their way back from the arena when Theo had found them. It wasn't the training fatigue that concerned him though. It was the dark circles under Alia's eyes and the sunken, pale cast to her face. She must not be sleeping well. Something must be wrong.

"I'm guessing things didn't go well," she said, assessing his disposition just as he had been assessing hers. A hint of pride shone past all Declan's frustration at how well she had learned to read people. It wasn't a magic skill he'd taught her, but a way to use what information was already available, and she wielded it like a weapon.

"No," he admitted. Checking in with her would have to wait. "It did not. Someone has tampered with the submissions my designated contacts filed, and the Council is claiming ignorance to the whole thing. And they are claiming we *forcibly* recruited Galvin without his grandmother's permission."

"I shouldn't be surprised they're upset about me becoming a druid," Galvin scoffed. "Unlike the other faction heads, the fae courts have only maintained autonomy because they're on a separate plane. The Council's been trying to pull the fae under their rule for a long time now though. But I can't imagine they convinced Nanny to pursue charges. She hates letting them have a hand in anything."

Declan realized Galvin likely knew more about the World Council in it's current state than anyone else in the room. Since Icelyn was one of the faction heads for the fae, Galvin must have personally witnessed their underhanded tactics while attempting to seize control over the other factions. "It makes more sense why she didn't, now. She's still plenty angry with us and won't talk to me any more than necessary, but she is choosing to let you stay," Declan clarified. "The Council are the ones pressing the issue, not her. If she were, I'm sure the Council would use it as an opportunity to get us under their thumb."

"While you were in hiding, the Council took over the other factions through small legal matters like this. Any non-human supernatural faction head is now mostly just a liaison used to enforce World Council rules on the faction," Galvin explained. "If they don't comply, they get replaced or eliminated."

That was what Declan was afraid of. "As it is, they *are* requiring all new clan members to be registered, so we've been dinged for failing to comply *twice*." He took a deep breath. He could feel himself starting to lose his cool again. Above everything, he had to remain levelheaded. "They have put all of us on probation, and I've lost my standing with them."

His three charges stared back at him. Galvin's fists clenched at his sides, small flames flickering between his fingers as he glowered. He was twenty-five, an adult by fae lifespans, but still had a lot to learn about controlling his emotions. Alia gaped, looking a little confused and a lot worried. He should have done better to prepare her but he had kept her from having extensive dealings with anyone outside the druid community and had never taught her about the Council. Now, at twenty-three, she didn't know nearly enough about magic world politics. Theo's eyes widened slightly, so something in the conversation must have caught him by surprise, but he was the only one who didn't appear shocked. Likely because he was the second oldest person there after Declan and, while infuriating, the Council's corruption wasn't really anything new, considering the whole history of people, politics, and power.

Wow, I'm old.

"This all seems harsh for some misplaced paperwork," Galvin commented.

"It's deliberate. Why? I don't know yet." Declan watched each of their faces as they processed the information.

Theo, as paranoid as he usually was, seemed to be realizing how the Council's interference was going to affect him as well as the druids. He just wasn't aware of how much yet.

Galvin was the only one to visibly share Declan's frustration.

Alia raised an eyebrow at Declan's silent contemplation. "There's more, isn't there?"

Declan grimaced. Alia was too perceptive for him to try hiding things from her. He inhaled again before dropping the last piece of bad news. "Our probation officer will be staying with us until further notice."

"Wait, I thought that wasn't allowed?" Galvin asked, looking worried.

"Yes and no. In order to protect our way of life, the clan elders didn't let just anyone stay here. We don't like to share our secrets. However, we gave the Council special consideration when we first joined because we wanted to cooperate. That didn't guarantee them access to the Arbor Grove, though there was rarely a reason to deny them in the past. But since I've lost all sway and we don't have any elders anymore, I can't prevent them coming now. Look," he warned, "I've been advised not to trust this woman and, frankly, I don't get good vibes from her myself. It's not the first time an enemy has stayed here, and it probably won't be the last.

"We keep everything under wraps," he instructed. "If someone in the Council is targeting us, then I don't want them learning anything about us. They're already suspicious, trying to figure out what happened during the equinox, but I don't want them knowing anything. Not about how you two blended powers"—he gestured to Alia and Galvin—"nothing about the new grove spell, Tiberius, or Evelyn. If anyone asks about Theo, stick to the official story: I killed him to end the monster rebellion. And of course, not a word about our practices and rituals. The more the Council knows about us and what we're doing, the easier it will be for them to take over our clan."

"Is the Council a bad government?" Alia looked to each of them in turn.

"Corrupt," Theo supplied. "Human wizards have been attempting to accumulate power for a long time. When non-human supernaturals stood up to them, they were labeled 'monsters.' We embraced the name and started a rebellion. After we lost, any 'monsters' who helped in the rebellion were deemed too dangerous to control their own affairs any longer. They slowly started losing official positions until they were nothing but figureheads."

Declan noticed Theo left out the part where he led that rebellion and got himself marked as public enemy number one. Was he feeling guilty? Regret, maybe?

"What about Hallowtide?" Alia asked, but she knew the answer. "It's already the twenty-seventh. It's only three days away."

Declan could hear her disappointment and swore under his breath. With everything going on, he had completely forgotten about Hallowtide. He and Alia thankfully didn't partake in most of the druids' spiritual rituals for All Hallows' Eve, mostly because Declan didn't like to, but they always harvested the tree's fruit when they could. The magic fruit only grew during the three days of Hallowtide—October thirtieth and thirty-first and November first— and was an important part of the druid's whole year. Once harvested, it could be made into all sorts of drinks, pies, and preserves that would boost a druid's magic. Many thought the boost ended on the next Hallowtide, while others believed the increase was permanent, something to grow with each year, though Declan wasn't sure which was true. The fruit would be processed and preserved to keep for spells as well. It could be turned into body paints for blessing and protection during special ceremonies. Everything that couldn't be saved was left to compost and fertilize the grove tree.

When Mathias had been hunting Declan and his apprentices, they had only ever done the bare minimum for holidays and ceremonies. Now that they weren't in hiding and with no hint of Mathias for weeks, both Alia and Galvin had been looking forward to all the holiday traditions. It was all new to Galvin of course, but even Alia, who had heard so many of Declan's stories about past druid celebrations, couldn't wait to experience the ritual herself. Their excitement made Declan look forward to bringing some of the old ways back to life as well.

They couldn't do it now though, it was too risky. They would just have to continue to wait. "I'm sorry," he told his charges, "but Hallowtide is out. I don't even know if we'll get a chance to harvest the fruit without this witch finding out. It will be difficult enough to hide that we won't have any powers for a few days."

"Wait, what? We won't have any powers?" Galvin started, surprised, glancing between Declan and Alia.

Declan closed his eyes, his shoulders sagging as he sighed. That was right. Galvin didn't know yet. Declan had planned to tell him as they prepared for Hallowtide, but he wouldn't have time now. "Correct, but it's a bit more nuanced than that. Alia, I'm going to need you to explain it to him later."

Alia crossed her arms, dropping her weight to one foot and glaring at him. "And how do you plan to keep it a secret when we can't use the most basic of spells?"

"Carefully," Declan retorted.

"Okay, and how are we going to keep the fact that Theo is alive a secret when he lives here?"

Theo shifted uncomfortably. Declan felt bad for locking him away at the estate so long—almost as long as Declan had been in hiding himself. Theo had chafed and railed at his confinement at first, but after a while had come to embrace being hidden away. Forcing him back out into the world was going to be tough. "He and I will talk about that shortly, but know that he will have to disappear for a while."

Galvin's eyes lit up and he reached in his pocket. "I finished these just in time then." He passed two cellphones to Declan. "I've tweaked the circuits inside to not only withstand magic but also to use it. You shouldn't ever have to charge these," he proclaimed proudly. "I've only got the two ready so far but I can make others."

Declan marveled at the smartphones piled in his hand. Technology on this level would be a big step into the modern world for magic users, and it was nice to get a bit of good news today. He patted Galvin on the arm, and the boy beamed. "I'm impressed. These will be incredibly helpful. Great work."

"Technology that can withstand magic." Theo whistled and nodded his approval. "That's going to be a hot commodity. If the Council was already mad at you, then finding out about these will ensure their desire to get rid of you."

"What do you mean?" Declan asked.

Theo frowned, his gaze raising to nothing in particular as he thought. "The Council wants to keep the non-magic world separate from the magic world. It's easier to keep everyone scared of each other. Technology that works with magic would make it too easy for the magic and non-magic worlds to get along."

Declan sighed, realizing the truth of Theo's claim. The phones were just two more things to keep secret then. He lay them on his desk behind him. "He's right. We'll need to keep this quiet too." Thankfully, he knew just what to do with them.

He turned back to address his apprentices. "I'm not sure what kind of time we have. I'll have to pick her up at the train station, and she has yet to tell me when she's arriving. It could be today for all I know. You two start going through the house, putting away anything we don't want the Council to know about. Lock any doors we don't want her wandering through unsupervised."

Alia and Galvin nodded, and Declan dismissed them to their tasks.

Theo crossed his arms, staring off into space. "I suppose I can hide out in one of the Arbor Village houses. They'll need to be fixed up eventually anyway."

Declan picked up one of the phones, rolling it in his hands, trying to gauge how Theo was going to take this. He was a smart half-dragon and likely knew what Declan was about to say.

He held one out. Without looking, the half-dragon's hand came up automatically. Theo trusted Declan more than he trusted anyone else on the planet. More deeply than most would experience in their lifetimes. Declan hoped he would continue to do so after the pain he was about to deliver.

"I think it's time to release you."

Theo's eyes snapped up to Declan's, growing wide, and his hand froze halfway to Declan's, now hesitant to obey.

"You have been cooped up here for too long," Declan explained, closing the distance between them and placing the phone in Theo's palm. "You need to get out, meet people. Go hunt one of those magic objects I know you've been researching."

Theo's fingers closed around the phone and he regarded it with an unfocused stare. Was he seeing shadows of his past mistakes?

"I can't be trusted." It came out small and frightened, like when he had been a child.

Declan's heart clenched. He squeezed the half-dragon's shoulder like he had when he was young. He had to reach up to manage it now since Theo had grown so tall. In some ways, he was so much older than when Declan and Tiberius had rescued him, but in other ways he was still a tiny scared boy. "I think your concern shows you can. Your imprisonment was only ever supposed to allow you time to think about what you've done. All that consideration led you to the right conclusion. You don't *want* to be like that anymore." Declan sighed. He had heard before that it always hurt parents more than their children when the time came to push them out of the nest. "This will be good for you."

His words didn't seem to reach through the fog of Theo's mind, but Declan was confident he understood. One at a time, he took each of Theo's wrists in his hands and ran his fingers over the silver bands he had placed on them all those years ago. With a little bit of magic, the markings filled with green light and the handcuffs that had dampened his magic fell away, releasing him.

Theo rubbed his wrists, a mixture of emotions shadowing his face—relief, fear, excitement. It took a moment, but Theo managed to gain control of his thoughts, his face relaxing into his normal bored expression. Only Declan, who had known him all his life, could recognize the turmoil still rolling behind his purple eyes.

The last time Declan had sent Theo out into the world, he had just become an adult. The younger Theo stood in the foyer of the Arbor estate, looking forward to the new experiences awaiting him.

Excitement had shone in his almost human purple eyes and he even smiled, though his fangs were much smaller then. Declan had barely wished him well before he bounded out the front door, promising to write often.

This time, there was no smile and Declan saw only worry in Theo's modified, more felid eyes. He fiddled with the phone, taking his time setting up the contact info for its pair in Declan's pocket. When finished, Theo slipped it into his jacket and adjusted his backpack on his shoulders but still did not leave. He was dragging his feet.

"I feel like I'm being kicked out."

Declan chuckled. "You kind of are, but it's for your own good."

Theo grimaced.

"It's just until things blow over."

Running footsteps echoed down the hall. Alia and Galvin rushed over, still in their pajamas, Galvin rubbing the sleep from his eyes. It did not surprise Declan in the least that they had come to say goodbye.

Alia scooted past Declan and threw her arms around Theo's neck. He lifted her off the ground, giving her a good squeeze. "I can't believe you tried to sneak out without saying goodbye," she told him.

"You know I don't like mushy stuff." He put her back on her feet and let go. "I made you some extra ammo. If you start to run out before I get back, have Declan call me."

Alia rubbed Theo's arm. "Be good out there."

"That's the plan, but I can't make any promises." Theo looked up and held his open hand out to Galvin.

Galvin's grogginess disappeared in an instant. He took Theo's offered hand, his eyes wide and a smile tugging at the side of his mouth.

"You can use the lab," Theo said, not letting go of Glavin. "Just keep it clean. I don't want to come back and not be able to find anything. And keep the door closed while the Council lady is here."

"You got it."

Theo turned back to Declan, an almost pleading look in his eyes. Declan's heart twisted, seeing the scared little boy who still lived deep inside the terrifying half-dragon. He shooed Alia and Galvin away. "Go on you two, there's plenty to do before Grace gets here."

With waves goodbye, Alia and Galvin walked back up the hall and around the corner toward the kitchen.

Declan pulled Theo into a hug, Theo bending down so Declan could reach. "I'm so sorry I kept you here for so long, but you need to be in the world. You can't stay hidden forever."

Theo's voice came out small, quiet next to his head. "I just don't want to disappoint you again."

Pulling back, Declan looked into Theo's eyes. The angry young man wasn't completely gone. The rage at wizards that had gotten him into trouble before was still there, but tempered. With the right stoking, Theo could easily return to terrorizing the world.

Maybe this was a bad idea. Was Declan dooming the world to another horrifying monster reign?

No. He couldn't think like that. Theo was different now. The angry half-dragon who was supposed to be dead wouldn't have been so reluctant to leave.

And it was time for Declan to put more faith in the people he promised to look after.

Declan patted Theo's shoulder. "I trust you. Call to check in every now and then, okay?"

    Theo nodded. With a last look at the place he had called home for the past two hundred years, he took a deep breath and walked out the door.

8

Galvin was still smiling from his goodbye with Theo as he got dressed. It turned out Alia was right and Theo had accepted Galvin into their little Arbor family.

He pulled a T-shirt over his head as he walked out into the hallway. He was looking forward to breakfast since Alia was making it. Anytime she cooked, Galvin knew it was going to be good, regardless of what it was. After breakfast, they would get started locking up anything they didn't want the World Council PO to find. As soon as he emerged into the hall, his heart leapt into his throat and he would have fallen through his bedroom door had he not already latched it. The scream he stifled would have been embarrassing too.

A man Galvin didn't know floated across the hallway, smiling at him. He was soft blues and grays, and translucent, his legs fading away into nothing. Galvin had only seen one other ghost before: the one he and Alia had summoned to ask about Evelyn.

This man was tall, able to meet Galvin's eyes. His dark, messy hair looked a lot like his own, and there was something familiar about his face. Galvin didn't know many humans, but he could have sworn he'd seen this man somewhere before.

The ghost reached out, laying his hand on Galvin's shoulder. The touch was weightless, but left a slight cool, tingling sensation.

The graveyard. That was where Galvin had seen him before. The man had been sitting on a tombstone as he and Alia snuck into the church to do their summoning.

Alia's bedroom door opened, and Galvin jumped again. He spun, stumbling into the wall where the ghost had been floating, clutching at his pounding heart. An undignified squeal escaped him this time.

Alia stood in her doorway, blinking at him. She looked up and down the hallway, then back at him, tilting her head slightly. "Everything okay?"

Still breathing hard, Galvin checked up and down the hallway also, but the ghost was gone. He nodded. "Yeah. Fine, but I have questions."

One of her eyebrows rose. "Okay."

"Declan mentioned something about losing our powers during Hallowtide. Do we get different ones instead?"

Alia *ah*-ed. "Yes, we will lose our powers during Hallowtide, but no, we don't get new ones. However, a druid with spirit abilities will still be able to use those gifts, even when our other powers are depleted."

Galvin nodded, thinking it over. Did he have spirit abilities? Was that why he could see ghosts? Then he shook his head. "Explain, please."

"Right, I still need to tell you about that. Let's get breakfast started and I'll answer all your questions." She started down the stairs. "Halloween, for everyone, is the time of year when the veil between realms is thinnest. All magical people have their own ways of celebrating."

Galvin followed her into the kitchen and sat at the island counter. "Like the Wild Hunt and the balls the fae have."

Alia started a pot of coffee and pulled some eggs, tomatoes, and cheese out of the fridge. *Yum.* Galvin loved Alia's omelets. There wasn't anything Alia cooked that Galvin didn't love.

"For druids," she went on, getting out bread and putting a few slices in the toaster, "it's also the time of year when our patron, the Archangel Gia, channels our power back into the earth. The power is used to restore the groves. They repair themselves and refuel their magic for the year, and the trees will grow a magic fruit."

Magic fruit wasn't uncommon in the fae realm, whether it was fruit the fae infused with magic or a variety that grew with magic in it. "What is the fruit used for?"

"It's made into a lot of different things druids use throughout the year in celebrations and rituals. We can also eat it plain. Hopefully we'll find a way to harvest and process some without the World Council's spy poking around. Then you'll get to see where it all goes."

Galvin's hopes echoed Alia's. He had been excited to learn all the druid celebrations that hadn't been observed in centuries.

The World Council really knew how to ruin the mood.

When the toast popped up, Alia put a couple slices on a plate and slid it over to him with a jar of bluish purple jam. Galvin had never seen jam that color anywhere else, but he liked it. He smeared some on his toast.

"So how early do our powers begin to fade?" he asked around a bite of toast and jam.

Alia poured the eggs into a hot pan. "Only the day before Halloween, and they come back the day after. The fruit matures and the groves repair themselves during those three days, so we observe the whole period as Hallowtide."

Made sense so far. "Okay, so what about the spirit stuff? If Hallowtide revolves around the groves, then what's the deal with the ghosts?"

"The harvest is only part of Hallowtide. Halloween is the one day of the year when the veil is thinnest and spirits can visit the mortal plane."

"And the spirit abilities let you see and communicate with the ghosts?"

Alia rolled her head and shoulders as she dished out the omelets. "Talking to ghosts isn't the *only* thing someone with spirit abilities can do. Supposedly they can use spiritual energy for spells too, but that's supposed to be rare. There aren't many recorded names of druids who had that ability. But all the spirit abilities and spells, regardless of the level, were only taught by someone who also had those abilities, so I don't even know where the records would've been written down."

Galvin's stomach twisted a little. That meant he would have to figure out what was happening to him on his own. Alia probably had some insight from everything she had read, but she didn't have the abilities herself. She didn't have context for what any of the records were talking about.

She laid a plate and a fork in front of Galvin and another in front of herself as she took a seat next to him. Galvin picked up the fork but didn't start eating. His mind returned to the man who had disappeared in the hallway. He gulped, wondering how many more times he was going to experience something like that. "When do the ghosts start showing up more often?"

"Is that what happened in at your bedroom door?"

Galvin nodded. He groaned, picturing how awkward he must have looked, freaking out by himself. "Yeah. Should I ask Declan about it?"

"Honestly, he always turns a little pale and sick-looking when we talk about ghosts and changes the subject so quickly. You can try, but I don't know how much you'll get out of him. I've always had to dig around in the library to find any information about ghosts. But since I don't have spirit abilities, I haven't had much need to do any research. Besides"—her face scrunched up—"spirit stuff is less a science and more an art."

Galvin laughed. "That's why you don't like it."

"What's that supposed to mean?"

"You like spells and skills you can master. If a skill can't be conveyed in precise and exact language, you rarely want anything to do with it."

Alia frowned at him but Galvin could feel her agreement in her thoughts before she spoke it. "What can I say? I like facts."

Alia was waiting in the common room when Galvin came up from Theo's lab. After saying goodbye to Theo and going through the house with Alia yesterday, his cellphone and other technology projects were the last bits to hide. Plus, Theo had asked him to make sure his lab stayed shut. Once closed, Theo's lab would not be found by anyone who didn't know the secret to get in. Of course all the druids here knew but the probation officer would not, and if the grove wasn't off limits to the Council anymore, then he certainly didn't expect their rooms to be either.

Alia still looked worse for wear. He regretted agreeing to spar with her the other day because now she was dead on her feet. Her bleary eyes peeked at him from under heavy, slow-blinking lids. Some of those blinks stretched so long, Galvin thought she'd fallen asleep where she stood. She had put on a nice blouse and re-braided her hair, but he could still see the shadows of something wrong. Her face was pale and drawn, and the bags were getting darker. He wished she would tell him the truth about what was going on. She needed rest and the way she was dealing with her trauma response was not healthy.

"Declan's back with her," Alia announced, cutting off any questions he wanted to ask. "We've been summoned to his office to meet her."

Galvin nodded, turning to grab the lab door. Alia waited as he pulled it shut. Silently, it slid closed, revealing nothing but another bookcase filled with innocuous tomes and decorative knickknacks. Galvin felt the faint but cool magic of Theo's shadows hiding the door from sight.

After the lab was secure, he faced Alia once more. She turned before he could say anything, heading up to Declan's office.

Galvin fell in beside her, taking the hint to not push the issue of her exhaustion. "Have you seen her yet?" He was curious who the face of their enemy was, if it was someone he knew. She had to be dangerous if she was willing to spy on the druids in their own home. She was heading into potentially lethal territory alone, where she would be outnumbered, so whoever it was couldn't be helpless. Declan had also been warned ahead of time this person couldn't be trusted, further confirming Galvin's suspicion.

Alia shook her head. "Not yet." Her voice was thick with fatigue.

Galvin's heart ached at the sound. Besides Theo, Alia was the toughest person he knew. She was confident and wouldn't take cheek from anyone, not even the terrifying half-dragon. She was the one who'd taught Galvin how to fight, not just physically, but for the life he wanted too. It was likely because she was so strong that she was trying to handle her trauma on her own. He hated seeing her so downtrodden but as much as he wanted to help, she was keeping him out.

Before he could prod her again, they reached the office door. Alia politely knocked to announce their presence but didn't wait for an answer before striding in. Galvin hesitated a breath before entering behind her. He was still surprised by how casual life was here sometimes.

He gazed over the room, analyzing the situation. Declan's office was usually filled with ancient tomes and stacks of paper. He was always either taking notes on Galvin's and Alia's new powers, making quick enchantments to keep handy in the packs, or digging through old texts. Now, his office was tidy, almost empty. Even his old-fashioned wood desk was completely cleaned off. Galvin wondered where he had managed to hide it all.

The other desk in the office, the one that was once Tiberius's, remained clear and untouched. It hadn't had anything on it anyway, but the thick layer of dust was undisturbed.

The cleanup job was impressive, but the blood drained from

Galvin's face when his eyes landed on the woman standing next to Declan. She wore a white dress, dark hair hanging loosely around her shoulders, cold blue eyes glinting as they entered. *Oh shit.*

Grace Edenbrach.

She was bad news. Galvin remembered many days when Nanny returned from Council requests angry enough to freeze the Summer Court on the Solstice. Nanny never shared specifics with Galvin, since it was not his place, but he knew this woman had thwarted and tied the Queen of the Winter Court's hands up in red tape more than a few times.

Through gossip between Nanny and Bianca, Galvin had learned that Grace Edenbrach held a high position in the World Council. Rumors claimed she was of the lower witch class of magic user but had climbed the ranks through deception and seduction. Others said some mysterious benefactor gave her powers beyond a human witch's normal capabilities that outshone the more highly trained wizards. She also had a reputation for treating the non-human creatures the Council deemed "monsters" with little to no respect and was working toward oppressing those groups the wizards didn't fully control yet. Fae included.

If she was their spy, this was going to be *very* difficult.

Alia squeezed his hand hard enough to pinch, making him jump. *You're staring,* he felt her say, though she never spoke the words. He didn't dare look at her and give away their connection. He quickly erased the glare sinking onto his face, composing himself just as Declan began the introductions.

"Ms. Edenbrach—"

She stopped him by placing her hand on his arm, and he visibly attempted not to recoil.

Galvin wasn't the only one who got bad vibes from her.

"Grace, please," she said sweetly. Galvin had to make the same effort as Declan to not roll his eyes and gag.

"These are my apprentices," Declan continued without making the requested correction. Grace didn't show that she noticed, just slipped her hand through Declan's arm. He frowned, his forest green eyes darkening in irritation, but made no move to displace her. "Alia, Galvin, this is… our probation officer."

Galvin suppressed a chuckle as Declan struggled with his words. Apparently her name left a bad taste in his mouth too. Galvin couldn't blame him.

"Grace. Edenbrach," Declan finished out of necessity, each syllable punctuated as he forced himself to speak.

Grace released Declan in her haste to approach Galvin first, and her excitement sent chills up his spine. She extended her perfect, well-manicured hand, offering him the back. He glanced down at it, hoping she didn't expect him to bow over it or kiss it like she was a princess.

"You must be Icelyn's grandson, the Prince of Winter."

He took her hand between his thumb and index finger, touching her only as much as necessary to be cordial. He gave it a brief shake and dropped it like it was disgusting. "I abdicated my royal position, but yes. Icelyn is my grandmother."

She watched him with slight bewilderment at his answer, but she composed herself again in an instant. "I wasn't aware a fae royal could abdicate without permission from the ruling monarch." She smiled, delighted. "How interesting. And you are a druid now?"

Galvin felt a pinch from Alia through their connection. *Fix your face.*

Galvin erased the sass that was starting to scrunch up his features. Why would Grace ask that when it was one of the reasons she was here? Did she expect him to deny it? He stole a glance at Declan who, looking a little worried, gave him a quick nod. "She did give permission, actually. And, yes. I am a druid now."

"Hmm. I didn't know that could happen either. I thought druid magic didn't mix with other kinds of magic." There was a heavy pause as she continued to search into Galvin's expression, waiting for him to add anything extra.

Galvin clenched his jaw shut, forcing himself to keep a neutral look in response. He knew better than to answer.

"How fascinating," she conceded, breaking the stare first.

Galvin breathed deep and swallowed hard. Fear and irritation left him at a loss for words. How could she possibly know anything about him and Alia blending magic? Somehow she did know more than she should and was digging for information. This woman was trying to catch them in a lie or manipulate them into accidentally exposing some secret. As the newest Arbor, he was of course the weak link and the reason she'd singled him out, but she was going to be disappointed if she thought him an easy target.

"It is a long process to turn newcomers," Declan explained on Galvin's behalf, "but since our numbers are notoriously low, we welcome who we can right now."

It wasn't an outright lie, but certainly not the true reason he'd become a druid—completely by accident. Declan said it so easily too, so naturally. His ability to play the diplomat, despite his clear anger, was probably why he had once been an ambassador for the druid clans.

The fiendish woman regarded Declan with confusion, which Galvin didn't believe for a second. "But on the forms you filed before leaving the Council offices, you claimed they were in the completion stage of their training."

Declan's face remained neutral, despite realizing his slip.

"You must have been training them both for quite some time then." Grace turned her toxic sweet smile back to Galvin. "But you only recently abdicated. Is that correct?"

"I—" Galvin stammered, searching for the right words. He'd never been good at the fae version of lying. This wasn't going well. "Um, well." He might be easier to crack than he realized. How did Declan make it look so easy?

"It's a rather complicated and personal story for him," Declan interjected. "To put it simply, circumstance has only recently allowed Galvin to abdicate, so yes, you are correct. For the full story, you'll have to ask him if he feels comfortable sharing with you."

"I see." Her demeanor changed from friendly and innocent to professional seriousness when she directed her attention to Alia for the first time since they had entered the room. "My understanding is the two of you are capable of performing missions on your own now. Is that correct?"

Alia hesitated, and Galvin followed her lead. She pursed her lips but made no other sign of irritation. Choosing missions wasn't an apprentice's decision to make, and Alia refused to be forced to do so.

Her silence didn't matter, since Declan answered without waiting to hear what either of them would eventually come up with. "That's at the discretion of the elders and their mentor," he explained. He straightened his stance, crossing his arms over his chest and glaring at Grace. His tone and look clearly stated the topic wasn't up for discussion.

She nodded, pleased. Galvin wasn't sure she actually cared

what Declan said, only that she'd heard what she wanted. "I'm glad to hear you two are so capable."

Declan huffed, his glare deepening into something more threatening.

Grace ignored him. "I have a task for you both."

"I just said no," Declan interrupted. "The World Council does not have the authority to assign missions to my apprentices. Anything the Council needs has to be submitted for approval by the clan elders."

Another sweet smile spread across Grace's face. "Since the Arbors don't currently have any clan elders and, as your whole clan is under probation, thus revoking your privilege to act autonomously, it falls to your probation officer to accept and assign missions." She tsked and tapped her chin with one delicate finger. It made Galvin want to melt her face off. "And since that's me, those decisions fall to me." She turned back to Alia and Galvin, further ignoring Declan's incredulous glare. "You're dismissed to go pack your things. You will need to report back to me here in the morning for further instruction."

If Declan had ordered it, Galvin would defy this woman in a heartbeat. Alia harrumphed, jamming her fists on her hips, shifting her weight to one foot and throwing her hip out. He silently reached out to her, her mind already open and waiting for him. She agreed: they wouldn't do anything without Declan's approval, whatever Grace claimed. They looked to him in unison, seeking his confirmation or denial.

Anger boiled behind Declan's eyes even as he kept his face an irritated but stoic mask. He was losing the power struggle against Grace, and none of them were happy about it. As a clan, the three of them were not strong enough to defy the entire Council and their warlock army. Maybe they'd stand a chance if they had Theo, who had done it once before, but even he'd had a band of rebels behind him.

Declan huffed a sigh but gave his apprentices a curt nod. He was surrendering the battle in favor of hopefully winning the war.

Once more in perfect unison, Galvin and Alia spared a glance at one another, turned on their heels, and left. Galvin caught the soft groan Declan tried to hide. Neither of them had planned to be so in sync, it just sort of happened sometimes when they were connected. But even Galvin had to admit their identical movements must've appeared odd. Grace would surely interrogate them about it later.

The whole situation was not off to a good start. Galvin rarely agreed with Nanny, but she had it right on this one: there was something about Grace Edenbrach he did not like or trust.

9

Declan waited until it was well past midnight and their required house guest was asleep before he got to work.

He and Tiberius had been gifted personal apartments in honor of their services in creating the first anchor groves. Within Declan's personal suite, he should have been safe from surveillance, but he didn't trust Grace as far he could throw her. He'd heard rumors she had stronger magic than she should've been capable of.

From the cabinets in his living room, he pulled out a small satchel of preserved flower clippings, a jar of water from the grove, another jar of meat snacks, a pen, and a small square of paper. Before Grace's arrival and while Galvin and Alia had been securing their druid things, Declan had managed to replace several of the potted plants in the mansion with decorative, flowerless shrubs that didn't have any known magical uses but would work great for concealing his own surveillance system. He even took special care to match the species of each bush he swapped.

Now, he pulled out the bag in which he had stored some clippings from the plant just outside his rooms in the hallway. He laid the clippings on the coffee table and unscrewed the top of the jar of grove water. He always kept a stash of water from the river flowing behind the Arbor Grove's tree—not a lot, but his spells never required too much of the magic-infused water. It was quite potent and, while it would add a significant boost to spells and rituals, it needed to be used with caution in moderation. He dipped his fingers in the water and quickly traced out a circle and a few druid symbols around the clippings before it dried up. Once the circle was complete, he secured the lid back on the jar and replaced it in the cabinet.

Declan kneeled in front of the miniature circle and cupped his hands around the water and clippings, taking a deep breath and clearing his mind. He called up energy for the spell, whispering the words as he touched the water. It sparkled and glowed with Declan's green magic, and the contents of the circle began to swirl—slowly at first, but gaining speed, faster and faster, shrinking in and engulfing the clippings. The concoction twirled and tumbled like a tiny cyclone on the coffee table. After a few seconds, the clippings arranged themselves into a living shape. The configuration absorbed all the water as it formed until the cyclone dissipated.

In mere moments, a small creature stood on the coffee table, shaking the excess water off its leaves, sending glittering droplets everywhere. Some splashed Declan in the face and he chuckled, wiping them away. The sentry would be active until Hallowtide started and the druids lost their magic.

Since it was after midnight, it was already the twenty-ninth, so Declan had at least the whole day to use magic, maybe a few hours longer. He never knew exactly when their powers would stop working. When the clan was at its height, there had been a team who took information from previous years to more accurately guess when Hallowtide would begin, but with only one day left and a spy in their house, there wasn't time to learn how to make those predictions. There wasn't a lot of time to figure out what Grace was after either, but he would work with what he had.

Declan's sentries always ended up looking like little dragon leaf bugs. He held out his hand to the sentry, who scurried up and sniffed him before climbing on. Its sharp twig claws poked into Declan's skin, but it didn't hurt. With a finger, he scratched the sentry under the chin, and it made a sort of croaking purr.

"All right, little guy, I have a job for you."

Its twig face turned toward Declan, holding him in its gaze as it fluttered its leaf wings.

"We have a 'guest' in the house. First elder's suite down the hall." Since Declan had created the sentry, it possessed his knowledge of the house so he didn't have to explain specifics, just the job he needed it to do. "She's a wizard, not a druid. I want you to keep an eye on her for me. Let me know if you see her sneaking around where she shouldn't."

The sentry fluttered its leaf wings and purred again.

"Good." Declan brought the sentry to the door. He listened for noise through the wood before opening it a crack, then checked up and down the hallway, ensuring everything was still quiet and dark. After ensuring the hall was still empty, he knelt, lowering the creature. "Her room is that first one on the left over there," he whispered, pointing in the direction of the elder's suite she had taken for herself.

The sentry fluttered its wings once more before hopping out of Declan's hand. It slinked out of the room and was gone in a wink, disappearing into the darkness.

Declan closed the door, taking extra care to not make any noise. He returned to the coffee table and pulled out the card Ophelia had handed him in the World Council offices. It was the business card of some nightclub in New Orleans. One side was all black with red lettering in a font like dripping blood, advertising a vampire-themed bar. The Princess of Denmark, it was called. It looked like a tacky, stereotypical place where mortals could have an experience a little more real than they bargained for. As a rule, the supernatural world stayed hidden, but there were plenty of mortals who managed to learn the truth. This sort of kitschy club was not something Declan could see Ophelia associating with.

The other side of the card was light blue with a swirling font of the same name. This side claimed to be a nighttime bistro. It looked elegant and expensive. Declan chuckled, shaking his head. This was more Ophelia's style.

On the elegant side of the card, she had written two words in her precise hand.

Date? Time?

Declan grabbed the jar of meat snacks, the pen, and the square of paper on his way to the balcony connected to his bedroom. His suite was the only room with private access to this balcony. He opened the doors to the night air. It was a clear and the stars were bright—perfect for nocturnal rituals. This late in October, though, it was starting to get cold. He didn't bother with a jacket or a blanket because he didn't plan to be out long. He stepped up to the railing and whistled, using the railing to scribble a reply as he waited.

29th. 10 PM.

A small boreal owl landed on the balcony, softly hooting at him.

"Hello, Nova." Declan smiled at her, rubbing her beak, and she nibbled at his fingers affectionately. It had been several years since he had last seen her. He was glad nothing had happened. He folded up the note and offered it to her.

She ruffled her feathers indignantly and refused to take it. He sagged his shoulders and groaned, knowing exactly what she wanted. He twisted the lid off the jar and shook a few treats into his hand. She hooted excitedly then scarfed them down.

"Pigeons are never this demanding," he told her as she snacked.

She clicked her beak and snatched the note from his hand. She tucked it into the pouch hidden under her wing. Before leaving, she playfully snapped at his fingers for good measure.

Declan frowned. Owls were sassier than pigeons. Smarter, too. Pigeons couldn't think critically like owls could. It was why Declan put up with them. "Please deliver to Ophelia Polonius."

She trilled, much more polite now she'd been fed, and took the last of the treats. When she was finished eating, she spread her wings and flew off.

Once she was gone and his tasks were finished, Declan slipped back into his room, locked the door, and drew the curtains. He was off to bed. Today was going to be a long day, and he needed to rest.

10

Alia was back in endless, empty hallways of empty near darkness and. Her internal compass only spun. Her heart raced, inky black fear already clouding her thoughts. She pushed it away, trying to rely on the skills Declan had taught her: keep a level head and she'd stay in control. As long as she could do that, she could conquer anything.

She searched up and down, trying to spot any clue to end these dreams, but there was nothing. Even if she had found anything, what would she use it on? Every room was empty. There were no windows, no doors to unlock. Everything was gray, dim, and identical. If there was a way out, Alia couldn't find it.

It was only a dream. She had to be missing something. Maybe there was something she couldn't see. Despite the apparent lack of a light source, she could navigate, but shadows filled every corner, lurking just out of reach. When she was brave enough to approach, the darkness receded, revealing more nothing. Perhaps magic hid whatever she was supposed to find. She held her hand above her head, wanting to use her sunlight powers to illuminate the place and dispel any shadowy illusions stopping her from getting to what she needed.

But the room remained dark. Her stomach twisted and she snapped her hand back down, staring at her empty palm. It should have been filled with tangible light she could mold to her will, but nothing had come. Her chest tightened and she tried again and again to call on her light, but her hand remained empty, her surroundings dark.

Very dark.

Familiar laughter echoed in the space around her, coming from everywhere and nowhere. Her heart pounded in her chest and she gasped, searching for signs of Lucian. She had to escape before he found her.

"Tsk, tsk. Your magic won't work here, Little Druid."

Alia closed her eyes, trying to calm her thoughts and emotions. Lucian created fear with magic. This dream was her mind dealing with the trauma of him almost killing her a few weeks ago. It wasn't real.

It was just a dream. She had to control her fear.

"I'm not scared of you!" she shouted to the emptiness where she knew he was waiting. She had to fight his magic.

His chuckle echoed. "Yes, you are. I've already told you, I make sure everyone is afraid of me."

Silence fell again. Her breaths came small and shallow as she tried to make as little noise as possible. The hair on the back of her neck stood on end. Danger approached.

Her eyes flew open. Lucian's shadowy form stepped out of the room in front of her and she gasped, terror overtaking her. She turned on her heel and ran as fast as she could away from him. She didn't know where she was going and it didn't matter. All she knew was that she had to get away.

His laughter followed her as she flew down hallway after hallway, each the same as the last. She paused, chest heaving, her head swiveling back and forth. Had she been down this way already?

"Run all you like, Little Druid." He sounded close.

She bolted. As she skidded around a corner, she stole a glance back. She didn't see him but kept running. Seconds later, she collided with something solid and her head flipped forward.

Lucian grabbed her arms, lifted her off the ground, and slammed her back into the wall. His black hair was slicked back like a greaser, giving her an eerie view of his eyes glowing through the dim shadows. He lowered his face into the dull light radiating from her, and she perceived the discoloration from where she had burned him in their previous battles. Dark, rough patches covered his skin, giving him a particularly monstrous appearance. He was smiling, baring his fangs, chuckling. "Every path you take here will lead you right back to me."

Her body shook. *Wake up*, she told herself. *Wake up, it's just a dream! Wake up and it will all go away!* She couldn't slow her breathing as blood pounded in her ears. She struggled in his grip, trying to break out of his hold. She just needed to wake up!

Black tendrils crawled over her arms. The cold, slick chords were the same as before when they had bound her, preventing her from moving. She screamed, wiggling and kicking her legs, but Lucian laughed. She wasn't hitting him.

"Yes! Scream for me." He dropped his mouth to her neck, breathed in deep, and sighed in pleasure. "Your fear is so delicious, and I have been so hungry."

Alia kicked and squirmed but the tendrils squeezed, restricting her. As they slid up her neck, she began to hyperventilate. She snapped her mouth shut as they continued up over her chin, sliding toward her mouth, her eyes, her ears. She screwed her eyes shut and tears spilled down her cheeks. She whimpered, swinging her head back and forth, desperate to shake them off but not daring to open her mouth to scream. She struggled, trying to break free from his grasp.

Wake up!

A tendril slithered over her lip, pushing at the corner of her mouth. She bucked, bending away from him any way she could.

Wake up! It's the only way!

Another slid up her cheek and toward her nose, Lucian laughing.

Wake up! Wake up! WAKE UP!

With a final burst of strength, Alia pushed against him with an explosion of light. Her arms and legs were released, and her light pushed in every direction she could reach. The force of her desperate fight sent her toppling to one side and she fell to the floor, landing on her shoulder.

The quiet sounds of the Arbor estate greeted her. Her eyes flew open and she found herself lying on the floor of her room, her legs tangled up in the bedsheets hanging off the edge of the mattress. She gasped for air. She sat up, arms shaking and tears running down her face. Her skin tingled where his tendrils had slid, the sensation slowly fading as the dream grew more distant.

Pulling her knees to her chest and burying her face behind them, she wrapped herself up tightly. She let the tears fall as, slowly, her breathing and heart rate returned to normal. "Just a dream," she muttered to herself, rocking back and forth. "It was just a dream."

11

Galvin sat straight up in bed, gulping in air, his heart racing and hands shaking. He was certain he hadn't been dreaming so it couldn't have been his own fear that had awoken him. The sensation was coming from Alia and was much worse than a nightmare. He recognized the feeling: thick and greasy, sliding over his emotions to smother them. He knew only one demon who could elicit that reaction.

This was fear magic.

Alia hadn't been fully honest with him. Why wouldn't she trust him with something as important as Lucian? Did she think Galvin wasn't strong enough to help her?

He rubbed his face, forcing himself to wake up. The trembling in his hands subsided. He flipped the covers off, slipped out of bed, and marched across his room to the door. He was going to get to the bottom of what was bothering her and they would figure out how to get rid of it. He would prove she could rely on him. He certainly wasn't going to sit back and watch her suffer.

Galvin strode the few steps between his and Alia's doors and knocked. He wasn't interested in politeness at the moment and didn't wait for her to deny him entry before barging in. This time he planned to demand she tell him what was going on. No more letting her brush him off. If he had to, he would lock them both inside until she spilled.

But one look at her stole all the fight out of him. She was hunched on the floor next to the bed, hugging her legs to her chest with her forehead resting on her knees. The blankets were a tangled mess, half hanging off the bed, and her hair was escaping her usual braid, a curly mane around her head. She hadn't bothered to fix either of them, even though she was typically a very neat person. She hid her face, tremors wracking her frame as she sobbed.

The sight wrenched his heart. He had never seen her like this. She was so strong and confident, even when Declan had been captured and they had been left on their own. He always suspected a small portion of her attitude had to be bluster, as with most people, but he had never known her to be truly scared of anything. Something was certainly wrong, and he couldn't let her face it alone.

Galvin sank to the floor next to her, reaching to lay his hand on her back. Alia, lost in her fear, jumped and cried out. She scooted away, fighting him off as the dream cleared from her vision. Her beautiful hazel eyes were unfocused when she looked up, red and filled with tears.

It took her a few moments to realize it was him as she blinked, staring at him. Red marks marred her neck and cheeks, like the skin had been rubbed raw. She tried to pull herself together, wiping tears from her face and attempting to smooth back her hair, but the damage was done. He had already seen her distress. "I'm fine, really," she lied. "It was just a—"

"That was not just a nightmare." He kept his voice soft, but cut off her argument. There was no way he'd believe that anymore.

She stammered incoherently, trying to brush him off and deny anything was wrong.

Galvin cupped her face, his thumbs rubbing her freckled cheeks, forcing her to look him in the eye. She fit perfectly in his palm. He was gentle but held her in place. He didn't know how else to get her to stop and listen. "Alia Charlotte Arbor," he said, his voice as firm and gentle as his hold on her.

She froze, blinking some more as if seeing him for the first time.

When she trailed off, he sighed in relief. His thumbs wiped away the wet stains from her cheeks before he dropped his hands to her shoulders. "No more lies," he told her, softer now he'd gotten through to her. "Something's wrong, and you need to tell me what it is."

Her whole body sank farther to the floor. Tears flowed freely now. She took big breaths, trying to control the sobs threatening to overtake her. Her voice quivered. "It's the nightmares. Lucian traps me in some house where I can't use my magic." Her voice cracked and squeaked. "He's trying to finish what he started." She clenched her hands into herself to not tremble.

That was enough to give Galvin chills. Based on her description, he doubted her dreams were simply night terrors resulting from trauma. He traced the fading red mark on her cheek. "So what happened to your face?" He remembered Lucian controlled a tar-like substance resembling disgusting tentacles, like slick chords of boneless muscle. Galvin freed her from them in the Nome Grove. The memory was enough to churn his stomach.

She flinched away from him, her eyes growing wide and the trembling in her hands becoming more violent as she reached up to touch the side of her mouth. Her breathing became erratic, her chest heaving. "M-my face?" Her voice came out small and shaky.

"It's not so bad anymore." He downplayed his unease to keep her from losing all her composure but, as a half-fae, he couldn't fully lie. "I barely notice it now."

Alia started hyperventilating. Galvin felt the fear building in her in a thick fog, spiking his heart rate and clouding his mind, making it harder for him to remain level headed. He needed her to calm down so at least one of them could think clearly.

He did the only thing he knew to force her mind away from the fear. He pulled her into his arms, laying her head on his shoulder. It was almost like the time she had distracted him from his panic at the train station. He couldn't help but blush as he remembered how close they had been, but the plan had worked. He'd been too flustered to pay attention to the soldiers looking for them.

Her face pressed against the bare skin of his shoulder, her cheek on the white vine of his druid tattoo. She was so warm compared to the coolness of his own body. He'd never really noticed before, but even at the train station they hadn't touched like this. Each shuddering breath against his skin.

He pulled her into his lap, pressing her close. She hid in the crook of his neck, one hand coming up to rest on his chest. She spent so much time trying to be strong; did she ever let herself just feel? There, in the safety of his embrace, she cried.

He wasn't sure how long they stayed like that. It felt like hours and mere moments. He didn't mind. He would be happy to sit with her like this all night. He was comfortable, even on the floor.

While he cradled her, his gaze wandered. Alia's room was like her—rustic elegance. A bed decorated with druid stories, light greens and blues in the sheets and fabrics of her chaise lounge and armchair. A bookcase filled with her favorite titles.

Nothing like his. Galvin's room was mostly bare. It contained standard bedroom furniture—bed, nightstand, desk—all masterfully picked to match the dark wood and old style of the house. What it lacked, though, were things that made it Galvin's. He had only recently moved in with the Arbors and even more recently had they all come to live here. In that time he had gathered books and little tinkering projects on the desk and nightstand, but nothing that screamed, *This room belongs to Galvin*. The difference was Alia had decorated her room over the many years she and Declan visited the estate. Galvin's would have to evolve over time as well.

Her fear subsided. Slowly, the rise and fall of her chest steadied, though her heart still seemed to want to beat through her ribs. Which was probably why his heart was pounding so hard too. Her hands dropped to her lap and she lifted her head off his shoulder. The absence of her warmth where their skin had touched left him chilled.

As much as he wanted to sit with her forever, the night's events needed to be addressed. "Alia, this is serious." He tried to speak as soothingly as possible. "Something is wrong. Have you talked to Declan?"

"Not yet." Her breath was warm on his chest, raising goosebumps. "It started just before he left for his hearing. I wanted to tell him how much worse it had gotten when he came home but now that wizard is here, and we can't let the Council see our weakness."

Galvin quieted her, brushing back the tangle of hair from her face. The soft curls snagged on his fingers but she didn't seem to notice the slight tugs.

She sighed, melting into him and resting her forehead against his neck again. "That's nice."

Her lavender vanilla scent mixed with the musk of her sweat wafted up as he brushed her hair, reminding him of their sparring matches. She always came up with new ways to overcome his height advantage. Many of them involved wrapping herself around his shoulders and neck.

His heart lurched and his cheeks heated. He shoved away thoughts of her tackling him to the ground and pinning him underneath her. It was not the time, and he did not want to think about why his body reacted like that—or worse, for those thoughts to travel down the bond and into Alia's mind.

Galvin adjusted her so she could look at him but he kept her secure on his lap, his arm curled protectively around her. He tilted his head till her eyes met his. "This is what we're going to do. We're going to go downstairs and make you some moon milk, then I'm going to help you get back to sleep." Unease filled her eyes, but he shushed whatever argument was forming on her lips. "No, you need sleep. Your body will shut down if you don't get some good rest, and we're going to need you in top form to deal with whatever this wizard is sending us into. You know it's going to be bad."

Alia nodded. There was no denying Grace had picked the mission as some form of punishment. Of course it was going to be bad.

"In the morning, we'll find a moment alone with Declan before we're sent off." Galvin helped Alia to her feet, wrapped an arm behind her, and led her toward the kitchen. They had made it to the end of the hall before she paused and squinted at him.

"How did you know my middle name was Charlotte?"

He chuckled, shrugging a shoulder and urging her on down the stairs. "We've been in each other's heads. I'd be surprised if that's the only one of your secrets I've learned."

12

Declan had been stuck at his desk all morning under Grace's watchful eye. She had told him he needed to fill out some paperwork to replace the lost files of his life in hiding. Declan wasn't sure how much of it was necessary but under the circumstances he didn't have much choice but to play along, at least until he had a more effective plan.

He tried to remember where he had been one hundred and fifty years ago for one of the forms. Had his alias been James or William? Why did they even care this far back? 1868—just after the American Civil War. He had worked very hard not to be part of the war, instead helping supernatural refugees escape to safe places on both sides of the battle lines. He had traveled back and forth so much it was hard to remember exactly where he had been that year.

Standing, Declan stretched his back. It had been ages since he had spent so much time at a desk. Perhaps a break would be good. He wanted to check on Alia too. She looked so tired lately. He needed to make sure she was sleeping and everything was all right.

"And where are you going?"

Declan bristled. Grace's attitude irritated him. Since arriving yesterday, she had been giving him orders like she ran the place, like she were a clan elder. Even at the height of the druids' power, Declan had rarely taken orders he didn't agree with, and the elders never tried to force him into a subordinate role. He'd been on the Council once; they knew his position in the clan, which was likely why they'd stripped him of his authority and sent Grace, in the hopes she could do what the others could not. He wisely kept his mouth shut now, but the time would come when he would remind her of her place as a guest.

"I'm just going to take a break." He kept his voice as polite as possible, making his way around the desk toward the door. "I'm going to check on Alia and Galvin and make sure they have everything under control."

"What is there to control about a quiet day at home? Is something wrong?"

Declan paused a few steps from his desk. He didn't like the implication in that question. "No."

"Are they not adults? Why do they need constant supervision from you?"

Almost an accusation. "Yes, they are adults, but I am their mentor. I should be supervising what they are working on."

"Are they not skilled enough to handle things on their own? I thought they were completing their training."

Declan's jaw clenched. "They are—"

"Then should I be concerned about the capabilities of your apprentices?"

"No," he snapped, "of course not."

"Delightful." She smiled, her cold blue eyes shining in triumph. "You had me worried. But since everything is fine, we really should get back to this paperwork. It won't fill itself out." She giggled at her own joke.

Back turned towards Grace, Declan mimed an unflattering imitation her laughter as he took his seat at his desk. With the right spell, the paperwork probably could fill itself out. What a waste of time.

After another hour of trying to remember hundred-year-old aliases and locations, Declan was about ready to beg for a break. But before he could, Grace walked up, a small case file in her hand. It was different from the ones she'd brought him before. It must've been information on where she was sending his apprentices.

"Go ahead and take a break from that paperwork," she instructed. "I need you to inform Alia and Galvin to come here so I can brief them on their mission."

Finally! She was handing him the perfect opportunity to meet with his apprentices alone. He was standing from his chair before his pen hit the desk.

Grace stared in bewilderment, holding her palm out to slow him down. "Where are you going in such a hurry?"

Declan blinked at her, his lip curling. She couldn't be serious. "To get Alia and Galvin. Like you asked."

"Surely you have ways of communicating in a big place like this that don't require you searching the estate high and low on foot."

He frowned, sinking back into his chair. Of course he did, but that wasn't the point. Irritated, he pulled out an inactive sentry—a wispy thing, more flower than twig. He whispered to it, his green magic flowing into its petals, waking it up. It stretched gracefully, awaiting instruction. Declan instructed it to collect Alia and Galvin and tell them to come to his office. The little sentry floated off like a flower on a breeze.

Grace watched, intrigued. "What sort of spell is that?" she asked. "Are there limits to what the creature can do?"

Declan remained silent, leaning back in his chair and crossing his arms. He had no intention of answering.

Grace' mouth turned down at his insubordination. "I feel I must remind you that, as your probation officer, you are under my purview."

He didn't care if she was the Queen of Sheba. He wouldn't reveal anything he didn't have to. "You may be our PO," he retorted, more irritation in his voice than was wise, "but that does not make you privy to our spells."

Her disappointment turned into a glare. "Cooperation will work better in your favor."

"Duly noted." Declan wasn't easily intimidated and he had suffered worse than Grace's threat in others' attempts to persuade him to divulge secrets.

Thankfully Alia and Galvin entered then, preventing Declan from digging himself further into his hole. To his relief, Alia seemed quite a bit better this morning, her face less pale and drawn than it had been yesterday. Bags hung under her eyes but they looked less dark. She must have finally gotten some sleep.

Galvin, on the other hand, appeared more tired than normal. He was usually a deep and heavy sleeper; once he went down for the night, it was almost impossible to wake him. Whatever had kept him up must have been either important or intensive. Declan wondered if his lack of sleep had anything to do with Alia looking better.

With their connection, anything was possible. The bond seemed to evolve every day, and there was still so much Declan didn't understand about what had happened to them during the upgrade spell. He tried to guide them as much as he could but he wasn't sure how helpful he was all the time. Neither was in top shape right now but Declan knew he couldn't argue to keep them home. Especially not after his obstinance.

Alia handed him the sentry, raising an eyebrow at his open use of the spell in front of Grace. Declan glanced in Grace's direction and rolled his eyes. Alia nodded and pursed her lips.

The sentry, its task complete, curled up in his hand and turned back into inanimate flower petals and twigs, which he tucked into his desk drawer.

Without waiting, Grace handed Galvin the file, confirming Declan's suspicion about its contents. He found it odd she would mark Galvin as the leader of the pair. While he had come a long way from the naïve boy who had arrived on their doorstep over the summer, he wasn't the type to take charge. Alia carried a natural authority that typically singled her out as the leader. Now Declan thought about it, Grace had barely acknowledged Alia since she had arrived. He wondered what that was about.

"We need you two to assist our warlocks in the Redwood Forest. There is a dangerous creature causing havoc for the small town nearby. The mortals and civilian wizards living there are frightened and many have moved away for the safety of their families. The Council needs help figuring out what the creature is so we can stop it before it destroys the village. The warlocks have agreed to give you until November first before they solve the problem themselves."

That information seemed off to Declan. He didn't remember a village that close to the Redwoods, but it had been a long time since he'd been anywhere near Northern California. A small grove could have grown since the last time he'd been in the area.

Alia narrowed her eyes at Grace. "How, exactly, are we supposed to help?"

"The creature seems to be connected to the forest. Even though the warlocks have instructions to treat the area with respect, the creature is aggressive. We're worried it will attack more than just the mortals who live nearby. We need the two of you to find out what it is and destroy it."

Something wasn't right. Declan couldn't recall any type of creature who developed a connection to a particular forest and wasn't completely docile unless provoked. Supposing it had been provoked, then subduing it was out of the skill range of all three of them combined. It must have either felt threatened or been tainted by dark magic. In the case of either scenario, he wasn't comfortable with the Council's involvement.

His stomach twisted at the thought of Grace sending his apprentices out alone and knowing he couldn't do anything about it. They were walking into unknown danger, and he wouldn't be able to protect them from behind his desk.

"The two of you are expected to report to Captain Ashblade by two this afternoon. I have been assured that should be plenty of time for you to travel there by whatever means you see fit. You are dismissed."

Despite her attempt at authority, both Alia and Galvin turned to Declan. Like at the meeting yesterday, they weren't going to follow any orders without his approval.

Their habit of moving in unison sometimes made Declan uncomfortable. They couldn't help it, he knew that, and it startled them more often than it did him—but it was eerie, like they didn't have full control of their own thoughts.

He sighed, silent but heavy, nodding just enough for Alia and Galvin to see. He didn't want them to undertake the mission, certainly not alone and in their current condition. Especially not after what had happened the last time he'd left them alone. By some miracle, they had survived then but that didn't mean they were ready to take on another divine-level creature.

Despite his effort to hide his reaction, Grace noticed. He caught her glare without making eye contact, instead watching his apprentices leave, a familiar fear settling in his stomach as they disappeared around the corner. He'd felt the same apprehension watching the storm roll in on the back porch of their Appalachian home right before he and Alia had left Galvin and set off into the woods to attempt her master ceremony.

Right before everything had gone wrong.

13

Alia stopped by her room to gather the pack she had put together this morning. There were things she thought may be helpful to bring now they knew a little more about what their assignment entailed. Her pack was on the chaise at the foot of her bed, but what she was looking for was in her closet. She slid the door open and searched on the floor in the back for the enchanted camping gear she and Declan had used over the years. If they were going to be roughing it in the woods, they would probably want a tent, a couple mats to sleep on, flashlights, and a way to keep warm at night.

She grabbed the small box everything was neatly and magically tucked away in. The box was small and wouldn't take up too much room in her bag but contained everything she and Galvin would need to be comfortable while camping. She closed the closet door and turned toward her pack.

She almost ran into Lucian, who lurked right behind her. His eyes were black, wide mouth spread in a fang-baring grin.

Alia gasped, dropping the box and backing into the closet door. He pinned her, covering her mouth before she could scream. Her legs trembled so bad she wasn't sure she could keep herself up. She whimpered, shaking her head under his hand.

He leaned in, his mouth next to her ear. "Shh," he whispered, "I don't want anyone coming in to spoil my fun."

She squirmed, but his body pressed her flat to the door, giving her no room to escape. Lucian was supposed to be dead. This couldn't be happening. He couldn't be here. She had to be dreaming again—that was the only explanation.

But when had she fallen asleep?

Black tendrils wrapped around her, restrained her arms to her sides and binding her ankles together. She tried to shout for Galvin, Declan, anyone who could hear her, but his hand dampened the sound.

Lucian sniffed up her neck to her hair, and she recoiled, gagging. His fangs elongated over a wicked smile. Her blood ran cold and she chocked back a sob. The tremors in her arms and legs grew violent as she stared death in the face.

He lowered his head, fangs brushing the skin at her neck. "Don't worry, Little Druid," he purred. "I'm not going to kill you yet. I just need a little refresher to grow stronger for you." Sharp points pushed into her skin.

She screamed and struggled, doing anything to stop him from taking her blood. But her cries were too muffled and he bound her too tightly.

The door burst open, slamming against the wall as Galvin ran to her side.

In the moment it took her to look toward Galvin, Lucian had

disappeared, gone as if he had never been there.

Galvin scooped her up in his arms, holding her close as her trembling subsided.

She sobbed into his shoulder, curled into him. "He was here! Lucian was here, he was going to bite me."

"Alia," he said softly. The concern in his voice drew her gaze. Worry etched lines on his face. Worry for her sanity. "Lucian is dead. Declan killed him. We both saw him do it."

Her voice was small and uncertain. "I know, but he was here." It was impossible, yet it had happened. "He touched me. He was going to hurt me."

"He can't hurt you," Galvin reassured, but he didn't sound completely convinced. "But these nightmares might. We have to tell Declan what's going on. You can't go on the mission like this."

She knew he was right. Lack of sleep was no longer her biggest problem. Now she was hallucinating while awake. Or had she fallen asleep and not realized it? Which was worse? She couldn't afford to do either while on a mission.

Galvin helped her up, never letting go of her hand. He wrapped his arm around her shoulders and led her out of her room. She was thankful for the assistance. Her legs shook from the adrenaline. She leaned into him, letting him guide her as they made their way to Declan's office.

In addition to the physical support, something about Galvin's presence was comforting. If the nightmares were dark rain clouds, then he was the wind and sunshine that banished them. The terror made her thoughts fuzzy and it was difficult to concentrate but when Galvin was near she felt like herself again, though tired. Some of the peace traveled to her through their connection but it was also more tangible than usual, more measurable. It had to be magic.

If he had to resort to using magic to calm her, then her fear was more than normal: it was magic too. If that was true, Lucian would have to still be alive.

The thought scared and angered her at the same time.

Alia let Galvin walk her all the way to the office door, but she stopped him before he knocked. She straightened, taking a deep breath. Galvin huffed and opened his mouth to argue but she held up a hand. "I'm not going to back out. We're here to get Declan's help. But I'm not going to let this—let *him* have the better of me." She swallowed hard, gathering her strength and bit the bullet. She squared her shoulders and reached for the handle. Her fingers brushed the metal and a sharp pop snapped at her fingers. She jerked her hand back, shaking out the static.

"What was that?" Galvin asked.

"Static, I guess."

He looked around before eyeing her. "Where would you have built up static? There's no carpet." When she shrugged again, he turned back to the door. "Well, we have bigger things to worry about. C'mon."

He at least knocked before pushing into the office. It was a good thing Declan had an open door policy, Alia thought. He sat at his desk, a stack of papers on either side of him. He had paused in the middle of filling one out to rub his eyes.

Alia felt bad for him. Declan put up with paperwork when necessary, but he found it tedious. He was certainly no bureaucrat. He also looked angry, and Declan was rarely genuinely angry. True, Alia didn't know many people and hadn't ventured into the outside world much, but Declan seemed to possess the patience of a saint. Others with more worldly experience than her had claimed the same. Grace must be getting under his skin.

When Declan saw them, his expression changed to worry. His gaze passed over Galvin, expertly determining he was okay, but lingered on Alia as he took in her haggard appearance. He lept to his feet. "What happened?"

"It's Alia," Galvin explained, not giving her the chance to chicken out of telling the truth.

"What's wrong with Alia?" Grace emerged from somewhere behind them. First, Alia balked at her sudden appearance, concerned Grace would learn about her weakness, but the feeling was soon replaced with irritation at her constant presence. Why was she always hovering? Didn't she ever give Declan a minute alone?

"Well?" Grace probed Galvin. "What's happened to Alia?"

Alia locked eyes with Declan, willing him to understand. Of all the things that could not happen, Grace finding out about Alia's nightmares—or even worse, possession—was at the top of the list. She could tell him in Gaelic, but then Grace would know something was up and demand to be told what they were saying. It was no use; she couldn't say anything to Declan right now.

"Nothing is wrong," she lied. "I just wanted to borrow Declan's sentry." She turned a neutral stare on Grace. "In case we need to communicate with the two of you." The spell for the sentry was actually very simple. Declan had taught Alia how to make one years ago. Every druid carried infused water from the grove. Not that it mattered because Alia wouldn't be able to activate Declan's sentry anyway.

Declan knew all this, but he opened his desk drawer and handed her the bundle of flowers and twigs as if there were nothing strange about her request. Her fingers shook slightly as she reached out, and of course he noticed. He took her hand in both of his, steadying hers as he placed the useless sentry in her palm. Like everything was normal.

Declan held her briefly. "We'll talk more when you get back."

"Of course we will." Grace pushed into the room to stand next to Declan. "We'll need to be debriefed about the mission."

Since Grace couldn't see his face, Declan silently mocked her, lifting Alia's spirits. She gave him a small smile in return. How she wished she could tell him.

"Now that you have everything," Grace said, ushering Alia and Galvin out the door, "I'm guessing you'll be heading off." She flashed one last grin that gave Alia an icky feeling. "Good luck." And she closed the door behind them.

The two of them walked back up to their rooms, where they had left all their things in their rush to talk to Declan.

"I'm sorry," Alia said. "I wanted to tell him, I really did, but Grace *can't* know."

Galvin dropped his hands on her shoulders, shushing her arguments. "I know. Don't worry. I don't know how we'll do it, but we will get you through this."

Alia hugged him, squeezing him and burying her face in his chest. She felt him pause before his arms wrapped around her, returning the hug. She was more scared now than she had been to tell Declan the truth.

14

Declan stared at the door after Alia and Galvin left. They had wanted to tell him something and Alia had been frightened. She was rarely scared but there was no mistaking the tremor in her hands. He hoped it didn't have to do with the lingering effects of Lucian's magic but his gut told him that was exactly what it was—that, or something worse he didn't want to give a name to. If her symptoms were getting stronger, being sent off to fight some unknown creature would only put her in more danger. Magic side effects were unpredictable and could hit at the most inconvenient times. But she rightfully didn't want Grace to know something was wrong. So how could he keep them from going on the assignment without telling the Council his apprentices weren't up to the task? Or being openly rebellious and inviting a whole army of warlocks to their doorstep?

He sighed. He couldn't.

He looked around the room, locating Grace working on her own paperwork. She had taken over Tiberius's desk, which left a bad taste in his mouth. Tiberius hadn't used it much in life but it was still his space. Even during their falling out, Declan hadn't touched that desk. Despite all the genocide, a small part inside Declan had been convinced Tiberius was only pretending to be a traitor. Mass murder wasn't in Tiberius's nature.

Declan should have trusted that instinct.

He shook the memories away. He had issues to deal with now. Grace did not belong there. She didn't belong anywhere at the Arbor estate, but he hadn't figured out how to get rid of her without inciting a rebellion. The Council was corrupted and the best way to fight it was from the inside.

Grace seemed focused on her work, not paying him any mind. If he snuck out quietly, he might have enough time to check on Alia.

When Grace had announced she would be staying at the Arbor estate, Declan had assumed she would be the one constantly looking to sneak off and snoop around the house. Instead, here he was trying to sneak out of his own office. He gently turned the handle, trying to make as little noise as possible.

"You really shouldn't procrastinate on that paperwork," she called without looking up.

Declan kept his shoulders from slumping and suppressed the groan he felt to his soul. He said a silent prayer to any angel listening for patience before facing her. "It's their first assignment alone. I thought I'd see them off."

She put her pen down and got up from Tiberius's desk. "That's actually a lovely idea. I'll come with you."

Declan attempted several protests as she approached, but Grace ignored them all with a smile. She slipped her arm into his and pulled him out into the hallway and down the stairs. She pressed close against his side, making him uncomfortable. Was she flirting? He inwardly groaned. He hoped not so he wouldn't have to disappoint her. That would only make things more awkward.

Then again, it was possible she was doing it to throw him off. Hopefully it was that.

They turned the corner at the bottom of the stairs and walked through the hall to the ballroom and the doors leading to the courtyard in the back. Declan's sneakers squeaked on the polished wood floor and Grace's short heels clicked in the empty room. He opened one side of the French doors and led her out into the crisp autumn day.

Even with the sun up and shining, the air was cool. The surrounding trees and shrubs had turned all the beautiful reds, oranges, and bright yellows of fall and in about a week they would be brown and falling off. In the distance, Alia wore a warmer sweater instead of her normal flannel overshirt, but Galvin wore a thin one, hardly bothered by the chill at all. They paused at the entrance to the hedge maze that would take them to the grove's sacred tree, Alia checking Galvin's pack.

"We don't want a repeat of what happened last time. I doubt we're going to run into another laundry service out in the woods with a bunch of warlocks."

Galvin blushed, muttering under his breath.

Declan cleared his throat, alerting them to their company. Alia raised an eyebrow at Declan and Grace's linked arms but all he could do was shake his head and mouth a silent apology.

"We came to wish you luck," Grace announced. Declan wasn't sure why she sounded so delighted, it hadn't even been her idea. But at least he got to see Alia and Galvin off.

Detaching himself, Declan approached his two apprentices.

"Are you all right?" he asked Alia in Old Gaelic. Galvin wouldn't understand, but he had taught her the language from a young age for just this reason. This would only work once, since Grace would surely find a spell to translate when they went back inside.

Alia smiled, but it didn't reach her eyes. The hazel was more brown than green today. It could have been the brightness of the sun or her own bad mood. *"Not really,"* she admitted, *"but you can't help with Grace around, and I don't think you can fix it in a few seconds. Even in an almost dead language."* They chuckled together but the mirth died quickly. *"I have Galvin. Whatever he does, it seems to help. We'll figure it out when we get back."*

Declan brushed her cheek, *"All right, bug. The dragon and I have Galvin's phones, but send me some sort of message if you need anything. I'll come right away."*

Alia hugged him. *"Don't do something you'll regret.* Try not to worry too much, Galvin and I are together," she said, switching back to English.

Despite Galvin's recent addition to the druids, that did give Declan some comfort. "Sure. You'll be fine. Compared to Mathias, this should be easy, right?"

At least, that was what he needed to remind himself.

He turned to Galvin, who gave him a lopsided grin. He had changed so much in the short time he'd been with them. His black hair was a mess now and he had filled out nicely from their physical training. He was proving a fast and capable student.

"We got this," he said.

Declan gave each of his young apprentices one last hug before sending them off. Long ago, when the clan had been at its most powerful, it had always been good publicity to help other factions when they could. The Council would want the rest of the world to think the druids were dangerous to make it easier to control them. Despite their situation, they needed to do everything they could do to dispel that lie, even at the behest of someone they couldn't trust. Eventually, karma would tip in their favor. The strategy had worked for druid clans in the past, and it would help them again now.

Alia and Galvin walked into the hedge maze outside the grove's entrance, side by side. Declan was struck by how much they reminded him of Layla and Noah. Alia's parents had been his apprentices before these two. A pair lost before their time. His stomach clenched as he watched them leave.

All of them. Declan had lost every single apprentice on their first mission alone. But that had been when Mathias was killing them all off whenever he got the chance.

They hadn't seen a demon in weeks, though, and Mathias had to know where they were. It was the only grove left undamaged and Declan's longtime home. Clearly, Mathias wasn't interested in continuing the fight. But someone had started the feud between them. Was that person still out there? Would they too hunt his apprentices?

He said a silent prayer to Gia, God, and whatever angels were listening to keep Alia and Galvin safe. *Whatever you do, don't allow them to survive my worst nightmare just to be lost to a new one I'm not ready for.*

"What did you say to Alia?"

Grace's question jarred him out of his gloomy thoughts. It was for the best. He didn't want to accidentally manifest ill fortune by dwelling on his fears too long. He supposed he should be grateful to her, but he just couldn't muster it.

"Gave her some spell advice. There's no translation in English that would make any sense." A lie, through and through.

"It must be difficult to watch them go on their own."

Declan's blood ran cold as he turned to her. She gave that sinister smile before walking back up to the house without him. His heart fell into his stomach as he watched her. It might not have been a threat. It might have been her attempt at empathy.

It was no use. He couldn't convince himself.

He looked back to the hedge maze where Alia and Galvin were surely already using the sacred tree to grove hop to the Redwood Forest. He fought the urge to chase after them, knowing Alia would never forgive him if he didn't put his trust in her now, when it meant the most.

15

"Are you sure this is the right place?" Galvin looked over Alia's shoulder at the map Grace had provided once more, as if his inability to differentiate north from south made him the authority on map reading. She bristled, wondering how on earth he thought he was going to be able to do better.

Stop it. She forced herself to take a cleansing breath. Galvin was not commentating on her navigation skills, only wanting to be helpful. Her frustration was more with the vague map and lack of sleep than with Galvin.

She looked up at the path again, trying to make sense of the differences between the path and the map. Fall had come to the Redwoods as well. Unlike the Black Forest where the Arbor Grove was, sunlight glowed through the canopy, casting a golden hue on the colorful fall foliage. It wasn't quite as cold here as it was back home, but she was grateful for her warmer sweater.

She checked the map again. All their instructions had been

vague. The information Grace had given them in Declan's office was reiterated in the file along with orders to report to a Captain Ashblade when they got to the camp. A survey sketch was included as their map.

"Yes, I'm sure." Her tone was snappier than she would have liked, but thankfully Galvin didn't notice. The camp had to be nearby. Alia could read a good map blindfolded, and they were in the woods. She had a knack for knowing where to go. A druid's inner pull always led them toward a grove—even Galvin had that ability. But her power was something stronger. Like having a GPS in her head.

Her navigation wasn't the problem. While the map Grace had provided wasn't what Alia would call top quality, it was passable for discerning directions, minimal as they were. She knew she had read it correctly, but they should have arrived by now. "We should be standing right on top of it. It's probably hidden with wards but I know we're in the right place."

Galvin squinted around the empty pathway. "If they're here on official Council business, why would they hide the camp?"

That was an excellent question. Even if the Council didn't want mortals finding out about magic, they should still have the camp to be visible. They could call the creature a dangerous animal to send mortals on their way if a big military camp didn't warn everyone to avoid the area in the first place.

Plus, Alia and Galvin were *expected*. How could you expect allies to arrive if you hid the location and didn't tell them how to find it?

Everything since Declan had been summoned to his hearing had felt off, and Alia didn't like it. She stuffed down the frustrated groan she wanted to utter. They should be trying to find out what happened to Evelyn but instead they were here, searching for a bunch of warlocks.

"Hands where I can see them," a voice demanded behind them.

Alia rolled her eyes but both she and Galvin complied. Between her fatigue and the difficulty of locating something they were instructed to find, she wasn't in the mood to be mistaken for intruders. The last thing she wanted was to spook any of the warlocks.

One man stepped in front of them, a hand held up, open palm facing them in a ready spellcasting position. He glared at them, not angrily but more like with professional wariness. If it could be said he had any expression at all. His square face, softer cheekbones, and round ears told Alia he was human. In the magic world, appearances were a wildly inaccurate way to assume age, but he looked like he couldn't have been much older than her and Galvin. His platinum blond hair was in a military-style buzzcut, indicating his status as a warlock, but it was his silver eyes that marked him as a Raptor, one of the elite soldiers the warlocks trained. He wore all black tactical gear and had two solid, silver bands on each of his wrists. Weapon bangles.

A dual wielder, then. Alia remembered Galvin telling her dual wielders with weapon bands were rare, even among Raptors. She could understand why. Her single gun took enough mental focus and magic energy to aim effectively. The idea of two formed from pure thought, concentration, and magic energy was impressive. And those bangles would create whatever weapon he needed.

As irritated as she was with the inconvenience, they had been right to comply with his commands; this man was a highly trained and highly skilled fighter.

"Identify yourselves." His voice was a rich tenor.

"Alia and Galvin of the Arbor Clan. We were assigned here to help get rid of a dangerous creature." Slowly she reached into her bag to retrieve the dispatch. He watched her closely, neon lines scrawling across the silver bands, but no weapons appeared and he made no move to stop her. She pulled out the papers and handed them to him. "We are supposed to report to Captain Ashblade."

The Raptor looked over the offered paperwork. He must have found everything in order because the glowing lines went out and his stance relaxed. His expression—if you could call it that—never changed, though, but remained an intense sort of neutral. Like he was focused on what he was doing but didn't have an opinion on it one way or the other.

Alia had read Raptors underwent extensive conditioning when they were accepted into the program and rarely showed any feelings afterward. That had to explain his strange reactions. Like the emotions had been trained out of him. She found that sad.

He slipped the dispatch into his pocket. "This way."

He turned away and led them farther down the path Alia had chosen. Any satisfaction she might have felt at being proven correct was replaced with a reinforcement of the thought that something was off about the whole situation. If the camp had been in front of them, then where had the Raptor come from?

The Raptor waved a hand in front of himself as they walked and the camp shimmered into view, like a mirage solidifying in front of them. The protective barrier felt like a sheet that clung and dragged across their skin as they passed the threshold, and then she felt it sink back into place behind them.

The camp was much bigger than she had anticipated. She'd thought there might be a team of ten warlocks at most. Instead, a dozen tents lined each side of the dirt road with rows extending behind into the grassy clearing, and they passed twice that many warlocks going about their duties. At least it appeared they hadn't felled any trees to make the clearing, but the building of the camp and the warlocks' trampling had turned the place into a muddy mess.

What kind of creature needed this large of a force to subdue it? What did Grace expect her and Galvin to do against a creature this many warlocks and their Raptors couldn't manage?

Alia looked closer at the milling warlocks. If there were any other Raptors stationed here, Alia didn't see them. So this mission required a large militant force but only one Raptor? It was possible the others were somewhere else. She had read they were powerful, but only one for a force this size seemed strange.

The Raptor led them to a tent at the end of the row, larger than the others, with a warlock on duty outside, a silver flag posted behind him. This must have been the authoritative center where the leaders met to strategize, not a place to rest. The Raptor walked straight into the tent without stopping to announce himself or ask permission. The guard didn't flinch as he strode by.

Alia paused and Galvin stopped behind her. She wasn't sure of the appropriate protocol but the guard made no indication the Raptor had behaved strangely and made no attempt to prevent them from entering after him. She turned to Galvin and he shrugged, no less confused than she was. With nothing indicating not to, they followed the Raptor inside.

The Raptor had already presented their dispatch to what had to be Captain Ashblade, who was reading it over, a second dispatch in his hands.

So that was why he came from behind. He's reporting here too. Alia had assumed the Raptor knew where the camp was hidden. Was it possible he could see the magic veil? Perhaps his instructions to find the camp had been better than theirs.

Captain Ashblade's dark brown hair was also cut in a military buzz. He wore all black as well, but his clothes were cleaner and slightly more formal than the Raptor's. The other warlocks had worn mostly forest-colored fatigues: browns, greens, and a little black. Alia wondered if the black marked them as officers or just Raptors. She hadn't seen any others in all black.

The Raptor and the captain had some other similarities too. They were both human and, when they turned their heads just right, Alia saw a sort of dot pattern tattooed behind their left ears. Without getting closer, she couldn't tell if it was the same pattern or not. The captain also wore a silver band on his right wrist, but just one—as was more common, according to Galvin.

The captain folded up the dispatch, turning silver eyes to Alia and Galvin, confirming her suspicion: the captain was also a Raptor, making her running count two. "So you two are the druids I've been expecting." He coldly evaluated them, his expression blank and unreadable. "You look a little green but I suppose there aren't many other options."

Alia frowned. That wasn't exactly a warm welcome, but then again they had been marked as troublemakers by the Council. Orders or not, she was ready to show him just how "green" they were.

"I'm Captain Ashblade. Your activities here will be under my purview." He turned to the other Raptor. "And you requested to *assist* at this post? Excellent, you can be the druids' liaison."

The Raptor's brows twitched downward, only the shadow of an expression. "I didn't—"

"Hawthorne here," the Captain said, looking back at Alia and Galvin and gesturing to his fellow Raptor, "I'm assigning to the two of you to provide any assistance, but everything you do will still need to be approved by me."

Alia glanced at Hawthorne. He met her gaze, but if he was frustrated or delighted Alia couldn't tell. Clearly something was happening between the two men though.

"The rest of the force here is for defense only," the captain explained. "You should already be up to date on what your task is. You have until November first to do whatever it is you plan to do. If the creature is still running loose by then, I'm giving the order to burn the forest down with the creature inside. Do you have any additional questions?"

It wasn't exactly a briefing, and his definition of "up to date" was a lot different from hers. "What can you tell us about the creature?"

Hawthorne eyed them and answered first. "You don't already know what it is?"

What? Alia narrowed her eyes. "How would we know what it is? We just got here, same as you."

Captain Ashblade gave Hawthorne a hard stare, and the blond Raptor looked away, going quiet. Ashblade turned back to his work, but his face remained frustratingly unreadable. "I can't tell you much, unfortunately. The warlocks who encounter it don't usually come back, so there's not a lot on record. The ones who return have little more to report than shadows, growls, and claws. We know it attacks unprovoked and that it's big, it has magic, and it's hard to locate when it doesn't want to be found."

"That's nothing to go on." Galvin glared, crossing his arms. Alia elbowed him but couldn't argue with his statement.

Captain Ashblade considered them quietly but made no

comment.

"If that's all you have, then I'll need to observe the creature to get a better idea of what we're dealing with," Alia explained.

"It's marked as more active at dawn and at dusk. Do whatever you need to do."

Alia pursed her lips. He really didn't want to be involved more than necessary. So it was just going to be the three of them: she and Galvin with Hawthorne.

It was barely mid-day when they had walked into camp. They had plenty of time to get settled and prepped before going out. "Is there a place we can set up our tent?"

Captain Ashblade gestured to the Raptor. "Hawthorne will take you to the barracks. You'll be put up there. Any magic prep work can be done in your assigned tent. I can't authorize any expansion of the camp at this time. Charlie-niner," he told Hawthorne. "My instructions are to provide you anything you need outside of what Hawthorne can manage." He waved them off but didn't so much as glance at them before going back to his work.

Alia recognized a dismissal when she saw one.

Hawthorne apparently did too, but before moving he gave them each a look. Not angry—a sort of examination. Then, without a word or explanation, he ushered them out of the tent and led them farther into the camp.

Several more rows of tents extended across the clearing next to the forest path. Hawthorne led them down one with tents long enough to house several people and stopped at one labeled C-9. "Every barrack tent has a worktable inside the entrance that should suffice for anything you need to put together, but you will be required to share with the others assigned here."

Alia *humph*-ed, "Privacy isn't exactly a thing for warlocks, is it?"

Hawthorne's eyes darted down, and she caught the smallest twitch of his face muscles contracting. "I suppose, since I am assigned to facilitate you, if you need additional, unshared space for your magic, you can use my tent. It is private."

"Wait." Alia frowned. "You get your own tent? But we can't set up ours?"

"Raptors are always kept separate from the warlocks." There was something unsaid in his words. Like it wasn't a privilege but a restraint. "I don't know why you were assigned to barracks," he added, almost apologetic. "It's not customary for non-warlocks to be thrown in with a troop. If I could, I would let you set up your tent."

"Well, can we at least stay with you?" Galvin asked. "It's not the same as having our own but we also wouldn't be setting up an additional tent."

Hawthorne shook his head. "I cannot disobey orders. I'm sorry."

Alia scrutinized him. Hawthorne was following Ashblade's orders, but something odd was going on. The two Raptors were so difficult to read, though, she couldn't quite place what it was.

"Oh, one more thing," she said. "Captain Ashblade didn't mention the village. Is there anything we need to do to make sure we keep the creature away from it?"

The Raptor narrowed his eyes. "I wasn't told anything about a village. I will ask, see what I can find out."

Yup. Definitely something going on. If the village was the priority, why didn't the Raptor know anything about it?

When neither asked any more questions, Hawthorne agreed to meet them in a couple hours to brief them before their departure to investigate the forest at dusk. Then he gave them an awkward goodbye and strode off before Alia thought to ask him what he was going to be doing. She didn't think his curtness was because he disliked them but just the sort of personality he had. Direct and to the point with no need for excess socialization.

Exhaustion hit hard all at once. Alia yawned, rubbing her face and attempting to gain a second wind. She was going to need some coffee before heading into the woods.

Galvin put his hand on her shoulder, making her look at him. "We have plenty of time before dusk—"

"No." She knew where he was going. She could not risk the warlocks witnessing her night terrors. The captain already wasn't impressed with them. They didn't need to give him any reason to kick them off the job. She couldn't go the whole time without sleep but she needed to wait until they wouldn't be observed.

Galvin tilted her head up to meet his eyes. "Now is the perfect time. The warlocks should be on duty," he answered her unspoken concerns. "I'll hold you while you sleep. It worked last night."

Butterflies barrel-rolled in her stomach, her face burning at the memory. She tried sputtering any argument that came to mind, but he just shushed her. "C'mon. You need sleep and I can help keep the nightmares away."

16

Galvin stroked Alia's hair as she slept. They had picked one of the empty cots, dropping their stuff on top of the footlocker provided. Galvin sat propped up, leaning against the pillows with Alia in his lap, her head on his chest. He held her and smoothed the hair back from her face as he pulled away a gray fog that gathered around her head. The thicker the fog grew, the more restless her sleep. It had been easier last night to clear it, but this afternoon it was forming faster, as if trying to counter his soothing efforts. He had hardly noticed he'd used magic last night, but now he had to work at it.

The fog collected around Galvin's hands as he removed it, hanging momentarily, swirling while its magic changed. He wasn't sure how but he knew his own magic was nullifying the fog. As Lucian's magic was cleansed, the fog turned black and sank, disappearing from sight but not entirely gone. He felt it hovering around his hands.

A thick amount formed around Alia's temples and she

whimpered, clutching tighter to Galvin. He scooped the cloud away and she relaxed once more. It pained him to know she was suffering. He was frustrated they hadn't been able to talk to Declan about whatever was causing Alia's nightmares before leaving. It was clearly not some sort of emotional trauma she had to heal from; it was an attack, and there was only one person he could think of who would drag it out. Any attack Lucian made on Alia, he took deeply personally.

But Lucian was dead, wasn't he? Galvin had seen Declan stab him in the Alaskan grove—his body turned to mist and was sucked into the rift the dagger had opened.

Chills ran down Galvin's spine as the realization struck him. *He had been sucked into the demon realm.* Lucian *wasn't* dead. And he was trying to finish what he had started with Alia. What had that book said about him? Something about fixating on his victims until they perished.

The heat of Galvin's flame ignited in the pit of his stomach. That wasn't going to happen. Not if he had anything to say about it.

He cleared away more of the gray fog from Alia's head. Lucian's fog. Trying to penetrate her dreams and feed on her fear. He looked down at her. Even with most of Lucian's magic removed, her resting face was pinched and she clung to him. His hold on her tightened. He was going to do everything in his power to keep Lucian off of her. He just had to protect her until they could get back to Declan.

Two warlocks entered the tent in the midst of their horseplay. Alia stirred at the noise and Galvin tried to shush and soothe her. She had been sleeping for about an hour, but that would only keep her going a little longer. She needed a full eight hours.

The warlocks clopped past Alia and Galvin's cot, no concern

for the amount of noise they were making. "Well, lookie here," one of them said, pausing. "The druids everyone is talking about were assigned to our tent."

"Ooh, look." The other gestured to Galvin. "A half-fairy too. No surprise the druids had to recruit outside of humans." He leaned over them, and Galvin shifted Alia in his lap to shield her. "Humans don't want to be associated with monster sympathizers."

Galvin scowled at the two warlocks as they reared back, laughing.

Alia stirred in his arms. She rubbed her eyes, groaning. Galvin tried to hush her back to sleep, but she sat up. "How long was I out?" she mumbled, voice thick.

"Barely an hour," Galvin told her, glaring at the snickering warlocks. "We still have time before we need to prep. Try to get some more rest."

"Ah, and they're a couple. Can't find yourself a human, sweetheart?"

Alia stiffened, pulling away from Galvin, her eyes growing wide and her face turning a bright shade of red.

Galvin huffed, the heat in his stomach growing. He breathed deeply, using one of the calming techniques Declan had taught him to keep his flames under control. The last thing he needed was fire to erupt from his hands while Alia was still in his lap.

"It's fine," she told Galvin. "We need to start prepping anyway." She scooted to the foot of the bed but leaned over her legs, sighing and trying to rub the exhaustion from her face. Then she began to put her boots on.

Galvin clenched his fists, his anger growing. These two

warlocks were crass. He didn't care much what they said about him but he couldn't bear the insults about Alia. They had made light of her struggles, embarrassing her when they had no clue what she was facing. He doubted either one of them could fight off Lucian's magic half as well as Alia was, and she still thought he was dead.

"Sweetheart, you're good-looking enough to have your pick of men if you just ditch the monsters."

"That's it!" Galvin leapt to his feet and stomped up to the warlock so they were toe to toe. His blood boiled. He was tall enough to glare down at the warlock. "How dare you talk about her that way!"

The warlock matched his stare, bemused, and with a little smirk on his face. "And what's the sissy fairy boy going to do about it?"

Galvin grabbed the front of the warlock's shirt, yanking him up so that their noses almost touched. He narrowed his eyes and the warlock's smirk faltered a little, but Galvin was close enough to see his expression darken. The black smoke that had lingered unseen reappeared, swirling around Galvin's hands, creeping up the warlock's shoulders and neck.

The heat of Galvin's flames filled him, but it was the shadows bleeding into the edges of his vision that responded. "This sissy fairy boy is going to show you what real nightmares look like." His voice echoed strangely.

Alia pulled Galvin off the warlock. Galvin released him, but the smoke clung to his head and shoulders. Alia tugged him toward the tent's entrance, eyes wide.

The warlock stood dazed, the black smoke swirling around his temples. His buddy was shaking him and patting his cheeks, trying to get his attention. Apparently he couldn't see the smoke because he did nothing to clear it away. Was Galvin the only one who could see it?

Outside, Alia turned him to look at her. "What is wrong with you?"

"I'm sorry, they were so rude, I lost my temper. They're lucky I didn't set the place on fire. By accident," he clarified at the distressed look on Alia's face. He was actually a little surprised he hadn't lost control of his flames.

"And the dark eyes?"

"Who's dark eyes?"

"Yours! I know you cast something, I could feel it. What was that?"

"I didn't mean to cast anything! There was this smoke that forms while you're sleeping. I pulled it away and I guess I pushed it onto him. I don't know what it was," he admitted more soberly. "I've never done that before. It was like I was running on instinct."

"You transferred Lucian's fear magic onto someone else?" Alia closed her eyes and rubbed at her head. "You cannot lose control like that. We have to be on our best behavior. We're all in bad standing with the Council and if we go picking fights with warlocks, we could get in bigger trouble than we already are. Not to mention getting our butts kicked. There are only three of us, and they have an army."

Galvin snorted, crossing his arms. "We could take those two meatheads."

"And what would happen if they reported us and it got back to Grace? They could have us arrested before we get out of the camp. Who knows what they would tell the other supernatural groups about us." Alia shook her head. "We have to figure out how to get that off of him."

He deflated, realizing she was right. He had been reckless.

"Yeah. I'm sorry. I wasn't thinking."

"We have to be the very definition of model citizens." She pointed an accusatory finger at him. "You promise?"

Galvin nodded, holding up his hands in defeat. "Model citizen. I promise."

Alia relaxed with a sigh, looking him over with interest. "What's going to happen to him, anyway?"

"I'm not certain," he confessed. "I'm reasonably sure I've given him night terrors, though. I don't really know if it's Lucian's magic or mine now."

"Let's give you both time to calm down. Then we'll come back and try to take it off. No one deserves being tortured by Lucian."

"You're right. I'm sorry."

17

Alia was worried. She knew Galvin hadn't meant to go so far, but now that he was a druid and didn't have to hide his emotions, he tended to feel them strongly. Particularly when he thought he was protecting her or Declan. Hopefully whatever he'd done was mild and the warlock would be able to cleanse it. Maybe she could have Hawthorne check on the warlock in a bit.

Hawthorne's tent was located slightly apart from the rest of the barracks, tucked away in the back. It was within the perimeter the captain had claimed could not be expanded but definitely separate from the rest of the camp.

He had tied the opening flap back, leaving the entrance wide open. Still, it felt strange and rude to push in. Alia leaned over, peering inside. "Hawthorne?"

"Yeah," he replied, "in here."

He may have gotten his own tent, but it wasn't much of a luxury. It was smaller inside than Alia expected. The same standard issue cot and footlocker were in their tent. Aside from a place to sleep and a small worktable covered in various magical tools, there was little room for anything else.

Hawthorne was sitting inside on a short stool, a utility belt laid across the cot along with an assortment of small vials of colored potions, some utility tools, and seemingly random objects; rocks, coins, and was that a plastic army man? It appeared like he was going through what he would need and organizing his various pockets and pouches.

"Raptors *always* get separate tents?" Galvin asked, looking over Alia at the bits and bobs. He was likely eating this up. Galvin had always been fascinated by wizard magic and had wanted to be one before he became a druid. The first time he'd seen Theo's lab, she'd had to remind him not to drool. Thankfully, he was a little more restrained this time.

"Yes, it's standard practice to be kept separate from the warlocks," Hawthorne explained.

Separate and private but with no better accommodations than those in the warlock tent they just came from. "Does that make you an officer" Alia asked.

"Depends on what I'm doing. I'm not the ranking officer on this mission."

Alia wasn't sure what that meant. "Um. What?"

He lifted his gaze from his work, blinking when he took in Alia's appearance but showing no other sign of surprise. "You look like hell."

A tickle crawled across her skin as she bristled. "Gee. Thanks."

Hawthorne showed no indication he paid any heed to her

sarcasm. He simply returned his attention to his task. "Raptors are the elite force. It's rare to be qualified to train as one, and an even smaller number complete training. The warlocks have their own officers and hierarchy, but we come in as a supplement when a mission needs our skills. But usually we are considered more so the World Council's forces. Raptors get their orders from the Council. Warlocks are just the wizards' military force, though most of the wizards who hold positions in our faction also hold positions on the Council and their orders outrank other magic Council members, so the wizards and the Council are almost one and the same."

He had basically admitted the wizards were taking control of the Council. Alia wondered how much trouble Hawthorne would be in if anyone knew he said that.

"I'm guessing you're ready to get started." He finished up with his belt. "It's still too light out to go to the woods, so what's the plan?"

"I want to talk to the warlocks who encountered the creature. See if I can learn anything else from what they saw."

"All right." Hawthorne closed his last pouch and strapped on the belt. "I asked around while you were getting settled. I'm told they are all in the infirmary."

Alia eyed him, but Hawthorne continued to secure his utility belt. He seemed to know as much as she and Galvin did, which was almost nothing. Raptors were supposed to be the Council's elite warriors, but Alia got the impression they were treated more like undesirables. "Hawthorne."

He looked up at her.

"Why were you assigned here?"

He shrugged. "I'm not supposed to ask questions when I'm given orders."

Alia frowned, searching his metallic-colored eyes. Something was off about him, but she couldn't place what.

His eyes twitched in a couple of semi-blinks as she stared at him. "But"—he added, giving in—"I do know the request came from one of the faction heads."

"Which head?" Alia pressed.

Hawthorne shook his head. "I told you, I'm not supposed to ask questions. I probably wasn't even supposed to know that."

"Surely you were told who you need to report our movements to."

The smallest hint of a glare appeared on Hawthorne's face. "I was not given orders to spy on you."

Alia dropped her gaze and her hand went to her pocket, fidgeting with the wedding coin as she tried to grasp the thoughts running through her mind. Her exhaustion made it so much more difficult. Someone on the Council wanted to help them. It had to be one of Declan's friends.

That explained the tension between Hawthorne and the captain. Now the question was how much could they trust him? Had their ally asked for Hawthorne specifically or had he been picked at random? Was he more their ally or the Council's?

"So, how did you know I wanted to talk to the survivors?"

"I didn't," he admitted, "but if you didn't want to talk to them, then I sure as hell did."

She sighed, rubbing her eyes. She was too tired to thoroughly examine his motives. In the end, it appeared their goals were aligned so she really shouldn't try to split hairs. Since he seemed to have taken the time to learn his way around, perhaps he could help further. "Is there somewhere we can stop for coffee first?"

Hawthorne looked her over, scanning her face before drifting farther down. Galvin, thankfully, didn't notice. She didn't need him picking a fight with their only ally but she couldn't help her own irritation. Again, that tingling tickled across her skin as she glared at him. There was nothing predatory or lustful in his gaze, just cold calculation in his eyes.

Eyes, she realized, that had been altered. In the center of his silver-gray iris, a band of glittering metallic looped all the way around the pupil. Like a tiny band of metal had been carefully inserted. She couldn't tell if the loop was glowing or just reflecting the afternoon light coming in through the tent's opening. Whatever it was made of, it held magic. She wondered what he could see with those eyes.

"You don't want coffee," he finally told her, stepping over to his footlocker.

Alia blinked, watching him with a raised eyebrow as he dug through his stuff. "I don't?"

He pulled out a small, flat cartridge filled with liquid the color of sunshine and a vape. He stood up, closing the trunk. "No, caffeine is too aggressive. Gives you a high, then makes you crash. Does the same thing to your body as cocaine. You also become dependent on it. Gets harder to function normally without it." He loaded the cartridge into the vape as he approached. He checked the bottom, toggling a switch before handing it to her. "Use this. Its effect is much more stable and doesn't create any chemical dependency."

She narrowed her eyes. She had never smoked anything in her life and had no plans to trade one drug for another.

Galvin peered over her shoulder at the vape in her hand. "What does it do?"

Hawthorne's shoulders sank, but he didn't quite sigh, and his voice remained patient. "It's a potion. Raptors use it on missions when we don't get the opportunity for much sleep but need to stay awake." He pointed one finger at Alia. "Only take one hit and keep it small." His raised eyebrows emphasized his instructions. "Too much at once can make you lightheaded, and you don't have the tolerance I do."

Galvin was fascinated. He gapped at the potion in her palm, a slight grin on his face.

Alia wasn't sure she trusted it. "If it's a potion, why is it in this thing?"

"It vaporizes the potion so it begins taking effect in seconds instead of minutes. Makes a big difference when you're about to enter a fight."

"Whoa," Galvin breathed, "that is so cool." Alia tried not to roll her eyes. This was serious, and he was more interested in the magic than the consequences. He watched her closely, waiting for her to take her "hit," as Hawthorne called it. She knew he was dying to see it work, but he should have been more concerned.

"I don't want drugs," she said, holding the vape back out to Hawthorne. "I've read about what these things can do to people. It's no better than smoking."

Hawthorne pursed his lips. "I don't do drugs. Mortals were introduced to the technology and, of course, abused it. I don't recommend you buy the potion on the black market, but I made that one myself. It will hit your bloodstream before it ever reaches your lungs. Follow my instructions and you won't hurt yourself."

"How do I know we can trust you?"

Hawthorne's face pinched, the only indication of his irritation. "How do I know I can trust you two?"

Alia threw her arms up. "If you didn't trust us, you would tell me to take something that would hurt me!"

Conceding, Hawthorne nodded. "That's fair. Let me put it this way instead: I'm assigned to you with no other assistance. We're about to go into the woods to hunt down a reportedly dangerous creature, and you"—he pointed to Alia—"are obviously the person who will know what it is and how to defeat it, but you are dead on your feet. Those are not ideal odds in my opinion."

Galvin nudged her. "He makes a fair point."

Alia sighed, giving in. She couldn't argue with that logic either.

She put the opening to her mouth and gently sucked, not sure how strong the resistance would be. She thought it would be hot, like breathing in steam, but she didn't feel anything. No resistance, no heat, nothing. It was just like sucking air through a straw. She could taste it though. Her mouth filled with orange juice and sunshine.

Within seconds, she felt the fatigue leaving her body. The weight lifted from her limbs and the gritty feeling was gone from her eyes. Her mind began to clear of the fog, and she could think again. Even the staticky tingle across her skin began to subside along with her ever-present irritation.

A shadow of smugness ghosted over Hawthorne's face as he watched her reaction. "Feel better?"

"Yes, thank you." She was genuine. It was the most refreshed she had been in the past few days. She looked to Galvin, who smiled warmly.

"It's not a replacement for sleep," Hawthorne warned, "but it will help for the next several hours."

Alia nodded in understanding, offering back his vape.

Hawthorne's face scrunched up in disgust—the most intense emotion he had expressed thus far. "Keep it. I have others."

Alia grinned. So their Raptor was a bit of a germaphobe. She slipped the vape into her pocket. "Thank you."

"Let's go talk to those warlocks."

18

Declan finished another form. He groaned, rubbing his face and stretching his back. He had never envied the elders, sitting in their offices with their administrative tasks. He'd had plenty of his own when was an ambassador for the Arbor Clan, but far less than what the elders had to deal with and immensely less than the infernal paperwork he was dealing with now. He filed the form and pulled out the next. He could not figure out why there was so much paperwork.

Grace put down the book she was reading and stepped out of the room. Probably heading to the bathroom. Like several other times today, he pretended not to notice, continuing to fill out the next form in the huge stack she had laid on his desk this morning. *How many heads of cattle did Coyote Ridge have in 1820?*

Declan shook his head. *I worked as a ranch hand at Sagebrush Ranch. How would I know what they did at Coyote Ridge?* Where was she even getting all this paperwork?

When she slipped out the door, Declan started counting. He had timed all her previous absences and estimated he had approximately four minutes until she returned. He waited a few moments to give her enough time to get to her destination and be out of the hallway. He dropped his pen, hopped up from his chair, and rushed to the door, opening it just enough to see into the hallway.

The coast was clear so he slipped out. Using every ounce of stealth training he had, he snuck down the hallway, hoping to hurry down the stairs without being noticed.

One of the elder's suite doors opened behind him. "Declan?"

He froze, foot on the first step, trying not to audibly groan.

"You're not neglecting your paperwork, are you?"

Holy Gia, she was relentless. He lifted his gaze to the ceiling, praying to the Supreme Being and whatever angels and saints might be listening for the ability to remain polite and for his frustration to not be evident on his face. He fixed an innocent look on his expression before turning towards her.

She was coming out of the room she had claimed as hers.

"Of course not, I was just feeling a bit hungry and thirsty. Thought I'd pop down to the kitchen for a short break."

Her face lit up and Declan's irritation flared. "Oh, that sounds like a fantastic idea. I'm feeling peckish myself."

Declan's shoulders sagged. "Would you care to join me?" he asked with as much fake enthusiasm as he could muster. It wasn't a lot.

Grace slipped her arm into his and Declan lamented Theo's absence. He could scare anyone away with just a look. Something Declan had never been able to manage. Too bad.

He walked them both down to the kitchen where Grace made

herself comfortable at the island table. Declan daydreamed about lacing her food since she was freely letting him prepare it for her. A sleeping potion? Something strong enough to knock her out for the whole evening and through the night. That should be long enough for him to make his meeting with Ophelia. It wasn't a bad idea...

"Can I ask where all the Halloween decorations are? I thought All Hallows' Eve was an important holiday for druids."

Declan shrugged, looking through the fridge for something easy to lace. A large pot of Alia's leftover stew would make a good place to hide a sleeping draft. The stronger flavors, enhanced from sitting overnight, would hide the subtle taste of the potion. He pulled the container out and poured the contents into a pot on the stove to heat up.

"It is, but it's just the three of us here and you sent two of them away." He had to make sure he counted correctly. It would have been a wasted effort for Theo to leave if Declan couldn't manage to keep it secret. "We've been doing small celebrations, but there won't be anyone here this year so we didn't pull anything out."

"Is it true the druids used to have a huge festival?" Her questions sounded suspiciously like she was fishing for information. So far, she was only asking things anyone could look up in a history book, but Declan suspected she was warming up to ask about something she shouldn't.

"Yes, that's correct."

"And non-druids were invited to celebrate with you?"

"It wasn't open to just anyone," he explained. "Only certain mortals with close relations to the Arbors."

"Is it true the druids channeled the dead for them?"

Declan froze, his blood running cold. He didn't dare face her to answer. He gripped the spoon tighter to keep his hands from shaking and swallowed, trying to keep his voice neutral. "Who told you that?"

"I read about it," she answered casually. "It would certainly be a comfort to many."

He managed to keep his expression as unconcerned as he could when he faced to her. She was watching him closely, scanning his face. Declan didn't like it. It was like she was searching for confirmation. Like she already knew the answer but wanted to gauge his reaction.

"No one has been able to do that in a long time."

Her eyes glinted and she raised an eyebrow at him. "So it takes a special ability?"

"That information is classified, but something tells me someone else already answered that question for you." He turned back to the stew and stirred to keep it from burning on the bottom, hoping to hide his trembling and pale face.

"And *you* don't have that ability?"

Sweat beaded along his brow. He wiped it away, feeling slightly sick. How could she know? The only people who had ever known were Tiberius and Evelyn. Theo suspected by Declan had never confirmed it for him. Who could Grace possibly have been talking to? He racked his memories, trying to think of any time it might have slipped to someone.

"Declan?" Her voice was warning, like a parent reminding a child not to lie.

He swallowed the lump in his throat, forcing his voice to remain steady. "I don't do that, no."

"Hmm. Interesting." That was all she said.

He pulled the sleeping draft out from the cabinet, hiding it among some spices, then ladled the stew into bowls, seasoning his with extra herbs and hers with the spell. The spices he replaced into the cupboard, but the jar with the magic herbs he slipped into his pocket.

Ophelia was right. She couldn't just not be trusted; this lady was dangerous.

Declan fidgeted with his pen, watching Grace for any sign of the sleeping draft's effect. The potion had a particular taste that was easy to distinguish so he'd wanted to be careful not to use too much in the food earlier. Now he was concerned he may not have put in enough, but that might have been his nerves making him feel like it was taking longer than normal. He just needed to be patient. Any minute now...

When she finally yawned, standing and stretching from her chair, Declan heaved a sigh of relief but made himself sit calmly, holding his pen above the latest form. She mumbled her goodnights as she passed on her way out of the room, not even sparing him a glance.

With the door safely closed, Declan whispered a new order to his little twig sentry still hiding in the hall. "Tell me when she's in her room and the only thing you hear is her sleeping." He waited, the fidgeting of his pen turning to tapping on the desk.

The sentry sent its message back a few moments later. *She's asleep.*

Declan leapt out of his chair. He ran to his room and grabbed his pack, partially worried Grace would catch him again like she had earlier that evening. The meeting with Ophelia was too important to miss.

He rushed down the stairs, taking them two at a time, and out into the courtyard, not slowing until he passed the barrier to the grove. He walked the rest of the way to the tree, starting to undress. He had a long way to go in a short amount of time and flying after grove hopping would be the fastest.

When he reached the center of the grove and approached the sacred tree, he noticed the beginnings of the budding hallow flowers, named for the holiday they bloomed on. This year, the little buds glowed in the tree with the new spell like the large bulb Christmas lights that would be filling stores even now. The hallow fruit would start growing as soon as the buds bloomed tonight, which didn't give him much time before his powers began to fade.

He dropped his pack and finished undressing. The new glow around the trunk and in the leaves provided enough light for him to see by. The coolness of the night hit his bare skin and he shivered. Thankfully, his animal form would keep him warm. He folded his clothes and put them in his pack, then strapped the pack over his shoulder and focused his energy. His body shrank, pushing into a smaller form; his skin sprouted brown feathers and his mouth formed into a beak.

The transformation took longer than normal; he hadn't done it in so long he was a little rusty. He shook out his feathers and stretched his wings, getting comfortable in his owl shape again. He settled his pack, which had shrunk to match his size, and, flapping, took to the air. He flew toward the edge of the clearing to give himself room, then swung back around.

A knotwork symbol formed in front of his beak as he activated the grove hopping spell. The symbol matched the glow of the tree and the glitter and flash in the leaves and in the markings on the ground. That was new. But so was everything else about the grove—its constant florescence was evidence enough of all the changes.

Declan flew straight at the tree and disappeared into the trunk.

Declan was running late. The bistro Ophelia wanted to meet him at was not easy to find. The only hint on the card was *French Quarter*. That got him to the right city, but then he'd had to obtain directions from a restaurant hostess who told him it was three blocks away.

Now he was in a seedy alleyway surrounded by dilapidated buildings. He had only managed to find the place by following some oblivious young mortals who were dressed all in black and yammering about going to The Princess of Denmark. Only when they got closer could he hear the thumps of club music.

When he finally turned a corner and saw the place, he wondered how he'd had such trouble. A huge crowd waited to get in, and the heavy techno rock coming from inside was so loud Declan felt the vibrations in the street. It was the only place with any activity for a block.

He pulled the hood of his coat farther down to hide his face as he got in line for the door. He hadn't considered there would be a bouncer, and now he was concerned he might be turned away. He didn't match the aesthetic by any means. The crowd was full of goth makeup and clothing. Mortals mostly, all wanting to mimic various vampires in pop culture. Normal, non-magic humans who, he guessed, had learned just enough about the supernatural world to go looking for trouble. He caught sight of a few non-mortals like himself, but they too were dressed to blend in. He was the only one who looked more for hiking than clubbing in his blue jeans, boots, and worn jacket.

The guard at the door, a big, real vampire dressed in black leathers, was weeding out the unacceptable patrons from the line before letting the desirable ones in. Declan wasn't sure what the bouncer's criteria for judging the mortals was, but he was apparently quite particular about who passed inspection. As Declan watched, several people were turned away, but he couldn't quite discern the pattern. Likely the vampire's heightened senses picked out something Declan's human ones could not.

When it was finally Declan's turn, the bouncer stopped him and his glare dissolved into something more like alarm. Or confusion. He looked Declan over carefully, sniffing—confirming Declan's theory about his enhanced senses.

The music pouring out into the street was deafening and didn't allow any sort of conversation so Declan flashed Ophelia's business card. The bouncer's attitude shifted from suspicion to respect. He nodded in almost a bow but instead of letting him pass, he gestured behind him, leading Declan off to the side.

Another vampire, as large and broad as his cohort but dressed in a fine suit, materialized from the shadows, his appearance eliciting delighted gasps from the mortal onlookers. He led Declan around the line to an entrance away from the general population. People watched him go, chatting to themselves about the mysterious VIP. Declan sank farther into his jacket, hoping no one got a good look at his face.

The interior was as cliché as the clientele outside. It was warm, almost uncomfortably so for Declan in his jacket. It wasn't surprising: a warmer temperature wouldn't bother vampires and ensured mortals shed more clothes. Everything was decorated in blacks and reds, light-absorbing velvet and Victorian-style wood furniture. It was so hard to see in here the few mortals coming for a "real vampire experience" wouldn't know most of the décor was fake anyway. Intoxicated patrons lounged on plush sofas and huddled together in darkened booths. Declan spotted a few actual vampires sinking their teeth into seemingly willing victims. He grimaced at the confirmation of his earlier thought—just enough supernatural knowledge to get themselves in trouble.

It was early in the evening by vampire standards, but Declan saw many already getting sustenance in exchange for, mostly, physical pleasure for the mortals. Declan couldn't judge too harshly, having exchanged blood for his own gain in the past, but never in a public space. Or with so little disregard for his own safety. It was too dangerous to not pay attention to your surroundings in the open like this, and he had the means to defend himself, unlike most of these mortals.

When Ophelia had given him the card, he assumed she owned the establishment, based on the name. It wasn't like her to set up secret meetings in places she didn't absolutely trust, but she had never much cared for the dark vampire aesthetic or the base debauchery displayed here. He had a hard time picturing her anywhere near this place.

Declan's guide led him through the room on a special path behind the bar, blocked off from the main crowd. He showed Declan to a heavily curtained doorway where the barest glimpse of light shone through.

The vampire pushed back the curtains, revealing a completely different establishment. This room was brilliantly lit; warm and bright as a summer afternoon. Declan had to shield his eyes until they adjusted after the near pitch black of the tacky vampire bar out front.

This area was designed to look like an elegant Parisian cafe at midday. The floor was made of cobblestones and the walls were painted with a picturesque daytime cityscape, complete with the Eiffel Tower in the background. The bar was a beautiful redwood, elegant enough to feature in a fae royal palace. Booths lined the walls but the center was filled with cafe tables, all only large enough to accommodate no more than three people. Declan immediately felt relief as the temperature dropped to a more comfortable level. No need to keep people barely clad in here.

More than just vampires and mortals sat at these tables and the dress code was significantly more refined than out front—if Declan didn't fit in before, he certainly wasn't dressed appropriately now. There were all manner of creatures: several fae, a werewolf, and one he thought who might be a siren, but no human wizards. They all met at the little tables or at the bar, huddling together, quietly engaged in mutual exchanges but of a much more white-collar variety. He saw money, locked cases, sealed envelopes changing hands to the accompaniment of hushed whispers.

Now he knew he was in the right place. *This* was more Ophelia's style. Elegance and refinement. Even if he imagined the World Council wouldn't approve of the clandestine exchanges. Especially considering some of the vibes from the items passing from the supernaturals to the mortals. Declan tuned down his senses so he couldn't eavesdrop. He preferred plausible deniability.

At the back of the room, farthest away from the entrance and the bar, beautiful maple trees growing from richly decorated planters incorporated into the cobblestones covered a raised dais. The pristine cleanliness of the planters led Declan to believe the trees were actually fake. The leaves were a mix of golden yellow, brilliant orange, and deep red. The dais held the largest table in the whole room, a booth with plush white benches.

The bouncer led Declan toward the dais where a small but elegant woman sat. She wore a short black dress, and a very large sun hat covered her face. She leaned back in her seat, her legs crossed, dangling a stilettoed foot in the air. Her delicate hand twirled a wine glass. Declan was not naïve enough to be fooled by the glass. He knew the thick red liquid inside couldn't be anything other than blood.

As he approached, Ophelia lifted her head, revealing her pale, beautiful face from under the wide brim of the hat, once more made up to perfection. She smiled broadly, flashing her perfect white teeth and sharp fangs from behind blood-red lips. "I was starting to get worried," she purred. "Have trouble escaping your nanny?"

19

Hawthorne took Alia and Galvin to talk to the injured warlocks. The infirmary tent was on the other side of the camp from the barracks and closer to where food was cooked and served. Galvin figured they would to stop and ask some questions, and the answers would tell Alia everything she needed to know about what was hiding in the woods. They'd come up with a plan with Hawthorne's help, shut it down, and be going home by tomorrow morning. Not bad.

That idea shriveled up as soon as they walked inside. Galvin's stomach turned as he realized how difficult this was going be. More difficult than upgrading the groves and avoiding capture by demons.

Four warlocks lay in cots. Cuts covered their faces, necks, and arms. Three were unconscious, a nurse at each of their sides trying to clean a black goo dripping out of their eyes, their mouths, and from a set of deep gashes on each of them. Only one sat up, staring into space. Bandages wrapped around his chest, one leg propped up in a cast. He noticed the trio as they walked in, a haunted look clouding his expression.

Hawthorne led them to the conscious warlock's bedside. "How are you feeling?"

"I got lucky." He glanced at the others, sadness on his face. "They won't be suffering much longer." He nodded at Alia and Galvin. "They aren't warlocks. What do they want?"

"This is Alia and Galvin of the druid Arbor Clan. They would like to ask some questions about what you saw in the woods."

The injured warlock snorted. "Just what we need, *druids*." He crossed his arms and turned away from them.

When the warlock continued to ignore Alia and Galvin, Hawthorne cleared his throat aggressively. The warlock meet the Raptor's glare. "Fine," he snapped, glaring in return. "But there isn't much to tell. We went into the woods to scout when we were swarmed by a murder of crows. I was thrown hard against a tree, cracked a couple of ribs. I couldn't see anything through the birds but I heard this high-pitched and deep, earth-shaking cry, then the others screaming. I shot up a flare to call for help, then something huge stepped on my leg.

"The crows finally let up when the rescue team arrived. All I could see were the others, lying on the ground and oozing that goo." He shivered. "I never saw the creature."

That wasn't much more to go on than what the Captain had told them. Galvin saw Alia's shoulders sag in a sigh.

"You're druids, right?" the warlock asked.

Alia nodded.

"I hope you pick the right side this time."

Galvin raised an eyebrow and looked at Alia. What was he

talking about, "this time"?

Alia frowned and shook her head. She apparently didn't know any more than he did. "What do you mean?"

The warlock waved them off like they were hopeless. "When that famous druid stopped the monster rebellion by killing the leader. You druids need to get on the right side a lot earlier than at the very end this time."

Galvin bit his bottom lip. Declan had taken a long time to stand with the Council during the rebellion, leading to the belief that druids were monster sympathizers.

Alia's brows furrowed. "Well, we are going to try and stop this creature before it hurts anyone else."

The warlock shook his head and turned away, looking disappointed.

Is that what the warlocks thought was happening? That the non-human "monsters" were planning another rebellion?

Hawthorne was scrutinizing Galvin. Galvin blinked a few times, wondering what that meant. Hawthorne's glanced at Alia but returned to studying Galvin. He shifted uncomfortably under the Raptor's gaze. Why was he staring at Galvin?

"Well, thank you," Alia told the warlock, "for telling us what happened." She gestured for Galvin and Hawthorne to follow her. Outside the tent, she paused, regarding the tree line. "I guess we're just going to have to find out for ourselves."

"Do you think you two will be fine without me?" Hawthorne asked, looking in the direction of the camp. Galvin thought he was watching at the captain's tent. "I'm not sure how much I will be able to help identify the creature, and I want to check on some things that warlock said."

"You don't think he was being honest?" Galvin asked.

"He's being honest. That's what worries me."

"Without knowing what it is, it's hard to say if we'll need help or not, but we'll try to keep to gathering intel for now."

Hawthorne nodded. "Come to my tent when you get back and we'll exchange notes."

Alia and Galvin parted ways with the Raptor, heading to the woods.

Galvin didn't have nearly as much experience being out in the woods as Alia did but even he knew there was something off about this place. The scent of rotting vegetation permeated the air, and all the color in the plants, ground, and brush looked like it had been leached out, leaving everything dull and gray. There wasn't a clear view of the sky through the canopy, so the light had started as a wan and had stayed like that until the sun set, casting the woods in darkness, with no stars to guide them or offer additional visibility. Even Alia's ball of sunlight, held aloft in her hand like a lantern, lacked its normal golden hue. Galvin felt an unsettling chill, and he was not affected by cold. He expected small animals, birds, and bugs chirping or rustling, like back at the Arbor Grove, but they didn't come across any, and it was too quiet.

They didn't come across much at all. They walked the paths, going deeper and deeper into the woods, but didn't find anything out of the ordinary. Well, any more out of the ordinary than the whole place was. Galvin had been sure of a high-stakes hunt but instead, for a creature who was supposedly aggressive, it was proving difficult to provoke. So far, all they had done was go on a brisk hike though some spooky woods.

At least Alia was able to find some clues, though Galvin didn't know what they meant. He wasn't even sure what they were looking for, so he just followed Alia's lead as she wandered through the trees. She didn't say anything as they hiked, but he did get snippets of her whispered thoughts through their connection. *Hoofed. Bipedal. Chased warlocks, then turned north.* A few times she collected what appeared to be tufts of fur and some molted feathers into her pack.

Through their connection, Galvin felt her focus. He did not interrupt but watched and followed, allowing her to think through the strange problem they had been tasked with. The best way for him to help right now was to guard her back while she investigated. Since she was trained, they were relying entirely on her knowledge. Even though he was catching on quickly, he knew she would always be a few levels more advanced than him.

Something caught Alia's attention and she bent to the ground to examine a dark pool.

Galvin kept his focus of their surroundings but he couldn't help his curiosity. Or maybe it was Alia's curiosity leaking through to him. Either way, he stole a peek over her shoulder. The strange pool was shiny and black. Its surface was perfectly still until Alia stuck a twig into the center of it. The thick liquid stuck to the piece of wood like tar.

Alia pulled a small vial out of her pouch and dripped the strange goo in before dropping the whole stick in after it. She corked the bottle, squinting and staring at the substance. *What are you?* he felt her ask.

The loud snap of a branch made them both jump. Alia shoved the vial into her pouch and drew her gun just as Galvin drew his own weapons. Theo had loaned him batons when they upgraded the anchor groves, but he had made sure to return them as soon as they got back. Since then, Declan had outfitted and trained him with a matching set of blades.

Alia and Galvin stood back to back, searching for whatever had made the noise. Crows cawed, and a rustling circled their position. It sounded like something large, and the hair on the back of Galvin's neck stood up. They scanned the area for their intruder, but nothing showed itself. Neither spoke aloud, not wanting to give themselves away, but their minds remained open to one another. Galvin felt Alia's every thought as she searched the distance. *Something* was there, but what?

A thick fog began to swirl around their feet. It smelled funny, like smoke from the dry ice the Winter Court used to create fog in their decorative displays for special occasions, but that stuff wasn't straight water either. This fog rose, growing and obscuring their vision of anything farther than a few feet in front of them. It left a slick, dirty feeling on his skin he didn't like.

Alia's thoughts buzzed, but as if she were farther away. *I don't like this,* he sent to her.

Alia pulled away from Galvin's back, he assumed to get into a better stance if their intruder snuck up on them. Something was here. He felt it watching them, angry. A chill ran down his spine and his heart rate spiked. His breathing quickened in anticipation of an attack and he squeezed the handles of his knives. He narrowed his eyes, stepping back, trying to find Alia's foot with his. Her thoughts were too quiet for comfort.

Alia!

The fog sank, dissipating as quickly as it came, taking with it the sense of impending danger. The forest quieted, returning to the eerie, unnatural silence they had experienced since arriving.

Galvin lowered his weapons, no longer expecting an attack, but something was still wrong. He looked around suspiciously, wanting to locate Alia. What would sneak up on them, prepare to attack, and then just disappear?

His fears were confirmed when he couldn't see her. He spun around, reaching for her with his senses, but she wasn't there. Galvin was alone.

20

The fog sank into the ground, revealing an entirely different part of the woods. Galvin was gone, too far away for Alia to reach through their connection. How had she gotten here? She was completely alone.

No, not completely. Something lurked in the woods just out of sight, and the hair on Alia's neck stood up. Her heart began to pound and her breathing quickened. Her thoughts raced too quickly to hold onto any of them. It was like she was back in the haunted mansion. She felt Lucian stalking her, but she couldn't see where he was hiding. Lurking. Waiting to pounce.

She had to get out of here.

Alia let her senses sink into the ground, trying to pinpoint her location. She was still in the woods the creature called home. She found south and, turning that direction, ran as fast as she could toward the camp.

There was a rustling in the brush and the sound of footsteps trailing close. She glanced back to see Lucian, chasing her at full speed, making no more effort to hide. Her heart leapt into her throat. She faced forward, focusing on not losing her balance or her small lead.

She heaved as she ran, bringing more air into her body, prepping to use it to propel her forward with super speed, but the ability wasn't coming as easily as usual. A slithering at her feet warned her just as his black tendrils reached for her ankles. She gasped, losing the air she had been building up as she hopped out of the coils. She avoided their grasp but nearly tripped over a bush in the process. Damn, she would have to start over.

She didn't get the chance. Her slight slip was enough for Lucian to close the gap. He pounced, locking her in his arms and pinning hers to her sides. The weight of his tackle sent them both tumbling to the ground. The scuffle forced her gun from her hand, leaving her weaponless.

She wouldn't have been able to raise her arms to use it anyway. Lucian straddled her hips low to prevent her using her legs, her wrists stuck under his knees. She flailed, trying to kick him off, but couldn't get the leverage. His black tendrils wrapped around her, binding her arms and legs together. It was just like at the Nome Grove. She screamed for Gavin, Declan, anyone to help her, but the forest seemed to dampen the sound.

Lucian covered her mouth with his hand, pushing her head to one side, leaving her neck open and vulnerable. He laughed, breathless from the effort of subduing her, and leaned in close. "I'm going to make sure you can't keep me out, even with the help of your fairy prince." He sank his teeth into her neck.

Pain erupted across her skin, her blood spilling into his mouth as he drank it down. His fear magic flooded her mind. She couldn't think. She couldn't fight him off. She screamed and struggled against her restraints, desperate for any help.

A large claw swiped above their heads. Lucian unlatched from her neck, ducked, and rolled away to avoid being swatted. His concentration broke. So did his magic. Alia's mind cleared of fear, and she could think again.

Lucian's black tendrils had loosened in the distraction, but he still held her as he staggered to his knees on the ground next to her. It was enough of an opening. She bucked up and smashed both feet into his face as hard as she could. Lucian was flung away, crashing to the ground on his back. She scrambled upright and grabbed her gun.

Having lost the upper hand, Lucian's form began to fade in an attempt to escape. Alia wasn't going to let him get away that easily. In one practiced motion, she pointed the gun at Lucian, took aim, and fired two shots.

That was when she saw it. A tall creature had appeared behind him, emerging more from the darkness than the trees. It was skeletal, with long arms that practically dragged on the ground. Its head was an animal skull with glowing eyes and tall, branching antlers. Its legs were bent, furred, and hoofed like a goat's. It smelled like damp and rotting wood.

One shot sank into Lucian's arm as his form faded, but the other was too late and missed him entirely.

Sinking, instead, right into the creature's thigh.

The creature reeled backward, emitting a great scream—equal parts bass that shook the ground and a high-pitched piercing wail that made Alia clap her hands to her ears. Black blood oozed from the wound, but it recovered quickly and crouched low as if getting ready to pounce.

Alia sheathed her gun and reached into the ground, calling on the native vines to rise and engulf the creature. She hoped to immobilize it, perhaps calm it down and get a better look at it. The trees groaned, attempting to bend to her request. Vines meekly crawled through the dirt to the creature's feet but strained to do anything more than wiggle at its hooves.

Alia's heart sank when she quickly did the math. While searching the woods, the day had slipped from the twenty-ninth to the thirtieth.

Hallowtide had started.

She wasn't going to win this fight.

Alia turned and ran.

The beast stomped after her, trampling everything in its path. Alia struggled to keep ahead of the beast; one great stride from it was equal to about three of hers, and she was going at top speed. It swiped a thin, claw-like hand at her. She ducked, rolled away, and vaulted back to her feet to continue running.

The temperature dropped, and Alia smiled. She spared a glance behind her, recognizing the feel of Galvin's magic. Ice formed over the beast's extremities and thickened, slowing it down. Alia paused to see Galvin rushing to her aid from the creature's side. She had never been so relieved to see him and his ice powers. The question was, how long would he be able to use them?

He bolted toward her and grabbed her arm, pulling her along. His eyes were wide, and he appeared to be in a panic. "Don't stop now. We need to move! Now!"

No sooner had Galvin said the words than the ice around the beast began to crack and fall away. Alia pulled out her gun again—the only weapon she had that would be of any use—but she didn't dare stop to fire it. The standard bullets she had loaded hadn't done much more than anger the beast, and she would lose too much ground trying to dig out one of the other cartridges.

They fled for their lives, Alia leading Galvin to the only thing that could help: back to the warlock's camp and reinforcements.

21

Galvin followed Alia, occasionally throwing ice spells behind them. It was the only thing he could manage right now, and it was hardly useful. It slowed the creature for them to gain a bit more distance but didn't do any real harm to it.

He had tried fire too but he hadn't been able to conjure more than a few sputtering sparks. The *only* magic he could get working properly was his fae magic. Alia seemed to be struggling too. Her sunlight barely glowed enough for them to see where they were going, and the filigree on her gun wasn't as bright as normal. She also seemed to be doubting her usual keen sense of direction. Maybe it was the dark obscuring landmarks, but she was taking a long time to figure out how to navigate back to the camp.

She was also bleeding from two puncture wounds on her neck, and they didn't look like anything the creature could make. It had sharp teeth but with that long, skeletal snout, Galvin wasn't sure it could bite anything without tearing it to shreds.

"What is this thing?" he shouted over the beast's roars.

"I have no idea!"

Oh boy. If Alia didn't know what it was, this was going to be a lot harder than he had anticipated. And without their magic? They might be in trouble this time.

It only took a few large strides for the beast to catch up to them. The creature swiped a large skeletal hand. Galvin gasped and pulled Alia to the ground just in time for the creature's sharp claws to swoosh over the tops of their heads.

Alia rolled to her back and aimed her gun. The beast grabbed at them, and she fired two shots into its hand. The creature yanked it back, black ooze spraying from the wounds, splattering the forest around them.

Galvin lifted himself off Alia's legs and hauled her to her feet. The creature's roar both vibrated and pierced his body, sending chills up his spine and shaking the ground at the same time.

Once up, Alia tugged on his arm, and they raced off.

They had put a little more distance between themselves and the creature when they realized it had stopped chasing them. Instead, it picked up a huge boulder, easily large enough to crush at least one of them. The creature pulled its arm back as if the stone weighed no more than a baseball.

Galvin gasped. He pulled Alia up short and crouched, tucking her body under his as the creature flung the boulder. He threw up a magic shield, hoping Hallowtide wouldn't prevent his fae magic from working. To his immense relief, glowing symbols appeared in the air around them just in time to take the full brunt of the boulder.

It connected with Galvin's shield with painful solidity that sent sharp jabs shooting through his head. It didn't so much as bounce, but fell next to them. They hadn't been squished into jam, but the force of the impact broke Galvin's shield and left him dazed, his head throbbing. The world spun around him and the ground came up to meet him.

Alia managed to get to her feet and caught him before his face met the dirt. She pulled him along, keeping him upright as they continued trying to escape. Galvin heard alarms ringing but he wasn't sure if they were from the camp or the strike to his head.

The camp finally came into view. Alia and Galvin must have been right at the edge of the woods when the creature threw the boulder, which was good because there was no way they could outrun the beast, hobbling as they were. Warlocks hustled into position in a line around the camp, prepping for a massive combined spell. They moved in practiced unison as they began to cast a shield around the camp. Magic grew outward from their hands, symbols glowing in a multitude of each caster's unique color, speedily building a wall.

Galvin's stomach lurched as he realized how quickly the shield was expanding. Once it was up, nothing would get through.

Noticing the same, Alia called to the warlocks to wait. They did not. She tried using her wind magic to speed them up, and hope filled Galvin. The last time she had used that power, she had covered a hundred yards in a few seconds.

This time, there was a yank as she gained the smallest increase in speed. Their hobble turned into a run for a moment but soon petered out. Galvin's heart sank. He wasn't sure her spell would be enough, but he didn't have any others that would help.

The wall was going up with trained proficiency. As the shield grew, the holes between each warlock shrank, along with any way for

Alia and Galvin to get to safety. They weren't going to make it.

"Druids!" The voice was familiar, and they turned in unison to see Hawthorne. He was holding his shield steady with a gap large enough for them to squeeze through, but the warlocks next to him were trying to fill it. "Hurry up, you two!"

The creature emerged from the cover of the woods, still on their tail. Alia dragged Galvin behind her as she changed course for Hawthorne's direction. It charged, head down, attempting to reach them before they reached the shield, its massive hand stretching to scoop them up.

The warlocks had managed to shore up the area, reducing the breach to a small opening at the bottom left, directly under Hawthorne's spell. Alia dropped to the ground, pulling Galvin with her, and rolled in before hauling him the rest of the way through the as the gap closed.

They barely escaped the creature's claws, its swipe connecting with the warlock's shield instead. Galvin watched in amazed horror as the claws left deep gashes the magic. Warlocks dropped to their knees, straining to keep the shield up as the attack on the spell damaged their minds. Even the Raptor gritted his teeth and screwed his eyes shut against the assault as the claws ripped through his neon blue symbols.

Galvin's eyes went wide at the display of strength on both sides: the creature tearing through powerful magic like butter and the Raptor taking the attack with nothing more than a flinch. The thing had destroyed Galvin's own shield with one boulder, nearly dropping him and knocking him silly. But Hawthorne was on a different level. He wasn't just taking it, he was still attempting to keep his shield up.

More warlocks arrived, taking position in a precise formation behind the shield. They moved in easy unison as they cast, forming fire in their hands and throwing it over the wall at the creature.

Galvin lamented the fact his own flames hadn't worked. The creature recoiled from the fireballs, covering its head, and turned back to the woods with a piercing shriek—one missing the deep tones it had emitted earlier—and disappeared into the protection of the canopy. Its thundering stomps faded as it retreated. Clearly, fire was the creature's weakness.

Galvin worried the warlocks might continue to attack even after the beast had fled, possibly setting the thick forest on fire, but they were apparently better trained than he had guessed. The assault stopped once victory was established.

"I want the braindead goblin who led the creature to our camp in front of me now!" Captain Ashblade was walking up the ranks, glowering as he shouted.

The warlocks stepped away from where Galvin and Alia were still on the ground.

Captain Ashblade rounded on them. "I should have known it was the undisciplined toddlers I was saddled with."

Galvin frowned and felt Alia bristle next to him.

"Any of my scouts would know better than to lead it back to our *base!* What the hell were you two thinking?"

"That we needed backup!" Alia rose to face him.

Galvin was just as angry as Alia but it was amusing to see all of her five feet, three inches challenging Captain Ashblade, who had to be at least as tall as Galvin and had the better part of a foot on her. Amusing enough to almost make him chuckle despite his anger. If he was going to put money on a fight, he'd bet on Alia.

"And what was the deal with that shield? If it hadn't been for

Hawthorne, we wouldn't have made it!"

Captain Ashblade shot a glare at Hawthorne, who matched his commanding officer's gaze. "You were given orders to get that shield closed, soldier."

"I did get the shield closed," Hawthorne stated with no hint of argument.

Captain Ashblade's glare deepened. "Are you in need of some *quiet time* to remind you how to follow orders to the letter?"

Another soldier approached. Instead of a standard field uniform, he wore a buttoned shirt and tie, all white, with a band around his arm labeled *MP*. He stopped several paces behind Captain Ashblade and watched but didn't move closer, waiting for instruction.

Hawthorne's face paled, his eyes growing wide. Galvin noticed him swallow hard and stand a bit stiffer. "No, sir." His voice was almost pleading.

Captain Ashblade turned back to Alia, crossing his arms across his chest. "Don't think I don't know you two have been causing trouble in my camp."

Galvin's heart leapt into his throat. He knew about the confrontation with their bunkmates.

"One whiff of a formal complaint and you will be out of here."

What? The warlock Galvin attacked hadn't reported them yet?

"I will not risk the lives of the warlocks under my command for a couple of amateurs," Ashblade went on. "Even if it had been a warlock trapped out there, we would not have held the shields for him. The life of one individual is not more important than the lives of many." A malicious grin spread across his face. "Besides, you made it, didn't you?"

Alia ground her teeth, clenching her fists. She had just lectured Galvin about being on their best behavior but now struggled to keep her cool and follow her own instructions. Not that he could blame her—this guy was a jerk. Still, Galvin stood and placed a hand on her shoulder, hoping to bring her back from the edge.

She visibly relaxed, taking a subtle deep breath to calm herself. She had been right about keeping out of trouble, even though he wanted to punch this guy in the face too.

Captain Ashblade leaned in, his grin dissolving into an angry scowl. "I had better not catch you putting my Raptor or any more of my warlocks in danger. Dismissed."

Alia wanted to say more but Galvin stopped her, squeezing her arm.

Even Hawthorne shook his head at his retreating captain. "C'mon," he said, his voice small, "I need something for this headache, and you need that wound tended. How did you even get that? It looks too small for that thing to have given it to you."

Alia's eyes went wide and her whole body went rigid. She brought a shaky hand up to her neck, wincing as her fingers brushed the two puncture wounds. They came away stained with blood, tacky from trying to seal her skin. She gulped, staring at her fingers. Galvin had only ever seen her scared when dealing with one thing: Lucian. She must have had another waking nightmare.

But how had a nightmare bitten her?

Knowing she wouldn't want an audience while discussing her troubles with Lucian, he had to get her out of here. "You go on," he told Hawthorne, guiding Alia away from the crowd. "We'll take care of this."

She was silent the whole way back to the tent and Galvin didn't push. He led her inside and sat her on the end of her cot and took her bag from her. He dug inside, pulled the first aid kit out, and went to work on her neck. For once, she let him tend to her without complaint. He didn't dare let it show how deep that went to soothe him.

"What happened out there?" he asked, wiping away the dried blood, careful not to reopen the wound. He screwed the lid off the jar of M.U.D.—Medical Utility Dirt. He still had to suppress a snort every time he thought of the name Declan had given the magically enhanced herbal balm he had invented. He was quite proud of his pun.

There wasn't much left now. "One second you were there and the next you were gone."

"I don't know how we got separated." She sighed as he gently rubbed the M.U.D. onto her neck.

She hadn't seemed so bad when they had gone into the woods but now the energy she had gained from Hawthorne's potion and the couple hours of sleep she had gotten were gone. She looked like she could pass out at any moment. "Lucian appeared when you weren't there. He's the one who did this." She gestured to the bite mark. "But he got interrupted by…" She shrugged. "Whatever that thing was."

Galvin laid his palm on her neck, trying to sense any residual magic. Her skin was hot, and she relaxed against his cool hand. He left his hand there, hoping his natural temperature would soothe her. He brushed her cheek with his thumb, her eyes fluttering closed.

He hated Lucian. Not only for the torture Galvin had personally endured, but for the continued torture of Alia. Galvin couldn't remember ever truly wishing death on anyone, but he wished it on Lucian. And he wished to personally make it happen. "When I get my hands on him—"

Alia opened her eyes, meeting his gaze with her beautiful hazel one. He felt himself lean closer, but she laid a tired hand on top of the fist at his side. It was a gentle gesture, entirely at odds with the fury in her eyes. "If anyone is gets to kill him, it's going to be me."

He pulled his hand away, embarrassment flushing his face, not sure why he had been so forward. They were just friends, weren't they? After the fuss he had made at the train station, getting flustered when she had pretended to kiss him, that was likely all they were going to be.

Besides, she was right, of course. She didn't need him to protect her. She was always the one protecting him. Which was probably why he wanted so badly to help her now.

"We need to talk to Declan," she added, changing the subject. "I have no clue what that was, and I need to hear his thoughts."

"About all of it," he insisted, "including Lucian."

22

"Can I offer you something to drink?" Ophelia asked, signaling to a waitress—a young vampire, by the looks of her. Her bright red eyes still held some of her living color. Declan saw the moment she caught a whiff of him because her pupils expanded and her face scrunched up in furious concentration. Control was still new to her.

There was something familiar about the perfect golden curls hanging around her shoulders. Then it clicked: she was the fledgling from Declan's hearing. That was good, at least. Under Ophelia, the vampire would have protection from the Council and Ophelia would provide the best education she could get.

Declan wondered if she'd been able to pull any strings for the young male too.

"Just coffee," he told the fledgling, and she hurried away. "So, was it the perks of being ambassador or queen that got that young girl into your care?"

Ophelia huffed and took another long sip. "We figureheads still have some pull. And it's queen regent," she corrected in a lower voice, "but I would prefer you keep that quiet. I've worked hard to make sure this establishment is up to Council code."

Declan looked around at the illegal activity and raised an eyebrow at Ophelia, but she pointedly ignored him.

"Besides, if *he* wanted it, the crown would be his immediately upon his return. The Underground Monsters are all still very loyal to him."

"Seeing as how he's *dead*"—Declan emphasized the word to remind her—"that's not likely to happen. Besides, he wouldn't want it back." He didn't know how, since he had never told her, but Ophelia knew Theo was alive. Thankfully, she was also one of few people who could keep a secret. It was why Declan had trusted her to be one of his liaisons when he was in hiding.

Besides, Ophelia liked having the power. If anything, she would keep Theo's secret to prevent him from coming back and taking it from her.

She leaned over the table, resting her chin on the knuckles of her hand, smiling sweetly at him. "Is that what he told you or what you hope?"

Declan glared at her. Theo was trying to turn a corner and *had* said he didn't want the rule of the Underground Monsters back. He had gotten into enough trouble leading the world's non-human "monsters" in a personal vendetta against the wizards. He would have won too, if Declan hadn't talked sense into him.

But Declan couldn't deny it was his own hope that Theo wouldn't take back the crown. Declan had seen change in him while he was cooped up at home, but would he revert now that Declan had kicked him out into the world?

The phone Galvin had made vibrated in his pocket, making him jump. He had forgotten he brought it with him. After sending Theo away with the other one, Declan had decided to keep it on him, just in case anything happened and Theo needed… well, probably just a pep talk to stay on the wagon more than any actual assistance. Theo was strong and resourceful, but confident in not reverting back to the criminal he had been? Not so much. Declan wanted to make sure he was there for him in case he needed to talk. He hadn't thought it would be so soon, though.

Declan's heart sank when he realized it was Galvin calling. Seeing as how Declan and Theo had the only two magical phones, he was a little surprised to see Galvin's name at all. But if his apprentices had found a way to call him without a phone of their own, then they needed help with something.

"I have to take this," he told Ophelia.

She waved her hand in approval, leaning back in her chair to wait until he finished.

He hit the green button to accept the video call. Alia's and Galvin's faces came into view, surrounded by a sort of blue shimmer. Galvin looked disheveled and perhaps a little tired but, thankfully, mostly in good shape. But Alia was near collapse. Her face was pale, the bags under her eyes had grown. He almost gasped when he noticed a glob of M.U.D. on her neck.

Nightmares and already wounded? Things were not going well.

"What's wrong?" he asked.

Alia sighed. "A lot of things." Declan's stomach churned as she confirmed his fears. "For starters, it's already the thirtieth and this job is every bit as difficult as promised."

Declan's eyes darted to the time displayed at the top of the screen. It was past midnight already. Just one more item to add to the list of things going wrong. "I'm sure you're not surprised by that. What problems can I actually help you with?"

She described a creature that rang a bell, but he couldn't quite recall what sounded so familiar about it. "I can't place it," she told him, "but something about it feels…" She shrugged. "Wrong."

"Nothing about this feels right," Declan agreed. "First, I have to ask: are you in over your head? I don't care what that witch says, I'll drop what I'm doing to come to you. Don't blow me off," he scolded, seeing the beginning of an eye roll. "I'm serious. There are too many I don't like happening. If you need me—"

"I'm sorry," she said, cutting off his building lecture. "I know you're worried. If we get in over our head, we will tell you."

He noticed the sidelong glance Galvin gave her, his eyebrows raising slightly, though he didn't contradict her. She wanted to do the job on her own.

"Fine, but how do I call you back if I want to check on you guys?"

Galvin's face scrunched up. "Sorry, this is kind of a one-way thing. I set the phones up to take calls from communication spells, but I haven't figured out a way to allow the phones to call people the same way. You'll only be able to contact other enchanted communication items right now."

Impressive, Declan had to admit, but not ideal in this situation.

He let out a breath. "All right. Then from the appearance you described, the creature sounds like a leshy, but there are some major inconsistencies with what you recounted."

"Leshy?" Alia looked confused. "But those are creatures that live in old woods that have openings to the fae realm. Mostly Eastern European. Northern California isn't exactly parallel with the fae realm."

Declan nodded. "One of many things that don't match up. I've never heard of any creature with black goo for blood, and a leshy won't attack unprovoked unless you threatened its woods. And the Redwood Forest is a nationally protected park."

"It's plausible the creature feels endangered," Galvin added. "The warlocks have a whole regiment out here, and I'm not convinced the intelligence we've been given about what their activities is reliable."

"Good observation," Declan commended. "Threatening its rule over a territory would provoke it, if the warlocks are trying to root it out."

"I thought leshies could communicate verbally as well?" Alia asked. "This thing has only growled and roared."

Declan nodded. "You are correct. It should be able to communicate." He gestured to his neck in the same spot as Alia's wound. "Did something else do that to you? A leshy wouldn't make such a small wound."

She looked nervous at the question, and her face paled further. "No," she stammered. "That was another thing we wanted to talk to you about."

Declan felt his blood pressure rising. How many creatures were they up against?

Galvin opened his mouth, but voices in the background caught their attention. They both glanced over their shoulders before Alia's face zoomed in on the screen as she hunched over to hide the phone from view. Declan heard Galvin greet someone as she whispered, "We've got to go. We'll talk to you soon."

Declan nodded. He wasn't where he was supposed to be and didn't need anyone else finding out. "Be safe." It was half instruction and half plea.

She nodded and ended the call.

He hated that they were on the assignment alone. Especially with something sinister going on. During Hallowtide, to boot.

He stuffed the phone in his pocket, turning his attention back to Ophelia. "Sorry. Where were we?"

"A phone that works with magic," she purred over her wine glass. "Impressive."

"So I've heard."

Her expression was soft as she watched him. "I know you're worried about them."

Declan nodded, not bothering to deny it. Ophelia was particularly gifted at reading people. There was no point in trying to hide from her.

"Try not to worry too much. I've managed to send them a little help."

Declan blinked at her. "How?"

"I told you, I still have *some* power on the Council. And I asked for the one I know will see the truth through his training."

Declan frowned. He had no idea what that meant.

She finished her drink and set the glass down at the end of the table to be collected. "Now, I believe I was about to warn you about your little house guest, but it seems you're already aware she's no friend to you."

"You told me that much when you said not to trust her. If that was all, then why did you want to meet?"

Ophelia's eyes narrowed and she leaned over the table. "Because what you don't know is that she's an agent of someone working against you. I don't know who this person is or why they hate you, but they are out to destroy you."

Declan wondered how many enemies the druids had. Mathias had cornered the market for a while, reducing their numbers to near nothing. But their fight at the end of the summer had revealed that someone else had been behind their feud. They had been tricked into eliminating each other—Declan into trapping Mathias in the demon realm and Mathias into killing off all the druids.

Was Ophelia talking about a new enemy, or was it the same person behind the feud with Mathias?

Recent events started to make more sense. The Council's strangely severe punishment for Declan's lack of documents. Documents they claimed had gone missing due to a mistake. Ill intent was more likely.

"How do you know this?"

Ophelia's eyes darted around the room, no doubt checking for any signs of suspicious activity, before she gracefully got up from the table. She glided down from the dais, not sparing a glance back at him, only crooking one slender finger.

Declan rolled his eyes but obeyed, following her down the dais and around the fake shade tree to a hidden door. A key appeared in her hand, likely pulled from some tight fold in her dress he didn't want to know about. She unlocked the door, revealing a narrow staircase. She ushered Declan in first and closed and locked the door again behind them.

The hallway was tight, not built for heavy foot traffic. Ophelia gave him a sultry grin as she squeezed by—her hands tender on his sides, then dragging along his torso as she positioned herself ahead of him on the stairs. Despite her cool hands, her touch always left him feeling heated, and his cheeks flushed. He wasn't the only one she did this to. She knew exactly how to get the reaction she wanted.

It had been a long time since he was with a woman, and he didn't realize how much he'd been neglecting that particular need. He prayed for strength, closing his eyes and thinking about anything except her backside as it swayed up the stairs toward a door at the top. He did not want to get sidetracked with a tryst today, despite how tempting the idea was.

"Ophelia," he warned, giving her a hard stare. "I don't have time for this."

She gave him a mischievous smile, placing one of those delicate fingers to her soft lips. "Shh, not yet," she whispered and crooked her finger again, pointing to the door. "Inside."

Declan groaned but followed her up the stairs.

She used the same key to unlock the thick metal door. He felt a gentle release of magic in tandem with the sound of the lock turning. She swung the door open and entered first, stepping to the side to allow him through behind her.

Inside, her apartment was all light colors and classic, elegant furniture that fit Ophelia's style exactly. She had never liked modern, but wouldn't be caught dead with anything rustic either. She found dark colors too gloomy and surrounded herself with bright pastels instead. She felt she deserved princess treatment and, having been denied it in her living life by the whiny Danish prince, gave it to herself in her immortal one.

It was a small place, with a kitchen just inside the door that opened into the living room, and one bedroom off the main room. That was Ophelia style too. She was picky about who she brought up to her home, and the only visitors privileged enough to stay overnight did so in her bedroom. Declan, being one of the few she always welcomed to her previous apartments whenever he wanted, didn't plan to stay that long.

She closed the door behind them and locked it. The magic fell back into place, dampening the noise from downstairs like they had entered a musician's sound booth. It was impressive, since vampires had limited magical skills. A vampire's ability to use magic was determined by how much magic they had performed while living. Since Ophelia had been a mortal before she turned, she couldn't cast spells.

"Nice silencing spell. How did you get it on the door?"

"I paid a wizard to set it up for me." She sauntered into her bedroom, but this time Declan did not follow. He was determined to keep the meeting strictly professional today. He was on a time limit and couldn't stay out forever. As it was now, he could diffuse the tension she had built up in him, but not if he let her continue.

He crossed his arms, leaning against the counter separating the kitchen from the living room. "Tell me how you know Grace is working for someone who's trying to destroy me."

"Because she brings me orders from the same person," Ophelia called. He heard her rustling through her closet and dresser drawers.

He sighed, shoving away memories of the little lacy thing she'd worn the last time he spent the night with her. He really hoped she wasn't putting that on.

"So you work for them too?" It was a question of trying to understand the logistics. Declan had known Ophelia too long to think her a traitor. Besides, she wouldn't be telling him any of this if she was. "Do you know who it is?"

"No. He's careful to keep his identity hidden."

"But you know it's a man?"

"Only by the way Grace pines for him. Otherwise, his written instructions are clinical at best. I can't get anything from his handwriting or language style."

"How do you know Grace isn't into women?"

Ophelia didn't bother to answer his question. She was too good at what she did to entertain his doubts.

"Okay. Point taken." Declan didn't like how long she was taking to change. He shifted on his feet. "So what kind of orders does he give?"

"From me, he mostly wants the Underground to cause trouble, justify the fear propaganda the wizards are pushing. The more scared and separated the non-human supernaturals are, the easier they are to control. But he also wants information on you. Where your safehouses are, if other druids have tried to contact you, what other non-humans are loyal to you. I'm supposed to report back if anyone tries to contact you through me."

"It's not like you to follow orders," Declan pointed out. "What does he have on you?"

"You mean other than me being the queen regent of the Underground? Not much. Just the threat that he could take it from me. My understanding is he could take my crown as easily as Theo could."

"And you believe him?"

"He's proven his point with other rebellious groups, if that's what you mean. Some werewolves tried to organize peacefully a few years back, but something happened and now they're all diehard supporters of the World Council."

Declan balked. Squashing a whole group as a message for Ophelia to fall in line was some display. Plus, the supernaturals the wizards called "monsters," like werewolves, only responded to strength. Who else but a dragon could throw around that kind of power?

Only someone with that much would be able to so completely fool Mathias into believing the Arbors, specifically Declan and Tiberius, had attacked his temple. But why? Declan couldn't think of anyone he had made enemies with who could hate him so deeply. Someone like that would be difficult to forget, and Declan didn't forget much.

But why would a dragon want control in the mortal realm or want Declan destroyed? He couldn't remember ever dealing with dragons. Dragons stuck to themselves and had never required an ambassador with the druids, or any group for that matter. The only dragon—or half-dragon, in this case—he knew was Theo, and he had been alone when Declan and Tiberius rescued him from his abusive mother. They never found a father, and dragons didn't abandon their young. If Theo had a father, they would have found him by now.

Who could Declan have hurt so thoroughly to cause such enduring hatred?

Gia above, Ophelia was taking way too long to get dressed and it was getting harder to not picture what on earth she was putting on. It had to be more fastener than clothing at this point.

"I actually have a secondary reason for wanting to meet with you."

Declan closed his eyes, licking his lips. She was going to make him fight for every ounce of self-control tonight. "Ophelia, I told you I don't have time for a romantic diversion today."

She came out of her room, and Declan took a bracing breath before slowly opening his eyes. She was fully covered, wearing protective hiking boots, dark leggings, and a black, hooded, heavy sweater, her knife sheath peeking out from underneath. To his immense relief, she was dressed for stealth.

She smiled, showing her fangs. "Of course not, we have somewhere we need to be first. But," she added, batting her eyelashes, "if we finish early, and the rogue look does it for you…"

Declan stared at his shoes and counted slowly to ten, reminding himself there was someone out to get him and he needed to find out more about them to beat them at this cloak-and-dagger game.

When he once again had control, he lifted his head. Ophelia watched him with a amused smirk. She was enjoying his struggle.

He gestured to the door. "Don't sway your hips. Let's go."

23

Alia shook her head, rubbing her eyes, and tried reading the last line for the fourth time. She resumed flipping Declan and Evelyn's wedding coin in her hand, hoping the fidgeting would keep her alert. It worked a little. Her eyes didn't droop this time. She'd rather search for clues to find Evelyn but she had to figure out the strange monster in the woods before she could get back to that.

No use. Her eyes were open but she had no idea what she just read in the grove book.

She stretched and stood from the cot, trying to wake herself up. Sleep was a bad idea right now and, unless she was moving, she would nod off. The cold outside didn't help. She'd wrapped herself in a thick blanket but she needed something else. The potion Hawthorne gave her was working, and he was right about the side effects of coffee, but she needed to warm up and to move around or she would be sawing logs in seconds.

Galvin had offered to help her sleep, like before, but Alia

declined. Lucian had already warned her he was going to attack her, Galvin or not. At least one of them needed to be rested, and Galvin was starting to get worn out. At her insistence, he'd lain down and within moments his breathing deepened and slowed.

Alia, however, had stayed up. The truth was she was too scared to close her eyes. Her encounter with Lucian in the woods made her seriously rethink what was happening to her. He'd not only manifested enough to do physical harm, but the supposed leshy had seen him too. She hadn't noticed at the time, but it hadn't come after her at all until her bullets hit it. Plus, if Lucian hadn't really been there, he wouldn't have needed to dodge the creature's attack.

He wasn't just alive, he had been released from the demon realm.

If only she had gotten to talk to Declan longer during their phone call, but one of the patrolling warlocks had interrupted them, telling Alia and Galvin they couldn't loiter on the border of the camp. Rather than an actual rule, Alia suspected Captain Ashblade wanted reports on their doings, but she and Galvin had cleared out like good little soldiers and headed back to their tent. Galvin had wisely suggested they try to get some shut-eye before the night was totally gone and maybe they could go back out at dawn.

Alia's pack sat on the trunk at the foot of her cot. She rummaged through it quietly, not wanting to wake Galvin or any of the warlocks. She had a tea that would help her focus. Between that and Hawthorne's potion, she would be able to keep going until she could get back to Declan.

Hopefully.

Now she just needed to find some water. There had been a tent next to the infirmary that looked like the kitchen. Alia put the tea in her pocket and tiptoed out.

As she stepped out into the camp, she saw the soldier Galvin had attacked earlier. He had deep bags under his eyes and his face was pale. He looked a lot like Alia right now. Her stomach twisted in worry.

He didn't notice her as he made his way to their shared tent so Alia reached out. He stopped short before her hand touched him and glared. "What?" he snapped.

"I'm sorry about what happened. Galvin is... new to some of these abilities. He wouldn't have done it if he knew—"

The soldier scoffed and made to shoulder his way past her. "Whatever."

"Wait," Alia tried again.

The warlock stopped and looked at her.

"I'll wake Galvin. We'll see if he can figure out how to lift it. We can help."

He gazed burned down at Alia. "And have you do something worse to me if he can't?" He sneered. "Get lost before I change my mind about reporting you and your boyfriend."

Alia had been wondering about that. "Why didn't you report us?"

The warlock froze, hand holding the tent flap open. He was silent and didn't move. Alia was sure he wasn't going to answer, but he shot a scowl over his shoulder. "You think I need to tattle every time I get into it with another magic user? I can take care of myself." He turned away and stalked inside.

Her heart fell. She was sure they could help if he could stop being a bully long enough to let them. But Declan had told her many times that some people would never accept help. With a sigh, she turned away from the stubborn warlock and back to locating the mess tent.

The camp never seemed to sleep. Warlocks passed her on the way to and from their duties like they had earlier in the day, though perhaps not as many. This time, she noticed many of them staring at her as she passed. *That's new.*

The mess tent was easy to find. The camp was set up in orderly rows, and Alia remembered the path they had taken earlier.

Lights glowed from inside, indicating it was still open so she walked in. On one side stood a table containing plates, drinks, and cutlery, and the rest of the tent was filled with long tables and benches. Warlocks sat in a few small groups, eating and drinking. She didn't see anything like a kitchen, but the warlocks had food. Maybe it was made with magic. She hoped she could still get some hot water.

A warlock headed toward the flap, so Alia reached out to stop him. "Excuse me."

The warlock narrowed his eyes at her, and her stomach did a little flip.

"Hi," she tried sweetly. "Sorry to bother you, I was hoping you could tell me where can I get some hot water for tea?"

The warlock glared at her for a long moment before pointing to the end of the tent past all the tables, where she could make out a carafe, hiding a bit behind the dishes.

Alia smiled. "Thank you." But the warlock just grumbled, stomping away. Alia wondered why he seemed so upset with such a simple question.

But it wasn't just that warlock. As Alia made her way toward the table, she noticed all of them throwing small, angry glances her way. When she looked at them, their heads turned back to their companions, leaning in close to whisper.

She had a feeling the discontent had something to do with what happened earlier, though she didn't know why. A simple need for help had led her and Galvin back to the camp. Surely the warlocks didn't expect them to lie down and die out there instead of running for help?

Considering most of the others did *not* return, perhaps they did. Maybe by looking for help, she and Galvin had broken some sort of warlock code?

A group of three, sitting far away from the others, were the only ones who didn't pay her any attention. Two of them wore all white, like the MP officer they had seen earlier. The third wore the same forest colors as the regular soldier warlocks, but in the same suit-and-tie style as the MP officers. He had a similar band labeled *MP* around his upper arm.

Alia turned away from the stares and got a disposable hot drink cup from the stack. She put the cup under the carafe, but a large hand grabbed her by the arm and forced her away before she could fill it.

A broad and blocky warlock sneered down at her. "That was some stunt you pulled earlier, leading that beast back here," he growled, confirming her suspicion that they had broken some sort of code.

She stared blankly up at him, not revealing her surprise or nervousness at the confrontation. Instead, she showed all the warlocks looking that she wasn't about to cowed. She tried to yank her arm out of his grasp. "We needed help."

"Help from the beast?" he sneered, squeezing her arm harder and making her flinch. "Or help destroying—"

"Let her go," Hawthorne's voice was firm behind her. He must've come in without her noticing while she was getting shaken down.

"You siding with *them* now?" the warlock challenged, but he released Alia's arm as Hawthorne instructed.

Hawthorne also just stared at him. "I'll side with anyone getting picked on. I don't like bullies. I don't care what magic class they are."

The two squared off, one glaring and the other just waiting. Alia's heart raced and she was worried she was about to witness a brawl that would get them all in trouble. She placed a hand on Hawthorne's arm, hoping to convince him to let it go.

The Raptor's whole body went rigid as he shifted to stand at attention. The group of MPs had left their table and walked over. The two in white remained silent, watching Hawthorne, while the third frowned at Alia. "Is there a problem here?" he asked.

Hawthorne began to tremble under Alia's hand. She glanced up to see his face had gone completely pale, just as it had when the other white-clad MP had approached them at the barrier. His eyes were wide and pleading, darting between the two in white. His pupils had contracted to pinpoints. He swallowed hard. "No, sir." His normally confident voice was small.

Hawthorne was scared. Something about the two in white frightened him, and Alia couldn't help but feel sorry for him.

"No, sirs," the bully warlock echoed, though not nearly as contrite.

"Wellby." The MP in forest green was the only one speaking. The two in white stared at Hawthorne, silent and unreadable. "Get out of here."

Wellby saluted before marching off.

The third MP shifted his focus to Hawthorne and Alia. His gaze flicked down to her empty cup before returning to Hawthorne. "Hurry up, then escort your druid charge back to her tent. Make sure there's no more trouble."

"Yes, sir." Hawthorne's eyes never left the two MPs in white and it wasn't until all three officers had left the tent that he finally stopped shaking.

He looked down at Alia, expression wiped completely blank. "Get your water. Let's go."

"But—"

Hawthorne fixed hard, silver eyes on her, cutting off any argument she might have made. "I told you. I cannot disobey orders."

Alia frowned at that choice of words. He *couldn't* disobey orders, not that he *wouldn't*.

Something odd was going on, but she didn't voice her thoughts as she got her water.

Once her cup was full, Hawthorne led her out of the mess tent and through the camp. He remained silent and Alia wasn't quite sure what to say, so they walked back without speaking.

He stopped when they reached C-9. "I'll check on you a bit later, but I think you should probably stay here for now."

"Thank you, Hawthorne."

The Raptor nodded, then turned and left.

Alia ducked inside as quiet as possible but noticed Galvin yawn and stirring. Galvin was such a heavy sleeper he had not been disturbed by the sounds of the bully's stubborn nightmares farther down the row. Normally, Galvin would sleep through half the morning if Alia didn't wake him up, and she wondered what trick he'd used this time to do it on his own. Maybe he was just that worried about her.

It would still take Galvin a good few minutes to be fully awake, so Alia went back to her cot and the grove book. Her hands wrapped around the steaming cup of tea while it steeped. She sipped it, careful not to burn her tongue. The warlocks apparently liked their beverages boiling because the water was still hot, even after the walk back. The warmth spread through her body, perking her up.

Galvin sat up, groaning, but Alia continued to flip through the grove book. She doubted she would find anything of use in it. It contained knowledge Declan had practiced and, for the most part, perfected pertaining to the groves. Which wasn't much help in either the leshy or the Lucian situation.

She turned a page to a full spread detailing grove guardians. They were creatures tied to a grove by the druid who tended it and were fiercely loyal to their druid. It was not often a guardian connect with another druid after their original one was gone. Guardians usually defended the grove from intruders, mostly animals like bears or wolves. Alia and Declan had lived near a few groves with guardians when she was growing up but had rarely seen them. They once visited a grove in the desert with a mountain lion guardian. Alia had gotten only a glimpse of its magical glittering fur before it had disappeared in the rocks.

The knotwork of the druid language in Declan's handwriting covered both sides of the two-page spread. He explained how guardians were not actual animals but manifestations of the grove tree's magic in conjunction with the druid who tended it. *These guardians are almost always called forth by a druid with the ability to speak with animals since they are the only druids capable of fully communicating with the creatures. However, unlike their animal counterparts, guardians will have some distinctly magical features that make them easy to distinguish, such as gold in the fur, mist that gathers at their feet, or glowing eyes and markings. Each guardian is unique in this way.*

Galvin yawned, stretching. "Were you able to get much sleep?"

Alia peered closer at Declan's illustrations, avoiding the glare she knew would be coming. There was no point lying to him, he'd know anyway. "I didn't sleep at all. I didn't want to risk it."

She felt the stern look drilling into the side of her head but refused to face him. "Alia," he started, his voice more full of worry than she would have guessed. "You must sleep. You're already running on empty—"

"Stop." She cut off the lecture she had heard several times already. He wasn't telling her anything she didn't know. She put the book aside and swung her feet over the side of the cot. "Something dangerous is happening. Either Lucian is haunting me and I'll just keep waking up anyway, or he's actually alive."

Galvin didn't argue or even flinch. He must have already reached the same conclusion.

"Either way, my nightmares are real and somehow give him unrestricted access to me. I can't keep giving him *any* access. Especially not now." She didn't elaborate in case others were listening, but Galvin knew what she meant. He was experiencing the loss of his magic too. "The only thing that seems to shield me is you, and I don't know if you'll be able to do that for the next couple of days. Besides, if you stay awake so I can sleep, then you'll be the exhausted one, and we're right back where we started."

Galvin's shoulders slumped, his face full of concern. "I would do that for you. I am happy to do whatever it takes to help you."

She reached over, cupping his cheek and giving him a warm smile. She knew he insisted because he cared, but his idea just wasn't going to work right now. She ran her thumb over his cheekbone, no longer covered in frost like when they had first met but colored a bit from the late summer sun. His hair was getting longer too. He'd need a haircut soon if he didn't want it hanging in his face.

But it was his eyes that always made her heart skip beats. What used to be a clear, ice blue from the heavy snowflakes coating his irises had melted into a deep, gemlike blue. She brushed his dark locks back, tucking them behind his ear. His eyes drifted closed and he leaned into her hand, his own sliding up her arm to wrap around her wrist. Her breath caught and her cheeks burned. A smile tugged on the side of his mouth, his lips brushing her palm. He really had no idea how handsome he was.

Alia snapped out of her daze, slipping her hand out of his before stuffing it into her lap and glaring at the offending appendage, wondering what on earth had gotten into her. That was wildly inappropriate. Galvin was her friend and partner. One who had made his position on physical contact quite clear at the train station when she pretended to kiss him. Not to mention, it was never a good idea for partners to become romantically involved. She didn't even like him that way anyway.

At least, she didn't think she did.

She sheepishly lifted her gaze back to his face. He was rubbing the back of his neck, looking up at nothing in particular, as if he had gotten caught doing something he shouldn't. Her stomach felt like she had swallowed a rock. In reality, it was Alia who had done something she shouldn't. She had made him uncomfortable again, after promising not to. She wasn't even sure why she had done it. Exhaustion maybe?

Galvin swallowed hard, clearing his throat. "So what's the plan? I'm sure you've made one since you weren't busy sleeping."

Changing the subject was generous of him. She knew how much he disliked unsolicited attention. Maybe he thought it was the condition she was in too and was going easy on her. Either way, she would take the opportunity to move on and forget what had just happened.

"Right. Well, I think we should check out the creature's lair. If it *is* a leshy, then something is affecting it and the source is likely in the place it's most connected to." She rolled on her side, reaching for her pack. She didn't bother to pick it up but dug inside for the little vial of black goo and handed it to Galvin. "I've looked at this a couple times, it doesn't seem like a natural substance. I think this might be part of what's messing with the creature. Maybe even this whole section of forest."

Galvin squinted at the goo. It moved slowly as he tilted the vial, more solid than liquid. It had a sheen to it, sort of like a metallic glitter. "Okay, but how do we keep it from attacking while we dig through its home?"

"You're so good at loud, flashy diversions," she teased. "I thought you could come up with another one."

He grinned. "You know, I may have an idea, but we're going to need some help."

Alia frowned. She got the sense Hawthorne wasn't very impulsive and couldn't see him being okay with an off-the-cuff plan.

Galvin made a dismissive sound when he saw the doubt on her face. "I think he'll help. I think we're starting to grow on him."

She wasn't sure of that.

24

Ophelia led the way through shadows and back alleys a few blocks up the road from her vampire bar and cafe. She and Declan both pulled the hoods of their jackets low over their heads to keep from being identifiable. Theo had done an excellent job updating the old cloaks while maintaining the magic woven into the fabric. The spell tingled over Declan's arms as curious eyes glanced past him, the magic diverting their attention. Declan hoped he wouldn't learn the limits of the spell's strength tonight. Thankfully, on Ophelia's practically abandoned side of town, there weren't many people milling about who weren't also looking to avoid detection themselves.

 As they moved through the city, Declan noticed the buildings and roads becoming more populous but no less seedy. There was more graffiti, working lights, and plenty of unsavory folks out and about on their business. Most were mortal humans and—with Declan's cloak, Ophelia's natural threatening vibes, and the fact they didn't want people poking around in their own affairs—they didn't bother the duo.

In this area, people didn't stick their noses into others' business.

Since his encounter with Mathias in the Nome Grove, Declan had not seen a single demon but that didn't mean he threw caution to the wind. Even if Mathias had called off the hunt, it was unlikely word had gotten to every demon in the world in just a couple weeks. There were bound to be one or two who hadn't heard. Or had a grudge of their own after a few hundred years of fighting.

While Mathias had acted as if he didn't believe Declan and Tiberius when they claimed not to have attacked his temple, he was a very intelligent individual. Declan could call Mathias many things but illogical was not one of them. Declan had no doubt he had quickly discovered they were telling the truth, and the lack of outright attacks led Declan to believe he was rethinking his hatred of the druids.

Declan also knew if a powerful demon such as Mathias could be tricked, then it was entirely possible he had been as well. Mathias had seemed genuinely confused by their accusations and made solid arguments against them. Declan had also begun to reconsider his own perception of Mathias, though that did not mean he was ready to forgive and forget the whole thing.

Ophelia brought Declan to an old pub so unlike her style he was surprised she even knew how to find it. Clearly it wasn't her chosen meeting place, which told him they were here to see someone. Inside, everything was dark, old wood and nineties-esque restaurant furniture. The bar and tables had a sheen that could only come from bussers constantly trying to clean up grease and sticky drinks. It wasn't what Declan would consider a busy establishment but it had a good number of patrons tonight. A biker gang took up a larger area over by the pool tables and dartboards, having a grand, raucous time. A handful of people sat at a large corner booth on the opposite side of the room. Low growls amid the chatter and their reflective eyes told Declan they were werewolves. A small pack, by the looks of it. They were engaged in some sort of discussion. The few mortals at the bar took no notice of the pack, likely wrestling with their own problems at the bottom of another glass.

A man sat at a table in the center of the room, his back toward the door. He had long, dark brown hair with Viking braids on the side of his head. The mass of thick locks were piled up in a messy bun. His beard was long, but at this angle Declan wasn't sure how long. From what Declan could see, the man wore an open flannel over dark jeans, the sleeves rolled up to his elbows, and—Declan's heart skipped a beat—a vine tattoo wrapped down his arm, ending at his hand.

He must have been who they had come to see because Ophelia walked right up to his table without so much as a greeting and sat down. He barely acknowledged her, taking a long pull from his mug, trying to finish now he had company.

As Declan approached, he noticed a large scar on the right side of the man's face, starting just above his eyebrow, going down across his eye, and ending at his lip. The milky white eye was marred with thin lines following the path of the scar, with only the faintest hint of where his useless iris and pupil were hidden. Declan knew from the many years he had spent with the Viking that, even though he could no longer see the physical world through that eye, it now gave him a constant view into the spirit world.

Declan recognized the bulky block of a man immediately. "Blessed Gia," he managed around the lump in his throat, overcome with joy and bewilderment. The last time he had seen Erik Arbor had been holding off a group of five demons from some young druids. That had been well before the two hundred years Declan had been in hiding. "You're alive!"

"Keep your voice down," Erik scolded, but he was smiling

under the bushy beard. He stood up, taking Declan's hand.

Declan didn't know how to feel. All he could do was gape at the man he had known. A clan member still alive!

"Stop gaping, sir," Erik teased, thumping Declan on the back. "You look like a fish. Besides, if anyone should be gaping, it's me." He clasped Declan's arm in the old warrior's embrace before lifting the shorter man off his feet in a great bear hug—which was an accurate description, since Erik could turn into an actual bear.

Erik was the fourth son of a Viking family and, with nothing left to inherit after his three older brothers, had been given to the Arbor Clan to train as a druid. He had been a little older than most trainees when he joined and kept a lot of Viking traditions, but he had advanced quickly.

"It's good to see you vertical, sir," he said.

With all the air squeezed out of him, Declan couldn't answer even if he had the words to answer with.

Erik set Declan back on his feet and gestured for him to take a seat next to Ophelia, who had spent her time during their reunion attempting to wipe the surface of the table clean enough for her standard with a napkin. Apparently she had not succeeded, for she abandoned the napkin and wiggled the dirt and germs from her fingers with a disgusted grimace before demurely placing her hands in her lap.

"I can't believe it." Declan was grinning so wide his face hurt, but the prickling of tears had already been replaced with barely contained laughter. If Erik was alive, there could be more druids out there. He and his apprentices were not alone. They wouldn't have to rebuild a whole people from nothing again. "I thought everyone else had been killed," he confessed, the words spilling out. "What happened to you? You look like a hipster. Why didn't you come back to the Arbor Grove?"

Erik chuckled and waved to the bartender for another round. "I hope you don't mind, but I already told her what you'd like. If we had more time, I'd give you the whole story but, in a nutshell, I didn't know there were any more of us either. At least, not until your students came and restarted everything. Very loudly, I might add." He gave Declan a judgmental side-eye with his good one. "And I didn't return because I was still in hiding. You remember better than anyone that, when we stayed in large groups, the demons found us that much easier. I really shouldn't even be contacting you now."

The waitress placed two mugs of a brown brew in front of Declan and Erik, with a glass of red wine for Ophelia, who only took it to be polite. The waitress likely had no idea she couldn't actually drink it. Not that she would anyway—any vintage this establishment served would not be high enough quality for her.

"You won't have to stay away," Declan said once the waitress was out of earshot. "I don't think Mathias is hunting us anymore."

Erik huffed and took a long pull from his drink. Erik could easily drink Declan under the table, and had on several occasions. Like Declan's own oldest habits and traditions, most of Erik's were probably long gone now. Except for the drinking, it seemed. "Don't be fooled into thinking you and two apprentices killed him by yourselves."

"Of course not. But our last fight unveiled some truths. On both sides." Declan shrugged and gestured around the room. "Come on, I bet you haven't seen a demon in weeks."

Erik bobbed his head to the side, confirming Declan's claim. "I did find that suspicious. I had a tail about the time your kiddos were doing their thing, then it just dropped off without warning. Thought it was regrouping with some friends." He waved his hand, brushing the topic away, and leaned toward Declan over the table. "Look, the demons—or lack thereof—aren't the only threat. The World Council is slowly taking control of all the different groups, but I'm sure Miss O here has told you all about that."

"I got a firsthand look at it," Declan drawled, stealing a glance at Ophelia. He was surprised she allowed that sort of familiarity from Erik.

"Before, I thought if I just stayed hidden, I wouldn't have to worry about it, but you very loudly announced our presence to the world. I'm grateful to not be alone anymore and I want to help. I followed you then, and I'll do it now."

An idea began to form in Declan's mind. "Have you been back to any of the anchor groves?"

Erik shook his head. "Not since your apprentices were there. I have seen their exemplary work on some of the smaller ones, though."

Declan glowed with pride for Alia and Galvin but pushed it away to bask in later. "I'll be sure to pass along the compliment. Go to Ingadi," he instructed. "It took the least amount of damage during the upgrade. When you get there, send out signals through the network for any druids still alive and in hiding to come home. Rebuild. Retrain. Take anyone who wants to become a druid. But do it all quietly."

Erik was nodding. "Build our numbers back up under their noses so, by the time they notice, we're too big for them to step on." He grinned. "I like it."

Ophelia placed a hand on Declan's arm. "I hate to break up your touching reunion, but anything else should be discussed a little closer to home. Plus, we need to get back."

He sighed. "She's right. I have to get back to the Arbor Grove before I'm missed. We have a… guest who can't know I've been out."

Erik stood with them, clasping arms with Declan as they did when they were warriors. "It is so good to see you. My heart is lighter knowing there might be more of us out there."

"Mine too." Declan smiled.

Erik was about to release his arm but changed his mind and pulled Declan into another rib-cracking hug. He set him back down on his feet but did not let go of his arm. "Before you go, I have a message for you. It's one of the main reasons I asked O to arrange this meeting."

The blood drained from Declan's face and all lightness his heart had was gone. "Messages" from Erik usually came from the other side. This one was apparently important enough for Erik to contact him. He didn't know Declan could have easily received the message himself. No one except Tiberius and Evelyn knew Declan had spirit abilities, and even they didn't know to what extent.

"She's been trying to get this message to you for a long time," Erik continued.

Ever since Evelyn's death, Declan had shut off his spirit abilities. He ignored ghosts who tried to communicate with him and eventually was able to stop seeing them if he focused. He had never known for certain if Evelyn was on the other side, terrified he would find her if he looked, and so refused to talk to any of them. Now, he was forced to face the possibility that her spirit wanted to tell him something.

Declan swallowed hard. "Can I say no?"

Erik hummed, nodding, but went on. "Just listen. It's a young woman, human."

Declan's heart clenched.

"Frail-looking, thin, wispy hair." Erik fixed him in an ocean blue stare. "It's not her, Declan."

He almost sobbed with relief, briefly closing his eyes and taking a steadying breath. Erik would never know how much that confirmation meant to him.

He didn't want to get involved with spirits, but if this one had sought out someone he knew, then she was likely persistent enough to find him. "Is she here now?"

"No, but if you need to talk to her further, I can send her your way. Tell her you are more... receptive?"

Declan glared. Erik had always suspected he had spirit abilities but had never called him out so openly like that. "Just tell me what she wants."

"She wants you to help her 'mate.' Says he doesn't know the truth and that's why he's lashing out."

Spirit messages were always a little cryptic, but this one was strange. Someone was lashing out and the spirit thought Declan was the best one to help. Could it have something to do with whomever was giving orders to Grace and pulling the Council's strings?

"Humans don't usually have 'mates' unless they end up with someone who isn't human," Declan mused. "Did she give you a name?"

"I asked but all she could say was her mate is known as 'the dark one.'" Declan stared, waiting for more, but Erik shrugged. "Spirits lose connection to the living world more and more the longer they're dead. She must think it's important, but it's all she can remember."

Declan turned to Ophelia but she shook her head. "Doesn't mean anything to me."

"It could be an old name," Erik guessed. "If you're staying at the Arbor Grove, do some digging, see what comes up."

"Erik, I've lived through most of recorded history. You've lived through at least half. If we don't know that name, then it wasn't used."

"Not by anyone in this realm," Ophelia added.

25

Galvin felt Alia fidget in the dark behind him and Hawthorne. He knew having to rely on the two of them was driving her crazy, but her human eyes couldn't navigate the pre-dawn dark like his and Hawthorne's could.

"Are you sure about this?" Alia asked, echoing the same question she had asked Galvin at Ingadi before he had cast the demolition spell. "The forest already looks like it could go up from one errant spark." She waved at the dry brush. "We want to distract the creature, not set the whole forest on fire."

Galvin huffed as he and Hawthorne dumped more leafy branches onto the last pile. The spell Galvin had used for their distraction at Ingadi needed to be delicate and precise. This plan required more oomph than finesse. They'd be fine. Besides, Galvin wasn't even casting the spell this time. She didn't have anything to worry about.

"You asked that last time I was in charge of a distraction," he reminded her, "and it turned out great."

Alia crossed her arms. "You mean when we both got captured and you were beaten so bad you could hardly stand?"

Hawthorne turned to Galvin with raised eyebrows.

He gave an uneasy giggle and waved his hand dismissively, hoping Hawthorne hadn't seen the flush of embarrassment coloring his face. "My spell was executed perfectly," he argued to the Raptor. "The rest was just bad luck." He left out the part where he had never actually cast that spell before.

"You better not have the same luck this time." Hawthorne had agreed to help quite readily but gave them both a look of doubt now. "I don't think that monster takes prisoners, and I have no aversion to leaving you both here."

Galvin huffed another laugh.

"Duly noted," Alia bit back, shifting her glare between the two of them.

Galvin cleared his throat. He thought Hawthorne was teasing, but apparently Alia didn't agree or she wasn't in the mood for jokes. She probably didn't realize the Raptor's cold exterior was from his training. Galvin had met a few Raptors when he had accompanied Nanny to some of her World Council duties. Hawthorne was the life of the party compared to them. If he was really as unfeeling as he acted, he wouldn't have agreed to help them in the first place.

She was also tired, though, and it had been difficult lately to make her laugh.

"So." Hawthorne gestured to the last pile they had made, which would actually be the first pile when they started the distraction. "I'm guessing your plan is to keep the monster moving by lighting all these smoke signals?"

Galvin nodded. "Yes. When it approaches one pile, we'll move on to the next one and light it."

"How are you going to get it to come close to fire? It ran away terrified before."

"The forest's safety will be more important to it than its own," Alia explained. "Plus, a forest fire is different from having actual fireballs thrown at you."

"And what happens when it approaches the last signal fire?"

"Hopefully we'll be done by then," Alia answered.

Galvin let out a chuckle and a smile twitched at the sides of Hawthorne's mouth. At least she hadn't completely lost her sense of humor in her fatigue.

Alia rolled her eyes but her face relaxed into a grin with them. "We'll make sure to count the smoke plumes," she assured Hawthorne, without going into more detail.

She and Galvin had agreed not to share the whole plan with Hawthorne. Galvin had to admit, just because the Raptor liked them, it didn't mean they could fully trust him yet. It was clear he and Captain Ashblade were not working together, but it wasn't clear how loyal he was to his commanding officer.

"When we see the last one lit, we'll finish up and get the heck out," Alia added. "Once you light the last signal, all you have to worry about is getting back to the camp before the creature sees you."

Realization dawned on Hawthorne's face. "Oh, I'm the bait?"

Alia and Galvin beamed at him in unison. They didn't tell him he had to light the fires because they couldn't conjure a spark between them and didn't want him asking why. Galvin doubted his smile was as innocent as Alia's, with her big eyes, batting her long eyelashes at him. Galvin never could resist those eyes but Hawthorne just harrumphed.

"Figures." He crossed his arms. "I'm ready when you two are."

"Great. Just give us a few minutes to get there before you light the first one." Alia gave him an encouraging thumbs up, and Galvin wished him luck before trailing behind her.

They followed the trail of unlit signal fires back to where Alia had first found the tracks. Thankfully, they could still rely on her tracking training, since their abilities were all but gone now. With her skill, they found the opening of the creature's lair after a brisk hike along an animal trail.

They approached a wall of stacked stone in a clearing as the first plumes of smoke rose above the canopy. An archway stood at one end, reminding Galvin of some of the grove entrances Alia had shown him. It was certainly built by hand, not nature, and he couldn't help but wonder if the creature had done it. It had hands after all. The plants had more life here than in the rest of the woods, but they were barely holding on. The same black goo they had found before and on the warlocks dripped from several of the stones, confirming Alia's theory that it was affecting the leshy.

"Do you think it's left already?" Galvin whispered.

Alia didn't answer, just silently shushed him. They didn't have to wait long to find out. As they watched, the creature emerged from the stone archway. It lifted its head to the sky, sniffing the wind, and stalked in the direction of the smoke.

Once it stepped out of sight, Alia dashed toward the opening, pulling Galvin behind her as they passed under the archway…

And into a satellite grove. The magical tree sat off-center in a grotto of rock. The stone walls were tall, reaching far above the tree and tapering down to the archway of the entrance. Brush and shrubs grew along the far wall and close to the tree, creating a hidden space behind the tree at the back of the smaller side of the circle. The larger portion of the grove was open and empty.

Alia stopped short, Galvin almost slamming into her back. She stood still, taking in the horror, and Galvin's heart sank at the sight. The grove was small, maybe fifty yards from one rock wall to the other. The new markings from their upgrade spell on the anchors were present but they should have been glowing on the ground, around the trunk, and in the leaves. Instead, the whole circle was dark and dull, like all life was leaching out of it. The tree had wilted, the foliage turned gray, and black goo dripped from the chalky, shedding bark.

"This can't be right."

"It's not." Anger and unshed tears colored Alia's voice. "Someone did this on purpose. Galvin, we have to figure this out. We can't let the warlocks burn down a grove."

Hawthorne was waiting for them outside his tent when they returned to the camp. "Well?" he asked. "What did you find out?"

Alia stomped up to him, glaring every step of the way. "Did you know there was a grove here?"

His eyes widened in surprise for a moment but otherwise remained unaffected. It was a testament to his surprise, since he wouldn't have reacted if he had already known. He furrowed his brows in suspicion. "A grove? I only know about the monster." His face pinched. "But it doesn't make any sense for the warlocks to withhold that information from you if they asked for your help. How come you didn't know one of your sacred spots was here?"

"It's a little one, not exactly a metropolis." She rounded on him again. "Why has the World Council sent all these soldiers to a druid grove?"

"I told you." He frowned. "All I know is there's a monster and, when I got here, Ashblade gave me orders to make sure you two didn't go rogue and start helping it destroy the regiment."

"What!" Alia fumed. "We are here to *help* because a creature is threatening to *hurt civilians!*"

"Well, someone is lying, and it's the two of you who keep acting like you're up to something."

"Someone is." Alia's hand went to her pocket and pulled out the wedding coin. She flipped it as she thought. "But it's not us."

Hawthorne nodded like she had just confirmed something for him. "I was thinking that too. No one here knows anything about a village nearby, and Ashblade refused to answer me when I asked." He paused, looking them both over. "You two don't know anything about a monster rebellion, do you?"

Galvin laughed. "The one from the eighteenth century where the supposed king of the monsters nearly took out the World Council? That monster rebellion?" He shrugged and shook his head. "What does that have to do with the creature here?"

"Certain members of the Council have been pushing the narrative that vampires, weres, and the other monsters are growing restless under Council rule again."

"But what does that have to do with the creature here?" Galvin asked again, since Hawthorne hadn't answered him the first time.

"My orders said it was created by a rebellion group called the Underground Monsters as a weapon against the Council."

Alia groaned. "And the warlocks think we are monster sympathizers and are part of this rebellion group. That's why you had orders to look after us."

Hawthorne gestured toward Alia, indicating she had it correct.

She growled in frustration. "Something is wrong. Grace is setting us up, but I just can't put my finger on what she's after, other than framing us." She frowned, and Galvin could see as much as feel her mind racing. Her fingers moved faster as they flipped the coin and she began to pace. She was fighting against a fog of sleep slowing her thoughts and making it more difficult to decipher the evidence. She was working far harder than she should be.

Galvin and Hawthorne watched her. "Grace Edenbrach?" Hawthorne asked in a hushed voice.

"Yeah. She was assigned as our parole officer."

"If it was anyone but her," Hawthorne said, fixing Galvin with an unamused stare, "the fact that you *have* a parole officer would not help your argument."

Galvin could feel Alia's mind continue to chase thoughts flying just out of reach. He couldn't take it anymore. It didn't matter what arguments she made, she couldn't keep going like this. He took her arm, turning her to face him.

She read the thoughts on his scowl, and all at once the steam went out of her. Galvin pulled her to him and she sagged against him.

"She's exhausted," he told Hawthorne. "We can't do this now. Let's discuss it later."

Hawthorne nodded. "I told you that potion was not meant to

replace sleep." He addressed Galvin. "I'll see what I can learn on my end. If someone here is plotting against you, I'm not sure I want you going back to the barracks."

"I *did* ask for our own tent," Alia grumbled, stuffing the coin back into her pocket.

"Use mine."

Galvin and Alia looked up at him in tandem, perfectly in sync without meaning to be.

Hawthorne sighed, either not noticing or choosing not to acknowledge their matched movements. "I'm not totally convinced you're not up to no good but, whether you two are causing trouble or need help from it, it'll be much easier to keep an eye on you if you're close by. Go to your tent and get your stuff and bring it back here. I'll poke around a bit, see what I can find out." He scanned them again and scoffed. "Honestly, the state you guys are in, it's hard to picture you two up to no good. If Alia's not sleeping, I'll pick up some stuff from the infirmary tent for you to make her a dreamcatcher."

"Wow." Galvin stared at Hawthorne. The Raptor was really helping them, even though they hadn't given him any reason to trust them. "Thank you."

"Don't thank me yet," he warned, heading toward the infirmary. "I may still decide to arrest you both."

Galvin grinned. Yeah, he liked this guy.

With a hand on her back, he ushered Alia away from Hawthorne's tent. The walk was quiet, each in their own heads. Galvin felt Alia fading, despite her efforts. She kept dragging behind, and he had to gently pull her along.

"You're either going to get some sleep or you'll end up

collapsing where you stand. No more arguing," Galvin scolded when she protested again. "I'll stay with you, though I don't know how much I can help now our powers are gone."

"I think you used spirit powers before, so they should still work," she said sleepily, wrapping her arms around his middle and clinging to hold herself up.

Galvin went hot and cold at the same time. "Spirit powers?"

"Yeah," she mumbled into his chest. "When we summoned that ghost and you could see her but I couldn't? That was your spirit power. It's a connection to the other side, mostly taught by other druids with the talent. We don't fully understand how it works, but they're the only powers you don't lose during Hallowtide."

"Then I hope that's what it is," he told her, pushing back the flaps of the tent, "so I can watch over you and you can rest."

It took Galvin all of a minute to gather what little they had left in C-9. He half carried Alia back to Hawthorne's tent. He just dropped their stuff on the ground and pulled Alia into the cot with him.

It took some time, but Alia finally settled in his arms. He sat against the head of the cot, holding her against his chest. He rubbed her hair away from her face, trying to soothe her.

Just when Alia was beginning to drift off, Hawthorne stormed in, glowering. "What did you do to that warlock?" he demanded, startling her awake.

Galvin froze, the blood draining from his face. Alia was right, his lack of control had come back to bite him in the butt. "Oh. That. Um…"

Hawthorne stalked over. "Don't bullshit me," he warned. "I can see through lies. You'd better have a good reason."

Galvin gulped. "Well, I uh… may have lost my temper when he started harassing us."

"A lot of the druid powers are new to him," Alia interjected.

It wasn't a lie, exactly, but Hawthorne rounded on her. "That's not the truth. I want him to say it. Spill it."

"It *is* true," Galvin tried, "that power is new. I'm not exactly sure what I did, but I think I used some of the stuff affecting Alia's sleep to give him nightmares. He *was* harassing us, and I *did* lose my temper. Alia told me off right afterward."

"Nightmares," Hawthorne clarified.

"I think so." Galvin cringed.

Hawthorne leaned closer, staring into Galvin's eyes. "Well, you gave him nightmares all right."

"Is he okay?" Alia asked.

Hawthorne looked at her, then sighed, his glare fading. "Physically, he's fine." He stood, dropping a hoop, some twine, and a small bag of beads and feathers onto Alia's lap. "He's in the infirmary, and they have him under some blessed dreamcatchers that seem to be helping."

"So," Galvin tried as Alia picked up the materials. "Are we okay?"

"I'm not going to report it, if that's what you're asking. I don't want Ashblade getting a hold of you before I figure out what's going on here. And you two are telling me the truth, which is more than I can say for the captain. I've also met plenty of warlocks just like that one. Unfortunately, some guys are bullies all their lives and becoming a warlock only adds fuel to that fire."

"And you just believe us." Alia gave him a sidelong glance.

Hawthorne scoffed. "Of course not. I heard the same thing about him from the nurses. Guy's a jerk and on his last strike for getting into confrontations. Probably why he hasn't reported you himself. But I had to be sure you would both tell me the truth. Plus, Galvin here is not very good at fairy deception."

Galvin blinked.

Alia tried to stifle her giggle.

"What do you mean I'm not good at fairy deception?"

Hawthorne ignored him. "I'm going to see what else I can find out." He turned to leave. "I'll be back after a while."

26

Declan barely made it back inside the small grove's border in New Orleans before he was forced out of his owl transformation. Thankfully he only fell about a foot to the ground. As he got his clothes back on, he noticed the grove pulling its power back into the tree.

The upgrade spell Alia and Galvin had completed left glowing markings all over the groves: the leaves, circling the trunk in a band, and across the ground. As Declan dressed, the markings on the ground faded, crawling inward toward the tree. Even the leaves dimmed, only the blossoming flowers glowing in the branches. Declan dressed faster; he was running out of time.

He hurried to the trunk of the tree, reaching for whatever magic he still had. He cast the spell to grove hop but opening the pathway was like trying to start a fire with flint and steel instead of a lighter. It took a few extra strikes, but the bark finally began to glow, ready to take him home.

Not wasting any more time, Declan pushed against the trunk. There was more resistance than normal but no more than he expected. As soon as he passed through the bark, his body became weightless, floating down the path toward the Arbor Grove tree. The sensation felt like the tail end of a jump, when gravity pulled you back to earth.

Not surprisingly, the grove hopping spell had changed with the upgrade to the groves as well. The pathway used to be glittering vines, but now it was how Declan imagined traveling through a fiberoptic cable might look. The tunnel he fell through was all light—the same neon, bioluminescent color as was in the groves now. There were no more vines, but symbols moving at different speeds made up the walls of the tunnel. The symbols sounded like different voices chanting the same thing at varying speeds and volumes. The fastest ones were just streaks of light, but Declan could make out the ones moving at his speed. All of them said, "The Arbor Grove," his destination.

The portal shrank, pressing in uncomfortably. Declan pushed, willing himself to move faster. Being caught in a collapsing grove hopping portal was not something he had experienced, and he wasn't ready to try it now. He shoved his way through the constricting path in the anchor tree and stumbled as he broke through the bark into the Arbor Grov. The pressure of the tunnel released. He fell to one knee but recovered without getting a face full of grass.

The tree was covered in huge glowing flowers, larger than he had seen in many years. The glow was new but then again, with the upgrade spell, a lot of things could be different this year. Declan wondered if the size of the flowers were an indication the fruit's growth or it's powerful. Unfortunately he didn't have time to do more than glance at them. He pushed up and hurried out of the inner circle and back toward the house.

The sun wasn't quite up yet but dawn lightened the world.

The whole trip had taken a lot longer than he had planned. Thankfully Ophelia had rushed him back after seeing Erik, but it had taken more time to get back to the satellite grove than he had wanted. He hoped he had used enough potion to make sure Grace slept well into the morning. If he had measured correctly, he would be able to sneak back in and get an hour or two of shut eye before she came looking for him.

If Grace did catch him, he would have to figure out how to smooth things over using old-fashioned diplomacy. He didn't want her poking her overly curious nose into whatever he was doing. Already she was asking questions about things she didn't need to know. Particularly about things he didn't want *anyone* to know.

If she found him, he could play it off like he was tending to the everyday running of the house, but he didn't favor the idea of staying up after an all nighter. It sure felt like Hallowtide was hitting hard and fast this year—likely because it was another problem the druids had to deal with at a time when they couldn't afford any more setbacks—but he hadn't been this sapped so early during Hallowtide in many years.

Usually, a draining Hallowtide meant the fruit would grow extra magically charged, which was a favorable omen. But right now, he'd feel better if he had more magic. Hallowtide already made him nervous, the loss of power making him feel vulnerable, but this year, with a spy in his house, it was just bad timing.

Declan took a casual look around the courtyard as he strode up to the house. No Grace. No surveillance he could spot. So far, so good. He slipped through the double doors and made his way through the ballroom, then over to the hall closet where he dumped his pack, boots, and cloak to store them out of sight until he could put them away as if he'd never left.

Before going up the stairs, he made a detour to the kitchen for a glass of water. As he drank, the long night caught up with him. He yawned, leaving the glass at the sink, then headed up the stairs toward his room.

He checked the hall to make sure he was still in the clear. He was so close to a few uninterrupted hours of shut-eye. Only a couple dozen feet left to his room. Everything was quiet. No spells lay in wait to detect movement.

As tempting as his pillow was, he wasn't quite done yet. Before going to his room, he ducked into the council room, where the elders held private council with one another and public council with everyone else in the clan, as well as communicated with druids of other clans. Right now, that was exactly what Declan needed.

The doors had been locked for many years. Declan had not had reason to enter after the genocide started. Regular contact between druids was what had gotten most of them killed, so all the clans had agreed to stop. Now, with Erik and possibly others alive, Declan needed the lines back open.

With the estate's magic down and the key hidden, Declan had to rely on his lockpicking, to his immense frustration. At least he didn't have to worry about anti-lockpicking charms. He hated to admit it but he had let this particular skill get rusty. Once he finally got the door open, he slipped in and closed it behind him.

A crescent-shaped table took up most of the space in the room, with eight chairs lined up on the outside: four for the clan elders and four for the master druids in training to succeed them. He dared not turn on any lights in case Grace was awake or waking up, but he didn't need them since he was familiar with the room well enough to navigate it without sight. He knew exactly what he was looking for and where it was.

He skirted the table and chairs to the cabinet in the back corner.

Inside was an arrangement of things he had never personally used: a scrying bowl the elders had for insight on how their decisions would impact the future; something that looked like a magnifying globe, which could see into a druid's heart or mind and was only used when passing judgment on a convicted druid; and many other items Declan had never bothered to identify. A master would possess the magic necessary to use any of these, but they were very serious objects to be activated with the utmost discretion. Even the elders were not supposed to use them unless they reached a unanimous decision to do so, and only with all the elders present. Since Declan hadn't been an elder, nor trained to be one, he never had reason to try any of them.

The communication line was the only thing in the cabinet Declan had any experience with because it didn't fall under the elder-only rule, and he located it easily on one of the lower shelves. It was bigger and bulkier than most of the other things and looked like a mix between an early telephone and a telegraph, and worked in a similar way to both. After Declan activated the device, it would remain on and open to receive verbal and written communications from any other activated device. Erik would set one up once he got to Ingadi.

Declan ran his fingers over the back, searching for the slightly raised symbol that powered the device. He brushed over it and sent a little magic into it. At least, he tried, but the spell fizzled.

He fought the urge to curse and tried again. It was too bad cellphones were so difficult to keep alive and expensive to replace. Maybe Galvin could make Erik one of his fancy upgraded cellphones when he and Alia got back.

This time, the magic obeyed him. The little glass leaf at the top lit up like an old incandescent bulb. It was ready. Once Erik turned on his device, they could send messages back and forth. At least, they would be able to after Hallowtide. He'd still have to find a way to sneak in and check it, though.

With the device activated, Declan slipped out of the council room, making sure to lock the door before pulling it shut behind him.

His sentry scurried up to him. It moved in bursts, taking many rests on the short journey down the hall. Declan's stomach twisted as he watched the poor thing struggle. With his magic down, the little bit Declan had used on it was petering out. He was impressed it held together long enough for him to get back. He scooped it up, eager to hear what it had to tell him before it fell apart but not daring to receive the message in the hall. He put the sentry in his pocket and strode quietly to his room.

The closer he got to his door, the more he started to relax. Everything was going according to plan and he was going to make it back without being noticed or missed. He sighed, relief giving way to the exhaustion he had been holding off, and he opened his bedroom door, looking forward to the soft bed waiting for him.

"Declan?"

His whole body tensed. His eyes dropped closed and he put all his effort into suppressing an audible groan.

"It's awfully early. Aren't those the clothes you were wearing yesterday?"

He had to decide fast how to handle this, which was getting harder with his increasing tiredness. He turned to face Grace, sagging his shoulders. "Yes," he admitted, "I was up later than I should have been." That was true, but not for the reasons he was implying.

Her face said she was concerned. She was a better actor than him. If he hadn't been warned about her multiple times, he'd probably believe she was concerned. "You're only just now going to bed?"

"Yes," he started, thinking maybe if he'd been up all night doing paperwork, she'd let him get some rest before resuming. The failing sentry squirmed in his pocket, reminding him his magic was running out and he wouldn't have a way to keep an eye on her. "I mean no. I was going *back* to bed. I had gotten up for some water and was planning to go *back* to bed." He wasn't looking forward to a day with no sleep, but he couldn't leave her alone unsupervised. "But I'm actually too awake now, so I guess I'll just get up for the day."

She pursed her lips, as if debating letting him get away with the blatant lie. "All right, well, then would you like some coffee?"

"I would love some." He was probably going to need energy drinks to make it through the day at this point. And they'd be safer than letting her handle his coffee too. "Let me change my clothes, and I'll meet you in the kitchen." At least she couldn't stick her nose in anything there, but she could cause plenty of trouble. He needed to check in with his sentry first, though.

Grace nodded, and Declan ducked into his room, locking the door behind him. He headed straight for the coffee table, taking out the little sentry to hear its message.

When Declan opened his hand, his heart sank. All that remained was a small pile of leaves and twigs.

27

Alia was in the woods this time. The same gray and lifeless woods the creature called home. Her feet made no sound. The usual forest scents of dirt and wood were not present either. Not even when her hand brushed the bark of a shedding tree did she feel or sense anything.

She was running, trying to keep ahead of Lucian, and searching for something. The way out? Something to make the dreams stop?

Lucian was snarling and angry, calling out threats for bringing *him* with her. He had to mean Galvin. She couldn't see Galvin, but his presence was one of the only things she felt in this place. Galvin, Lucian, and… she felt someone else too. Was that who she was looking for?

"I know you don't have your powers, Little Druid." Lucian's voice was close, and she made a sharp turn away from him. She saw him send fear her way, great long and oily shadows reaching for her. But she dodged them easily, he didn't seem able to pinpoint her. "Once

I catch you, there won't be anything you can do to stop me!"

She grinned triumphantly, avoiding him again and watching as his shadows missed her entirely. *If you catch me.*

The grove, a deep voice whispered in the wind. It certainly wasn't Galvin, even though she still felt him stroking her hair. The voice was guttural and rough, one she had not heard before but almost recognized. Who had she met who could reach her in these dreams? **The grove will protect you from the demon.**

Realization washed over her like light from the dawn. Whoever the voice was spoke truth. The grove would always protect her.

She reached out with power to locate the grove's location in this dream forest. Groves always quietly called to a druid like a compass pointing north. Dream or no dream, the grove would call a druid home.

But she felt nothing. Her power was totally cut off. She'd have to find the grove the old-fashioned way.

Alia slowed, examining her surroundings more closely, trying to find the path they had taken earlier today, but all the trees were the same. Nothing looked like the real woods. Everything was too cookie-cutter and fake. *It won't be like the real woods,* she reminded herself. *This is another dream.*

She searched for the grove tree's magical roots but couldn't see those either. She huffed. Stupid dream. She was just going to have to continue hunting and hope to will the grove to show itself, even though she had no idea how to do that manifestation fiddle-faddle.

"What are you looking for, Little Druid?" Lucian said in a lilt.

Her heart leapt into her throat and she nearly gasped out loud. His voice was too close but she couldn't pin down from which direction it came. His fear magic would find her soon.

Gray walls began to appear between the trees the farther she ran. Her stomach twisted, her mind fogging. *No, no, no!* She veered to the left to escape from Lucian and his horror hallways. She felt Galvin struggling to maintain his grip on her, but his was growing weaker.

Her heart pounded in her chest and she forced herself to keep breathing normally. She fled, turning every time the walls began to close in on her, wanting to get back to the forest. She *had* to get back to the forest and find the grove. Galvin was trying to hold on, but as the empty hallways grew more prevalent, his presence faded more quickly.

She was heaving air, her arms and legs shaking as she scrambled to get back to the woods. "Where is it?" she asked the voice. "I can't find it! Help me, please!"

I cannot. You must help me first.

A loud crack thundered around her, and several things happened at once. Galvin's presence tore away from her as if he had been ripped from her hands. The trees vanished, and she was once again in that place of endless hallways and empty rooms. Her fear, which she had been able to outrun in the forest, was now overwhelming. Her heart beat so fast she thought it might fly right out of her chest. Her stomach churned, and she barely managed to not throw up. Her trembling limbs gave out and she tumbled to her knees.

She screwed her eyes shut, labored to calm her breathing and slow her heart rate. *Fight it!* she screamed at herself. *It's just magic! Fight it!*

Footsteps echoed through the halls and she opened her eyes as Theo stepped around a corner. She smiled, scrambling to her feet and bolted to him, but something was off. He was grayish, like the rest of the haunted hallways, and sort of soft around the edges.

He stopped several paces away, glaring down at her in irritation as he crossed his arms and scoffed. "Pathetic. Can't even complete one assignment without Declan's help. And you thought you wanted to be great."

Alia halted and took a slow step backward. He was right. She wanted to be great, like Declan, but she couldn't even finish one assignment on her own. Since the failed master ceremony a few weeks ago, she was doing everything wrong. She let Declan get captured and had performed a spell much too advanced, altering her and Galvin forever. She had gotten her master druid tattoos through the spell, not the proper ceremony, and forced Galvin to become a druid as well.

More footsteps sounded beside her. Galvin emerged from one of the empty rooms. He was grayed, like Theo, with the same soft, undefined edges. He frowned, scrunching his nose in disgust. "What makes you think you're so special?"

Alia's heart clenched.

"You're short, overbearing, and bossy. You're not as strong or beautiful as the fae women back home, but you think I'd pick you over one of them?"

Alia shook her head, backing up some more. She hadn't meant to make things awkward. She knew she couldn't compare to the fae women. Galvin was handsome and sweet and he could have his pick of anyone.

Theo and Galvin advanced as she retreated. For each step they took toward her, she took one back until she hit the wall. Another gray figure appeared from the opposite end of the hall, and her heart broke.

Declan frowned as he approached, gray and soft around the edges just like the others. He shook his head, sighing, and tears pricked

Alia's eyes. She knew that expression; it was the one she dreaded seeing on his face the most.

Disappointment.

"How could I have trained such a helpless weakling?"

Alia covered her mouth, trying to stop a sob bursting from her, tears spilling down her cheeks.

Declan turned his face away. "You're such an embarrassment."

Alia sank to the ground. They were right. She worked so hard to be strong, smart, and powerful because, buried deep, she knew she wasn't. Their words weighed her down as she sank farther onto the floor.

Lucian appeared at Declan's side, smiling wide. His arm was bandaged where she had shot him but he lifted it easily and laid it on Declan's shoulder. "I didn't get a lot of blood from you last time," he mused, "but it was enough to get inside your head."

Alia tried to lift her head to face him, but she was so heavy. Lucian was vivid compared to everything around him. He appeared to glow from within, so brilliant he was painful to behold. His skin was luminous and the scars she had given him from their fights at Ingadi and the Nome Grove seemed to lessen. She only managed to look at him for a moment before the weight on her head grew too great to lift again.

Her gaze fell to her lap, where she noticed the same radiance in her. It slid down her body and across the floor to Lucian. A light *was* glowing in him. Her light. She tried to get up, to scoot away, anything, but her body was too cumbersome. She couldn't get off the floor.

Lucian chuckled softly. "You were a difficult catch," he admitted, "but this light of yours is so vibrant. It was worth the trouble."

This is it. He's won. This is where I die.

Fight him!

The voice boomed, bass vibrating through her chest as well as the walls, making the shades of her family drift away like smoke. Lucian stumbled backward, clapping his hands to his ears with a groan as Alia's radiance fell out of him. It snapped back to her, relieving the weight holding her down.

Lucian's magic weakened for a moment, and Alia knew she had to seize the opportunity to break free. She sprang up and dashed away as fast as she could.

He recovered and shot his black tendrils out. They tangled around her feet and toppled her once more. He snarled, angry, but did not move toward her. Instead, his tendrils did the work. Alia yanked and kicked and squirmed, desperate to escape them, but there were too many to fight at once, not without her sunlight. Slowly, they dragged her across the floor toward Lucian.

Alia screamed—for Galvin, for the mysterious voice—needing to reach them wherever they were. Battling to call them back.

Lucian didn't seem bothered. His tendrils covered and entangled her body, dragging her closer, inch by inch.

Strong hands grabbed her arms, flooding warmth back into her, and light shone down on her. The hands lifted her off the floor and shook her, not roughly but enough to startle her.

She blinked awake and saw Hawthorne. His silver eyes were wide and worried and he was shouting at her to wake up.

He sighed when she met his gaze. "Holy fuck," he breathed, lowering her to the cot she had been sharing with Galvin. He looked truly alarmed. For the first time, she wondered what happened to her physical form when she was in the dream.

Hawthorne bent and propped Galvin up from where he was lying on the floor. How had he gotten down there? Alia gasped when she saw him, sliding down to help him up. Blood trickled from his nose as his head lolled to the side, much like when the creature had hit his magic shield directly. Lucian forcing him out of her dream must have hit his mind.

Between the two of them, they managed to get Galvin back up on the cot. Alia tried to get Galvin to focus, but Hawthorne just gaped down at them both. "What the hell was that?" he demanded. "First he got knocked senseless, crashed to the floor, bleeding from his nose, then you started screaming bloody murder. I thought you were being killed."

He wasn't far off from the truth. "I'm sorry," Alia pleaded, checking Galvin's pupils for signs of serious damage. "It's... a long story." She was embarrassed enough to be in a situation she couldn't handle on her own. A warlock, Raptor or not, wasn't the person she wanted to confide in. The only person she wanted to do that with was currently blinking bleary eyes at her and moaning.

"I get you druids have secrets but you have to give me something to work with."

Alia sighed. "I guess he's like a parasite." There really wasn't a better word to describe Lucian. "I sort of made an enemy of a demon, and now he's haunting my dreams and trying to kill me. I don't know how to get rid of him, and we were sent here before my—" She paused, realizing that while Hawthorne was the only warlock to help them so far, they still didn't know how much he could be trusted. It probably wasn't a good idea to tell him what newbies they were. "Before someone with more experience could help."

Hawthorne's face scrunched in disgust. It was the most emotion she had seen from him, besides the startled expression that had greeted her when she woke up. "That's"—he shuddered—"disturbing."

Alia rolled her eyes and glared at him. She felt her whole face turning red, but she couldn't argue his assessment. "You have no idea."

"He kicked me out," Galvin groaned, holding his head, but at least he was more aware now. "That bastard kicked me out!" He gave an apologetic pout to Alia. "I'm sorry. I tried."

"I know," she assured him, gently brushing the hair away from his face. She wasn't sure what she had done to earn such loyalty from her friend but she was glad to have it. "I know you did, but I don't think we're going to fix this on our own. I need Declan."

28

Alia told Galvin and Hawthorne about the voice in her dream urging her to keep fighting Lucian and trying to save her, and insisted they go back into the woods.

Galvin didn't like the idea. They had just gotten back. "We barely have any magic between the two of us," he whispered, unable to communicate with his mind, when Hawthorne moved to the other side of the tent. Their connection could convey feelings but actual conversation had stopped coming through. "I have winter and you have your gun. That's it until after Hallowtide."

"It's almost over," she argued. "After tonight, our magic will start to trickle back. Until then, we'll just have to convince Hawthorne to go with us again."

"You don't have to convince me. I'm going with you," Hawthorne told them, grabbing his coat, boots already on. "Especially if you two can't conjure anything," he added as he walked toward the entrance of the tent. "Don't bother whispering while I'm outside, I can hear you from there too."

Alia and Galvin watched him leave, Alia looking as surprised as Galvin felt. Humans were not supposed to hear that well. Galvin wasn't sure even he could hear through canvas.

Alia furrowed her brows at Galvin. "This isn't ideal."

"I don't want to go at all but, since I can't change your mind, we need him."

She sighed and pulled him along after the Raptor. "That's not what I meant."

So far, Hawthorne seemed like the kind of guy to do something because it was right, not to further his own agenda. "You have to give a little trust to earn it. He hasn't let us down yet. Besides, we don't have any other allies right now."

With a glance as they emerged from the tent, Hawthorne led them to the woods. At the edge of the trees, Alia took the lead and began her search for the mysterious voice from her dream.

This mission went against Galvin's good judgement. They were marching right up to the creature's lair with not nearly enough magic to fight back if it found them and only one Raptor to rely on like a crutch. The three of them out here, searching for strange voices who may or may not be helpful—he didn't like it. Not one bit.

"Alia, what on earth are you looking for? How do you know the voice came from the grove? How do you know we can trust it? Maybe it was all part of the show to frighten you more."

He could feel the eye roll through the back of her head. "Its shout affected Lucian physically, making him drop his magic focus. He lost control for a second, though not long enough for me to do any real damage. If it was part of his game, he wouldn't have lost control at all."

"Could be something worse than Lucian," Hawthorne added helpfully.

Galvin nodded. "Yeah, how do you know it's not something worse?"

Alia pivoted to glare them down, bringing both to an abrupt halt. "It's not something worse. It's something that needs help."

Frowning, Galvin crossed his arms. "That's exactly what something worse than Lucian would say."

She exhaled sharply, her shoulders slumping. She flipped on him again, but this time her face was pleading. Her beautiful hazel eyes stared into his, stealing his fight. How could he deny her when she needed him?

He dropped his arms to his sides, letting out a groan. She could ask just about anything of him with that look.

"Please," she begged. "I need you to trust me."

It wasn't going to end well. Rolling his head back, Galvin gestured to the path ahead of them. "Lead on."

The closer they got to the grove, the more the air seemed charged. Like something was watching them. The hour approached late morning—the end of the leshy's marked hours of activity—so it was probably asleep in its lair. If it wasn't, they would need to find whoever or whatever supposedly needed help while also avoiding the creature.

Without prompting, the three of them grew quiet. Galvin tried to keep his steps as light as possible. Even fully human, Alia and Hawthorne were much better at it than him. Not too surprising: they were trained, he was not. Every crunching misstep earned him a sideward glance from either one or the other.

When they reached the clearing, the three knelt behind the short wall of stone outside the clearing and watched the archway for any type of movement.

"I hope one of you has a plan," Hawthorne whispered.

"Of course I do," Alia retorted, her answer as devoid of emotion as any of Hawthorne's. She was stating facts, not boasting. "It's well past dawn. It should be asleep inside. Animals who live near a grove will go there when they're sick or injured. As long as we don't wake up the leshy, we can slip inside and look for the animal."

"Animal?" Galvin asked. "I thought you said a voice spoke to you."

"It did speak, and I think it's the voice of an animal." She clicked her tongue, scrunching up her face. "At least, it will look like an animal but be something far greater."

From the side, Galvin saw Hawthorne looking at him, waiting for further explanation. "Don't look at me, I'm new at this. She's the trained one."

Hawthorne pursed his lips and they all focused on the grove entrance.

They monitored in silence as the sun rose higher in the sky, but instead of warming, the atmosphere grew thicker as they waited. While they couldn't pinpoint the sun's location because of the trees, the daylight pushed the shadows farther back into their hiding places. The creature should have been snoozing away.

Unless the information they had been given was wrong, and the creature was still out and about.

The hair on the back of Galvin's neck began to stand up.

Something had changed, and he wasn't the only one to notice. Both Alia and Hawthorne subtly looked around the clearing for whatever had electrified the air. Galvin cast a glance over his shoulder. His heart lurched into his throat.

The creature stood right behind them, regarding them closely with dull, brown eyes.

His mouth went dry and his stomach threatened to bring up everything inside. How had something so large gotten so close without a sound? It leaned in, sniffing at Galvin. He remained still—more out of fear than training, but it was working. The creature was examining him but did not appear hostile.

As the creature checked his scent, Galvin noticed the fur on its hinged legs wasn't growing in tufts, but actually falling out. As it shifted, more fur fell to the ground, small sparkles catching the light.

Slowly, Galvin looked up at its head. The skull of its face was fresh bone, but the antlers were browned and dry, covered in familiar markings. It lowered its head and Galvin gulped. He reached behind him, grabbing someone's sleeve and gently tugging. Hawthorne, by the feel of it.

Alia must have noticed his fear because she was already turning. He hoped they didn't spook the creature into violence.

"Don't panic," Galvin whispered.

Hawthorne jumped behind him but otherwise froze where he knelt. The beast's gaze darted to the Raptor's abrupt movement but it still did not attack. It resumed its examination of the three.

"What is it doing?" Hawthorne asked.

"Determining if we're threats," Alia answered.

The creature turned its attention to her and snuffled some more, nudging her with its snout.

"And what happens when it determines we *are* threats?"

"Don't be threatening," she scolded the Raptor without looking away from the creature, "and we won't have to find out."

After checking her thoroughly, the creature whimpered at Alia. It sounded equal parts plea and misery. Galvin's brows furrowed at the odd behavior. Was something hurting it?

The wan light in the woods dimmed as a shadow blocked out the already weak sunlight. The effect on the leshy was immediate. The brown of its eyes disappeared as they began to glow an angry red. It threw its head back in an agonizing shriek in several octaves that both shook the earth and pierced Galvin's eardrums. All three of them scrambled as its clawed hand swiped down but they didn't manage to get far enough away. The creature swatted them over the stones and into the clearing.

Hawthorne was the first to recover with a speed that left Galvin in awe. He rushed the creature while extending his arms. His silver bangles glowed a brilliant neon teal and swords made of pure magic in the same color appeared in his hands. Conjured flames licked across the blades as he ran toward the beast.

"Don't use fire!" Alia was back on her knees, pulling out her gun and trying to switch the cartridge. Something must have changed her mind about which ammunition to use. She was moving as quickly as she could but neither she nor Galvin would be able to keep up with the Raptor.

Hawthorne cursed, but the flames died down without him slowing for more than half a breath. He slashed at the creature's legs, dodged its arms, and cut underneath to its backside. Galvin expected the blades to slice right through the leshy like the lasers they resembled but they left only charred lines on the creature's bovine legs.

Hawthorne had the same expectation and grumbled at the minimal damage. "Fire is the only thing that works against it!"

"I don't care!" Alia shouted, shoving the new cartridge in. "This whole place looks like it could go up, and we're way too close to the grove to risk it."

"You were fine with fire for the distraction!"

"That was smoke, not fire!" She shot two rounds at the creature, the bullets exploding into sticky glue on impact, covering its chest and face and limiting its vision but otherwise not hindering its movements. She needed to use a lot more than that to stop it.

The leshy swatted in irritation, knocking Hawthorne away and sending him crashing into a wall of stones. He made no indication of pain other than a grunt. He landed on his feet and charged the creature without missing a beat.

Galvin, much slower and far less trained, had managed to get his own swords out and was rushing in to help wherever he could. The only magic he had left he used in force, conjuring enough cold to bring about a small winter. Frost covered the blades and drifted off the metal like smoke, the chill of ice lingering in his wake as he rushed the leshy. It was completely occupied by Hawthorne and Alia, so Galvin took advantage of its distraction and tried his ice against its legs. They left a trail of ice where they struck but he didn't break through the thing's armor. The legs were only covered in fur and should have easily sliced open. Without breaking the skin, it would be a lot harder to seize up the beast.

"What the actual—whoa!" One large, hoofed foot bucked at him, forcing Galvin to retreat to the side or get his head smashed. He hadn't realized it could move like that. Or that it was so aware of what was behind it. Lesson learned.

Alia fired two more shots, each one hitting its massive torso and the creature reeled backward. The glue burst, expanding over its arms and chest. Alia had managed to get the glue around just about every joint, clearly frustrating the beast but not doing much else. Galvin wondered how freezable that glue was.

Before he could figure out how to get close enough, it regained its footing and turned a glowing red glare on Alia. It bellowed at her in the awful, layered scream, sending all three of them to their knees as they shielded their ears.

Crows appeared out of nowhere, swarming the clearing and swallowing them in a cloud of black feathers. It was like the injured warlock explained: so many crows the murder blocked out the remaining light of the setting sun. Galvin couldn't see anything except black wings, beaks, and claws. The birds scratched and bit at exposed flesh, especially his face, which he covered with his arms, safeguarding his eyes from being scooped out of his head by those sharp beaks.

Gathering all the cold he could, Galvin shoved a wave of frost. Crows went rigid mid-flight, falling to the ground in masses with heavy tinkling thuds as their crystalized bodies knocked together. Undeterred, more crows replaced the ones turned to ice, the murder still filling the clearing but thin enough for Galvin to move through the scratching claws and snapping beaks.

He continued icing walls of crows, searching for Alia and Hawthorne in the mass of black feathers. Birds still flew in, slashing at his arms and biting at his face when they could get through his cold front. Blood trickled from a number of cuts over his exposed skin, but he kept solidify birds out of his way.

Whatever magic the creature had over the huge murder of crows began to peter out, either because of Galvin freezing them or the creature running out of steam. The reason didn't matter. The clearing was visible again between flights of birds, and Galvin finally spotted Alia. She was down on one knee, protecting her face and eyes from the swarm.

Standing behind her was the monster.

Galvin's heart leapt into his throat, and he raced toward her as fast as he could. She couldn't see the creature practically on top of her, reaching out its skeletal hand. Galvin threw bursts of frost and ice, aiming for the sticky spots on the creature's hands, arms, legs, anything to slow it down. "Alia!" His frost hit the glue around its elbow, becoming solid ice, locking the creature's arm. "Alia, move!"

But she couldn't escape from under the crows. He had to save her.

The beast strained against the ice, and it began to crack.

Galvin threw more frost, hoping it would hold long enough for her to get away. Sliding to her side, he pushed as much ice around them as he could, freezing the last of the crows and freeing her from their attack. He grabbed her arms to pull her to her feet and a safe distance where she could keep firing that gun.

The ice shattered with a loud crack. They were out of time.

Galvin didn't look to see what the creature was doing, just half-pulled, half-shoved Alia away. Sharp claws raked down his back, sending him face-first to the ground. Pain erupted, burning his skin as if he were covered in iron. Warmth dripped down torso and legs, and he smelled the coppery tang of blood. His blood. The world spun.

Flames ignited next to him, adding to the heat blooming in his back. A warm orange glow and Hawthorne's voice came from the same direction but he couldn't lift his head to see what was happening without almost blacking out. His vision darkened. He might black out anyway.

Alia dropped to the ground at his side. She took his face in her hands and tried to make him look at her.

More pain shot through his body. He screamed, wanting to throw up.

"No, no, no," she pleaded "Stay with me."

His vision went blurry as nausea overwhelmed him. He leaned over her legs and vomited. Everything that came up was mixed with black goo. He blinked, startled. Where had that come from?

It didn't matter. He was tired. So tired. His eyes sagged closed, too heavy to keep open anymore, and the whole world faded into oblivion.

29

Galvin lost consciousness in Alia's arms, and her stomach dropped out her feet. She breathed in and out, calming her mind as she examined how severe his injury was. Above all else, Alia needed her not to panic. The slashes were deep, too deep to tend here. He was spitting up black goo all over her lap and himself while blood poured from the gashes on his back.

This was bad. So bad

She tried to lift him off the ground but his dead weight was hard to manage on her own. He was a lot taller than her and had bulked up in the almost two months since they started training together. She needed help to carry him out of here.

Hawthorne hacked at the creature with fire blades, driving it back into the woods. He shouldn't be using fire, but right now she didn't care. Galvin was what mattered.

The creature was retreating, backing up, away and out of the clearing, but not quite ready to give up the fight. It prowled the edge of the trees waiting for an opportunity to strike again.

Thankfully, the Raptor did not follow the creature into the woods. Instead, he back-stepped to Alia and Galvin, keeping his defensive position but sparing a glance down at Galvin. His eyes grew wide, the largest show of emotion she had seen from him.

Her heart clenched but she shoved the feeling aside. Hawthorne's expression told her everything she needed to know but she didn't have time for those thoughts at the moment. She needed to save Galvin. "We have to get him back to camp, to one of the healers."

Hawthorne shook his head. "He won't make it that far, and the healers won't know how to save him."

Alia looked around the clearing. There had to be a solution. She was not going to lose Galvin today, not like this. *Think, there has to be something.* Her eyes landed on the archway leading to the grove.

There was only one thing to do. She just hoped she would be able. "Help me get him inside the grove."

To his credit, Hawthorne didn't hesitate. He kneeled, laid Galvin across his shoulders, and lifted him off the ground with no more effort than he would a child. Alia hadn't expected him to handle Galvin by himself but she had to admit it was going to make things easier. She ran toward the grove and heard his footsteps follow, keeping pace right behind her.

The grove was enclosed, like the one at Nome, with no back exit. Hawthorne noticed immediately. "I sure hope you have a plan, 'cause we're trapped in here now. That creature isn't gone."

"I know, and I do have a plan. I just need a few minutes."

Thundering stomps outside in the clearing signaled the return of the creature. It had watched them as they retreated and did not seem pleased they were inside the grove.

"I'll do what I can but I don't know if you have a few minutes." Hawthorne set Galvin over a shoulder, holding him with one arm, and called forth his laser-fire sword in the other. Alia couldn't help but envy that sort of training and strength. She couldn't even lift Galvin on her own, and she didn't know anyone other than Theo who would be able carry a person one-armed in battle. Raptors really were on another level.

She ran to the grove tree and began her examination. The glowing writing around the trunk was split down the middle, the edges hanging like an open belt from its loops. They were clean—like when Lucian had sliced that grove tree with Declan's dagger—meaning it had been severed, not torn, so it should be fairly easy to repair, not unlike how she and Galvin had pulled the spell back together at Nome. The dagger wouldn't be in the way this time, but she also wouldn't have Galvin's help.

She laced her fingers through the symbols on both sides of the knotwork and tightened her grip on the magic as if she were going to cast a spell. With her hold secure, she started drawing them closer. The magic was warm in her hand, telling her the enchantment was still in good condition. She just had to get it sealed. "Please God, Gia, whoever is listening," she prayed under her breath, "give me just enough magic to make this work."

The cut had been made some time ago, it seemed, and the edges had frayed more than she would have liked; even pulled taut, it was difficult to shrink the gap. It didn't help that the smooth bands of symbols flexed in her hands. It felt like trying to tie a too-short string around something too wide, except the strings wiggled. She braced her foot against the roots, tugging with all her might on one side and then the other to bring the two halves as near to each other as she could.

Black goo oozed out of the bark as the magical symbols inched closer and closer, the same goo that seemed to be coming out of Galvin. She felt like she was lancing a boil, squeezing the goo out of the tree with the spell. The smell of it burned her nose, like gasoline.

Another earth-splitting screech poured in from outside the archway, followed by the swoosh of fire through air. She glanced over. The creature crouched at the entrance, attempting to push its way in despite Hawthorne's efforts to prevent it. Its rage must be outweighing its fear of the flames. Hawthorne couldn't keep it out much longer. She was running out of time.

Galvin was still unconscious and draped across Hawthorne's shoulders, the goo dripping from his mouth and tinging the blood spilling from his back. His blood was everywhere. Too much was on Hawthorne and the forest floor, instead of inside Galvin's body.

"Stop using flames!" she yelled over her shoulder, turning her focus back to the spell. "You're going to burn the forest down!"

"Then hurry up whatever you're doing so I can stop!"

Alia didn't turn to glare at him; she could finish scolding him later. Their survival relied on her success, and she couldn't afford any more distractions. She dug deep for any magic left in her. She *had* to get this spell to work. She heaved, her arms out wide and struggling to force the edges to unite in front of her, fighting against a pressure pushing them apart. She gritted her teeth, her arms shaking and her muscles cramping. But she was making progress. The edges of the spell at last came near enough to start knitting themselves back together. The markings on the ground and in the leaves of the tree began to softly glow, just like they should, from the upgrade.

Alia smiled, relieved *something* was going right.

She let go to help Hawthorne and, as soon as she did, the spell snapped apart and the markings went dark. She groaned, grabbing the two halves before they fell too far away and yanked them taut again. It was easier this time, either because she had already found the strength once or because she had lanced enough of the goo out of the trunk to eliminate the resistance. She didn't know why. Or care. She concentrated on keeping the spell intact.

The bark of the tree withered as the goo dripped down. What little grass had survived turned brown before the goo pooled and swallowed it. She made sure to be careful where she put her feet. She didn't want to find out what it would do to her shoes.

Once more, the edges of the spell repaired itself, the lights of the grove coming to life. She didn't dare let go this time. A few small Hallowtide flowers began to grow on the branches above her. She shouted for Hawthorne.

Galvin was secure over his shoulder as he swung his flames at the clawed hand of the beast still trying to push inside. As the lights around the grove got brighter, it reeled back with an awful screech, shielding its face.

"Get over here!"

Hawthorne extinguished his flames, locked Galvin in a fireman's hold, and ran toward her.

Alia heaved at her magic, calling up everything she had to start the spell. She didn't care how much it took, she would use every last ounce to make this work.

Please, she begged, hoping Gia was listening. *Please let me have enough to get home.* Her power sputtered at first, but she reached further into herself then she ever had and tried again.

Nothing. She was completely tapped out.

Hawthorne appeared at her side, keeping an eye on the leshy. "What now, druid?"

Alia didn't know. She searched around her, still holding the grove's spell together. She had no magic, Galvin was unconscious, and Hawthorne's magic wouldn't work. They were too far away from camp to escape. How was she going to start the spell?

Her eyes landed on a small illuminated flower above her, and her heart skipped a beat. If the groves took the druids' magic to grow the fruit, then she should be able to take some back from the flower.

"Grab that flower." She threw her chin in its direction. "I need you to smash it on my hands."

Hawthorne reached up and easily plucked the flower. He crushed it in his fist, and it released a gleaming sap that he smeared all over her hands and the grove spell.

She could feel it! Magic! She sighed thanks to Gia. It was a small trickle but enough to open a tenuous pathway through the grove tree. Sweat beaded at her hairline as she struggled to keep the path open. The bark of the tree shimmered, showing it was ready to take them through.

"Grab ahold of me," she grunted through gritted teeth.

Hawthorne shifted Galvin's weight and had barely touched her arm before she shouldered them through, tumbling, into the trunk of the tree and onto the pathway. Neon lights streaked around them in a thin layer of strings as magic pulled them along. The tunnel was usually lit up, a solid barrier that flung them from one tree to the next. This time, barely anything separated them from the black void beyond the strings. As soon as Alia was no longer holding the spell, the grove they just left darkened again, the pathway dissolving behind them, leaving no way back unless they wanted to be thrown into vast nothingness.

The jump was rough. Alia's stomach rolled into her throat as they floated through the magic tunnel, like falling from a great height in a dream. But it was also like trying to swim through sludge. They were moving too slow. The pathway was disappearing behind them at an alarming rate. Alia didn't know what happened if you got caught on the path when it closed. She pushed Hawthorne, trying to get them through before they found out firsthand.

At the end of the path, the Arbor Grove tree was visible, but not as brightly as she wanted. There was always some resistance when passing through trunks, but now it was quite solid, like the difference between cutting Jell-O and frozen ice cream, except they were trapped in the ice cream as it was being quickly eaten. She shoved them against the barrier as the pathway continued to disintegrated behind them.

Hawthorne put a hand on her back and helped her. He wouldn't be able to break through the magic, but his strength would assist her to do it. Together, they forced their way through the trunk and tumbled onto the grass on the other side.

Alia looked up at the illuminated leaves of the grove that was her home. Tears pricked her eyes at the sight, so grateful to be back someplace she knew was safe. And that Galvin would be healed. He was going to be all right. "Thank you," she said to the leaves and to any divine being listening. "Thank God."

"For fuck's sake," Hawthorne groaned, heaving himself off the ground. He swayed a bit, his face rather green. Grove hopping was known to leave some feeling nauseous. "Let's not do that again." He hauled Galvin back onto his shoulders. "And you might want to hold your thankful prayers, he's not okay yet. What's the next step in your plan?"

"Get to Declan." Hawthorne was right. There was a lot of garden between here and Declan's aide. Alia scrambled to her feet and led the way to the Arbor estate, Hawthorne on her heels.

30

It had been a long, boring day of paperwork. Declan was nodding off at his desk, looking forward to finally getting some shut-eye, when he heard Alia shouting. The sound jolted him awake, his heart racing as he blinked at Grace to see if she had heard it too. His mind had been wandering to his two apprentices, and he thought he had started dreaming about them. Perhaps it was his fear that sounded like Alia calling for him.

But Grace sat up in her chair, staring at the open door to the hallway too. So she had heard it.

"Declan!" Alia shouted again, and this time he heard pounding footsteps downstairs.

He leapt up and bolted down the hallway, not giving one hoot if Grace followed or not. He sat on the stair railing and slid down to get to the bottom faster. He landed on the floor and sprinted toward the sounds of stomping boots and slamming doors. His heart leapt into his throat as he realized where they were going. They were headed for the infirmary.

He ran into the room and skidded to a stop. His blood ran cold. The sight that greeted him was as bad as any his nightmares could invent. A Raptor was helping Alia lay Galvin on a medical bed on his stomach. Galvin's back was gashed open, what should have been red was turning black and spilling freely. All three of them were covered in mud and blood, but Alia and the Raptor appeared unwounded, so it was Galvin's most likely. A black sludge—Declan had no idea what it could be—was mixed in with everything else. It dripped out Galvin's nose and the corners of his eyes, dribbling out every time he tried to breathe.

Declan's heart clenched and he forced himself to focus. Galvin coughed, spitting up more black goo from his mouth and nose.

No, no, no! Not his apprentices.

Declan rushed over, rolling up his sleeves. "Slide that cart over here," he told the Raptor.

The boy nodded and quickly obeyed.

Declan grabbed a bottle of alcohol off the cart and splashed it over his hands up to his elbows. He tore the rest of Galvin's shirt off to get a better view of the wounds. "What happened?"

"What does it look like?" Alia snapped. "Galvin got clawed!"

"I meant the black stuff! What is it?"

"I don't know." She was practically sobbing, gripping tight to Galvin's hand. Declan shoved the lump in his own throat down. "We haven't figured it out yet."

"It's some kind of poison," the Raptor added. "Our medics have figured that much out but not how to counter it yet."

Evelyn had trained Declan a bit in healing and medicine a long time ago. Over the years, what she had taught him had saved his—and several other druids'—lives. But this was different. The wound he could fix, but the goo? He'd dealt with some magic poisons but this was outside his experience. If the warlock's medics hadn't discovered the cure, he wasn't sure he had the knowledge to neutralize it.

He'd have to work with what he knew. "Has anyone else been poisoned?"

"A few warlocks."

"What are the symptoms?"

The Raptor shrugged. "I never saw any other than what you see here. It turns their blood black, moves like tar. Fills their lungs and comes out their mouths, noses, then the eyes. They drown if you can't clear it from their faces, and that's if they live long enough."

Declan stared at the Raptor, his panic growing for his apprentice. "How long?"

The Raptor held Declan's gaze, his eyes sad even if his face was neutral. It was more expression than the other Raptors Declan encountered at the World Council had exhibited, and spoke volumes. It was that bad then. He turned his gaze to Galvin's barely moving chest. "Not long."

Alia lowered her shaking hand to Galvin's head and stroked his hair, silent tears falling down her face.

Grace shoved Declan out of her way as she quickly and clinically grabbed medicines from the cart next to Galvin's bed, several Declan recognized and just as many he did not. She collected jars of herbs without labels, identifying them with a glance or a sniff before shaking them into a mortar and grinding them up. "I need a base," she told Declan. "Something thick to coat the wound."

Declan rushed to the cabinets along the far wall and picked a beeswax salve he kept on hand for multiple types of medical remedies. He offered it to her.

She took one look, nodded curtly, and opened it. She poured the mixture in, and the room filled with a sharp antiseptic smell. She turned back to Galvin and slathered the salve generously over his cuts before setting the jar aside. She laid her hands over his back, careful to avoid the freshly administered medicinal cream, and began to chant under her breath, almost like she was thinking out loud through a chemical formula. Her hands glowed with warm light, one Declan recognized as healing magic. The same kind Evelyn used.

He stared in shock at Grace. He thought that brand of magic had disappeared long ago.

The salve reacted first, illuminating with Grace's magic like a golden blanket over Galvin. The magic sank into him, filling his body. Without losing her concentration, she motioned toward the bench. "Get a cloth for his face, please. Clear away what comes out."

Alia rushed to obey, fetching a clean rag, and wiped the graying goo away from his mouth, his nose, and the little bit pooling in the corners of his eyes. She was clinical in her ministrations but did them with a gentleness Declan had not seen her use with anyone else before.

With one more cough, the goo came clear out of Galvin's mouth. He gasped as air returned to his lungs, then was able to breathe easily for the first time since arriving home.

The light dimmed and faded from Grace's hands and she stumbled backward weakly, if a little dramatically. Declan had seen Evelyn expend much more energy and wait to collapse until she was out of the room. When she steadied herself, she smiled up at Declan. "After you stitch him up, he'll need rest, but he will live."

"How did you do that?" Declan asked, staring in open wonder as he gathered what he would need to finish tending Galvin's wounds. It was difficult to remain angry at her when she had just saved Galvin's life. With a type of magic he never thought he would see again.

But something nagged at the back of his mind. He threaded the suture needle and quickly got to work on the gashes. "How did you know what it was?"

"We've seen that toxin at the Council a couple times." Declan didn't look at her but something in her answer didn't sound right. "We have learned ways to expel it from the body, but we're not sure what it is yet."

Declan tied off the first set of sutures and started on the next. "Thank you. You don't know how much this means to me. To us."

"I told you I was here to help, remember?" She let out a heavy breath and headed toward the door. "Please, I must go rest now. I will administer to him some more tomorrow to make sure the toxin is gone."

Declan paused to watch her leave, his heart torn between gratitude and unease. She had saved Galvin's life, but he couldn't shake the feeling something was off. If the Council had experience with the toxin, why did the warlock healers not know how to counter it yet? And if Grace was a healer like Evelyn, why hadn't she been able to heal the physical wounds as well as the toxin?

And if she knew so much about medicine, how had he gotten away with drugging her?

31

Galvin's eyelids felt like they had been lined with stone and glued together with gritty mortar. It was quiet where he was, which seemed odd. He thought they had been in the middle of doing something quite loud. And important.

It slowly came back to him. He and Alia had been in the woods with Hawthorne. The creature had showed up, attacked. It had been about to claw Alia. He'd had to save her.

He forced his eyes open, trying to sit up. His body wouldn't cooperate, continuing to lie prone on the bed. His stomach churned at the effort, so he closed his eyes and took deep breaths to calm it.

Alia's hand laid on his arm and she placed a cool cloth on his head. "Take it easy," she soothed. "You're still in rough shape."

Rough shape? That was right, the creature had injured him. Galvin opened his eyes again. He blinked, noticing they were in the Arbor Grove infirmary. When had he gotten here?

Alia sat next to his bead, carefully administering to him. She couldn't have slept since they arrived because her eyelids drooped and the bags underneath were dark. Her face was drawn and her hair was a mess. She seemed to be holding herself upright about as well as Galvin. His injuries must be serious for her to be that worried.

"What happened?" His tongue felt like a lead weight and his voice came out thick and phlegmy.

"The leshy poisoned you. Hawthorne said you wouldn't make it back to the camp, so I manhandled the grove hopping spell and jumped us home."

That was impressive since they didn't have any power. His own well was uncomfortably empty. He wondered how she had managed to dig up enough magic to cast any spell, let alone a jump.

He had to admit, though, it was a comfort to know they were back home. "At least you made it to Declan so he could cure me."

"It wasn't Declan."

Her face was pinched. Galvin blinked. Who else was there?

"He didn't know what the poison was. It was actually Grace who saved you."

Galvin scoffed. "That's a frightening thought. I wonder what that's going to cost us."

Alia's mouth fell open and she quickly turned to Hawthorne, shaking her head. "That isn't what he meant."

Hawthorne had tucked himself away in a nearby corner. His face was a little green and fidgeted nervously, but he shrugged at Alia's comment. "It wouldn't be the first time I've heard about her extracting payment for favors."

The crease between her eyebrows appeared as it always did

when she was thinking. Galvin was amazed; he didn't know how she did it. She was running on fumes but still evaluating and calculating. Galvin could barely stay awake, let alone think through their predicament.

"So you've never actually worked with her before?" Alia asked.

The green color grew on the Raptor's face. He swallowed hard. "Captain Ashblade is her creature. Though I'm not sure how he can stand it." He shivered and his voice was small, almost as if he didn't realize he was saying it: "All that white."

Alia's expression glazed over. She was trying to have a thought but those fumes were running out.

"You look awful," Galvin told her.

She glared at him. "You should see yourself."

"You still haven't slept." It wasn't a question. Galvin knew what the answer was.

To her credit, she didn't try to argue. She sank lower into her chair, as if the effort of simply sitting up was too exhausting. It probably was.

"Go tell Declan."

She slipped her hand into his. "I can't leave you like this."

He gave her a squeeze before pulling away. "I'll be fine. I'm on the mend, right?" It only just occurred to him that he might not be. He lifted his head to get a good view of Alia and Hawthorne. "I am on the mend, right?"

Alia let out a soft laugh, and he relaxed back into the bed. "Yes, you're on the mend."

"Then it's your turn. Besides, Hawthorne's not going anywhere."

Hawthorne snorted.

They both looked at the Raptor, still green and huddled in the corner, but a small smile pulled at the side of his mouth. He noticed them staring and shifted away from them. "I don't have anything else to do, and I can't exactly leave without one of you 'jumping' us back through the tree, can I? I'll watch him for you." Alia's face relaxed, and Hawthorne crossed his arms, appearing bored. "Besides," he added, "your performance in the grove was lacking. You better have your boss sort you out if you want to stand a chance against that monster."

She turned back to Galvin. "Are you sure you'll be okay?"

Galvin laid his head back on his pillows. "You shouldn't worry, I plan to be sleeping too."

Hawthorne pushed up from the wall and came to stand behind Alia. He placed a hand on her shoulder. "He'll be fine."

Alia sighed. she knew she had lost this fight. She rose from her chair and leaned over to replace the cloth on his forehead. "I'll be back as soon as I'm able."

"Mhm."

With one more heavy breath, she stepped away from Galvin's bed. As she passed Hawthorne, she paused, looking up at him. "Thank you."

Hawthorne nodded, and Galvin thought he could see the a swell of pride. "You're welcome."

Galvin watched Alia leave the infirmary, and Hawthorne sank into her vacant seat, propping his boots up on the end of Galvin's bed.

Galvin saw him pick a book off the end table and flip through it. It was some sort of novel, worn, and not one Galvin recognized.

He found himself curious. Curious about Hawthorne's distinct lack of curiosity. He wasn't sure how many outsiders were invited into the groves, but he imagined any Council spy would have jumped at the opportunity to learn more about the druids' secrets. "Why are you helping us?"

Hawthorne didn't look up from the book when he answered. "My orders were to keep an eye on you both."

"I thought your orders were to make sure we didn't go rogue. The Council has been dying to get someone in here. Any other warlock would be eager to report information back. Again I ask, why?"

"I already told you, I never received orders to spy on you, so I'm not starting now. And most of my fellow warlocks have forgotten why they became so in the first place."

Galvin's eyelids were getting heavier. "Why did they become warlocks in the first place?"

"To protect those weaker than themselves."

That was more noble than Galvin would have thought for the thugs they had met at camp. His eyes sagged closed. Perhaps Hawthorne wasn't like the other warlocks. "Are you going to tell Grace?" His tongue felt thick in his mouth and forming the words was difficult.

"I'm going to avoid her like that creature in the woods avoids fire, but tell her what?"

"About our powers." He had heard them back at the camp. He knew they didn't have magic. Hawthrone would have seen Alia struggle to pull together a spell that should have come easy to her. He had witnessed firsthand how helpless they really were.

"I don't know what you're talking about," Hawthorne answered, flipping a page.

Galvin smiled as the sleep pulled him under. Someone had sent Hawthorne to them because they knew they would need him. At least not everyone on the Council was an enemy.

32

Alia paused outside Declan's door, trying to think of what to say. She knew Galvin was right but how was she going to explain that Lucian was still attacking her when he was supposed to be dead by Declan's own hand? Would he believe her? Would he be disappointed she had let Lucian get attached to her? And what about the disaster of a mission? Was she failing him by not solving the mystery by herself? Would he ever let her handle missions on her own again?

She stopped her spiraling thoughts. They wouldn't fix anything—to do that, she knew what needed to happen. Whatever resulted, she needed his help. She couldn't fight Lucian off forever. Disappointed or not, Declan loved her. She would probably have to convince him she could handle herself all over again, but he wouldn't make her suffer.

The memory of the gray Declan from Lucian's haunted hallways popped into her mind. *How could I have trained such a helpless weakling?*

She was spared losing her nerve when Declan opened the door. He was freshly showered and clothed, but on his face she could see how tired he was too. All the things she had considered saying died on her tongue. Her face flushed, embarrassed at being a useless child, and she dropped her view to the floor. Maybe if she wasn't looking at him, she could find where she had placed her resolve.

"Alia." Declan lifted her chin. His gaze was soft and without judgment, like it had been her whole life.

Her sight blurred, but she didn't cry.

"You look exhausted. Have you slept?" He noticed her unshed tears, clenched hands, and nervous expression. He sighed. "Will you finally tell me what's wrong?"

"No, I haven't slept," she confessed, glancing around, worried Grace might appear and overhear them. "But that's why I'm here. Can I talk to you? Inside?"

Declan ushered her in without question and closed the door behind them. He brought her to the couch and sat her down while taking a seat on the coffee table in front of her. He checked her over, stopping at the bandage on her neck, which really needed to be changed. He lifted it, clinically examining the state of her wound. "It needs to be cleaned again. I thought you used M.U.D.?"

"We did, but there wasn't much left and I haven't made any more since our trip to Ingadi," she admitted, feeling another layer adding to his certain disappointment. She was supposed to keep her pack well stocked at all times.

Such an embarrassment, shade Declan whispered in her mind.

He pulled the bandage off and Alia winced as it pulled at the tender skin. He poked it, sending hot pain radiating out. "Not quite infected, but close."

Alia shuddered at the thought of what sort of bacteria lived in Lucian's mouth.

"You never did get a chance to tell me what did this. By your reaction on the phone, I assume it wasn't the leshy. What else lives in that forest?" He stepped over to the cabinet that held all his jars of herbs, potions, and salves, as well as over-the-counter painkillers from the drugstore. He pulled out his med kit and returned to his seat on the table in front of her.

Alia wrung her hands in her lap. This was it. She was going to have to tell him. No backing out now. She'd win back his approval someday. Somehow… "That's actually what I wanted to talk to you about."

"Oh?" Declan raised his eyebrows but didn't look away from the antiseptic cream he was prepping. It wasn't M.U.D.; that was used for the field. Alia was familiar with the salve, though, and knew it was going to sting like hell when he put it on.

She swallowed the lump that had come back into her throat, her mouth going suddenly dry. "H-how sure are you that—" She licked her lips, trying to get moisture back into her mouth. "That L-Lucian is dead?"

He stopped mixing and regarded her, startled, for a moment. Then his shoulders sank, and he bobbed his head, lips pursed. "We had a portal open. He did this to you?"

Alia's heart raced and she couldn't get enough air. He knew. Declan had already known Lucian wasn't dead. Her hands shook as she took huge rattling breaths. She wasn't crazy, Lucian was alive and attacking her.

Declan dropped the bowl on the table. He sat next to her on the couch and pulled her into his arms. She was too big to fit in his lap anymore, but he tucked her head on his shoulder, gently rubbing circles on her back, holding her as she trembled. Tears ran down her face, and she buried herself in his shirt to hide them.

Declan continued stroking her like he used to do after her nightmares when she was young, gently quieting her sobs. "You don't have to be scared," his voice was gentle. "You are strong enough to fight him off, and you are not alone."

Slowly, her breathing steadied, but she didn't dare let go of him. She wasn't ready to deal with the world again yet.

"I'm sorry," he said, his hand making soothing circles. "I really thought he was dead. That's what I was going for, anyway. I completely forgot we had the portal to the demon realm open." He lifted her face to look at him, wiping the streaks from her cheeks. "I should have realized the signs sooner. I'm sorry, *Bug*. This is my fault."

Of all the things she had prepared to hear, that was not one of them. She wrapped her arms around his neck, crying into his shoulder. He shushed her, holding her close, the weight of Declan's shade falling off her with each stroke, his whispered lies dissolving under the real Declan's love.

Why had she been so scared to tell him? Declan was the closest thing she had to a father and he had never been anything but supportive. Not once had he expected her to succeed under unreasonable circumstances. He loved her and under no circumstances would he shy away from helping her.

Was it Lucian's fear that put those thoughts in her head? Or was he simply playing on her own insecurities, making everything seem worse than it really was?

Maybe Declan and Galvin were right. She did work too hard.

It didn't take long to calm down after reason came back to her as she rested in the safety of Declan's arms. It had been many years since they sat like this, and it felt good.

"Now," his warm but firm, "tell me what's been happening."

She told him everything. She told him about the nightmares, not sleeping, Lucian appearing while she was awake, Galvin helping keep him at bay, him drinking her blood, the room with no escape, the woods, the strange voice that told her to fight Lucian off, and the shades who spoke her fears.

"I'm so tired." The words came out with a sob. Despite everything, she could hardly keep her eyes open.

"Don't you worry." Declan propped her up. The effort roused her but it was a struggle to stay awake. Every blink felt like sandpaper and her limbs were almost too heavy to lift. "I'll make sure you get some sleep."

"You can make him go away?"

"Long enough for you to rest and for us to figure out what to do, but we need to take care of your wound first. Let's get you in the shower, and I'll prep the stuff I need."

She clung to him like the child she had been long ago. "What if he comes while you're gone?"

He shushed her, easing her to her feet and leading her to his bathroom. "My room is warded. He can't get in here while you're awake, and I'm going to lay an enchantment for you so he can't get in your dreams either."

"But it's Hallowtide."

"I still have one power," he admitted sheepishly. "One we don't lose during Hallowtide."

Alia blinked at him. Spirit powers were the only ones druids didn't lose during Hallowtide since they were connected to the time of the year when the dead reigned over the realms. Powers Declan had avoided at all costs and never once hinted he might have. "You have the gift of spirit?"

He sighed dejectedly. "Yes, and it appears I have ignored it for too long. Galvin will need to be trained with his as well."

"So Galvin keeping Lucian out of my dreams *is* spirit power?"

"Good guess." He pulled towels out of the linen closet. "Yes, it would appear so."

"But Lucian is a demon, not a spirit."

Declan nodded. "Yes, but he's attacking you in your mind and dreams, which are connected to your spirit."

From everything she had read, spirit powers were seen as a gift among the druids. Why would Declan ignore his? She had also read the ability to see ghosts and perform some minor protection spells was not uncommon, but the sort of spell Declan was suggesting was much larger and required a deeper connection to the other side. He was talking about protection for the living spirit, not just the dead. "What level of spirit power do you have?"

Declan was silent a long moment as he ushered her into the bathroom. She thought he might not answer, but he stopped in the doorway, holding the handle, his gaze turned toward the floor. "I have one of the rarest. Tiberius and Evelyn were the only two I ever told. They both knew how much it frightened me to see others lose control of their bodies during the Halloween channeling ritual. More than one druid has been lost to spirit possession because their guardians were not skilled enough or were careless. Tiberius and Evelyn always helped me avoid being nearby during the channeling ritual, and no one ever found out. Not even my mentor."

Alia stared at him in awe. Not only did he have the strongest form of the spirit gift but he had kept it hidden from everyone for over two thousand years. Even from his mentor. Her heart ached, imagining that burden.

Declan met her gaze, his expression sad but resolved. It was the look he had given her many times growing up, when she experienced a little too much of what life had to offer before he could prepare her. It was the face of a dad, desperately hoping to convey an important concept to his child. "You should never be scared to tell me anything. I will support you and I won't make you do something you don't want simply because it's tradition." He turned away and shut the door behind him.

33

With Alia safely sleeping in his room and Grace closed up in hers, Declan made his way down to the grove. It was the only time he would be able to gather anything from the tree without Grace wondering what he was doing. If he worked fast enough, he could even send Alia and Galvin off with a couple of the fruits. He stopped at the shed to pick up the three large baskets he knew he could manage on his own, along with the ladder, before making his way through the hedge maze and into the inner circle.

The tree was heavy with the hallow fruit, as he had suspected—a bountiful year indeed. Enough that, if all three of them picked all day, the branches would still be laden. The trees held more fruit than they would be able to use or consume in the whole year by themselves. Declan's three baskets would be plenty for their needs.

The fruit was shaped like a large peach but with the smooth skin of a plum. The flesh was soft and came in a myriad of colors, all ranging in blues, reds, and purples this year. The darker the color meant the juicier and sweeter the flesh. In previous years, the fruit had simply been fruit—fruit laced with magic, but still just fruit. Now, each glowed from its center. Some had a stronger glow than others, but the light didn't seem to have any correlation to the color. Declan picked one, examining it. The same type of power radiated from each, though the ones with a stronger glow exuded more. The upgrade spell was changing everything the druids knew, not just Alia and Galvin's magic.

Declan picked as much fruit as quickly as he could, filling the three baskets to the very top. He didn't want to spend too much time in the grove while Alia and Galvin were both unattended inside the house with Grace and that Raptor Alia had brought with her, but they needed the fruit for the upcoming year. Especially if they were going to bring back some of their traditions, since the fruit would boost spells and rituals. Declan put the ladder back in the shed and started bringing the baskets down to the cellar on the other side of the house.

Before leaving the grove with the last basket, Declan grabbed one of the redder fruits, a bright red like an apple that should have just the right balance between sweet and tart—his favorite kind. He bit into the soft flesh, the juice spilling over his chin and the warmth of the fruit's gift spreading through him from his stomach outward. This year was going to be very productive.

He nodded and grinned at the preciseness of his judgment. The taste was perfect. He finished chewing as he pulled the last basket into the cellar with the others. The room was cool and would keep the fruit fresh for a few days while the druids sorted things out before processing it.

Declan didn't go back outside but up the stairs that led into the pantry adjacent to the kitchen. The infirmary was at the end of the same hall so he made the short detour to check on Galvin. He quietly poked his head inside the door, expecting Galvin to be sleeping and not wanting to wake him.

Instead, he was sitting up with the Raptor, playing cards. Each had a hand and a pile of holographic poker chips on the bed between them. Galvin was staring hard at the Raptor's face, who matched Galvin's with a lazy one of his own. "You're bluffing," Galvin told him.

Nothing about the Raptor's expression changed that Declan could discern. "Am I?"

Declan hadn't seen enough of the game to know if Galvin was right or not, and this guy was a great bluffer—better than the warlocks he had met—but he was a Raptor. Declan didn't have much experience with them. He doubted he would be able to read the boy even if he had witnessed the game from the beginning.

Galvin looked at his dwindling pile of poker chips before tossing his cards down. "Frostbite take you, I fold."

He had a full house. Not bad.

The Raptor threw down a two pair and Galvin's mouth dropped open. Declan couldn't help but chuckle as the Raptor calmly collected his chips.

"I would have won again," Galvin lamented. He shook his head, baffled. "How are you so good at this?"

"Training." The Raptor didn't miss a beat as he collected the cards again and began to shuffle.

Training. It suddenly clicked. *Ophelia picked one she knew would see the truth through his training. This Raptor must be the help she sent.*

A tension Declan hadn't realized he had been holding left him and his shoulders relaxed. He'd have to remember to send a thank you to Ophelia for meddling on their behalf.

"Aren't you supposed to be sleeping?" Declan asked, stepping to the side of Galvin's bed. "How are you feeling?"

Galvin shrugged. "I was having trouble sleeping," he explained, "so Hawthorne taught me how to play poker."

"You just learned?"

"Yeah." He said it like Declan should have known. Now that he thought about it, he should have. Icelyn had no moral objections to others gambling but she did not approve of it in the nobility. Galvin had probably never even heard of poker until the Raptor had shown it to him. "He says I'm good with the cards but I need to work on my poker face."

Declan snorted. That statement accurately summed up Galvin better than anything Declan had ever heard. He held his hand out to the Raptor. "We haven't officially met. Declan Arbor."

"Hawthorne. Zayne Hawthorne." He took Declan's offered hand, giving it a good, solid shake. His grip was firm but not crushing, earning him points with Declan. Respect without the need to display dominating superiority. Few shook hands like that anymore.

"Did she come talk to you? Did you help her?" Galvin asked.

There was only one *she* Galvin would be concerned about. "Yes. She's sleeping peacefully for now but it's not a permanent fix." His shoulders sagged in disappointment so Declan gave him a reassuring smile. "We'll figure it out, don't you worry."

"Should you leave her unguarded?" the Raptor asked.

Declan turned to him. Hawthorne. Zayne Hawthorne. His stoic expression cracked ever so slightly to show the idea didn't sit well with him. "She's warded in my room and the door is locked."

That didn't seem to put Hawthorne any more at ease.

"You have concerns, though." It wasn't a question. Declan saw him debate whether to speak his mind or not. "Please, I'm all ears."

"Chair Witch Grace, she wanted to examine Galvin alone when he was sleeping. She approached at a moment when Alia wasn't here. She wanted me to step out."

Declan had allowed the Raptor to stay in the infirmary since he had helped Alia get Galvin here in time to save him but he had yet to decide if he should trust him. The answer to his next question would tip his feelings one way or the other. "Did you?"

"No, sir."

Declan was satisfied, though he probably hadn't needed to worry. Ophelia was a hard woman to impress and, if she had handpicked this particular Raptor, then there was no reason not to trust him.

"Alia only stepped away to use the bathroom and she asked me to watch over him. I was not going to betray her trust."

Further confirmation Ophelia was exceptional at what she did.

"Good. I know you don't have any reason to pick us over the Council, but I ask you to continue watching his back for me."

"Yes, sir." The answer of a good soldier taking orders from a respected leader. The guy was checking Declan's boxes.

He turned back to Galvin. "Hawthorne is right about not leaving anyone unattended. We should all stay in pairs for the time being. I'll go up to watch over Alia while she sleeps. The three of you need rest, so no one will be going anywhere for at least another day." Hopefully they could recuperate through the end of Hallowtide and he could feel better about sending them back out with their powers returned.

Galvin nodded that he heard but he was gazing down at the pile of poker chips without seeing them. His brows were furrowed and he flipped one of the chips absently in his hand. Declan imagined that was what the thought rolling around his mind looked like.

"What is it?" Declan asked.

"Why would Grace heal me if she was just going do something sinister afterward?"

That was a good question. One the silence that followed told Declan none of them had an answer for.

"Unfortunately," he said, "I expect we'll probably find out why very soon."

34

Light filtering in between the curtains on Declan's balcony doors woke Alia. Her arms felt heavy as she draped an arm over her face. The bed was warm and she was comfortable and didn't want to get up.

Declan came in, holding a steaming mug. "Good morning." He sat next to her on the bed. "How did you sleep?"

"Better." She propped herself up, rubbing exhaustion off her face. "But I don't feel a hundred percent yet."

Declan nodded, handing her the cup when her hands were free. "What about your dreams?"

It was warm in her hand, and the smell of tea perked up her senses. "No dreams, though I could feel him lurking on the edges of my sleep."

"That's a good start. I'll teach Galvin how to make that ward for you until we can figure out how to get rid of him for good."

"How is he?" Alia asked, then sipped at the tea. Heat filled her, easing some of her worries.

Declan smirked. "Last I checked on him, Zayne was teaching him how to play poker."

Alia snorted in her tea as she tried to take a drink. "Really? Galvin? He has a terrible poker face."

Declan shared her laughter. "I know." He stood up and gestured to the foot of the bed where her clean clothes laid out. "After you get dressed, we'll go check on him. It's probably time to change those bandages anyway." He walked out of the room, shutting the door behind him.

Gratitude swelled in her chest. Declan always knew what she needed, whether tea, clothes, or protection wards. Why did she ever think she couldn't come to him with any problem? Fear and sleep deprivation distorting her thoughts was the answer.

Alia drank the rest of her tea in big gulps in between putting on her clothes. She made sure to grab the wedding coin from her sleep shorts and slip it into her pocket before tossing her pajamas into the hamper. She went to the bathroom, then washed her face and re-braided her hair. The bags under her eyes were not quite so dark and a bit of color had returned to her face, but she still felt run-down.

And scared. She wouldn't be shielded once she left this room. Declan was going to teach Galvin to make the ward, and she trusted Galvin, but it wouldn't be the same. She wouldn't be under the watchful eye of the two-thousand-year-old and skilled druid who had protected her for her entire life.

It wouldn't be like a father looking after his little girl. It would be her and Galvin fighting to defeat Lucian.

She closed her eyes, hands gripping the edge of the sink, and took a few deep breaths. *I can do this. I'm smart. I can figure this out.* She opened her eyes, staring straight into her own hazel gaze like she was talking to another person. "You are not alone. You can do this."

Boosting her courage, Alia walked out of the bedroom. Declan was waiting for her in the living room. When she emerged, he glanced over her, checking her like he always did, to make sure she was all right and had everything. "Ready?"

She nodded. He led the way out of his apartment. As soon as she crossed the threshold, Alia felt the protection recede. She was once again vulnerable. She picked up the pace to the infirmary, wanting to get to Galvin as quickly as possible. Not only was she worried about him but things were always better when she was with him. They were a team and together they could tackle anything. Even cutting off Lucian.

That's right, I remember. Galvin had cut Lucian off once before. When Lucian had captured him at Ingadi, Galvin had somehow managed to prevent Lucian from feeding on his fear. If Alia did the same thing, it should work for her too, right?

Arguing voices reached them before they fully descended the stairs. "I am a member of the Council," Grace's voice demanded as Alia stepped onto the ground floor. "If you have that boy's best interest in mind, you should be obeying *my* orders and let me see him."

Alia exchanged a look with Declan. His shoulders sagged and he looked like he wanted to groan. "That woman is insufferable," he muttered, just loud enough for Alia to make out. He stepped in front of her and marched down the hall toward the infirmary.

"I'm sorry," Hawthorne told Grace, standing stiffly, blocking the infirmary doors. His face was pale but he did not back down. "My order to make sure he is not seen without supervision outranks your order to be admitted."

Grace scoffed. "That's ridiculous. Who here outranks me?"

"I guess that would be me," Declan answered, standing next to Hawthorne. Alia joined them.

"That's impossible," Grace snapped. "Your position and authority have been revoked."

"His position has, but he's been a Council member longer than you and outranks you as a faction head," Hawthorne added, helpfully.

Grace glared at them both. "I see. An oversight that will surely be corrected."

"No doubt," Declan said flatly.

"You're all being silly," Grace pressed. "I'm merely trying to check on the patient. And since it's Halloween, we really must test all three of you for the ability to talk to ghosts."

Declan's face paled like Hawthorne's, though his hard expression never left. His reactions made more sense now. "Why?"

A slight grin pulled at the sides of Grace's mouth. "A skill like that will be quite useful to the Council and is thus part of your registration."

Declan turned to Alia and she met his gaze. She could see him trying to mask his fear under pure resolve. "Go check on Galvin while Grace and I finish this conversation."

Alia nodded. With a glance back at Grace's triumphant smirk, she slipped inside the infirmary. As the doors closed, she could hear them arguing.

Galvin was sitting up in his bed, shuffling a deck of cards in his lap. He looked up when she came in and smiled. His face didn't have enough color in it but the warmth in his expression told her he wasn't bad off. Concern eased in her chest. She had been holding it so long she had almost forgotten it was there. But he was all right.

She wanted to run up and throw her arms around him but that would have probably been too much. Instead, she walked over and sat next to him. "How are you feeling?"

"I'm healing. Declan's been giving me some excellent pain meds and Hawthorne has been teaching me to play poker when I'm awake." He held up the cards. "How are *you* feeling?"

"Better," she said, her stomach twisting. "Still scared."

Galvin laid his hand over hers. Her stomach twisted again but for entirely different reasons. "We'll figure this out."

"Actually, I wanted to ask you about that. How did you stop him?"

Galvin's eyebrows raised. "When we were captured at Ingadi?" His gaze drifted off as he thought. After a few moments, he frowned, shaking his head. "It's hard to say. It's like I could see where his magic ended. I could see him leeching off my emotions so I just"—he shrugged—"cut him off."

"But *how*?" Alia pressed. "*How* were you able to see his magic?"

His expression turned sad and he squeezed her hand. Alia huffed, knowing what was coming. He couldn't tell her because he didn't know.

"I'm sorry. I know you want me to give you some sort of instruction so you can copy it, but I don't have that for you."

She looked away. She knew he wasn't trying to hurt her and she didn't want him to see it on her face.

"I hate how hollow it sounds," he tried again, "but I don't know what the trick is. You just have to keep looking. You'll find a way to fight him off. And I will do whatever I can to help you."

Alia smiled, though she knew it didn't reach her eyes, and patted his arm. "I know. Thank you."

The bickering outside grew louder. "Wherever you read about our Halloween ritual of channeling ghosts, that's where you need to check again. My name has never been on the roster as someone who participated in that," Declan said.

"Not participating does not exclude you from having the ability. That is why we need to test you," Grace countered.

"That's *exactly* what it means! Besides, don't you think that in two thousand years, *someone* would have noticed?" Grace started to protest but Declan cut her off. "No. My apprentices are healing before they have to go back out there to complete *your* assignment, and you will *not* be testing them before I have to send them into danger!"

The door swung open and Declan marched in, fuming. Hawthorne followed, face blank, and stood in front of the door, blocking it.

Declan paced back and forth a couple times, huffing. "Insufferable woman. Mark my words, I will get her out of here." He stopped, back facing Alia and Galvin. He took a deep breath and only after did he turn toward them. "All right, I've had the last word this time but I doubt she'll let me get away with it for long, and we have a lot to do before I'm sending you all back out there. Galvin, you need to learn the ward to guard Alia. While I teach him, Alia, you should start examining that goo. Let's see what we can learn about it and how to counter it before you have to face it again. Zayne." Declan nodded at where he was. "You keep doing that. We have to put her off for the rest of the day. We can't have her testing anything and finding out..." Declan glanced at Hawthorne again, "More than we want her to."

"Theo's lab has better equipment," Galvin offered. "You should take the samples there if you can sneak past you-know-who."

All three druids froze. Alia felt the blood drain from her face, her stomach twisting. Galvin winced, realizing what he said. Declan closed his eyes, letting out a quiet sigh. Then all three of them looked at Hawthorne.

The Raptor made tiny shakes of his head, lifting his face toward the ceiling. "I don't want any part of it. Don't." He cut off whatever Declan was about to say with a pointed finger. "Don't. It's cool a *dead* dragon left you all some sort of lab, but I don't need to know about it."

Declan shut his mouth and Hawthorne shook his head again, closing his eyes.

"Just don't."

35

A day of rest was just what they needed. Galvin felt right as rain as he and Hawthorne followed behind Alia on their way to the warlock camp. Since the grove in the woods was still corrupted, they had to travel the way they had arrived the first time. Alia had jumped them through a small grove tree as close as she could get and they hiked the rest of the way in. Hawthorne had needed a minute to find his stomach after another jump but only grumbled a little.

Things were better this time. After a couple sessions with Grace, under Declan's supervision, Galvin was healed, the wounds only faded lines across his back, and he had not coughed up black goo for a whole twenty-four hours. His skin was a bit thin and he tired faster than normal, but he was otherwise ready to resolve this mess. As long as he made sure his wound didn't take a direct hit, he would be just fine. Plus, Halloween had passed and his and Alia's powers were beginning to return, so they both had more to work with.

Alia was better as well. She had been able to sleep all of the previous day and night and had woken up more like herself. She was calm, confident again, and less irritable with Galvin and Hawthorne.

He could see she was still worried about Lucian, though. Declan had taught Galvin the spell to set the necessary wards while she slept, but it didn't break the blood bond Lucian had made when he bit her. Declan wasn't entirely sure how to get rid of that yet. Each bond was different and, to break it, he needed the specifics of how Lucian bound the two of them. Without that, it was up to Alia to figure out how to defeat Lucian on her own.

If anyone could find a way to break the blood bond, it was her.

Even now, as he and Hawthorne marched behind her, it was in the back of her mind. A looming threat following her everywhere, like a shadow. She hid it well from others, outwardly displaying her usual cool composure. Galvin only knew how worried she was because he could feel it. He could almost see it, percolating there in the back of her head. The dark, icy tendrils of fear magic lurking just out of sight, infecting her thoughts and waiting to attack when least expected.

He wished he could solve it for her. Push Lucian out of her mind and her life, breaking his nose for good measure like he had promised weeks ago. But it wasn't his fight, it was hers. The blood Lucian had taken from her made it impossible for Galvin to do anything but help shield her for a small amount of time. He wanted do more for her.

They were still a good distance from the camp when she stopped them. She faced them with all the authority she had inherited from Declan. Her hand went to her pocket and pulled out the wedding coin. "So, I don't have much of a plan."

Hawthorne blinked at her, and a nervous chuckle escaped

Galvin. "What," Galvin's voice came out too high.

Alia shrugged, flipping the coin in her palm. "We need to restore the grove before anything else. Since the leshy likes it so much in there, we need a distraction to keep it busy until Galvin and I can figure something out. That's what I've got."

"You're right," Hawthorne said. "That's not much of a plan."

"What about the warlocks? We can't have them run in and burn the forest down before we get a chance to fix it," Galvin pointed out.

"I'll go back to camp. See if I can hold them off to give you guys some time."

"That seems like a long shot," Alia lamented. "The warlocks don't like us very much. Besides, we could use your help."

"I'll come back as soon as I know they won't rush in after I'm gone." A small grin pulled at the side of Hawthorne's mouth.

Alia nodded with her own smile and slipped the coin back into her pocket. "Okay, then when you get back, you and Galvin can lead the creature around the woods for a bit, and I will signal you to bring it back when I've fixed the grove."

"Question," Galvin interjected. "How are we going to restore the grove? And how will that stop the leshy?"

Her head dropped to the side as she grimaced. "Well, Declan's actually still working that out for us. I left my samples with him, so he's running some tests to figure out how to at least clear that black stuff. He'll give me a call if he discovers anything but, in the meantime, we'll have to try different things to put the spell back together. But now that Hallowtide's ending, once the grove is restored, it should heal the leshy."

Galvin could only bite his lip. A good rest must have made her feel much better if she was good with this loose of a plan. "And once it's healed, the leshy will stop attacking?"

"You guys keep calling it a leshy," Hawthorne said. He frowned and slowly shook his head. "I don't think that's what it is. Leshies have totems and, if it's living in the grove, we should have seen it there. And you didn't find it while you were poking around its nest. I just don't think that's what it is."

Alia rolled her hands in the air. "I have no idea what else it could be. Nothing lives *inside* the grove, so I'm not sure what is attracting it there. You're absolutely right about the totem. And sure, it's not like any leshy I've read about. Declan thought it was a stretch as well but we don't have anything else to go on and that's the only thing that sort of fits. Besides, whether or not it is one, the grove should cure it of that stuff making it feral. The black goo might have altered its appearance, and healing it will give us a better idea of what it is."

Hawthorne scratched his chin. "We can't just kill it? If it's a danger, then maybe we should put it down. That would stop the Council's fearmongering about the non-humans using it as a weapon."

"One"—Alia counted on her fingers—"if we could kill it, I suspect the warlocks would have managed to by now, but it doesn't seem possible. For them or for us."

Hawthorne silently conceded she had a point.

"Second, if you kill it, it will only add to the propaganda that the non-humans *did* use it as a weapon. If you want to disprove those rumors, you need the beast alive."

Hawthorne crossed his arms, mulling that over.

"Look," she said, dropping her hands to her sides. "I'm really winging it right now. I don't have nearly enough information about what's going on, and we have until the end of the day before Ashblade burns this forest down. So, if you guys have anything helpful to add, I'm all ears."

She waited, looking at Hawthorne first but he held up his hands. "I don't like it," he admitted, "but I don't have a better answer."

When Alia faced Galvin, he just laughed. "I'm good at distractions, history, and tinkering. Outside of that, I rely on you."

Alia gave him a soft smile. "Then we should get going. You'll need time to get the warlocks together, and we need to restore the grove before sundown." She grabbed Galvin's arm, pulling him toward the trees and throwing a wave back at Hawthorne. "See you later."

The hike through the woods didn't reveal any changes. The forest was as quiet as ever, still gray and dead. The only sounds were of their crunching footsteps, as loud as if a whole army were marching through.

As they walked, Alia pulled two curious glowing fruits from her pack, one a dark blue and the other purple. Galvin had never known fruit to glow. They looked soft, with smooth skin like plums but were the size of grapefruits.

"Here," she said, handing him the blue one. "We'll want the boost."

"Boost of what?"

She kept the purple one for herself. "It's the hallow fruit that grows when Gia calls back our powers. Purple is my favorite," she told him, as if that explained everything.

"Purple is not a flavor."

"Purple is too a flavor. And Declan says the flavor doesn't change the power you get, but the more brightly glowing fruits felt stronger this year. He thinks it has to do with the upgrade spell."

"So this will boost our magic?"

"There's a lot more theory behind it than that but, for now, yes. I hope one will be enough. These are the only two Declan gave me."

He stared at the fruit in his hand while Alia took a big bite of hers. "So that's it, we just eat it?" The way Declan and Alia talked about it, there was a whole festival around harvesting these. He thought there would be something more you needed to do with it.

"For right now, yeah." She giggled, wiping juice from her mouth.

He shrugged and took a bite. He noticed a few things all at once. The fruit was sweet, with an almost heady flavor. The flesh was soft, like a ripe peach, and just as juicy. The scent and flavor were reminiscent of other fruits he had eaten but could not equally be compared to any of them. A tingling warmth filled him as he swallowed the first bite, satiating and recharging him. His powers had been growing since Halloween ended but, with each bite of the fruit, he felt magic surge in him. It must've been the boost Alia mentioned.

They finished as they hiked. There were no seeds or cores so they were able to consume the whole things, with nothing to discard. The dripping juice did leave his hand slightly sticky but Alia summoned some water to clean them both.

After their snack, Alia prepped her gun, switching the ammunition cartage to one of the magic ones. Fully loaded, she slipped it back into the holster on her leg.

The whole way, they didn't see any footprints or other signs of the leshy; they made it to the grove without finding a hint of the creature. But, after traveling all morning, it was now closer to midday and the beast was likely hiding out in its lair. That was a problem, since they wanted to traipse around the grove, fixing it, which would be difficult if the leshy were in there sleeping, or whatever it did during the day.

They paused behind the stone wall surrounding the grove's opening and checked the clearing in front of the stone archway. It wasn't the same spot they had been ambushed last time, but that didn't mean they needed to make the same mistake twice. Galvin watched their backs while Alia examined the clearing. Nothing moved and nothing except them made noise.

When Alia decided it was safe, he felt a gentle tug on his attention, like a soft touch of her hand on the back of his neck. He reached out with his mind to reciprocate, letting her know he was ready.

She moved first and he followed, still watching their backs as they approached the stone archway. He heard her take out her gun and the gentle clicks as she switched off the safety, prepared for any surprise intruders while Galvin continued to guard their rears.

An impulse to lure the creature out of the grove washed over Galvin. Alia was sending him a message, though their connection wasn't strong enough to transmit words yet. He felt her certainty that it's lair wasn't inside the magic circle. No animal would build a nest inside, but something kept calling the leshy to the grove.

Galvin nodded without taking his attention away from the woods but recalled what they had seen of the space when they investigated the first time. The grove was up against the side of a rock face, making it a sort of small grotto. They had focused on the tree the last time they were here, so there might have been more room hiding in the back. *I'll check the perimeter for any caves or exits outside the circle. You start figuring out how to restore the magic.*

Alia headed under the archway first and Galvin walked backward, following her inside. They shared one look before nodding and heading off to their tasks. He waked the edge of the rock that lined up with the outer rim of the grove. The magic was faded but Galvin could see the markings of the circle scored in the earth right up to the stone walls. There wasn't room for anything else in the small grotto. The grove's perimeter matched the stone so well the circle wasn't perfectly round. Its waves and juts aligned with the uneven stone, like water filling all the available spaces. As Galvin walked around the other side of the tree, he found the grove was completely enclosed. Which meant there was no place for the creature to make a lair and not be inside the grove.

But Alia said that was impossible.

That was when Galvin realized what he was looking at. At the very back of the grotto, in one of the rounded grooves of the stone wall, was the nest. A pile of brush and leaves Galvin hadn't quite picked up as different from the surrounding shrubbery filled the little alcove. Upon closer inspection, he saw the ground was tamped down from extended use, so something had to be sleeping here.

Galvin was no tracker but knew something was wrong. Animals picked homes that would fit them. And this one was inside the grove's magic circle, exactly where Alia had said no creature would live. Maybe she was wrong.

"Um, Alia, I think you should look at this."

She stood next to him, scrutinizing the nest area. "That's odd," she agreed. "Only guardians are able to live inside the circle but that's clearly where the leshy sleeps."

"So, Hawthorne was right. It's not a leshy."

Alia flipped around just as the hair on the back of Galvin's neck began to stand up. He looked at her, before a soft mewing call came from behind them. There was only one thing that would be inside the grove and make those eerie cries. Galvin turned slowly, fully expecting to see the creature.

There it was, standing over them, watching them closely. Black goo dripped from its dark eyeholes and from the nose hole on its skull head. It mewed again, the sound of something sad and pained.

Alia's mouth gaped, her eyes growing wide in alarm. Galvin's stomach clenched as he remembered the painful slash of its claws. It was too close to her and too fast for her to avoid when it decided to attack.

The creature stared at Alia, not paying any attention to Galvin. A glow bloomed in the eye sockets. It was still broad daylight but whatever made the thing feral was about to happen right now.

Galvin gulped. "Alia, we're too close."

Slowly, Alia reached a hand up toward the side of the creature's skull head. "Shh. You're all right."

Galvin's eyes darted between Alia and the creature. He couldn't believe she was going to pet it!

The need to lead the creature away just about overwhelmed him coupled with the familiar admonishment to fix his face. He snapped his mouth closed.

Her fingers barely brushed the side of its face when the creature stepped away. It threw its head back, making another of those loud and terrible bugle calls, shaking the earth around them. It pulled one skeletal hand back, winding up to swipe.

Galvin dashed between Alia and the feral thing, lifting his blades above their heads and summoning his fire. The creature's hand landed in the flames, its bony fingers singeing. It screamed in pain, retreating toward the archway. Galvin left Alia's side, driving the creature back with burning sweeps of his swords.

"We have to get it out of here," Alia said, raising her gun.

"I'll do it." She started to protest and he nudged her back toward the tree. "You know more about druid magic than I do. You have to stay here to fix the grove." He never took his eyes off his target. He felt her wanting to argue, but she knew he was right. Of the two of them, she could figure out what was wrong with the grove, not him.

The creature continued to back away from the flames. Galvin pushed it back to the stone archway. He just needed it to move into the clearing enough for him to get out too. It reeled back anytime the fire got too close but Galvin could tell it was getting irritated with him. This tactic would only work a little longer before its need to attack outweighed its fear of burning.

"Galvin!" Alia scrambled to convey something through their connection but it was coming over in jumbled segments. Doubt, excitement, and important information, but he couldn't pick up what she wanted him to know. It was like trying to lip read with no words. "Try not to hurt it, just distract it."

"You're kidding, right?" He didn't mean for his voice to come out quite so high. He swung his swords at the creature's legs. It stepped back again and into a position Galvin could use. There was enough room between the creature's hoofed feet and the stone for him to slip through if he was fast. "I need to find Hawthorne and even then I don't think it will be fair odds."

"I know it doesn't make any sense yet. I'll explain later. Just promise me you'll try!"

"Fine, I promise! You restore the grove before it hurts me!"

He summoned ice, freezing the area from the monster's feet to the stone archway while leaving an opening he could slide through. He rolled back to his feet as the creature broke free, sending shards flying in all directions.

Galvin ran as fast as he could out of the clearing, pausing only to toss a massive snowball at the creature's head for good measure. He knew he couldn't hurt it with anything other than fire and that he would never win in a one-on-one battle with it, so he didn't even try. The snowball hit its skull squarely in the eye, sending it reeling to one side, stumbling to stay upright. Galvin pumped a fist to celebrate his bullseye, grinning and chuckling. That should get its attention.

The creature glared at Galvin, bugling once more before stalking after him. Galvin dashed away, leading the creature into a fairer fight.

36

The equipment in Theo's lab was more advanced than anything in the infirmary or Declan's own rooms, so that was where he was currently hiding and looking over Alia's samples. This time, he had told Grace the truth. She had protested at first but, when Declan acted confused, asking if the Council *wanted* answers about the goo or not, she had begrudgingly agreed.

She was a little more surly and distracted than usual too. Something wasn't going according to plan. After he analyzed the goo for Alia and Galvin, he'd go looking for the reason why.

He stared at a goo sample at the end of the magi-scope, Theo's microscope that was able to magnify the bits of magic in things. But even with Theo's high-tech tools, Declan didn't discover much. The goo was magic but not any kind Declan recognized. That wasn't strange—life was ever-changing and adapting, and new forms of magic tended to evolve every few hundred years or so. What was strange was that it acted like old magic, not modern magic—more like how he cast spells than how Alia did. That wasn't much to go on, though, and told him nothing about what the substance actually was.

Declan switched the goo out for the fur sample, which he would examine under the magi-scope in a few minutes after he ran some tests on the goo. Knowing more about the creature would help them defeat it, which was all they would be able to do if they couldn't get rid of the black toxin and save it.

Declan put some goo in a secure container on the counter next to the scope, thinking about what he already knew. Galvin and Hawthorne had confirmed the creature was afraid of fire. Leshies were not afraid of fire as a rule, so its fear likely had something to do with the toxin. He had also witnessed a warm light, similar to a druid's sunlight powers, when Grace was healing Galvin, which had dried the goo up, but he couldn't replicate what she had done on the samples.

He tried both fire and sunlight on the goo. The fire, while effective, did not eradicate the goo but simply dried it out. The process was slow, more likely to burn and destroy the surroundings before the goo. In fact, the fire might do more damage than it helped to prevent. Useful information, but not a viable way to eliminate the toxin from a living being.

Sunlight had the most success. Anywhere Declan's concentrated sunlight touched the goo, it dried instantly and fell away into ash. That did bring up more questions, though. If sunlight so effectively destroyed the toxin, why was it still in the tree? It should burn up as soon as the sun rose for the day. Was the sunlight too weak, filtered through the thick forest canopy, to do the job? Was that why the creature was more active during the times of day with the least amount of light? If so, then why wasn't it active at night instead, avoiding sunlight altogether?

Perhaps he needed more insight into what the creature was than he originally thought.

Declan had told his apprentices the only thing that came to mind when they described it was a leshy but that he wasn't comfortable with the assessment. Leshies were intelligent beings capable of speech and negotiation. If it was a leshy, Declan would expect it to attempt to dissuade the warlocks and possibly make an example of one before attacking them all. Goo poisoning might account for its feral behavior but, after seeing Galvin's symptoms, he didn't find that likely either. The toxin hadn't turned Galvin feral, only tried to kill him.

Alia had told him about the ruined grove and, from the size she described, it had been there for some time, likely before the upgrade spell. Leshies didn't like to make their homes in forests already guarded by a druid grove. The grove's magic was usually problematic to a leshy, negating the power of its totem. And if the woods already had a grove, then it didn't need protection from a leshy too. There was too much about the whole situation that just didn't fit.

He turned back to the magi-scope and the other samples Alia had brought him. She had been confident the fur belonged to the creature. It was long, dark brown, and rather coarse. Elk, by the looks of it. They were native to the higher altitudes of the Redwood National Park, so it made sense. A familiar shimmer caught his eye and Declan adjusted the magi-scope to a higher power.

Magic laced through the fur in fragments. The magic was part of the creature, not the goo, but the toxin had morphed and mutated it, twisting it into something sinister. It was decaying the creature from the inside, similar to the way it had begun to corrupt Galvin. Declan found a small section of the creature's magic still intact and his stomach flipped as he realized what he was looking at.

The original magic was recognizable, with some slight

modifications. Modifications he was beginning to become more familiar with as he grew accustomed with the changes to the grove and his apprentices. "Oh, Supreme Heavenly Being," he breathed, his heart racing as the picture of the mysterious creature became clearer.

It was a guardian. Poisoned, feral, and impossible to kill without destroying the grove.

"I have to stop them." Declan sprang up from the table, not bothering to clear the samples before rushing up to the common room. He did remember to secure the door behind him. It slid into place, disappearing into the wall and keeping Theo's presence in the estate disguised. He rushed up the stairs, heading straight for his room and his things.

Grace happened to be passing in the hallway on her way to his office when Declan ran by. He didn't stop, forcing her to stumble back with a squeak as he barreled past and skidded the turn through his door. "Declan! What are you doing?" she asked, following him to the threshold of his apartment.

He rushed around his living room, grabbing his pack and throwing the extra things he might need into it: gravity stickers, a vial of grove water, and an elk call whistle, hoping his guess was right. "Alia and Galvin need my help," he told her, collecting all his medical supplies and stuffing them into his bag.

She scoffed, rolling her eyes and crossing her arms.

"They don't know what they're up against," he argued. He made one more glance over the room, trying to think if there was anything else they might need.

"You can't run to their rescue every time they have a problem. Besides, they just left. They can't possibly have gotten into any trouble yet." She sounded irritated, the biggest crack in her overly pleasant demeanor yet.

If Declan weren't more concerned about his apprentices, he would take more time to examine her reaction. Right now, though, she could shove it.

"The hell I can't run to their rescue." He pushed past her back into the hall and picked up his bō staff from its place next to door. She had to step back to prevent being knocked over. He was done playing nice for the sake of diplomacy. Neither Grace nor the World Council would stop him from helping his apprentices. To hell with what she said about them to the Council.

After locking his bedroom door, Declan secured his pack on his back, shrank his bō staff, and secured it to his belt. He was about to rush off but paused, then went to his office. At his desk, he opened the top drawer and took out the silver cuffs he had removed from Theo, then walked out and closed and locked that door as well.

Grace huffed, throwing up her hands at his behavior. "Why are you locking doors? You are not going anywhere."

Declan grabbed her hands and clicked Theo's silver cuffs around her wrists.

She gasped, yanking her arms back, trying to pull the magic cuffs off. "What do you think you're doing?"

Declan smirked at her attempt. If Theo hadn't been able to get them off, there was no way Grace could. They should at least keep her out of trouble while he was gone.

"Take these off me at once! You are *not* going anywhere!"

But Declan was already rushing down the stairs, ignoring her.

She shouted after him, "I have given you a direct order!"

"Fuck your order!" he called from the floor below. "Those are my kids, and I'm going to help them!"

37

Alia stood in the grove alone, not sure what to do. Galvin had led the guardian away but he didn't really know what he was up against. He was right about it being more likely to hurt him than the other way around. He was going to find Hawthorne, so he'd have help at least. Hopefully Galvin could enforce her promise on whomever Hawthorne trusted enough to bring with him.

The creature had spoken to her. Its voice was the one she had heard in her dream, telling her to help it before it could help her. She now understood what it meant. A few moments ago, it had pleaded with her to find a cure. Galvin hadn't heard it speak because he couldn't talk to animals like she could. Guardians only communicated with druids who could speak with animals.

Hawthorne had been right. Declan had been right. It wasn't a leshy, and all the things that hadn't fit now fell into place. It was the guardian of this grove and they needed to cure it. To destroy one would be to destroy the other, and that would be a death sentence to these woods.

She turned back to the poisoned tree. She had no idea how to fix it. She had her work cut out for her. Time to start trying things.

Lucian's scarred hand clamped down on her arm, yanking her back, and he clapped another hand over her mouth. Her heart leapt into her throat and her thoughts spiraled into a chaotic mess as he dragged her toward the stone archway. Magic fear flooded her senses and muddled her thoughts.

She struggled and squirmed, trying to break out of his grasp, but Lucian wasn't playful or teasing anymore. She called sunlight to her hands, hoping to burn him, but his black tendrils wrapped around her arms, pinning them to her sides and making it impossible for her to get a good angle.

He tsked. "Not this time, Little Druid."

She searched the fear, trying to follow Galvin's advice: find where Lucian's magic ended and her own feelings began. But she couldn't see anything. *Find it,* she told herself. *Find it. Fight back!* Everything was shadowed, blurred together, and all she knew was the panic clutching at her chest. She couldn't use magic, she couldn't reach her weapon, and nothing she did could stop him flooding her with terror. She shouted to Galvin through their connection, knowing there was nothing he could do to help her.

"I am tired of those guys coming to your rescue all the time with their wards and magic," Lucian snarled. "I'm taking you home where no one will be able to save you."

Alia whimpered, digging her heels in the dirt, grabbing anything within reach, anything to stop him from taking her out of the circle. If he did, she was as good as dead.

Fight, girl! the guardian shouted in her mind. ***Are you a***

damsel or a druid?

Anger bloomed. She was *not* a damsel. She glared and growled under Lucian's hand. Declan had trained her most of her life to fight. She could protect herself. She called her sunlight, screwing her eyes shut and forcing it out of her body in any direction she could. Lucian had her hands clamped down, but she would hit him with sunlight one way or another.

With her eyes closed, she finally saw it—the kernel of light in the midst of the darkness—and hope flickered through the fear. That must be what Galvin meant. Her mind latched onto that one small bit of herself, determined to fight back. Focusing on the glow, Alia poured everything she had into it, willing it to grow.

Tingling heat ran over her skin like a million static shocks and her vision filled with electric blue. A pressure released, a feeling like her whole body might break apart. She heard Lucian cry out, the sound accompanied by loud crackling and booming thunder. His tendrils retreated as his body was flung away from her, leaving behind a great weight on her shoulder blades.

What was happening to her? She wrapped her arms around her middle, trying to keep herself together as the crackling snapped around her, threatening to pull her apart and burn her up all at the same time.

The feeling finally passed, her vision clearing, but the world had turned dark around her. She heard Lucian growling in pain and smelled the burning of his flesh but she couldn't see past the great pair of wings encircling her.

Where did these come from?

They were lovely. The feathers were white, with touches of a stormy gray and blue throughout. Gold lined the tips and little sparks of electricity danced along them. The coloring reminded her of Galvin's fur in his wolf form and for a moment she thought he had come after all.

But there was no way he could have gotten back that fast, and he hadn't been able to change into a bird when they tried it before. She reached across their connection to double-check and felt him far off in the woods, distracted and running.

Slowly, she dropped her arms and stretched out to touch the feathers, but the wings unfurled and spread in the same movement. Her muscles shifted and pulled in her back and down her legs as the wings moved.

They were *her* wings. A breathy laugh escaped her lips. She had wings. Big, beautiful wings. It wasn't exactly an animal transformation, but it was amazing.

She whirled to face Lucian, wings spread and catching every gust of wind as she moved. She stumbled, nearly getting blown off her feet to one side. She was going to need practice to get the hang of her new appendages. She pulled the wings in until she found her balance and pinned Lucian with a hard stare.

He had made it back up to one knee but was struggling with the blacked wounds across his face and arms. He grimaced up at her, his flesh falling away from him like ash. Unlike the sunlight burns she had given him, these were deeper, more gash-like. The scars would leave zigzagging marks across his discolored skin when his body finally reformed.

His magic poked and prodded Alia's mind, trying to find a foothold. Each oily tendril yanking back with a sizzle when it came too close. Alia let him search, standing strong and steady in front of him, her breathing even and controlled. She met his scowl with a steely one of her own.

That was when he realized.

Alia wasn't scared anymore. No longer could he find a grip on her or poison her with dark magic. She opened her hand, summoning that same hot light that had exploded around them. Stormy blue lightning crackled around her.

Lucian's eyes grew wide and he recoiled. He tried to scramble to his feet but Alia lifted her knee and thrust a kick at his face. She didn't dare attempt a bigger kick with the unfamiliar weight of her wings but she had moved quickly and effectively. Her foot caught Lucian under the chin, throwing his head backward. Using the momentum, she stomped her foot into his abdomen, slamming him into the ground.

He crumpled, dazed, and she leaned over her knee to look him in the face and make sure he heard her clearly. She bore down on him, the lightning in her hands sparking and cracking. Lucian flinched from each bolt, his body dissolving into ash wherever he was struck, revealing the disgusting black bug-like endoskeleton underneath.

"If I ever see you again"—her voice was low but steady with the clarity of her certainty—"I will kill you in every realm to ensure you never come back."

She didn't have time to kill him today. The grove was more important. She'd have to finish him off another day.

Lucian sneered at her threat and Alia raged. Pressure grew in her again as lightning flashed around them and a stormy blue crept into the edges of her vision. Lucian's confidence disappeared at what he saw in her eyes and he sank away from her. For the first time, it was Lucian who trembled in fear of her.

She slammed her hand down on his chest and unleashed all the magic buildup. Lightning crackled over his body and burned him away, endoskeleton and all. He screamed and writhed in pain as he was reduced to nothing but ashes. She didn't stop until he had completely dissolved.

A gentle shake of her wings sent the ashes scattering through the wind. He wasn't dead, she knew that now. He had too much demon in him to be that easy to kill but she took some pleasure in the fact that the destruction of his body on this plane had hurt him like hell.

Alia breathed deep, feeling lighter than she had in weeks despite the new massive weight on her back. She had done it. She didn't know how but the new power had helped. She had broken the blood bond with Lucian and thus his hold over her. She wasn't sure she cared how it worked. She jumped, pumping her fist in the air and shouting in victory. Her heavy wings made jumping difficult and they mimicked the movements of her hands, almost sending her tumbling to the ground.

These were going to take some training. Already, muscles she didn't usually use—at least, not in this way—were burning. With concentrated effort, she folded the wings tightly against her back. That put her center of balance closer to a familiar spot. Slowly, she assessed herself and the grove for damage.

Thankfully, Alia was uninjured, a blessing that did not go overlooked. Her shirt had not been so fortunate. The wings had ripped it open from the back and now it sagged in front of her, holding on by nothing but the sleeves. She sighed, pulling the ruined thing off. Amazingly, her bra had survived completely intact. She stuffed the scrap fabric that had once been her shirt into her bag.

The grove had not fared so well. Scorch marks radiated out from where she stood. Nothing was on fire or smoldering, thank goodness, but dark marks were burned into the ground and the stone walls where her lightning had touched. She had given the grove stripes.

On the bright side, Lucian wasn't the only thing that had turned to ash when struck. The burn marks went through the black goo as well. While it still oozed out of the unmarred bark on the tree, the parts that had been hit were drying up and flaking away. That was progress, at least, but it was not a viable option to repair the grove. She clearly didn't have enough control over the new power to eradicate the toxin safely.

"Whoa," Declan's voice breathed behind her. Having learned her lesson, she slowly turned, making sure not to knock herself over, to see her mentor standing in the stone archway. His eyes were wide and his mouth hung open as he gaped at her. "Those are wings."

Alia grinned. "Yeah." She spread them so Declan could get a better look at them.

His surprise grew. The awe in his voice made Alia blush. "Those are *thunderbird* wings."

38

The creature's long legs easily kept up with Galvin, even as he ran at full speed to stay ahead of it. Of all the things he'd thrown at it so far, the snowball to the face had really angered it. Now he couldn't deter it to save his life. He just hoped he would be able to maintain his lead all the way back to camp. Then the warlocks could figure out a way to save his life.

A pile of boulders he recognized told him he was still closer to the grove than the camp and had quite a bit more running ahead of him. That was unfortunate. His lungs were burning and he wasn't sure how much longer his legs would keep going. He rounded the boulders and slammed into Hawthorne, knocking them both to the ground.

"Son of a—"

"C'mon." Galvin untangled himself from the Raptor, trying to push back to his feet. The effort was more difficult than it should have been but Hawthorne was already up, staring blankly at Galvin. "We need the others."

The creature emerged from behind the boulders, growling as it approached them, claws raised.

Hawthorne's laser blades were out and covered in flames as he squared off with the creature. Galvin readied his own blades in the same way but much slower and with shaking muscles. He wasn't as recovered as he thought he had been. The creature paused, eyeing the flames of Hawthorne's blades closely, just as Hawthorne and Galvin watched it.

Alia's scream for help hit him through their connection and his heart sank. Of course Lucian would wait until they were separated to show up, the coward. He mumbled a curse, never taking his eyes off the beast. At the same time, the creature's head perked up and it turned to look back the way they had come. Galvin thought he saw a flicker in the beast's eyes, the red fading slightly perhaps, but it was too quick to be sure. Without giving them a second glance, the creature headed toward the grove.

Galvin lowered his blades, extinguishing the flames, and stared in confusion as the creature stalked off. *That's odd, like it can sense Alia too.* Whatever the reason for its behavior, they needed to cut it off before it caught Alia by surprise. While she was fighting Lucian to boot.

"We better hurry," he said to Hawthorn's back. "Alia needs our help. The thing attacking her is there, and now the creature is on its way to join them."

But Hawthorne didn't move. The hair on Galvin's neck stood up. The Raptor's blades were extinguished but still out, hanging by his sides. He only needed to drop his concentration to put them away. To keep them in hand meant he was prepared to fight.

"Uh." It didn't even seem like Hawthorne was listening to him.

His gut told him something was wrong. "Hawthorne?" He made no move closer to the Raptor but gripped his blades in anticipation.

Hawthorne whirled with a speed Galvin hadn't seen even in Winter Soldiers. He slashed with his right, then his left, and Galvin barely managed to raise his swords in time to block.

Hawthorne was strong. Each strike reverberated through Galvin's arms and forced him to step back or risk losing his balance. He barely had a moment to wonder what was going on when Hawthorne came in again from above. He defended high, needing both blades to block both of Hawthorne's, his arms shaking and straining and leaving his torso wide open.

It was what Hawthorne wanted. He pulled away in a blink and kicked Galvin hard in the chest, sending him stumbling to the ground. He landed on his knees, which was better than being prone, but not a good situation. Hawthorne was rushing at him again, so Galvin manifested ice around him from the feet up, freezing him in place. As his arm cast upward, Hawthorne's blade came down and slashed across Galvin's forearm.

Galvin shouted and the sword fell from his hand as he yanked his arm back to his body. He didn't finish the ice spell. Blood spilled from the fresh wound, blood he really didn't have to lose.

Galvin pushed up to his feet, holding his remaining weapon up for defense. "Hawthorne, it's me! What are you doing?"

The only reply the Raptor gave was a steely stare made all the more frightening by its calm. No hate, no rage fueled his actions, simply cold, calculating evaluation. Galvin wasn't sure there was thought in Hawthorne's head.

The ice vanished with more ease than Galvin had summoned it, and Hawthorne rushed back in. Galvin couldn't block with his injured arm, so he conjured a shield just as Hawthorne began a relentless barrage of stabs and slashes too fast for Galvin to do anything other than block and try to stand upright.

What was going on? Hawthorne had been on their side no more than a few hours ago. He had given Declan reason to trust him when they were at the Arbor estate. He had defended Galvin from a Council member's nefarious intentions. What could have happened at the camp to so thoroughly change his mind?

Hawthorne moved and Galvin lost sight of him. How fast was he? He reappeared behind Galvin and, more importantly, behind his shield. The Raptor shouldered him hard in the back and pain shot through his healing slashes. The force and agony sent him crashing to the ground face-first.

He managed to roll to his back in time to see Hawthorne's neon weapon descended. The pain in his healing injury flared to life again and Galvin barely deflected Hawthorne's attack with another magic shield, preventing it from landing a fatal blow to his head and earning him a slice across the ribs for his efforts. The other blade came down fast, and Galvin brought his own up to block.

Hawthorne kicked the sword out of Galvin's hand and brought his foot down on his wrist. His other knee dropped onto Galvin's chest, pinning him to the ground. He clutched one blade to Galvin's throat and poised the other above, ready to sink into his left eye.

Galvin was about to die and the worst part was he didn't understand why. Hawthorne had gone mental and was about to stab straight into his brain.

Except he didn't. He stared at Galvin with those unfeeling silver Raptor eyes but he didn't move. Galvin didn't know why and didn't dare risk a twitch and making the final decision on whatever

Hawthorne was debating.

Hawthorne's eyes glinted and narrowed, the blade at Galvin's throat pressing into his skin. The laser burned but he did not make the killing blow. The one hovering above Galvin's face began to shake, inching closer and backing away. Galvin realized Hawthorne wasn't debating, he was struggling. His chest labored and his hands, along with the weapons in them, trembled with the effort of, Galvin hoped, not killing him. Galvin watched the beams of light waver between his death and his release.

Hawthorne's face contorted in what looked like pain and he screwed his eyes shut, shaking his head, as if he were trying to throw off a voice only he could hear. "No," he ground out between clenched teeth. "No, it's not right! I do not have to follow bad orders!"

The laser swords disappeared, Hawthorne's hands spreading open like he had dropped something dangerous. He pushed to his feet, scrambling away from Galvin, breathing hard and holding his head.

Never before had Galvin wondered at the Raptors' training. He thought it was extensive and advanced, for warlocks who excelled above and beyond the rest. Now he wasn't so sure and had concern for Hawthorne's mental stability. His reaction seemed more like mind control than training.

Galvin snatched up his own swords. His injured arm could only hold one up but he stood ready in case Hawthorne lost whatever battle he was fighting with himself and came at him again.

After a moment or two, Hawthorne's face and arms went slack as he dropped to his knees, staring into the distance.

"Hawthorne," Galvin tried, planning to gauge from his response how safe he really was, but the Raptor ignored him. Perhaps he should just make a run for it while he still could. "Zayne

Hawthorne, are you in there?"

"I disobeyed orders." He said it like he had committed an atrocious crime. Galvin didn't wonder what the order was. He'd seen it firsthand. "They told me you're part of the rebellion and my orders were to eliminate you, but it's not true." He scrunched his eyes closed. "I *know* it's not true. I know it's not *true*. I do not have to obey bad orders." He sounded like he was trying to convince himself.

Snowflakes, this was bad. Galvin wasn't sure Hawthorne could hear him so he waited, hoping he won over his personal demons. If he had orders to kill Galvin and Alia, it was probably safe to assume no reinforcements were coming to their aid. And now the creature was goodness knew where, Alia was fighting Lucian alone, and Galvin didn't dare move in case it triggered Hawthorne.

Footsteps crunched through the woods toward them and Galvin groaned. It wasn't the thundering sound of the creature so it had to be people. The last thing he needed right now was more trained soldiers coming to kill him.

Galvin was shocked when Declan and Alia run around the pile of boulders. Declan wasn't supposed to be here but his presence was a pleasant surprise. The bigger shock was Alia. Galvin almost laughed with joy that she was all right, but his mouth gaped when he got a look at her. Great white wings hung off her shoulders, dragging on the ground behind her. Colors of a stormy sky danced in the white feathers and the afternoon sun glinted off the golden tips. She had the wings of a thunderbird. They wrapped around her shoulders like a cloak and the bit he could see of her underneath was shirtless.

In November. Blessed snowflakes.

They both took one look at Galvin's bleeding arm, neck, and chest, with his blades out and ready, and Hawthorne, sitting on the ground, clearly not in his right mind. Declan already had his staff out, but Alia began to reach for her gun.

"What's going on here," Alia's eyes darted between Galvin and Hawthorne. "And what happened to the guardian?"

"Guardian." Galvin stared at them. "What guardian?"

Something about realizing they were not alone snapped Hawthorne back to his senses. He blinked several times, his face and eyes returning to the relaxed indifference Galvin was used to seeing from him. He turned toward the newcomers, his mouth hanging open at the sight of Alia's additions. "Holy crap! When did you get those?"

Galvin wasn't about to ignore what just happened. "Hawthorne," he barked.

The Raptor flinched slightly before looking over his shoulder at him.

Galvin fixed the Raptor with a hard stare, swords out and body tense in case he needed to defend himself again. Or the others. "We good or are you going to lose your shit again?"

Hawthorne nodded solemnly. "No, we're good."

Galvin huffed but put his weapons away.

"Someone want to fill us in?" Declan relaxed his stance when Galvin did but the staff was still in his hand.

"I think that's a great idea." Galvin frowned at Hawthorne. "I'd like to know as well."

39

Declan had arrived to utter chaos. Alia had the wings of a magical thunderbird in a partial animal transformation, which he had never seen a druid do before. Galvin was injured again from Hawthorne going berserk, and no one knew where the guardian was. Declan took a deep breath and gestured to the Raptor. "All right, let's hear it."

Hawthorne sighed. "I was given orders to kill Alia. And Galvin." Something about the answer felt odd to Declan, like the order was more for Alia only. Declan also wasn't mentioned. Of course, he wasn't supposed to be here.

Alia huffed, rolling her eyes and pulling her restocked first aid kit from her bag. "You might as well get in line. It seems like everyone wants to kill me."

"Your orders were just to kill Alia and Galvin?" Declan asked.

Recognition glinted in Hawthorne's face; he noticed it too—the strange wording of the order. His eyes dropped to the right as he recalled the event. "I don't think they expected you to be here but, to answer your question, yes. The order was specifically for Alia. Galvin was added as an afterthought."

"You had me as good as dead," Galvin admitted as Alia smeared M.U.D. over the gash in his arm.

Declan shushed him but couldn't help the way his stomach turned at the thought. Another close call for his apprentices. They may not like it but Declan was going to be a lot more involved moving forward. "How did you get the orders?"

"From Captain Ashblade." That wasn't what Declan meant but it answered part of his question. Hawthorne quickly altered his previous response after seeing Declan's expression. "Verbally. With the M…" His face paled, fear in those silver eyes. His voice came out small when he tried again. "The MPs…" He paused, swallowing hard, but his voice was steadier when he spoke again. "With the MPs present to ensure compliance."

A Raptor receiving an order verbally wasn't unusual but Declan had hoped for more information to prove his hunch. From Hawthorne's admission in the infirmary, it was common knowledge that Ashblade worked with Grace, so Declan assumed the druids' mysterious enemy was behind this. But a verbal order was impossible to prove. Clever.

And *she* was currently alone in their house, left to her own devices. She wouldn't be able to use magic and all the important doors were locked, but Declan didn't want to leave her there indefinitely to figure out how to break in.

Or out. The cuffs should keep her from leaving the grove but she would probably use that fact to add to the druids' criminal reputation if she managed to call for help. They needed to finish quickly and get back but…

Ensure compliance?

"But he didn't obey the orders," Galvin reminded them. "Are you going to be in a lot of trouble for helping us?"

Hawthorne cringed. "Yes. A lot."

"Why did you disobey?" Declan asked.

Hawthorne sighed again, running his hand over his buzzed hair. "God, I hate sob stories," he muttered. He shook his head but went on. "I became a Raptor because I wanted to play a part in bettering the world. At least, that's what I thought I was doing when I signed up. My disillusionment with my chosen occupation has been a long time coming."

That tracked with what Ophelia had told Declan but it almost hadn't worked out the way she planned. She had gambled a little more than Declan was comfortable with, and he'd be having a word with her about it.

"This whole mission has too many holes and it doesn't sit well with me," Hawthorne went on. "You were told the creature is dangerous. And it is but it only attacked us unprovoked one time."

"Something did provoke it." Alia put the M.U.D. away. "Something magical forced it into that feral mode and changed its eyes from brown to glowing. But I didn't want to take the chance of leaving it be if the mortals nearby were in danger."

"That's the other thing. You've been told you're here to protect a village but everyone I talked to in the camp didn't know anything about one. We were all told this creature—"

"Guardian," Alia corrected.

"I don't know what that means," Hawthorne sassed back. "But we were told *it* is a weapon of the rebellion."

"Wait," Declan stopped him. "What rebellion?"

"Hawthorne says the warlocks have been pushing the narrative of a second Underground Monster rebellion," Galvin added helpfully.

Things were starting to click into place. This mission had been orchestrated on purpose to split the druids up and make them out as bad guys to the Council. Specifically, to get Alia and Galvin away long enough to be killed and leave Declan alone. But why target them? And how many of their problems were caused by this plan? Hallowtide was just bad timing, since no one on the Council knew they'd lose their powers, but what about Alia's issues with Lucian? Was he still working with his father, Mathias, or with the mysterious enemy?

It was a good thing nobody knew about Erik.

"Ashblade also told me you druids might be helping the monster rebellion and that's why I was sent, to keep an eye on you."

So not just bad guys, Declan realized. Grace and their mystery adversary wanted the druids to be marked as criminals. They didn't just want him out of the Council but an enemy of it.

"That was a lie too," Hawthorne continued. "Alia and Galvin had no idea what the creature is and didn't know there was a grove here until they found it." He pursed his lips. "I don't think there is a new rebellion. Monsters aren't acting like there's one. They're not breaking laws and causing havoc. They're scared and cowering in the shadows."

Declan thought of Cyrus Nightshade, the vampire at his hearing. Hawthorne was right, that vampire had been scared and certainly not fighting back.

The only real question was how involved Grace was in the whole thing. Was she the orchestrator or a pawn setting the plan into motion? Was it she or her mysterious boss who wanted to destroy

Declan?

"What do we do about the warlock camp?" Alia asked. "Won't they look for you when you don't come back?"

Hawthorne shook his head. "The camp was packing up when Ashblade gave me my orders but a small group stayed behind to burn the forest. They gave me two hours to finish you off before they start setting fires. We're on our own for now."

This just kept getting better. Two hours wasn't a lot of time.

"Why did you struggle so much to not kill me?" Galvin asked a legit question, one Declan would like to know the answer to as well.

Hawthorne shrugged as if it were common knowledge. "Raptors are programmed to obey. We are conditioned, extensively. That's why not following orders is such a big deal."

Programmed, he said. As if they were machines. Declan had heard rumors about Raptor training, brainwashing and conditioning that made torture look like a vacation. Seeing Hawthorne now, he almost believed it. "Do I need to worry about you following your… programming at a later time?"

"Don't wear white and don't give me the silent treatment, and everything should be fine." Hawthorne laughed but no one laughed with him.

"Like the weird MPs who don't speak?" Alia asked.

Hawthorne nodded, face pale. "But I've made my choice. I'm done with that, and I'm here to help."

Declan let out a low whistle. Raptors were a lot more damaged than everyone pretended they were.

"Speaking of clothing," Alia said, somewhat bashfully with her teeth chattering. "Do you still have an extra shirt, Galvin? Mine was…

well."

Galvin snorted. "What happened to 'You should always pack an extra set of clothes'?"

"Yeah, yeah," she sassed, rolling her eyes. "In my defense, you already knew you could change before we left. I only just discovered these." She shrugged her wings a little to emphasize her point, dropping them to expose her shoulders covered by nothing but the black straps of her bra.

All teasing gone, Galvin jumped in front of her and pulled her wings back around her. "Yes. I have an extra shirt. Don't show everyone that."

"Okay," Declan declared, changing the subject. He had been caught without a change of clothes after a transformation too many times to care about nudity now, and they had more important things to worry about. "How much of the two hours do we have left?"

"About an hour and forty-five minutes."

As long as nothing went wrong, that should be enough time. "We have a lot to do and, the longer we take, the worse things are going to get. First of all, as I'm sure we've all figured out by now, we've been set up." He was pleased to see there weren't any surprised faces among them. He would have worried if he needed to spell it out for anyone. "I don't know if this is all Grace's doing or if she's just the pawn but, either way, she is unsupervised in our house, so we need to hurry.

"Secondly, the fact remains that this grove has been poisoned. Trap or not, we need to cure it and the guardian while we're here before the toxin seeps into the rest of the network. You can't kill the guardian without killing the grove and, frankly, we don't want either of those things to happen. Thankfully, Alia and I have everything we need to repair the grove."

"Using my lightning is not a viable plan," Alia said, trying to figure out how to get the borrowed shirt over her wings. So far, she was not managing very well. Every attempt to do more than cover her arms would result in the shirt ripping. "It could set the whole grove on fire. It's already left scorch marks everywhere."

"True," he admitted, "but you won't be using it in the grove. You know, you'd have more success if you put your wings away."

Alia huffed.

He ignored her and again addressed the group. "Here's the plan." He pointed to Hawthorne and Alia. "You two will distract the guardian."

"Wait, wait, wait," Galvin interrupted. "I don't know if I'm comfortable with that. Why don't I go with Alia?"

"One, because Alia has the sunlight power to eliminate the toxin, plus lightning powers that work in a surprisingly similar way, and she can communicate with the guardian. I need to work in the grove and I need you with me so you can signal to Alia when we're finished. Besides, I trust Hawthorne is in control of his decisions. He's not exhibiting signs that tell me otherwise. Alia."

She looked at him, still struggling with the wings.

"You're not wearing white, so just don't give him the silent treatment and everything should be fine."

"She's not actually wearing anything," Galvin grumbled as she continued to fight with the shirt.

"*In ainm Dé,* girl." Declan sighed. "Just put them away."

"I tried that," she snapped, but her frustration immediately turned into embarrassment. She hated not having something handled.

Or to not be immediately good at something on the first try. "It didn't work."

"If you need them for your lightning, then maybe you should leave them out," Hawthorne suggested.

Declan sucked his teeth. The situation wasn't ideal. Lightning or no, he had no clue what to tell her about a partial transformation. He didn't know partial transformations were possible. Of course, nothing was off limits for his apprentices now. But this was what they had to work with so they would just have to roll with it. "Any questions before we split up?"

"I still think I should go with Alia," Galvin protested.

"Didn't ask for complaints, only questions."

"What do you want us to do with the thing when we find it?" Hawthorne asked.

"Keep it busy, keep it out of the grove, heal it as much as you can, but, whatever you do, don't kill it."

Hawthorne crossed his arms and frowned.

"Yeah, I don't think you have to worry about that." Alia gave up on pulling the shirt over her head and just used it to cover her front and shoulders.

Declan hadn't worked with a team this raw in a long time. It was going to be interesting.

40

Hawthorne followed Alia as she wandered the woods, listening for the faint sounds of the poor thing's cries for help. She was getting worried about how well the guardian was holding up because the sounds were becoming less intelligible and more miserable. It was also heading away from the grove, like an animal looking for a place to hide before it passed.

Alia clutched Galvin's extra shirt tighter around her arms and pulled her wings in closer and shivered. Early November was not the time to be running around at higher altitudes without a warm top. Because of the wings, which did *not* want to go away for some reason, all she had managed to do was put her arms through the sleeves. Galvin, who never got cold and only ever wore a sweater if it looked nice, had packed a short-sleeved tee, which provided minimal protection. Cool air hit the back of her neck and she shuddered again.

"Oh, for fuck's sake," Hawthorne grumbled as he pulled her up short. He waved his hands at her wings, wanting her to open them.

If she thought he cared what her bare body looked like, she might have blushed, but she didn't get those vibes from him, so she did as he asked.

He pulled the shirt off her arms and gave it a tug when she didn't immediately let go. She narrowed her eyes, a doubt creeping into her stomach, but Hawthorne didn't seem like the type. She let him take the shirt.

He shook it and held it out flat with the back facing her. Snapped his fingers over the fabric and it disintegrated into tiny floating particles. He took the bottom and pulled it over her head. Once on, the particles came back together as a complete garment with room for her wings to stick out the back.

"Better?" he asked.

"Yes, actually," she said, relieved her gut had been right. "Thank you."

He turned and kept walking.

Alia had met very few other magic users, usually in passing or in secret dealings with Declan. Out of all those people, Hawthorne had witnessed the most about the druids and had, so far, pried the least. "You know, you're decidedly not curious."

Hawthorne raised one blond eyebrow at her, his face otherwise devoid of emotion. "Would you rather I ask about your wings?"

"Well, no."

"How about your inability to do magic on Halloween?"

"No—"

"Or the creepy brain thing you have with your boyfriend?"

"He's not my boyfriend!" He was right, though. She much

preferred him to not ask questions. "But point taken. Don't look a gift horse in the mouth."

She had to admit, while this whole experience had put her off warlocks, Hawthorne was the one redeeming factor that reminded her you couldn't judge an entire group from just a few people. Galvin certainly liked him. Probably because he was the first real wizard Galvin had talked to. For Galvin, that was like getting to meet a celebrity.

"If anything," she teased, "Galvin's your boyfriend."

Hawthorne clicked his tongue, scrunching up his face. "Are you even looking for this beast thing?"

"Yes, but it's harder to hear. We were close, but now it's not saying anything. It's like it's forgetting how to speak, or just giving up." Alia rebuffed his skeptical look. "And no, I don't really want you asking about that either."

He shrugged, the movement smug as if to further prove he was right.

Alia ignored him. She tried calling out to the guardian, imitating its bugle sound and making Hawthorne jump. She had never gotten the chance to physically talk to a guardian outside her dreams, but its call was similar to an elk's.

Nothing responded. She searched among the trees, hoping to see it approach. Hawthorne was staring at her but very considerately did not say anything.

Alia sighed, her shoulders and wings sagging. "I thought we were close but now I don't know where it's at. It's not answering me."

Hawthorne tensed just as the hair on the back of Alia's neck stood up. Danger was close by. He groaned, his gaze drifting upward with little amusement. "It's right behind us, isn't it?"

Together, they turned to see the guardian standing behind them.

Alia moaned, her heart sinking at the sight of it. It was just as bad as she had predicted. Black goo dripped from the skull's empty eye sockets as well as its nostrils. It wheezed, and the poison dripped from its mouth when it fell open. Alia's wanted to cry. The poor thing had been fighting for its life this whole time.

Help... me... please...

Gently, Alia lifted a hand toward its face, slightly unfurling her wings to free her arms, and shushed as it leaned in. "It's okay," she whispered. "We're here to help." Slowly, she filled her palm with sunlight, not daring to move too fast in fear the guardian might startle and attack.

Thankfully Hawthorne seemed to understand not to spook it as well. The bands on his wrists dimly lit up, preparing in case they did have to fight the monster inside before she could heal the guardian. Maybe partly because he was still nervous around it.

Needing more room for her arm to move, Alia continued to unfurl her wings. Just a little farther and the sunlight would touch the poison. She continued approaching gingerly, sensing the creature struggle. It needed help and knew Alia was the one who could, but it was scared she and Hawthorne would attack it.

Gradually, one light beam at a time, Hawthorne's blades took shape. He must have felt the guardian's unease too.

The guardian's eyes filled with red and it yanked its head back, shrieking into the sky, and pulled a clawed hand up to slash at them. Hawthorne stepped between Alia and the guardian, bringing his blades up in time to block it. He had opted for a less lethal style this time, the blades more like shields than swords. And not covered in fire.

Alia flared open her wings, summoning lightning and directing it toward the guardian's head, wanting to clear the toxin there first, hoping that would help it know itself better, but the creature dodged the bolts and roared at her. The lightning scorched the trees and rocks behind the creature, leaving black, smoking scars everywhere it touched.

While pressing Hawthorne with one hand, the guardian lifted the second, aiming to slash him under the shield. Hawthorne managed to get one shield down to his side just as the creature swatted him, sending him crashing into a tree.

Alia winced, feeling bad that he seemed to go flying every time they faced the guardian. At least the tree wasn't as solid to hit as stone.

Free, the guardian stalked toward Alia. Sunlight, though safer, took too long to form into a large enough net. Alia flapped her great wings to generate several lightning bolts, theoretically, the more she threw, the more likely she was to hit the creature. Lightning cracked with each wing beat, scorching the guardian across the arms and torso, destroying the bits of toxin it touched. Her wings blew a gust so strong the beast was forced to stop advancing and leaned into the wind to keep its balance.

Recovering quickly, Hawthorne rushed toward the guardian and dropped to his knees to slide in. "Do that again!" he shouted as he threw himself at its legs.

Alia flapped, sending a gale force wind that, with Hawthorne's tackle, felled the guardian to its back. Lightning snapped, singing not only the guardian, but Hawthorne as well. He grunted when he was struck, his body twitching and the skin burning under each bolt, but otherwise held his ground.

Alia dashed in, conjuring sunlight as she climbed the creature to get to its face. If she could clear the toxin from the head, perhaps it would be able to think clearly enough to calm down and let her do the rest of its body.

She had barely gotten on top of the beast when it picked her up by her wings and tossed her off. This time it was her turn to go flying through the air. Her wings were pushed forward, but out of the way, as her back smacked into a tree. She fell to the ground and a sharp twinge stabbed her knee as it took the full impact, making her wince. It would hurt like hell later when it swelled but thankfully no bones had broken.

Back on her feet, Alia decided she needed a new plan. The offensive approach was not working. Hawthorne was currently using his blades to block the guardian's attacks while not harming it. That was good, but he wouldn't be able to hold out forever. If she couldn't get close to the guardian to heal parts one at a time, then she needed to maximize the amount of sunlight she exposed the thing to. She needed water. Ice probably would have been better, but he wasn't here right now.

Alia stepped into to the fight, summoning water from wherever she could find it in the dry forest. It was a lot tougher than calling it from nearer sources like she had before, but the water obeyed her, beginning to form at her call. She swirled it around Hawthorne and the guardian, making twirls of ribbon like a reversed maypole. She then created sunlight, lacing it with the streaming ribbons to reflect off the surface. The water amplified the light, shining it over the guardian in a blinding wave of light.

The guardian paused, its arms going stiff at its sides and its head thrown back. Its whole body twitched like a seizure as big pieces of toxin began to turn to ash and drift off and away. It was working and, as more toxin was removed, the seizure calmed, relaxing the guardian. Alia could have laughed for joy if she didn't have to concentrate so hard to keep both elements going at the same time. Finally, something was working!

Hawthorne wiggled his way out of the shining vortex and stood next to Alia, watching with approval. "About time you lived up to your reputation and did something impressive."

"Remind me to hit you later," she huffed out. "I'm a little too busy to do it now."

The toxin came off the guardian in huge chunks that didn't appear to be lessening. Sweat beaded on Alia's forehead despite the chill in the air, her arms shaking. If Declan and Galvin were going to finish anytime soon, now would be perfect.

As if he had heard her, Galvin called through their connection. Alia needed no further incentive to release the magic. She dropped her arms, the sunlight fading into regular daylight and the water crashing to the ground, splashing all of them.

The guardian looked the same. Skeletal head and hands with hoofed feet. It shouldn't still look like that; it should look like an animal. If Declan and Galvin had healed the grove, shouldn't the guardian be better too? Maybe getting it back to the grove would complete the process.

Alia didn't wait to see what the guardian would do now it was released from her magic. She grabbed Hawthorne by the arm. "Time to go," she told him, pulling him toward the grove.

41

With nothing better to do while Declan worked, Galvin paced back and forth in front of the archway. He hated splitting up. He knew why Declan had picked the assignments but he wanted to be out there helping Alia. Instead he was stuck here. Useless while Alia was in danger.

Declan's sunlight was doing the trick but it wasn't a speedy process. He had to hold the glowing light in his hands directly against the black toxin to burn it away. Unlike Alia, Declan could not shape and throw the light and only had an endless reserve while the sun was up. The sun which was currently sinking lower in the sky. If only he could cover the whole tree at once like Galvin was sure Alia could.

Alia would probably have a better idea. He reached to her with his thoughts, checking to make sure she was all right. She and Hawthorne must have found the guardian because her thoughts ran fast. She needed water, lots of it. Ice would be better, but that was his power, not hers. She was brilliant and sparked a concept of his own;

apparently he wasn't useless after all.

"Hang on," he told Declan, pulling him away from the tree. He was sweating under the heat of the light and the effort, despite the coolness of the weather. "I know how to make this easier." He conjured a small wall of ice at the base of the trunk, taking great care to make it as smooth and clear as possible. He angled it inward toward the tree. He had to calculate the angle in his head, so the degree was off a bit. Fortunately, the ice was forgiving with any adjustments he needed to make.

Declan grinned, patting Galvin on the back as he saw what he was creating. "That's more like it." He went back to work with his sunlight, shining it directly on the glass-like ice. The light reflected up to the trunk, the ice amplifying it to cover whole sections of the bark at one time. The toxin turned to ash and floated away in the wind in large chunks, like an ember fire. Unfortunately, the light was still limited by the reach of Declan's hands and the intensity of it melted the ice quickly, causing imperfections and ruining the reflective surface. But it was better than nothing and would allow Declan to finish before the sun went down.

Assuming Galvin didn't tire out first. He couldn't reform the mirror forever. His arm and chest were sore from the open gashes. The M.U.D. kept them closed and protected from his stinging perspiration but it still hurt when he shifted and the skin pulled at the wounds.

Declan might not get it done before he tired out too. Moisture dripped down his face, neck, and arms from the heat, and his arms began to shake. It was impressive. Galvin would have been tapped by now, but Declan still had a lot of strength to go on. Galvin prayed it was enough to last.

After Declan made a complete turn around the tree, the ice all but completely melted at the base, he stood back, taking a break and wiping his face. He gestured Galvin to the clean trunk while he caught his breath. "Alia says you're good with spells, so now it's your turn. Let's see what you got."

Easy-peasy. He and Alia had memorized the upgrade spell and performed it four times now. He should be able to knit this one back together no problem.

He stepped up to the trunk, looking at the sliced ends of the spell. The band of glowing symbols that should have surrounded the trunk hung limply where it was separated. Part of the band had been eaten away by the toxin and was missing some key symbols. That complicated things a little but Galvin was undeterred. He knew Alia's part of the spell and just hoped him casting it instead of her didn't cause any problems.

Galvin dug in his pack and pulled out his stylus wand. It was short, no longer than a regular ink pen and not all that dissimilar to one. It was mostly wood, carved from a branch shed by the anchor tree back home, with a small pointed crystal at the tip. He had made this special wand for laying magic into electronics, and it would work for filling in the spell. It allowed him to draw more dynamically on a constantly moving spell than chalk, which was more static. He had also never liked carrying chalk in his pocket; it was messy, and he didn't like the feeling on his hands. He sent magic into the wand and, when the crystal lit up, he began to write.

He replaced in the missing symbols. When each band of the spell matched end for end, he pulled and welded them together. He winced as the gash on his arm tugged under the dried M.U.D. The M.U.D. cracked and a little blood dripped down his arm. He ignored it and kept going.

It didn't take longer than a few minutes to repair the spell, and the grove to right itself. The band around the trunk settled, glowing and writhing like those on its larger sibling trees. The leaves glittered, coming back to life along with the symbols on the ground. In a matter of moments, the grove looked like a smaller version of the one back home.

Declan watched in awe. "I never thought I'd get to see this." His voice was low, reverent. "Is that what it looked like when you two cast the spell?"

"Close"—Galvin shrugged one shoulder—"but not quite. Everything was already here, just dormant."

Declan smiled, running a hand lovingly over the bark of the trunk. "Still beautiful." When the moment was over, he turned to Galvin, all business. "We're ready. Let her know."

Galvin sent Alia the message down their connection. He didn't receive so much of an answer as a jumble of thoughts and adrenaline that felt like static. He grew nervous, wondering if Alia and Hawthorne were in danger.

Noticing his furrowed brows and pensive stare, Declan frowned. "What's wrong?"

"I think they're with the guardian but I'm not getting a clear answer from her."

He thought that over. "Does your connection get weaker with distance?"

"I don't know, we haven't been this far apart before. Not counting the stuff that happened with Lucian. I didn't think they were that far away now." He hoped she and Hawthorne weren't in over their heads. *Where are you? Are you all right?*

Pounding footsteps in the clearing drew both Declan's and Galvin's attention. Irritation slammed through the connection as Alia shouted from just outside the archway. "This isn't as easy as it looks!"

The same words echoed in his head as well. His hand came up to his temple to dampen the sharp pounding that accompanied her scolding.

Alia rushed in, grabbed Galvin's arm, and dragged him farther in. Hawthorne trailed her, blocking swipes from the guardian and trying to keep it out as it lumbered along. The guardian panted and wheezed, trailing black toxin with each step. Scorch marks covered its dripping wet body.

Declan pulled at Hawthorne, bringing him back with the others and making room for the guardian to enter.

Hawthorne tried shaking him off. "It's going to trap us in here."

"We *want* it in here, to heal," Declan explained, tugging him to keep coming.

The four of them backed up, watching the guardian duck the stone archway and step into the grove. Its red eyes flickered in and out as it whimpered between growls. Each labored breath rattled, gurgling with toxin as it struggled to get air.

"This had better work," Hawthorne said, following the druids but not losing his fighting stance.

"I agree," Declan mumbled.

Galvin was more confident, having seen the grove heal him and Alia before, but Declan's comment didn't seem to comfort the Raptor. Galvin had to admit, they didn't really know what was going to happen.

The instant the guardian's hooves stepped into the grove, the magic circle responded. The ground and leaves glowed brighter, filling the space with warm light. Hawthorne's gaze left the guardian as he nervously examined what the grove was doing. Galvin recognized the familiar tingling warmth, though. It was the magic of the grove saturating their bodies to repair and protect its allies and destroy any enemies.

The light died down after only moments, leaving everyone whole and healthy. Hawthorne's burns were gone as well as the deep cuts on Galvin's arms and chest. Even the gashes on his back felt healed.

Where the skeletal creature once stood, a beautiful elk now took its place. Its fur sparkled with the same bioluminescent light as the grove and its antlers were covered in the same illuminated symbols. Instead of red eyes, soft brown ones looked at them. Galvin had seen elk in the Winter Court's forests, but this guy was huge. Galvin, at just over six feet, barely topped its shoulder.

It reared up on its hind legs, making a sort of snorting chuckle. Galvin tensed, thinking it might still attack them. He reached for Alia's arm to but the guardian turned and ran from the grove.

Alia flipped on the three of them too, eyes wide. "The warlocks are burning the forest, we have to go help him!" She dashed after the guardian.

Galvin's heart lurched as he went after her, Declan and Hawthorne close behind.

The forest burned.

Galvin froze, his mind racing. He had never seen so much fire before. He felt Alia's panic as she shouted, *No! No! No!* The flames and the smoke singed his lungs, making him cough and gasp for air.

The warlock team was making its way inward from the edge of where the camp had been, but so much was already ablaze. Four warlocks cast fire spells onto the trees while three followed, carrying things that looked like the ends of firehoses but weren't connected to anything. Nothing came out of the hoses and they were not casting spells, so presumably they were there in case they needed to put the fire out before it got out of hand. A warlock officer and an MP in white followed at a longer distance, the MP holding up a magic shield to protect them both.

As Galvin was still wrapping his head around what he saw, the guardian took action. Head down and antlers aimed at its targets, it charged the warlocks. The four soldiers turned toward the magical elk and it swept its antlers up at them. An iridescent wave scooped them off their feet, sending them flying backward.

Alia rushed in behind the animal, chanting an incantation. Her wings opened wide, waves of magic rippling along her feathers. As she beat her wings, the magic dispersed around them, rising up into the air.

The three in the water brigade lifted their hoses at Alia. She turned glowing eyes on them as water shot toward her. Still chanting, she raised her hand, took control of the rushing water, and guided it toward the flames.

The guardian stalked around her, using his great antlers to keep the warlocks from approaching her, but they would need help. Galvin moved to rush to Alia's side.

Declan pulled him up short. Galvin turned back to yell but Declan was pushing Hawthorne toward Alia instead. "Zayne, go!"

Hawthorne ran, neon blue magic forming from the silver bands on his wrists into a two-handed gun that looked like it belonged in a sci-fi movie. He flanked the guardian and shot lasers at the warlocks. Between the two, they protected Alia as she worked to put out the fire.

Galvin wanted to argue but Declan pointed to the officer and the MP, who were joining the confrontation. "We have to keep that MP away from Zayne if we don't want him losing his mind again."

Declan was right. If they wanted to keep Hawthorne on their side, they needed to deal with the MP. Galvin nodded, and he and Declan rushed side by side into the fray.

As they approached, the MP's shield came down and he manifested a gun from his silver bangle as well. He raised it, firing multiple shots. Declan dodged to the side, circling round toward the officer, and Galvin went the opposite direction toward the MP.

Galvin sheathed a blade as he charged and used his free hand to conjure a thick wall of ice between him and the MP. He curved it up and over, creating a tunnel around the MP as he approached. A blast from the MP's gun tore through the wall like it was a thin layer. Even at top speed, Galvin barely managed to avoid the shots. One grazed his shoulder, burning through his shirt and blistering the skin underneath. He clenched his teeth, groaning, but did not stop running.

As the distance between them grew smaller, the MP stepped into Galvin's path, transforming his gun into a giant axe. He anticipated where Galvin was going to be and swung it down.

Thankfully, he was not as fast as Hawthorne. Galvin saw him raise the axe and spun out of the way at the last second. It passed close to his body, barely missing him as he dodged. Twisting, Galvin unsheathed his second blade, slashing down and brought the other up, trying to get inside the MP's open defense. They were close enough Galvin could see the MP's silver eyes. They were empty and lifeless, much as Hawthorne's had been when he attacked Galvin.

Was the MP brainwashed too?

The clang of steel on steel reached Galvin's ears before he noticed the axe, now a sword, block Galvin's downward attack.

But it didn't stop Galvin's upward attack.

The MP realized his mistake and stepped back to avoid the attack, but it was too late. It sliced across his torso. It wasn't deep but enough to cut open his uniform and leave a small trail of red that marred the monochrome white.

As the MP winced, Galvin saw it. Static hanging around the MP's temples. Galvin reached out, calling it toward him. It flew from the warlock's head to his hand. If felt odd. It wasn't magic but it had the same ability to muddle thoughts. Was this what "conditioning" looked like? Galvin shook his hands, not wanting to keep it or affect someone else like he had the bully warlock from the camp.

Holding his head, the MP started to scream, making Galvin nearly jump out of his skin. The sound was awful. He was terrified and in a pain Galvin couldn't begin to fathom. Galvin froze, unsure what he had done or what to do to fix it. He looked around for Declan to help him.

The screaming stopped the fight between Declan and the officer. The officer looked between Galvin and the MP, now on his knees and clutching his head like he was trying to keep it together. The officer's eyes went wide and he began to back away from Declan. "Retreat!" he shouted to his other warlocks. "Fall back!"

Galvin's mouth dropped open. He wanted to say something but had no idea what to tell them. All he could do was watch as the officer dragged the MP away and, one by one, the warlocks all touched something on their uniforms and disappeared.

Lightning split the sky and rain began to pour in sheets. Declan grabbed Galvin's arm and led him under the cover of the undamaged forest canopy. The rain dribbled through, soaking both of them, but at least they could see each other. "What happened?" Declan asked.

Galvin shook his head and shrugged. "I don't know. I saw this fuzzy stuff around his head and I pulled it away. Then he started screaming."

Declan's eyes turned sad and their quick dart to Hawthorne spoke volumes.

"I thought it would clear his mind but I made it worse. I shouldn't have done it."

Declan's face twisted and his shoulders raised toward his ears. "To be honest, I don't know what happened. But from now on, let's not remove anything out of anyone's head 'til we know what it is."

Galvin nodded.

"Hey," Alia called, waving them over. Hawthorne had picked up one of the discarded hoses and was pouring water on anything still burning, while the guardian used its magic to extinguish the flames. "Are you two going to help or what?"

Declan squeezed Galvin's arm, and they ran to help. Declan used another of the warlocks' hoses to blast any remaining flames. Using his control of fire, Galvin reached for the flames and quieted them with his will until they fizzled out. The five of them together, with the rain, managed the extinguish the forest before too much damage was done. After each put out their last fire, they retreated under the forest canopy and out of the pouring rain. Their clothes were soaked, mud covered their shoes and legs, their faces were smudged with soot, and Galvin's shoulder burned, but they had done it. The forest would be fine.

The guardian was the last to join them. It fixed soft eyes on

Alia, stepping slowly and gracefully up to her and lowering its head to her upraised hands. Smiling, Alia stroked its nose, rubbing gently up the beast's face. It nuzzled her lovingly and Alia giggled. It pulled back, making direct eye contact with her, before touching its forehead to hers.

Galvin didn't hear anything but he could tell they were having a conversation. Alia's head tilted to the side as she put her hand into her pocket and pulled out what was inside. Some empty vials, a couple magic bullets, some charms with the Arbor Clan symbol on them, and Declan and Evelyn's marriage coin sat in her open palms.

She held her these out to the guardian but it turned away and walked back into the forest. With each step it took, life returned to the earth around them. Grass grew under the guardian's hooves, the plants and trees regained their color, birds and insects chirped, and, somewhere close by, Galvin heard water rushing.

Galvin watched it go, feeling a little underwhelmed. "Why didn't it acknowledge us?" he asked Declan.

He shrugged, seeming resigned. "Guardians always favor the ones who can talk to them. Not much point with the rest of us, so they don't usually bother."

"Oh."

"Holy mother."

The three druids looked to the only warlock at his soft exclamation. He stood there, soaked through and as dirty as the rest of them. Blood leaked from cuts on his arms and chest but he didn't seem to notice. He looked at each of them. "Do all druids wait until the end to do all the impressive stuff? Or is that just a you guys thing?"

All three of them chuckled and Declan stepped up to him. "Zayne, I'm not sure how much trouble you're going to be in for helping us."

"A lot," Hawthorne confirmed. "But I'll figure something out."

Declan handed him a charm. "If you need someplace to go, our home has plenty of room and will always be open to you."

Hawthorne took the offered token, a slight smile at the corners of his mouth. "I think I have somewhere to go but I'll keep that in mind in case things fall through. Thank you."

"No, thank you," Declan said, "for giving up everything to do what was right. Please take care of yourself."

"Yes, sir."

Declan faced Alia and Galvin, hands on his hips. "All right, you two, I know we don't mean to heal and leave but we have to get home."

42

Declan was concerned about what they would find when they got back to the Arbor estate. After making the jump home, he ran ahead, Alia and Galvin following through the hedge and up to the house. He couldn't help but wonder what kind of disaster awaited them when they got there. An army of warlocks ready to arrest them? Traps all over the house? He shoved open the outside doors to the ballroom, bracing himself for what was on the other side.

He crossed the ballroom and through the inside doors, and the first thing that greeted him was the hall closet. The doors were pulled off the hinges and everything inside was scattered on the floor. His stomach sank and he felt cold and clammy. Out of all the scenarios that had played through his head, being ransacked was not one of them. There were any number of objects that would be disastrous if she stole, most of which didn't even belong to the druids but were part of Theo's horde.

Oh God, Theo's horde. Declan ran down the hall, skidded

around the corner, passed the foyer and the common room. The common room door sat open too, still on its hinges, and Declan caught a glance of books strewn about and drawers turned out. The shelves were snapped and splintered and fragile knickknacks were shattered everywhere.

Swinging around the next corner he saw, thankfully, the door to the Link Room remained shut and fastened, though the doors themselves looked worse for wear—deep gashes, splintered wood—but the damage wasn't enough to admit entry. It would've been more than bad if Grace had gotten unfettered access to the other anchor groves.

Declan slid to a halt in front of the hidden door to Theo's lab. It was thrown open, all the shelves on the hidden door broken, with the books and more knickknacks on the floor. The lock and handle were also in pieces. Declan's heart sank. This was so much worse than anything that could have happened. If he had his choice, he would have picked to take on an entire army of warlocks than for Grace to rob Theo's horde.

The lab was just as trashed as the rest of the place. Shelves broken, books everywhere, and altars destroyed. Theo was going to be furious when he found out. How had Grace managed any of this? The cuffs should have prevented her from doing anything but sit around and wait for them to get back.

Declan rushed to the bookcase where he knew Theo had hidden another door. This one too was open. He groaned, praying to the Supreme Being and whomever of His angels were listening Grace was intelligent enough not to take anything that belonged to a dragon. Declan wasn't sure even a miracle, would save *him* if any piece went missing under his watch. He rushed inside, hoping he wouldn't find the place completely destroyed like the rest of the house.

To his relief, nothing seemed to be touched. Theo displayed all the rare magical items he had collected over the centuries on rows and rows of neat shelves. Each item was clearly labeled with a name but not with a description of what it could do. Declan suspected that was because Theo already knew what each item could do but it might also have been to discourage others from taking things.

He walked up and down the rows of shelves, making sure each label had a corresponding object. Though he would gladly thank the divine if everything were present, he couldn't understand why Grace would come down here if she didn't intend to take anything. Still, nothing was out of place in every spot he checked, a thin layer of dust confirming even Theo hadn't been down here in a bit.

It wasn't until he reached the back of the room that he found what had been Grace's goal. A mount on the wall made for a small blade sat empty. The blood drained from Declan's face and he thought he might be sick. He had personally given that particular dagger to Theo for safekeeping. The card underneath confirmed the dagger connecting him, his best friend Tiberius, and the demon who hunted them, Mathias—locking each one in their respective realm—was gone.

Declan screamed in anger, pacing back and forth. Grace had stolen the one thing that could destroy everything the druids had fought for. Everything he had almost lost Alia and Galvin for just a few weeks ago. What they *had* lost Tiberius for. Had lost *all* the druids for. They had just gotten to a point where he thought they were safe from the constant onslaught of demon attacks, and Grace had stolen the object that would ruin all of it.

No, he realized, remembering there was something else that would be devastating if she had found and taken it. *Not all the druids.*

He ran out of Theo's vault and through his lab, passing a startled Alia and Galvin, and rushed up the stairs. Alia called to him as they tried to keep up with him but he didn't slow down. If Grace had discovered there were other druids, they would be in grave danger.

The door to the council room had been ripped off and lay splintered across the hall. Declan cursed under his breath. Not only was he going to have to change all the Arbor Grove's wards, he would need to look into better locks. He wasn't sure what sort of magic Grace had used to break through even Theo's seals but they would need to figure out more effective ways to keep intruders out.

The room was destroyed. The large council table had been snapped in half. The chairs were in pieces and every cabinet door had been torn off and everything inside tossed about.

Declan went straight to the open cabinet of powerful druid items and found most of them gone. Not scattered around the debris, but taken. Declan's blood boiled, but it made more sense than Theo's almost pristine horde vault. Apparently Grace did know what she was doing by only stealing what she absolutely needed from a dragon but taking freely from those she didn't see as a big threat.

Thankfully, the communicator was still there. It was too old and common to be of any value, and practically useless unless she knew someone who could translate the druid knots. It was turned on but Declan didn't see any messages. He quickly typed a warning to the other groves.

Arbor Grove breached. Must replace wards. Repeat last message. Confirm safety. D.A.

"What are you doing?" Alia and Galvin had finally made it up the stairs. Alia spread her arms, emphasizing her question, her wings rustling to mimic the movement. "Why is the house in shambles, and where is Grace?"

"We've been robbed." It came out snappier than he intended

and he made himself pause to check his tone with his apprentices. The anger and anxiety at the violation of their sacred estate and home was getting to him. It was an acceptable feeling after such a betrayal but that didn't make it right to take it out on them.

"I realize that," she shot back, glaring and crossing her arms. "But you've been running back and forth like you're going to catch her in the act." She sighed, placing her fisted hands on her hips. "It's bad if she took anything, but what has you so worried?"

The communicator clicked to life and a reply typed out on the roll of paper. Declan ripped it off, barely letting it finish.

Just arrived at Nome. No messages sent prior to this one. We are safe here. Everything in bad shape. What the heck did you guys do to this place? E.A.

Declan chuckled. He had told Erik to go to Ingadi, but perhaps Nome was better. The Nome lodge had taken quite a beating when Alia and Galvin upgraded the groves. It was the last one and had been unstable longer.

Erik had also written *we*, not *I*. Declan sighed. It soothed him a great deal knowing not only were there more druids, but they were safe.

Alia stepped up next to him, taking the missive from his hand and reading it over. "Who's at Nome? Who's E.A.?"

Declan smiled up at the two of them. "Things are bad but I do have some good news in all of this." He laid a hand on each of their shoulders. "There's a lot we need to catch up on, but we're not alone after all."

There was one more thing Declan wanted to check before trying to calm down with a shower. He closed the door to his office and hurried to his desk. He pulled Galvin's phone out of the top drawer and tapped the buttons, calling the only contact programmed.

After three rings, Theo's face showed up on the screen. He was lounging in a chair somewhere sunny. A pair of dark glasses covered his eyes, the sound of waves in the background. Was he on a beach?

"Yes?" he asked, his voice sounding sleepy.

"Where are you?" Declan demanded. "Are you all right?"

Theo sat up, pushing his sunglasses up, looking worried, and Declan got a glimpse of palm trees and sand behind him. Definitely a beach. Theo's expression turned irritated. "I haven't pillaged any cities or destroyed any governments, if that's what you're worried about."

"Theo," Declan snapped. *"Are you all right?"*

"I'm fine. I'm at The Brando."

Declan sighed. If Grace had found out about Theo, there was no way the Council wouldn't have attacked him by now. Theo was safe for the time being.

"Wait." Declan realized what Theo had said and shook his head. "Are you on *vacation?*"

Theo dropped the sunglasses down and lay back in his chair. "You kicked me out, remember? Said I needed to experience the world again." He shrugged. "I spent a long time in that cold forest so I went somewhere to warm my scales."

Declan couldn't argue with those facts. "You could have picked any beach anywhere, and you pick an exclusive and expensive private island in French Polynesia?"

"There's also an enchanted reef here I was going to explore in a few days." Declan shouldn't have been surprised. "Why did you need to know I was all right?"

Declan blew out a breath. "Grace set us up. The Council ransacked the estate. Don't worry," he said, cutting off the question Theo was sure to ask, "your horde is fine. I checked it myself. The only thing she took was my dagger."

Theo sat up and raised his sunglasses again. "Do you need me to come back?"

"No, stay on vacation. We'll handle things here. The most important thing is for you to remain hidden." Declan narrowed his eyes at the screen. "Maybe try to be a bit more inconspicuous."

Lying back down, Theo rolled his eyes and dropped his sunglasses again. "It's a private island. Who's going to find me?"

Declan smiled. Theo deserved a warm holiday, and he was happy to see him adapting so well already. Of course, the real test would happen when there were actual people around. "Fine. But don't forget to call and check in."

"It's only been three days."

Had it? It felt like a lot longer. "Theo, please."

"Fine. But only because I need to keep an eye on you guys."

Declan's grin returned. "Thank you."

"Yeah. Look, I have a beach nap to get to and it looks like you need a shower. I'll talk to you later."

"Bye. And be safe!" Theo had already hung up. Declan put the phone on his desk. A glance at his arm showed he was still covered in drying mud and soot from the fire. He was a mess. "Ah, man. I do need a shower."

43

Alia sat in the bathroom, staring at herself in the mirror as it fogged with steam from the filling bath, her new thunderbird wings sticking up behind her. The first night back at the Arbor estate had been the hardest. The three of them had been going nonstop for the past few days and Alia, like the guys, was completely drained. She had lost so much sleep that the little she got on Halloween wasn't enough for her to feel rested. Her wings were heavy, and so many muscles she had not used like this before were screaming and sore from holding them up.

They had come home from healing the grove to find their house had been robbed. Worst of all, Declan's dagger was missing. He had told them not to worry about it tonight and to go to bed.

Alia did worry about it, though. Just a few weeks ago, they had nearly died trying to get the dagger back and now it was gone again. Grace couldn't use it but she could go to Mathias or Lucian for help.

Alia finished off her calming tea, set the mug on the counter, and turned off the water. She looked down at the tub, wondering how her wings were going to fit. How was she to manage *anything* with wings? Not just the bath, but her whole life. Would she ever be able to put them away or was she going to be part thunderbird forever?

Alia closed her eyes and stopped the spiral of thoughts. Declan was right. Worrying wouldn't do any good and exhaustion made everything seem worse than it really was. She took a deep breath. *One step at a time.* Then let it out. *First the bath, then bed.* Another in. *Tomorrow is a brand new day to figure everything else out.* And out once more. With each breath, the tension left her shoulders. With her third exhale, the weight on her back shrank, leaving her scrambling to regain her balance and not topple face-first into the bath.

She opened her eyes and looked in the mirror. Her wings had disappeared, leaving her aching muscles begging for the warmth of the water. She smiled, feeling a little better as she slipped into the bath.

She soaked and washed, taking her time. When she was clean, the water had cooled and her eyes were heavy enough to droop closed. She dried off and put on her pajamas.

Now standing and staring at her bed, she wasn't as ready to crawl in anymore. She had broken free of Lucian's hold but how long would that last? Would he come back for her in her dreams? What if she was never safe again?

She shook her head. No, she had to stop thinking like that. She had defeated Lucian. Never again would he be able to make her afraid of him. Even if he was stupid enough to attack her again, he had lost his greatest power over her. She was safe now and forever.

So why did she still fear the nightmares?

She glanced at her bedroom door. Galvin had been able to keep her safe for a bit before, and she debated asking him. Would he be able to do it? Even if the nightmares weren't caused by Lucian but her own subconscious? He'd probably be irritated if she woke him up; he didn't wake up well when he was tired. She doubted he would be angry if she asked, since he had insisted on helping her before, but that was when she was in danger. Lucian was gone, so now she was just being scared. Would Galvin think her pathetic for being terrified of the thought of nightmares?

She looked back to her bed. She really should be tougher than this. She should stop fussing, get in bed, and get the sleep she needed.

A soft knock on the door made her jump. She turned to see Galvin standing there, his eyes barely open. He wore sleep pants and nothing else. She was lucky he wore even that, seeing as how he never got cold.

He had really bulked up in the past few weeks and the pants sat snugly on his hips. His white tattoo was on full display as the vines circled his chest, waist, and back, rising and falling over the muscle he was quickly developing. The healed gash from Hawthorne's attack marred his otherwise pristine skin. This adventure had left him with his first scars. It looked good on him, all of it. The scars, the muscle, that tattoo.

Alia noticed some leaves and the druid markings woven in the vines appeared a brighter white in places and more grayish and blueish in other areas. She was almost certain it hadn't been like that before. The tattoo had been one white color.

Galvin blinked heavy eyelids at her. "What's wrong?" His voice was thick and raspy with sleep.

"What do you mean?"

He stood there, too tired to argue. Too tired to even send his irritation down the connection. With a patience that always surprised her, he waited for her to tell him, trying to keep his eyes from falling closed for too long.

Alia's shoulders sank, defeated. "I'm…" She wasn't quite sure how to put her jumble of feelings into words. "I don't…" She was scared, but she couldn't bring herself to admit it. Especially not to Galvin, when she was supposed to be strong and put together. He'd relied so much on her when they were upgrading the groves. What would happen if he found out she really wasn't the badass he thought she was? He'd think her a silly girl. As silly as any of the courtiers he was used to who only wanted to use him. She turned away, hugging her arms and glowering at the bed. Why wasn't she stronger than this?

Galvin slipped his hand over one of hers, unraveling the protective barrier her arms had made around her. She looked up at him, terrified she would find him judging her. All she found was him regarding her warmly. Well, mostly sleepily, but she thought there was some warmth. He nodded and gently tugged on her hand, entreating her to follow. She let him lead her away.

He took her out into the hallway and she assumed they would go down to the kitchen for something soothing to drink. Instead, he walked away from the stairs. The only thing in this direction was his room, right next to hers. "Where are we going?"

"I'm tired," he replied, "you're tired. We're going to bed."

A nervous thrill went through her and she quickly stamped it out. She pulled back on reflex, but Galvin ignored her. His hand squeezed hers and he continued toward his bedroom. She had shared a sleeping space with him on several occasions at this point. He'd even held her while she slept to keep the nightmares away. This shouldn't be any different.

But it was. It was different because she didn't have to fight

Lucian anymore. It was different in the way he held her hand. In the way he said they were going to bed. In the way she had a hard time not looking at his bare back without blushing.

He had left his door open on his way out and easily led her into his room. He hadn't tidied up yet after Grace had gone through their stuff. Not like Alia had, but then he wasn't trying to avoid sleep like she was. She had also needed to do it, to remove Grace's presence from her room—a step toward healing what she had done to their home.

Galvin guided her to his bed, where he pulled the covers back and guided her in. He gestured for her to scoot to the other side to make room for him before lying down. He slid in after her and covered them both, unfolding the heavier blanket he never used at the foot of his bed to ensure she was warm enough.

Alia rolled to her side, getting as comfortable as she could in Galvin's bed, his body close. She tried distracting her mind by examining the things around her, hoping to calm it enough to drift off. He was beginning to make the space his. The decorations were the same as in the other unassigned rooms but he had started collecting his own things. A deconstructed electronic gadget on his desk, a radio and a couple books on the bookshelf. Despite being mostly empty, his room was comfortable, peaceful. The biggest difference was Lucian hadn't tainted Galvin's room like he had hers.

Galvin's arm wound around her waist, pulling her close. Alia's heart raced and she stiffened, turning feverish next to him. His cheek rested on the top of her head, keeping his face out of her hair even though she braided it when she slept. She wanted to snuggle closer but she shouldn't be thinking that. Instead, she scrunched her eyes closed, forcing away the traitorous feelings beginning to brew. At that moment, she regretted following him. She was never going to get any sleep this way.

He didn't move, just held her close, so neither did she. She was almost sure he was already asleep. The weight of his arm and head and his even breathing became a comfort, more so than being someplace Lucian had not touched her, where she didn't have to shove away memories of the nauseating things he had done to her.

She let Galvin comfort her. She lay still, eyes closed, focusing on his chest rising and falling against her back. Her own breathing slowed to match his and her eyes grew heavy enough that she didn't have to work to keep them closed. Her awareness of the room began to fade as her consciousness wandered from reality, slowly and softly falling into peaceful dreams.

44

Somewhere in the fog of sleep, Galvin was aware of Alia sliding out from under his arm and out of bed, but he wasn't conscious enough to think anything of it. He let himself sink further from consciousness.

That first morning after returning home had been all about strengthening their defenses before Grace returned with an army, and Declan was almost positive she would. The three of them had walked the perimeter of the village, using magic from dawn until dusk to lay new protection spells exactly as Declan showed them. It pushed them each to their limits and Galvin wasn't sure he would have been able to do it if it hadn't been for the fruit. But Declan assured them no one would get in after the wards were up and, if they waited and did it slowly, it was possible the spell would fall apart before the next morning and they risked someone sneaking in.

Galvin had thought the anchor grove's borders were limited to the house and garden where the tree was, but Declan explained that was just the inner circle, with the estate house at the entrance. Ingadi was probably the best example to compare to the Arbor Grove. The house was the temple, with the inner circle being the hedge maze and garden attached to the house. The actual border of the grove was much bigger, like Ingadi's surrounding city. The Arbor Grove, Galvin learned, was not quite as large but the size of a small village. Most of the village was abandoned and run down now, but there were enough houses and shops within the grove's borders to accommodate and employ a couple thousand people. He supposed he should have realized that after Alia had taken him to the church, but it hadn't clicked until they walked the entire thing and Galvin got his first real look at the whole place. Nome must have been very similar to Arbor, though he hadn't seen anything more than the lodge.

Alia squeezed his arm before shaking him. "Wake up, sleepyhead."

He absolutely did not want to wake up. He was exhausted. They had been home for a whole day and had still not finished all the work that awaited their arrival. He groaned, pulling the covers back over his head. Just one more minute.

Alia yanked the covers off him and gave him another vigorous shake.

He moaned again.

"I know you're tired but we still have so much to do. You remember the state of the house."

He did, but it could be cleaned when they were well rested. "We don't have to get up at the crack of dawn to fix the house," he complained, rolling up into a seated position.

"Galvin, it's way past dawn. It's almost ten in the morning."

He opened one bleary eye. She was fully showered and dressed in a soft, berry-colored sweater and a pair of leggings. He watched her dig through his dresser for clothes, admiring the fit of those leggings. Why didn't she wear those more often?

His view became obstructed when she threw a shirt at him over her shoulder. Even without looking, her aim was spot on, the garment landing over his view. He pulled it off and peeked at the clock on the nightstand. He hadn't realized he had dozed so late. He rubbed the sleep from his face as best he could and pulled on the shirt.

When his head popped out, Alia stood in front of him, this time with a pair of socks and jeans, grinning from ear to ear. Galvin grumbled, almost flopping back over on the bed. Whatever had her grinning seemed like far too much work for his liking. "I don't want to."

Alia rolled her eyes. "Trust me, you'll like this. Now hurry up." She bounced out of the room, giving him another delightful look at her leggings.

Galvin finished changing. He had showered before going to bed and his hair now stuck up at funny angles from drying on his pillow. He ran a brush through it to try and tame it.

As he ambled downstairs, the smell of sweet and tangy cooking filled the air. He followed it and the sounds of clanking pots and pans into the kitchen.

There he found Declan and Alia, both wearing aprons, with just about every pot, bowl, and utensil out on the counters. Any space not filled with a bowl or a pot was covered with the glowing, magical fruit from the tree. Declan was cutting them into small bits which he slid into the big stockpot on the stove, while Alia was making slices and laying them out on a papered sheet.

Galvin took in the mayhem. "What are you doing?"

They turned and smiled in greeting. Alia gestured with her free hand over to the only section of counter in the whole kitchen not covered in fruit. "I left some coffee and breakfast for you."

Declan approached, wiping his hands on a stained towel. "Well, you two wanted us to do Halloween. Here's part of it." He gestured to the fruit laid out in the kitchen. "We need to process all of this into stuff we can keep for the year."

"Like what?" Galvin asked through a yawn, making his way over to his breakfast. Alia had indeed left him some coffee—iced, just the way he liked it. She had also made some toast, bacon, and a few slices of the magical fruit.

Declan shrugged. "Some will be jam and butter, Alia is dehydrating some over there. I've also convinced her to make a couple pies for us, and I'm going to make something I haven't made in a long time."

"And what's that?" Galvin asked around a mouthful of bacon.

Declan grinned. "Wine."

It took them all day to process all the fruit. Alia politely declined Galvin's offer to help so he was instead assigned to Declan make the wine. Galvin had drunk plenty fairy wine in his time at balls and parties but had never seen the process of making it and was excited to learn. Plus, it was going to be made with the hallow fruit—hallow wine.

Declan and Galvin spent the first several hours picking out the just ripe fruit and separating them by color. Each color had its own flavor and mixing them could have either beautiful or disastrous results. Decan explained it was best to mix with intention, not by accident.

Once the ripe fruit was separated, Declan showed Galvin how to press them into juice. He pulled an old wooden machine out from the cellar and took it into the yard. It was simple, basically a bowl with a solid plate the operator twisted down to the bottom to smash the fruit with little effort. It took them well into the afternoon to press all the piles, the sun overhead warming the day and making Galvin sweat.

After pressing, they took the juice inside the cellar, where Declan showed him these great clay pots. He explained that the juice would ferment in the pots until the Winter Solstice before the druids did anything else with it, but first the pots needed to be cleaned. So they lugged the clay pots outside, where they washed them with soap and water to get the years of dust and dirt out of them. They left them in the sun to dry, going back inside to check on Alia.

It was a lot warmer inside the kitchen than it was outside. She had made a good dent in her portion of the fruit, with three different stockpots simmering on the stove. She was just pulling a beautiful pie out of the oven. Deep red fruit bubbled under a latticework crust, the smell sweet and spicy. Galvin's stomach growled as she set it on a rack on the counter next to two others. He knew firsthand how delicious Alia's cooking was and he was practically drooling to try it. Theo had taught her everything he knew about cooking, and he was better than any chef at the Winter Palace.

Galvin and Declan spent some time inside helping her, canning the jam while it was warm and Alia cleaning up behind them. They laid out about ten jars of delicious-smelling jam to cool on the counter.

Galvin looked at the clothed red tops and realized where he had tasted the fruit before. "I've been eating this since I got here."

Alia chuckled. "Yes, that was our last jar from the grove where we lived when you found us."

He put the warm jar back on the counter with the others. "And this stuff boosts our powers? How come we don't all just overpower everyone?"

Declan munched on one of the leftover fruits. "There has always been debate about how much of our power is boosted and how much is returned after Hallowtide, whether it's a permanent or a temporary boost, and if the strength of the boost is affected once the fruit is cooked. There have not been any definitive studies on the subject to prove one way or the other."

"But we've had Hallowtides when we couldn't get fruit before," Alia pointed out, handing Galvin a leftover too. He didn't hesitate before devouring it. "But we usually had enough preserves to last until the next Hallowtide."

"That's true. But even some years when I didn't have any, my power always returned to the same level it had been before it faded. As long as we challenge ourselves, we continue to grow in strength, fruit or not, so that's hardly a concrete answer."

Galvin and Declan each polished off one more before going back out to finish the wine. This time, Declan had an old recipe book. They first brought the fermentation vessels to the cellar and Declan began to brew.

He followed a couple of his favorite recipes. Some juices he mixed, some he poured in pure. Once each pot was filled with the appropriate mix of juice, he added sugar and yeast. Then he sealed up the containers.

Before heading inside, Declan looked through the old dusty bottles lining the shelves on the walls. He handed a few to Galvin and carried a few himself. The labels were from a time before Declan had gone into hiding. When their hands were full, he gestured for them to go inside. "Come on, let's see what Alia's made for dinner. I'm dying to try that pie."

45

It took them a few days to assess all the damage to the house. Broken doors, shelves, and antiques littered the halls and rooms. Not a single book had been left on a shelf or a picture hanging on the wall. Alia wondered how one person could have gone through the whole estate by herself, leaving such a big mess in the process. Perhaps a spell had done all the damage. Either that or she had let people in to help her. It was going to take them a long time to pick the place up by themselves.

Not to mention there was a whole curriculum's worth of more training to do. Alia had to learn to wield lightning safely and strengthen her skill, as well as how to use her wings. Right now, she couldn't manage more than some sparks without her wings out. After training, she came back from the grounds sore and barely able to walk. Learning to use muscles she didn't know she had to strengthen her wings enough to fly was a challenge. Another area she struggled with was separating the lightning power from her anger. She had seen from Galvin's practice how difficult that could be.

Declan was also working with Galvin on his burgeoning spirit powers. Galvin seemed hesitant to do anything with ghosts but Declan promised that the more he trained, the better he would get at dictating when and where ghosts could pester him. For now, he constantly heard and saw things Alia couldn't. It was unsettling at first, but she was getting used to it.

It was Galvin's spirit abilities that had helped keep her safe from Lucian and one of the reasons she was still sleeping next to him at night. She knew she had banished Lucian from her mind—he could not attack her any longer—but Galvin's presence made her feel safer.

Declan and Galvin worked diligently to hone Galvin's powers. Not just for Alia's sake but also because Galvin didn't want to accidentally give people night terrors anymore. Declan had assured him he could do much worse to people without intending to if he didn't master the proper control. Galvin had become the most dedicated student after that.

After three days of chasing the sick guardian, installing the new protection spell, processing the Halloween harvest, and cleaning up the estate, all three of them were drained. Alia wanted to get back to searching for Evelyn but they were tired both physically and mentally, and they still had so much to fix. Even the thought of using the simplest of spells to help was exhausting, regardless of how sore she was.

To lighten the load, each evening they picked a room. Some days each righted one by themselves but, more often than not, everyone was too exhausted for a whole room and barely managed one working together. So far they had put back their bedrooms, Theo's lab, the library, and the council room.

Thankfully, nothing seemed to be missing other than Declan's dagger and the stuff from the council room. Even Declan wasn't entirely sure what most of those things were, he just knew they had been there a few days ago and now they were not. Grace was more likely looking for information and had probably only taken the objects either because they were valuable or because she hoped it would hurt the Arbors in some way.

It was wonderful to be able to think of the whole clan instead of just themselves. Declan told them all about his meeting with Erik Arbor, another master druid from long before the whole fiasco with Mathias. It was a blessing to learn there were others hiding out there. Alia had been overjoyed, tearing a little when Declan explained it was possible many survived and were being called home. That had been Alia's greatest wish when she started training: to help Declan rebuild the world he had known.

To Alia's relief, today was a light training day. Her muscles were so sore from learning to use her wings she wasn't sure she could of handled much heavy lifting. Now she rummaged through Grace's room to see what she could find while Declan fixed his office and Galvin picked up the disaster in the common room.

Grace hadn't had much with her when she got here and didn't seem to have left anything behind. Alia didn't expect Grace would be foolish enough to leave things behind. Since she'd stayed in the room, Alia thought she would at least not tear it apart but here it was, in shambles, like the rest of the house. The door was ripped off like many of the others, shelves were broken, and all the drawers pulled from the end tables and dresser. Alia recognized scorching on some of the splintered wood, reminding her of her lightning when it had struck bark. Perhaps that was further evidence of Grace using a spell to search the house.

The only thing of note Alia found was some burned papers in the fireplace. Galvin probably knew a spell to reconstitute the papers, but only if she could collect all the pieces. She dug through the ash with the fire poker but only managed to get a few small scraps of paper. Alia suspected if Grace thought to burn the papers, she would have made sure they could not be read. She collected the ash anyway, thinking they might be able to learn something.

With nothing else to find, Alia spent her time stripping the tattered sheets from the bed and putting on fresh ones, cleaning out the broken furniture and fixtures, and doing her best to wipe off the scorch marks. She finished the room by righting an end table next to the couch in the sitting room, and its drawer fell out, spilling the contents. She picked up the drawer, replaced it in the side table, and excitedly looked through the stuff on the floor. This could be the clues they needed.

Except the sheets were blank. Just some scratch paper with a pen in case whoever was staying here needed to write something down. She returned the papers to the drawer.

She was about to move on when another object caught her attention. She bent over to pick it up, groaning when her sore muscles stretched. It was a small, old-fashioned brooch. Golden leaves surrounded a large moonstone. It was lovely and reminiscent of something Alia had seen before. Not on Grace. Alia was certain Grace had not worn any jewelry, but there was something incredibly familiar about it.

She flipped it in her hand, looking over the metal and backing, checking it with her senses for any signs of magic. She couldn't sense anything and didn't spot any magical carvings but that didn't mean it wasn't lying dormant or hiding. She would need some sort of activating word or spell for the magic to reveal itself. Theo would surely be able to find it if he were here but in the meantime she would have to figure it out with Galvin.

A gentle pleading from Galvin tugged on her attention. A minute yet desperate request for her help. She wondered if another ghost had come clamoring for his attention. She slipped the brooch into her pocket to examine more closely later.

Alia exited the room and spotted Galvin walking up the stairs, arm in arm with a glamorous woman. Her skin was deathly pale and her movements were a little too fluid and graceful. A vampire. She wore a black dress, the skirt snug on her hips and flaring out elegantly, ending just above her knees. Her heels were also black and had to be at least two inches. Even with the added height, she was tiny. Alia wasn't exactly tall but the vampire could only match her height with the heels. A wide brimmed hat covered most of her face with her face pointed downward.

Alia blinked at them, startled to find anyone unfamiliar within the new wards. They weren't expecting any visitors that she knew of. Her eyes narrowed at the intimate way the vampire pressed against Galvin's arm. She knew he didn't like being objectified and that sort of physical touch made him uncomfortable. Alia didn't like it either. Static built around her shoulders.

"She's here to see Declan," Galvin quickly explained.

Alia took a deep breath, blowing out the static. She was still on edge, despite Galvin's protective presence while she slept, and the practice with her lightning and wings had not made her mood more stable. She could tell he wanted to soothe her, not exasperate her anxiety, and he was right; they did not need her bursting out thunderbird wings and throwing lightning bolts through the hallways they had just cleaned up.

"He sent her a new charm to get in," he added, and that calmed her more. She still didn't like how the vampire pressed against him, though.

"You should come, too, sweetheart," the vampire cooed at Alia, looking her up and down, eyes bright and hungry. She did not appear to be picky, then.

Alia's eyes grew wide and her stomach flipped. She didn't like being the object of a stranger's attention. She wondered if this was how Galvin felt when he got sized up by those power-hungry women in the Winter Court. No wonder he didn't like it. She felt like a piece of meat.

"It pertains to all of you," the vampire clarified.

Alia raised an eyebrow at Galvin, questioning if he knew what on earth she was talking about. He shrugged. He knew as much as she did.

Her gaze dropped back to the vampire, down to where she gripped Galvin's arm. She patted his arm tenderly, and Alia huffed. She wanted to rip that vampire off of him and shove her into Declan's office and away from Galvin. Instead, she turned on her heel and marched toward Declan's office.

Did the vampire chuckle behind her? Alia felt the blush spread across her face and dutifully ignored it.

46

Declan's office was strewn with papers. Most were the ones he had spent the last several days filling out. He crumpled these and threw them into the fireplace to burn his personal information. Since he had only been completing them as a huge waste of time, if the World Council actually needed them, they could pay one of their lackeys to do it. It wasn't like he could turn them in anyway, since the druids were most likely labeled as criminals by now. He wasn't doing it again either way.

He couldn't understand what Grace had been doing when she had gone through their stuff; had she just been after the dagger? If Lucian *was* involved with Grace and the mysterious enemy, the dagger was more than enough to hurt Declan.

He had just finished tossing another stack into the fire when Alia stalked in through the open door. She was glaring as she stopped in the center of the room and jammed a fist onto her hip. Declan blinked at her frustration, wondering what had set her off. Slowly, he stood up and joined her but she didn't appear to have any intention of explaining. He was about to ask when Galvin strode in behind her, Ophelia hanging daintily on his arm.

Declan grinned, understanding Alia's attitude a bit better. Ophelia liked to irritate people. Especially ones she suspected of suppressing their feelings. "Welcome back, Ophelia."

She was wearing one of her typical black dresses that hugged her sensuous curves and her large sun hat. She'd appear put together if she were anyone else but was more rumpled than Declan expected. Like she'd had to rough it for a few days.

He had suppress a chuckle. Ophelia did not "rough" anything. The trip by train wasn't that long, so he could only wonder what had happened to give her such a hard time. "Whatever you wanted to talk about must be important if you came all the way here."

Ophelia glanced around the messy room, quickly assessing what the druids were dealing with. She swayed up to him, carefully removed her hat, and placed it on his desk. "It appears you know all too well how bad things are."

"Knowing how much you like manners," Declan teased, "let me introduce you to my apprentices, Alia and Galvin." He gestured a hand in each of their directions as he said their names. "But it appears you're already quite familiar with them." He folded his arms across his chest, leaning against the front of his desk.

Ophelia fixed a hungry expression to Galvin. "Yes," her gaze raked him up and down, licking her lips.

Declan rolled his eyes at the theatrics. Even if she were starving, she didn't behave like that other than to get a rise out of people.

"We've met," she admitted, "but I would be remiss not to get to know them a little better."

Galvin shifted uncomfortably. Poor kid. Ophelia was so far out of his comfort zone it was painful.

"You should snatch him up, sweetheart," Ophelia said, turning a predatory gaze to Alia, "before someone else does."

Alia's eyes narrowed as a blush crept across her cheeks and Declan could see her seething. He held back the massive grin crawling across his face. Alia and Galvin both needed some romantic entanglement in their lives. At their age, Declan had gotten enough experience that he was practically an expert at the opposite gender.

The world was different now. He was different now. And they were not him. He had kept Alia in hiding her whole life, socializing her just enough so she learned to navigate interactions without being too weird. Galvin didn't even have that practice.

Romance was part of growing up and they would likely experience it eventually. He suspected something might be growing between them. With anyone else, he might have been concerned but he hadn't seen two fit together so well since Alia's parents. Neither of them would like it but perhaps Ophelia would be a good catalyst in the right direction. In good time, though.

"Ophelia," Declan warned, knowing she would push it past their limits if left to her own devices, and this wasn't the time.

"I'm just teasing," she countered, rolling her shoulders as if Declan was being difficult. To her, he probably was.

"All right, tell me what happened, then."

Ophelia handed him an envelope. Its seal marked it as official from the World Council, but she had already opened it. Declan removed the thick papers, unfolding them to see what was important enough to bring her here so quickly. "Congratulations," she purred, "you're all wanted criminals now."

Inside was a warrant for the arrests of the Arbor druids. Declan's stomach churned when he realized it did not specifically name any of them. Which meant anyone with an Arbor Clan tattoo was a criminal. Perhaps Grace had found out about the others somehow. Perhaps it was a precaution for any future recruits. The warrant accused the Arbor druids as a whole of attacking a warlock camp with one of their magic forest creatures and fraternizing with known monster criminals.

It wasn't untrue, he just wondered which "monster criminal" they had been caught "fraternizing" with.

A second warrant listed Ophelia. So she was the "monster criminal" in question. Declan held it up questioningly. Ophelia pursed her lips, turning her nose up and away from the offending paper. "Yes, that one is mine. I have been outed as the queen of the Underground and thus been stripped of my seat on the Council as well as booted from my throne."

Declan sighed. It was just a ploy to get her out of power because Grace had somehow learned Ophelia was helping him instead of obeying orders. If what she told him in her bistro was true, then the same person pulling the World Council's strings was pulling the Underground's strings too. Funny, seeing as how the Council claimed the Underground was dangerous and not to be trusted.

"Do you know who replaced you?" Declan hoped it was someone willing to work with him.

"Lucian is king now." Ophelia's eyes darted to Alia, indicating she knew Lucian had been targeting her. Declan wondered how. Maybe she could smell him on Alia. Or maybe Lucian had said as much.

"What?" Alia paled, her scowl deepening. "How could he possibly return to this realm so fast? I just sent him back to the lower plane."

It confirmed a theory forming at the back of Declan's mind. "Whoever Grace is working for must be using him as well. Freeing him from the demon realm every time we send him back." He folded the warrants back up and replaced them in the envelope. At least they didn't say anything about Theo. That secret was still safe.

Declan crossed his arms over his chest, looking down at Ophelia. "I suppose that means you need a place to stay while you lie low."

She smiled sweetly. "Why, yes, how kind of you to offer."

He hadn't actually offered but, seeing as how he had no intention of turning her away, he let it go. "You can have any of the rooms you want except the ones already occupied. I think Alia just cleaned out the one Grace was using?" He met her gaze and she nodded. "Did you find anything in there?"

"Nothing of value. She burned some papers in the fireplace but I saved the ashes."

Declan shook his head. "We can try to restore them but I doubt she would have left her secret communications where we could discern them." That was disappointing but not surprising. He hadn't expected Grace to be careless.

"Pity about not finding anything," Ophelia agreed pragmatically, then turned a hungry grin to Declan. "Hmm, after our meeting the other night, I thought you might want to share a room." She fluttered heavy-lidded eyes up toward him, leaning in, her chest barely brushing his arm.

Declan looked skyward. "I absolutely do *not* want you staying in my room." His body didn't exactly agree with him, though.

"I've never known you to be shy, Declan."

Declan couldn't think of a more ridiculous claim. Alia and Galvin didn't care who he was with.

But when he glanced at them, he found both his apprentices looking at him like he had just morphed into an entirely different person. Alia had an expression of slight disapproval she would never admit to because Declan was her elder but Galvin, on the other hand, appeared green.

Declan groaned. "You're desperate tonight," he quipped, even if he was feeling it a little himself. Their meeting had left him hungry as well. "You're usually better at this game."

Ophelia bristled, pulling back with a growl. "I was turned out of my home days ago. I've had to keep a low profile. Because of the bar, I didn't have to stay adequately fed and now I've gone days without anything. I'm quite hungry, and you are a particularly rare vintage."

That explained it. Declan sighed, resigned. "How do you always manage to get me to agree to feed you?"

Ophelia grinned mischievously.

"We are still not sharing a room, though."

"If you say so," she purred.

47

Declan shut the door to his suite and leaned against it, reveling in the blissful quiet. After enjoying the moment of silence and stillness, he pushed up and dragged himself over to the kitchenette. He turned on the electric kettle and pulled out the special herb tea blend he used for relaxation before going to his room to get undressed.

There had been little to no rest since they returned from saving the grove. After resetting the wards, and between returning the house to normal and Ophelia's constant flirting, there was training they absolutely had to get on with. Alia needed to improve with her wings and lightning so she didn't accidentally call up a storm every time her emotions got out of hand. She had progressed to being able to command the wings, not having them pop out at inconvenient times, but she couldn't summon any of the powers the wings gave her without them.

Probably more important was Galvin. Somehow, he had

ended up with spirit abilities. It wasn't a total stretch since the Winter Court was home to some very spiritual fairies high up in their snowy mountains. Regardless of where he got them, he required instruction. Declan knew firsthand how dangerous some of the abilities could be if Galvin didn't learn to control them.

To his utter disappointment, Declan was the only one here who *could* teach him. Because of that, he'd been reawakening his own "gifts." Spirits appeared more and more frequently to him, leaving him anxious, jumpy, and paranoid. He'd given in to Ophelia's advances a couple times in an attempt take the edge off. It wasn't helping.

Declan's abilities far exceeded what he admitted and, without proper precaution, he would be vulnerable to the darker forces lurking out there. He had warded his room but those protections wore away as spirits tried to come through and communicate with him. Training Galvin increased the attention they both got from spirits, and his wards needed replacing a lot more often.

The kettle whistled, calling Declan back to his tea. He carefully measured the herb blend and put it into a pouch before pouring boiling water over it. A tingling at the nape of his neck told him two things.

First, he wasn't alone.

Second, it was time to replace the wards around his room.

Declan groaned, not looking up from his task because he didn't want to acknowledge the visitor. "Go away."

The spirit ignored him, remaining patiently behind him. This one was certainly more polite than the others, he had to admit, but he still wasn't taking requests.

He picked up his mug and headed to the couch where he planned to drink his tea and read a book to wind down. A petite lady, hands demurely clasped in front of her, smiled gently as she watched him. He scowled in his best imitation of Theo. "Office hours are closed. Go away."

She let him step around her, simply following him as he made his way to the couch. She seemed vaguely familiar, like someone he knew from a photo, but Declan wasn't interested in why. Many spirits made themselves feel familiar to get his attention.

He just wanted her to leave him alone. He sighed before turning back to her with a glare. "What?"

You must help my mate.

That was why she seemed so familiar. She must be the spirit Erik had told him was trying to contact him. She looked just like Erik described her. A young and frail human woman with wispy hair. Her eyes were large, her nose small, and her lips full. There was no color to her other than a smoky gray, so he couldn't tell much more about her. Her dress would have been the height of fashion in Tudor England. Evelyn had worn similar clothes, though from a couple decades later, so the ghost must have been a noble at some point. But they appeared threadbare. So she had fallen on harder times then.

Declan didn't want to do this. Spirits were dead, they didn't need to worry about what happened in this world anymore. "I don't know who you are or who your mate is." He had attempted a few times since his discussion with Erik to find some reference to a "dark one" somewhere because curiosity had gotten the better of him, but he hadn't found anything. Not one mention of that name anywhere.

The ghost woman continued to smile as she glided up to him. She took his free hand in one of hers and placed something into his palm.

Declan glanced down to see a large matte black scale. He closed his hand around the gift but lowered his fist to his side, scowling at her. "I have a whole bag of Theo's scales. What am I supposed to do with this?"

She sighed, her smile turning sad. She lifted his hand one more and tapped the scale with one slender finger. *Make sure my mate knows how well you have cared for our son.*

"Oh no, no, no." Declan knew she hadn't mistaken him for someone else, so she had likely made a translation mistake; ghosts didn't always remember how to communicate with the world of the living. But the two translations he could think of were both too close to a major accusation of something he was *not* responsible for, and he needed to clear the misunderstanding up now.

He set his mug on the coffee table and faced the ghost squarely. "I don't know you. I do not have your son. I certainly didn't father one with you. I raised one half-dragon, and I was there when Tiberius ended the abusive witch who birthed Theo. You are not her."

Apparently that was all she had to say because she faded immediately after delivering her message, not sticking around to hear Declan's clarification.

He dropped his head back, growling in frustration. After a moment, he looked down at the scale in his palm. It took a lot of energy for a ghost to manifest an actual object to leave for the living. While it also required immense effort, it was much easier to pick up existing items from close by, so it was more likely she had picked up one of Theo's scales, thinking it would be the key to make Declan understand what she was trying to say. The only problem with that reasoning was the same problem with messages in general. Ghosts didn't always get it right.

The black scale was so dark it reflected no light, like it absorbed the light around it. That wasn't right. Declan examined closer, realizing it wasn't Theo's. Theo was black, yes, but his scales were not matte and had a purple sheen, reflecting light as well as emphasizing shadows. This was some other dragon's scale, but Declan didn't know any other dragons. If his suspicions about Grace's mysterious boss were right, there was one who knew about him though.

Could the scale belong to Theo's father?

That was impossible too. Declan, Evelyn, and Tiberius had searched for Theo's dragon father after rescuing him. The only thing that would keep a dragon from their child was death. It was the only reason they had decided to keep him.

"Am I supposed to know what this means?" Declan called to the ghost.

Nothing. He hadn't thought she would answer since she obviously felt she had told him everything he needed to know but she might still be lurking around.

He put the scale on the coffee table and flopped down on the couch with a groan, covering his face with the throw pillow. He was too tired to figure it out now. "I hate talking to ghosts!"

48

After days of dealing with Ophelia's constant teasing, Alia needed to get away from everyone for a few minutes. With each innuendo from the vampire to her mentor, Alia wasn't sure she could look Declan in the eye without blushing or hitting him. They were searching for Evelyn! *His* Evelyn! The whole fiasco with Grace and the Council had derailed them from that goal but it was time to get back to it.

She had to remind herself she and Galvin hadn't told Declan anything about summoning the ghost in the church. She had confirmed Evelyn had never crossed to the other side but Alia wasn't certain that meant she was dead. Declan had said Tiberius's gut was right more often than not, and he had been so sure that Evelyn was alive that he sold his soul to demons. But perhaps Declan doubted more than he let on.

Then again, things were different when Declan was young. Druids didn't ask questions behind closed doors and monogamy wasn't as big of a thing to the ancient druids as it was to Alia. Intimacy was seen as a basic bodily and spiritual need that should be tended to. Declan had taken pains to hide that side of him from her when she was little, but as she got older she recognized it for what it was. It was just too weird for her.

The whole thing left her fighting off a headache too, and she couldn't deal with all the romantic tension. She didn't know how to reconcile Declan and Ophelia's weird flirting with the search for Evelyn. She also didn't want to face the feelings she got when Ophelia brought up Galvin.

She stamped down the butterflies in her stomach, reminding herself she and Galvin were friends and that was how it was going to stay. Regardless of how it felt when he pulled her close or the way his eyes stared into hers or how good it felt to be able to snuggle next to him at night.

Nope. Friends. Just friends.

She went down to the Link Room and slipped inside where it was dim and quiet. The grove had a number of meditative places, and usually Alia liked sit at by the sacred tree, but something called her to the Link Room this time.

The portals to the three other anchor groves were just as the druids had left them. The Link Room door had still been locked when they returned home, preventing Grace from coming in and messing up their connections to the other anchor groves. The paths, smaller imitations of the trees they represented, lighted the room in a soft glow that was much easier on Alia's aching head. She looked them over, checking the spells, reassured that if any of the other druids found their way to an anchor grove, they could get through. Grove hopping was a master druid spell, but Alia and Galvin were the only druids to ascend to that rank since the start of the genocide. Any new druids still in hiding would need the portals in the Link Rooms to travel to anchor groves.

Declan had sent out a message to all the groves the day they returned, telling them to come back to the anchor groves, to rebuild their cities, and reset their protective wards. Hopefully more druids were hiding out like Erik, and they would return to the Arbor Grove and to the other anchors from all over the globe.

Other druids. The thought lifted her spirits and soothed her soul. Ever since she had gotten her powers, it had been her goal to help Declan not just stay safe but to restore their people and culture. Help him rebuild a life in which they didn't have to hide anymore. It had been so important when it was only the two of them, a burden she had taken on herself to be great enough to stand at Declan's side and eventually become the one person he could rely on. Living up to the legendary name of her mentor and the man who raised her. She hadn't realized how heavy the responsibility was until now. Until finding out she wasn't the only one. Because now she didn't have to do it all by herself.

Despite the joy it brought her, her heart twinged slightly. She wanted druids to be alive and free again. She wanted the villages and cities to be full once more. But a small part of her *had* wanted to do it by herself. Had wanted to prove to Declan she was as strong as he was. To be as legendary to the rest of the druids as Declan was and be worthy of the privilege of being trained by him.

It was a silly thought, and selfish. The rebuilding of the druids should be more important than her own personal glory.

The one dark corner in the room caught her attention. The portal to the temple where Evelyn had lived with her priestess sisters sat empty and lifeless, as it had when she and Galvin first seen it. A thought kindled in her mind. If only she could find some sort of clue.

Maybe, now that Declan was working with Galvin on his spirit powers, they should tell him what they had learned from the ghost in the church. There hadn't been much point before. Declan did *not* like working with spirits, and now she knew why. But also because it didn't help them find Evelyn. All the ghost told them was her spirit hadn't crossed over. Alia wanted that to mean she was alive, but the ghost hadn't specifically said those words. Alia had decided not to break Declan's heart with news that didn't put him any closer to her.

Perhaps she had kept it from him for another reason. Perhaps a part of her desired to solve something Declan could not. Solve something so big it put her on the same level as her heroic mentor. Then she could surprise him by returning his lost love.

Alia cringed and shook her head, imagining that reunion with Ophelia in the house. She had no idea how any of them would react and her visions were likely worse than it would really be, but still. Probably not a good idea under the circumstances.

Except Alia wasn't close to solving the mystery. She had thought over the encounter in the church a lot. Just because Evelyn's spirit had never crossed over, it didn't definitively mean she had not died. Only that her spirit had not gone with her sisters and wasn't with them now. Though, if she had died and her spirit had gone elsewhere, then her sisters would have been able to find her. Unless her spirit was trapped somewhere that didn't touch the other side at all. Alia wasn't sure how something like that would work.

In her research of the Holy Order, she had learned that, when a priestess died, her gift was reborn in someone else. She asked Theo to look for her but he found no evidence that any Holy Order gifts were currently active anywhere.

Alia's hand dropped into her pocket and rubbed the coin she always carried now. Tiberius had been convinced Evelyn wasn't dead.

So much so he had teamed up with his mortal enemy just to keep her alive. He believed she was Mathias's prisoner, which didn't track very well, but Declan said his gut instincts were usually good, if not his deduction skills.

Alia's mind was running in circles again. She paced and cleared the thoughts out of her head. She started over, listing what she knew.

Evelyn disappeared the night Declan's mysterious enemy attacked her temple, disguised as Mathias and his demons.

Evelyn's spirit was somewhere but had not crossed over. Otherwise the Holy Order powers would've been reborn into someone else.

Mathias had used Evelyn's unknown fate to control Tiberius but neither knew where she was. Both were looking for her.

The coin meant something. Lucian had tried to connect it to the temple that was destroyed the night she disappeared.

Now Lucian was working for someone else. Probably the same mysterious enemy who had pitted Mathias against the druids in the first place.

But Alia had no idea how any of these things fit together. She was missing something.

It was maddening.

She was about to leave the Link Room when a soft golden glow caught her attention. It came from the previously dark corner of the room, and Alia turned toward it. The markings along the Grecian columns glittered faintly, only bright enough to be visible, which was strange since the portal had been abandoned after the attack. The spells weren't even finished.

Alia stepped closer to get a better look and, as she did, the markings came more and more to life. A gentle vibration started in her pocket, growing in intensity as light grew from the archway. She pulled out the coin and examined it in her palm. The coin too had a glow and was vibrating in response to her proximity to the portal.

Be careful of carrying unprotected keys in your pocket, Winged One. You never know where they will take you. The guardian's warning came back to her. She hadn't understood at the time what it was talking about but that wasn't unusual when speaking to animals in general, especially magic ones. She had assumed the message would make sense later.

And it did. The guardian had to mean this.

A key. It was common in Roman times to mint a coin for special occasions. Evelyn had given both Declan and Tiberius one for her pending wedding to Declan. What she hadn't told them was that it was a key. For a portal that had been secretly finished.

Alia smiled broadly, almost laughing. Evelyn had put a spell on the portal to activate with the keys she had gifted her dearest friends. In case of emergencies.

She had to have predicted something disastrous would happen to herself or to the druids. Why else would she give them keys and not Declan and Tiberius what they were? What had Evelyn hidden in her temple for them to find in case she wasn't around? Whatever it was, it had to be important if she kept it secret from the two people she trusted most.

Unfortunately, her plan had worked too well since neither one understood the coins were meant for emergency use. Or perhaps she expected them both to carry the coins with them at all times for sentimental value. Tiberius did. She couldn't have anticipated everything that happened between them to prevent them from figuring it out. Declan had locked the Link Room at the Arbor Grove for as long as Alia could remember, all of his stuff from Evelyn safely tucked away, so he had never brought the coin anywhere near the portal. Tiberius wouldn't have been in any grove long enough after taking up with demons to have wandered into a Link Room, even though he always carried the coin with him.

Was it that simple? All Evelyn's planning ruined because Declan and Tiberius had stopped trusting each other and wrecked their friendship.

Alia looked at the portal. Inside the archway, a cool mist formed the longer she stood there. The spell grew stronger the closer she got. She paused, debating. Any closer and she could make the portal fully functional. All she would have to do was step through.

Solve the riddle the druids' biggest heroes never could.

Reunite her mentor with the love of his life and fulfill the one goal Tiberius had striven for till the end.

Be strong enough that no one would doubt her. That Declan would never have to worry about her again.

The answers, as well as the glory, waiting on the other side of the swirling magical doorway tempted her. Only a few steps away.

Alia put the coin back in her pocket, backed away from the portal. The lights dimmed, the portal returning to its slumber and the coin going still and quiet. As much as she wanted to dive in, she wasn't ready to leave. She could not control her wings yet and didn't like the idea of leaving with an unpredictable power. They were still putting the estate back together figuring out what to do next, and she didn't know how being a criminal to the rest of the world would affect what she had to do. She could walk into a mess if she wasn't careful. Besides, she couldn't leave on her own without telling anyone. What would Galvin say? He was nowhere near ready to join her and would be devastated if she disappeared.

    Reluctantly, Alia walked toward the exit. The portal stayed dark and lifeless, just as she remembered it. "Soon," she whispered to the secrets awaiting her on the other side, and she slipped out of the room and closed the door behind her.

Like the World of the Arbor Clan and looking for more?

Visit www.samhickeyauthor.com to find a list of current and upcomming books.

Sign up for the newsletter and recieve an exclusive short story featureing Theo on his vacation.

www.ingramcontent.com/pod-product-compliance
Lightning Source LLC
LaVergne TN
LVHW091618070526
838199LV00044B/842